THE WISDOM
OF DEAD MEN

THE WISDOM OF DEAD MEN

The Wildenstern Saga, Book Two

Oisín McGann

OPEN ROAD

INTEGRATED MEDIA

NEW YORK

Cover design by Jason Gabbert

978-1-4976-6589-7

Published in 2015 by Open Road Integrated Media, Inc.
345 Hudson Street
New York, NY 10014
www.openroadmedia.com

FOR CHRIS,
WHO BELIEVES REASON AND FAITH
ARE NOT MUTUALLY EXCLUSIVE.

THE WISDOM
OF DEAD MEN

PROLOGUE

THE WITCH OF TINAHELY

VICKY MILLER STUMBLED DIZZILY out into the darkness, away from the house and the stranger who lay dead inside it—the man she had just killed. Beyond the rectangle of light thrown from the open doorway, the night's gloom swallowed the old woman and she stretched her hands out in front of her to feel the way.

She could smell smoke from somewhere. It was hard to tell where it was coming from, because she was so disoriented. Her head spun and her vision, which had long been fading with age, was even worse now. Everything was blurred. Everything was dark. There were blackthorn bushes at the bottom of her garden and she stumbled into them, pulling herself free with an exasperated gasp. What was wrong with her? Why was she so weak?

Vicky stopped as she realized that she could feel the damp

grass beneath her feet. Why had she left the house without her shoes? And she was in her nightdress. There was blood on her arm and it had stained the white cotton. The old woman stopped meandering about her garden, staring down at a line of cabbages that bordered the vegetable patch. Pull yourself together, girl, she thought to herself. What's wrong with you?

She remembered killing the man. Feeling pain as she woke, she'd acted on reflex. The stranger was just standing there in the low light of the lamp on the sideboard. He was unarmed, he wasn't attacking, but he was in her home and she had been scared. Old reflexes, born of a childhood spent among villains and killers— her hands had moved of their own accord. Then she'd noticed the door was open and she had staggered outside. And now she was here. Outside. In her nightdress . . . without any shoes.

The smell of burning was stronger now.

Gazing back at her house, Vicky became alarmed. Had she knocked over the oil lamp on her way out? Everything she owned was in that little cottage. The walls were stone, but the floor was wooden and if the thatched roof caught . . . She moaned with fear.

There was no other dwelling for miles around. Even if she screamed for help, there was no one to hear. Water! The well was on the other side of the house. Vicky made her way clumsily around the side of the cottage, past the shed and the small stable. It was only a few yards away when her legs finally gave out beneath her. With a wheezing thud, she hit the ground. No matter how hard she tried, she could not get up again. What was wrong with her?

There came the sound of a scream that was not her own. It came from somewhere near the house, piercing the night. Vicky let out a frightened whimper. She did not believe in the mythical banshee, the woman whose shriek foretold your death. She did not believe . . .

The odor was very strong now. Her nostrils twitched, her nose wrinkling. It didn't smell of paraffin, or wood, but . . . Her senses spun in a whirl, the world rolled around her. It was a wonderful relief to close her eyes, to just lay her face on the cool grass.

The night was cold; she could feel it in the air. But her skin felt hot, as if the fire was right beside her, instead of being inside the house. The house. Lifting her head from the ground, Vicky pressed her hands against the ground and pushed herself up. Her strength failed before she could even lift her belly off the grass. Collapsing with a grunt, she started crying, tears streaming down the spider's web of lines that age had woven into the skin of her face. Unable to do anything else, she called out hoarsely for help, knowing it was useless. Nobody could hear. By the time anyone saw the fire, it would be too late.

She heard the scream again. It sounded loud and raw in the empty night.

Her own cries used up what little breath was left in her withered breast and with a last, feeble call, she passed out. Her head slumped limply into the grass and she was dead to the world. Then flames began to flicker into life along her body.

The cottage had two small windows looking out onto the back garden. They were lit from within, not by a raging fire, but by the oil lamp, which sat undisturbed on the sideboard in her bedroom. The windows watched without expression as Vicky Miller's motionless body ignited, flames spreading over her back and shoulders and down her thighs.

Vicky was right. It was some time before anybody noticed the fire. By then, there wasn't much of Vicky left.

And that was how the Witch of Tinahely met her death.

I

A COUSIN'S GRIEVANCE

ROBERTO WILDENSTERN WAS THE PATRIARCH, the eldest living son of the late Edgar Wildenstern, Duke of Leinster and ruler of the family's vast business empire. As the richest man in Ireland—indeed, one of the richest and most powerful men in the British Empire and, therefore, in the entire world—he had extraordinary resources at his disposal. As Chairman of the North America Trading Company he controlled the fates of many thousands of people, and influenced the lives of millions more in dozens of countries across the globe. The Wildenstern business interests stretched east through Europe, south to Asia and Africa, west across the Atlantic to North and South America, and on across the Pacific. The Wildensterns had huge merchant fleets, as well as special charters empowering the Company to commandeer ships of the

Royal Navy and draft armies in Ireland. There were few countries in the world that could match the Company's might, and even fewer business empires that could. Roberto Wildenstern controlled it all.

And he was thoroughly sick of it.

"If I have to endure one more of these bloody meetings, I'm going to have a seizure," he moaned as he waited for another gaggle of visiting envoys. "I've seen furniture with more life in it than some of these yaw-yaws. Couldn't they just put it all in a letter?"

"We've been over this a hundred times, Berto," his wife replied. "It's not just the negotiations with these people that are important; they need to see you in control. Your father ran this business with an iron fist for decades and everyone has to understand that you're in charge now.

"You want to force this family to mend their ways; you've said it enough times. So you have to stamp your authority on everything your father left behind—especially the business—or we're going to have the whole family fighting over whatever piece of the pie they can snatch out of your hands."

"Good luck to 'em," Berto muttered, running his fingers through his carefully styled, dark-blond hair. "They can have it . . . and the bloody great headache that goes with it."

"Don't start that again. I thought you were beginning to enjoy doing some good."

"Hmph!" He began sticking the point of his dip pen into the back of his hand, leaving black-stained dots along it.

They were sitting in his study. Berto was behind his desk, a warm mahogany slab that did, he was forced to admit, make him feel very business-like. It also hid the fact that he was in a wheelchair, a state he had hoped would be temporary. These hopes were fading. From time to time, he would adjust the thin gold discs on the belt that pressed against his bare back. The Wildensterns had long ago found that applying gold to an injury helped speed up their unique healing powers. Every day he grew less confident that it was doing any good.

The heavy blue velvet drapes had been pulled back from the tall windows to let in the late-afternoon light. This corner room, high up in the towering house, looked out on the Wicklow Mountains to the south, with the coast visible to the east and, if one stuck one's head far enough out of the window, the near edge of Dublin, blanketed in smog, to the north. The study was sumptuously decorated, with dark green ivy-printed wallpaper, mahogany furnishings, two large bookcases and an impressive collection of Japanese prints.

Berto's wife, Melancholy—or Daisy, as she preferred to be known—was sitting in an upright, but comfortable, chair with a notebook on her lap and a pen in her hand. Daisy had decided as a child that one's name could affect one's fate, and she would not spend her life as Melancholy, despite her mother's love for tragic romance novels. And what Daisy decided in her family home more often than not became policy. Now, she managed her husband's affairs with equal deliberation. Her dark hair was pinned up, her blue crinoline dress and matching shoes were as comfortable as fashion would allow. She kept the minutes of the Company meetings and, discreetly, acted as Berto's adviser. Many of the men who came to meet the Patriarch were amused by her interest in her husband's business affairs and tolerated her womanly whims with a patronizing civility. They would have been appalled to know just how much power Daisy was capable of wielding—and not just by nagging her husband until she got her way. Berto relied heavily on his wife's analytical skills, but he was slowly getting to grips with the massive responsibilities heaped upon him.

"I'm just *bored*," he sighed, adjusting his tie and patting down his waistcoat. "They're all such dry sorts—and you've never met such a bunch of asses and toad-eaters in all your life. I haven't had a good laugh in ages." Waving to Winters, his manservant, he sighed again and added, "All right, then, show the next lot in. I know how to take punishment—I went to public school, you know."

"Begging your pardon, Your Grace," Winters spoke up. "Master Simon would like a word. If I might be so bold as to say, he seems a bit . . . restless, sir."

Berto let out a breath and nodded. Simon—'Simple Simon,' as he was known to crueler members of the family—was a somewhat distant cousin who, at the age of seventeen, had the mind of an eight- or nine-year-old. Berto, a sensitive individual at heart, patiently put up with Simon's constant need for attention. It wasn't the boy's fault he was dull-witted, after all, and he had a lightness of heart that was sorely lacking in most of the rest of the family.

But Simon's usual gormless smile was missing as he stumbled into the room. His suit was as rumpled as always, despite the fact that he was provided with a freshly pressed one at the beginning of every day. His wild tufts of brown hair stood out from his head in every direction. He stood by the door looking furtively to right and left as if reluctant to come any further inside.

"What's on your mind, Simon?" Berto asked.

"Need to talk," Simon muttered. "Just with you, Berto . . . if I may."

It was unusual for the boy to speak in anything other than a breathless gabble and Berto looked at him with concern. He glanced at Daisy, who nodded slightly and stood up, straightened her bulky skirts and walked towards the door. Simon turned towards Winters as if afraid the footman might jump on him. Tall and thin and immaculately groomed, Berto's manservant had been trained from childhood not only for domestic service, but also as a bodyguard.

Berto lifted his chin to the servant and Winters nodded, following Daisy out the door and closing it softly behind him.

"What's on your mind, old chap?" Berto asked again.

Simon wouldn't meet his gaze, fixing his eyes firmly on the floor. He kept plucking at the collar of his suit jacket.

"You sent my mother away," he said in a near-whisper.

"What's that?"

"You sent my mother away!" Simon growled, tears welling in his eyes. For a moment, he glared at his older cousin.

Berto saw the expression on the boy's face, but could not believe what it was telling him. So he was slow to react. The knife was already drawn from inside Simon's jacket—what the boy lacked in wit, he made up for in speed. With a flick of his wrist, he hurled the blade at Berto's heart.

Berto was already pushing his wheelchair back from the desk, turning his body to bring it side on to the path of the knife, which cut across his chest, but missed its target. It thudded into the wall behind him.

"What the bloody hell—!" he shouted, before Simon leaped onto the desk, another knife in his hand.

The door was thrown open. Voices cried out. Simon raised the knife, but Berto was by no means defenseless. Grabbing the sawn-off shotgun clipped under his desk, Berto wrenched it free and swung it in one smooth move, sweeping Simon's legs out from under him. The boy fell hard on his back onto the desk, but was up again with the slickness of an eel. Berto could not bring himself to shoot the youngster. He fired both barrels into the ceiling over Simon's head, the blast and then the burst of exploding plaster above making the boy flinch away. But the shot was rushed, the recoil of the gun tipped Berto backwards and he tumbled out of his chair.

Before Simon could follow through on his attack, four strong hands seized him from behind and threw him to the floor. A foot kicked the knife out of his hand. He was rolled onto his front and gripped roughly in a ground hold that pinned both his arms behind him and pressed his head and chest to the floor. Berto's younger brother, Nathaniel, continued to hold the boy while Winters snapped a pair of handcuffs onto Simon's wrists.

"You sent my mother away! You sent my mother away!" Simon yelled over and over again, tears streaming down his face.

Nathaniel and Winters pulled him to his feet and the servant dragged him away. Berto was sitting up, trying to set his chair back on its wheels. He wrenched at it, swearing at his limp and useless legs, his movements jerky with confused anger and embarrassment. Nathaniel righted the wheelchair and helped his brother into it as Daisy hurried into the room.

"Oh my God!" she gasped. "Berto, darling, are you hurt?"

"What the hell was that about?" Nate asked, as he picked up the smoking shotgun.

Berto ignored both questions until he had settled his nerves, straightened out his clothes and hair, and taken a few deep breaths.

"No, I'm fine . . . and I have no idea what that was about," he said in a shaky voice. "But I mean to find out. You should have seen the hatred in the boy's face. I never knew he had that kind of venom in him. What do you think he meant about his mother?"

"Don't know," Nate replied, breaking open the shotgun and letting the spent shells fall out onto the desk. "I'll have a word with him when he's calmed down a bit."

"Don't be unkind to him," Daisy cautioned her brother-in-law. "This didn't come out of nowhere. It's clear that someone put him up to it. We must discover who has been pulling his strings."

"Obviously. Are there any other aspects of my job on which you'd like to offer instruction?"

"You seem to have it well in hand," she replied brightly. "Except, of course, for the simpleton who managed to slip *two throwing knives* past your *security*."

Nate's face went red, but he did not reply. He took a couple of shells from a drawer in Berto's desk, reloaded the weapon and swung it closed.

"All right, so we've a snake in the house," he grunted as he clipped the shotgun back into position under the desk and assessed the damage to the ceiling. "Some treacherous cur with murder on his mind."

"So it seems," Berto said sourly. "The family's all home at the moment. Do you think we should mention it at dinner?"

"If you like. But frankly, I don't think any of them would own up."

"It's probably better not to say anything," Daisy sighed, shaking her head as she wrapped her arms around her husband. "You don't want to go giving the rest of them ideas."

Berto nodded grimly.

"Ah. There's no place like home."

II

A VISIT FROM
THE ROYAL IRISH CONSTABULARY

NATHANIEL WILDENSTERN WAS BROODING in the breakfast room late in the morning, when the police inspector came calling. He was alone; the rest of the thirty-odd members of the family resident in Wildenstern Hall had eaten and left. The rich, wake-up scent of eggs, bacon, kippers, tea, coffee and fresh bread hung in the air. The maids had cleared the tables and only his manservant, Clancy, hovered unseen nearby. The large fireplace was filled with a display of flowers during these warm summer days and the paintings on the walls had all been changed to pastoral scenes to suit the season. Not that any of this could improve his mood.

Nate was sitting in the light of the east-facing French windows, indulging his taste for hot buttered toast—cooked on one side only, as all toast should be—berating himself for failing to anticipate Simple Simon's attack.

It was true that the boy was thought so innocent he could not constitute a threat, but even so, Nate should have taken the proper precautions with him, as he did with everyone else.

Berto had become Heir after their older brother, Marcus, had been killed by Edgar, their father, in self-defense . . . and had then been elevated to Patriarch when Edgar was murdered by a group of very old, very savage relatives. The upheaval that had resulted in the family had forced Nate to give up his boyhood dreams of wandering the world in search of adventures and instead, to support Roberto in his new role.

Nate had committed himself to the protection of his older brother—a serious undertaking for a nineteen-year-old who had spent most of his life avoiding responsibility. But he was well-trained in armed and unarmed combat, poisons and explosives, and had been given a thorough education in the family's history of plotting and conspiracy. He had an intimate knowledge of the house's defenses—the booby-traps, hidden rooms and passageways, the armories and secret weapons caches. And he could count on the support and expertise of Winters and Clancy, along with a team of loyal and able footmen. He had convinced himself it was enough.

After Edgar's death, there had been a rash of plots to remove Berto, some bordering on the absurd, others planned with chilling precision. Nate had succeeded in foiling all of them before they could get close. As Patriarch, Duke of Leinster and Chairman of the North American Trading Company, Roberto controlled the Wildenstern Empire and its vast resources. There were many among their flock of uncles, aunts and cousins who wanted Berto's power and would stop at nothing to seize it. Roberto was trying to reform the family, but his efforts were simply creating more enemies.

Berto was not perturbed by the family's resistance and was determined to force them to change their ways. And he was certain that they would, eventually. Nathaniel found it difficult, sometimes, to share his brother's optimism.

Not for the first time, Nate cursed the Rules of Ascension and the predatory practices they encouraged. For the Wildensterns were no ordinary family. Ordinary families did not think it acceptable to betray those closest to them in order to get ahead. Ordinary families did not tolerate murder.

It was Nate's job to weed out the conspirators and deal with them. Anyone who defied Berto's will had to be dealt with. Nate had thought himself up to the job, but he was beginning to have his doubts. He had thought that giving up his dream of a life filled with travel and adventure showed that he was maturing. But now he was feeling the pressure, and his initial confidence was giving way. He was desperately afraid of failing and beginning to fear he should have left this task to someone with more experience. But who could they trust?

The Wildensterns were bred to be cunning, deceptive and ruthless. Simple Simon's unpredictable attack was just the latest proof of just how dangerous they could be.

Nate had questioned the boy, but could get no sense out of him. Simon had sat at the table in the small boxroom where he was being held, his face in his arms, moaning incessantly about his mother. As far as anyone seemed to know, Simon's mother had died of tuberculosis when he was three or four. His father had passed away a few years later.

Nate chewed his toast thoughtfully. His tea had already gone cold. He was about to call for more, when his manservant appeared behind him and softly cleared his throat. Clancy was a Limerick man who had been raised to serve the Wildensterns. For many years now, he had been Nate's personal manservant and bodyguard, as well as his tutor in the family's unorthodox survival skills. Dressed in a black suit with tail-coat and buckled shoes, he was a short, solid man with a straight back, square shoulders and graying hair. His inscrutable face was shadowed by bushy eyebrows and looked as though it had been shaped out of wood with a blunt hatchet. Nate had seen Clancy's short-fingered hands sew the finest seams and break bones with equal ease.

Nate could sense Clancy's eyes on him and suddenly resented the degree to which he relied on his manservant. The older man often seemed more like a mentor than a member of staff and he had saved Nate's life on more than one occasion. Nate had the definite impression that Clancy disapproved of his more reckless behavior and expected better of him—a ridiculous attitude to have. That feeling was even stronger now that Nate had actually taken on some responsibility.

"Inspector Urskin of the Royal Irish Constabulary requests a moment of your time, sir," Clancy informed him now, handing over the policeman's card on a small silver platter.

Nate picked up the card and gave it a curious look. He nodded to Clancy, who retreated to the hallway, returning with a narrow-featured man dressed in a long gray coat, a mediocre brown suit and cheap but tasteful shoes. He held a slightly scuffed bowler hat in his hands. The policeman had a prematurely crumpled face sporting a bushy lip-whisker that was a shade lighter than his auburn hair. His eyes were intense and intelligent. He was accompanied by a young constable dressed in the RIC uniform of dark green with black buttons and insignia.

"Inspector Urskin and Constable Mahon," Clancy announced. "Nathaniel Wildenstern."

Nate avoided using all the titles to which he could lay claim—they made him feel old, and besides, his family name was more than enough to impress anyone.

"Thank you, Clancy," he replied. "What can I do for you, Inspector?"

"Thank you for seeing me, sir," Urskin addressed him, speaking with a guttural midlands accent. "If I may be so bold, I was hoping you or your brother could shed some light on a case that has come to my attention: the unfortunate death of an old woman in Tinahely."

Nate restrained himself from asking if any death could be considered 'fortunate.' The policeman had a very solemn look about him.

"And what makes you think we could help?" he inquired.

"Well, it seems the woman might have had some connection with your family," Urskin replied, handing over a small framed daguerreotype of a man and woman sitting in a formal, posed portrait. "That is your father, I believe."

Nate gazed at the silvery image, intrigued by it. He had never seen this picture of his father before. The daguerreotype was old and faded, and crude by the standards of modern photography, but there was no mistaking the countenance of Edgar Wildenstern, the most fearsome Patriarch ever to rule the family.

"And this is the woman?" he asked, nodding to the other person in the picture.

"Yes, sir. Vicky . . . Victoria Miller was 'er name. She was well known in the area. Had the reputation of being a . . . well, a healer an' all that."

"I see." Nate studied her face, noticing for the first time the likeness to his father's. Was it possible she had been related in some way? "My father was not fond of having portraits done, and certainly not with common folk. Perhaps some of my older relatives might recognize her. I can ask at dinner. How did she die, if you don't mind me asking?"

"Ah, well . . . " Urskin shifted uneasily on his feet. "That's one of the more . . . puzzling aspects of the case. It seems she burned to death. We just can't for the life of us figure out *how*."

"I'm not sure what you mean."

"I've seen enough deaths in my time, Mister Wildenstern. Bodies burn a certain way. You'd have to see the scene to understand why it's so damned odd."

"Well, then, Inspector," Nate said to him, "why don't you show me? We can go now if you like."

It did not occur to Nathaniel that the policeman would refuse. Nor did he. Urskin knew that the Wildensterns owned most of Wicklow and had almost as much influence in Ireland as Her Majesty's government. They were accustomed to getting their way.

"I'll be waiting for you in the square in Tinahely," Nate told him. "Try not to be too late."

Daisy knew that Nathaniel did not want anyone else to question Simon, but she also knew that her brother-in-law could be something of a blunt instrument at times. Despite her strict Christian values, she could appreciate that Nate's keen survival instincts and somewhat ruthless edge helped keep Roberto safe, but she didn't always agree with his methods. His maturity left a lot to be desired too. She suspected that shouts and threats were not the course to take with Simon. Some finesse would be required to bring him out of his shell.

Roberto's fifteen-year-old sister, Tatiana, had learned of the attack and insisted on joining Daisy for the interview. Daisy had objected at first, but then thought better of it. Simon was fond of Tatiana, and that might help open him up. There was the matter of protecting Tatiana's innocence to consider, but Tatty had seen more violence in the previous year than most girls see in their entire lifetime, and had come out of it relatively unscathed . . . although it seemed to have left her with a taste for penny dreadfuls and some of the more sensationalist news articles.

Daisy was on her way to the garden, trying to find Tatty, when Tatty found her.

"Daisy, have a look at this!" the younger girl exclaimed, waving the newspaper she was carrying as she scurried along the sumptuously decorated hallway towards her sister-in-law in a manner that made her thick, green, layered skirts look like she was running through a tumbling bush. Her golden curls bounced around her cherubic face, her cheeks rosy with color. "There's a new highwayman preying on the wealthy who travel by the roads over the mountains. They say he can't be more than sixteen years old! Isn't it splendid? They're calling him 'The Highwayboy.'"

"Marvelous, Tatty," Daisy replied, taking the paper from her hands, glancing at the questionable article. "I've been looking all over for you—"

"Do you think perhaps we could take a ride out over the mountains this evening and see if he might rob us? It would be awfully exciting!"

"Tatiana," Daisy said in a stern voice. "One does not allow oneself to be robbed for the sake of some cheap titillation. It would be most unseemly. Not to mention the inevitable loss of your valuables."

"We could wear costume jewelry. Besides, you're always saying that it's a lady's right to be able to pay for her own entertainment."

"Being cleaned out by a teenage cutpurse was not what I had in mind. Now, do you want to help me talk to Simon or not?"

"Of course. I'm just taking the opportunity to broaden my mind."

"A little *depth* wouldn't go amiss either, Tatty," Daisy admonished her. "I've told you this paper is a rag. Why don't you read something more reputable?"

"This one has the best illustrations!"

Daisy sighed and, holding her sister-in-law's hand, led her to the elevator that would take them up to the fifth floor, where Simon was being held in a small, bare boxroom.

The boy looked awful. His face was drawn and pale, his eyes red from crying. When a footman opened the door to admit the two young women, Simon looked at them with palpable relief. Women were not inclined to ask questions with their fists. She and Tatty gathered their skirts and sat down at the table opposite the prisoner. The footman went to stand inside the door, but Daisy motioned for him to wait outside. The man gave Simon a hard look to warn him to behave, and then left.

"What are they going to do to me?" Simon wailed as soon as the door had clicked shut. "Berto must be furious! And Nate hates me, I know it! They'll kick my bucket for sure!"

"There will be no kicking of buckets, Simon," Daisy assured him. "Don't you worry. We know you didn't mean to—"

"Of course I *meant* to!" Simon protested. "That's why I brought the *knives*. For stabbing Berto. That's what they were for."

Daisy sat back, exchanging glances with Tatty.

"But why would you want to hurt Berto?" Tatty asked gently. "He's only ever been good to you. I thought you were his friend."

"He sent my mother away," Simon explained, his eyes welling up again. "When I was little, she went away and it was him who made her." This last sentence was spoken with the peevishness of a child. He had always been one for biting his nails and now there was little left of them, but still he chewed at the remains.

"Didn't your mother die of consumption?" Daisy took his hand in hers. "You were four, you must remember? And anyway, Berto would only have been nine years old. How could he have sent your mother away?"

"But h-he was in charge of th-the estates back then," Simon stuttered, frowning. "She wasn't sick at all. He sent her away because she was a troublemaker."

"But he was only *nine*, Simon. How could he have been in charge of anything?"

Daisy knew that the boy did not have a firm sense of the passing of time. He could think in days, but not many of them. Weeks and months were yawning gaps in time and years were impossibly long. She was not surprised that he could make such a mistake. It was the conviction that his mother had not died, but had been sent away that bothered Daisy.

"Who told you she was sent away?" she pressed him.

"Nobody!" he retorted unconvincingly.

"Simon, we're trying to help you," Tatty said in a soothing tone. "Somebody's tricked you and we want to find out who it is. Who told you Berto sent your mother away?"

Simon's eyes flicked from one young woman to the other and back again. His chin was trembling, his hands moving constantly from the tabletop to his mouth and back again. There was a very visible struggle going on in his mind; the exaggerated expressions on his face would have been comical if the situation had not been such a serious one.

"I got letters . . . " he said finally. "They told me what happened."

Daisy closed her eyes. Tatty let out an exasperated growl.

"You tried to kill my brother because some *letters* told you to do it!" she snapped, standing up so suddenly the chair fell over behind her. "You blithering idiot! I should—"

"Tatiana," Daisy said quietly, trying to calm her sister-in-law. "There's no need to be unkind. Simon, would you be willing to show us these letters?"

"No," he said quickly.

"I'm sure Berto and Nate won't ask so politely. You don't want them messing up your rooms, do you?"

His imagination played with that one for a moment. Simon had several books of lewd cartoons stashed in the back of his chest of drawers. It was the worst-kept secret in Wildenstern Hall, but he didn't know that. Preventing their discovery suddenly became uppermost in his mind.

"All right, then," he said.

A maid was sent to fetch the letters from their 'hiding place'—a drawer in Simon's bedside table—and they were brought back up to the boxroom. Daisy and Tatty inspected them carefully. There were four of them, all written in an awkward and unfamiliar hand. If it was a member of the family they were disguising their handwriting, feigning a lack of education. Simon had not kept the envelopes, so there was no telling where they had come from—the writer might not have even been in the country when they were sent—but Simon said he had received each letter a week after the last.

The two young women read the first one carefully:

Dear Simon,

I am a friend. Please forgive me for not telling you my name.
I am scared of what Roberto and Nathaniel will do to me when

I tell you what happened to your mother. She did not die of tuberculosis, as everyone has told you. She was sent away for causing trouble in the house. Roberto sent her to a place where they put mad people. Please, please DO NOT TELL ANYONE ABOUT THIS LETTER. If you tell anyone, I cannot write to you again. I cannot help you take revenge on Roberto.

   I will write again soon with more information.

Yours faithfully,

A Friend

The other letters told much the same tale, each one adding a little more tantalizing detail. Daisy could imagine Simon stewing away for days at a time as he waited for more information about his mother's fate. The language was of a rudimentary nature throughout, so that Simon could read it without assistance. The writer claimed that Simon's mother, Catherine, had fought with Edgar Wildenstern over some land upon which he wanted to build a workhouse. She claimed it was hers, left to her by her father when he died. According to the letters, Roberto was in charge of building the workhouse. He had Catherine taken away to an asylum, where she was imprisoned until she too passed away.

Daisy and Tatty stared at the correspondence in amazement. It was a fiendishly blatant lie from beginning to end, but Simon had fallen for it. It was a ludicrous idea that Roberto would have been put in charge of anything at that age; even when he became old enough for such responsibility, he had spent the entire time defying his father's will at every opportunity and was not trusted with the most mundane task.

Catherine could not have been left land by her father because women had no right to own property or, indeed, to own or run a business, take part in government or even vote, all of which caused Daisy no end of irritation. Legally, women were under the complete control of either their husband or father—sometimes even their brother. And that got Daisy thinking about the one part of these letters which could be investigated.

"Simon, you've been told a horrible, horrible lie," she said to the boy. "You've been tricked into committing a terrible act. You must apologize to Berto and ask his forgiveness. I'm sure if your heart is pure, God will already have forgiven you. I might take a little longer. But I promise you this: as God is my witness, I'll find out what really happened to your mother."

"I will too," Tatty added, nodding. "We can't have people going around writing down whatever nasty ideas pop into their heads and sending them off to be read by gullible souls."

Daisy was about to comment on the kinds of newspapers Tatty had taken to reading but restrained herself. Her mind was already seething with thoughts about this blackguard who had poisoned Simon's mind. Whoever it was, they knew Simon well enough to choose just the right means to manipulate him. He had hardly known his father and idolized his mother. He had no less than six portraits of her on the walls in his rooms.

Merely by implying that Berto was responsible for her death, the conspirator had sown the seeds of murder; instincts bred into Simon by his upbringing would have done the rest. Despite his limited intellectual resources, Simon had received much the same martial training—although in a less comprehensive form—as all of the other boys in the family.

The Wildensterns were special, not only for their wealth and influence. They were one of the very few families in the world who benefited from *aurea sanitas*. They enjoyed extended life spans, superb powers of healing and excellent fitness and health. Their superhuman recuperative abilities could even be boosted by the application of gold to any injury. But they needed every advantage they could get. Generations of bloodthirsty ambition had resulted in the secret family tradition known as the Rules of Ascension.

With the intention of honing survival instincts and promoting aggression, cunning and ruthlessness, the men of the family were permitted to assassinate those of a higher rank in order to improve their own position in the Wildenstern Empire. The family would cover up any killing committed according to the Rules, which had been drawn up to maintain order and enforce the ideal of 'civilized murder.'

Daisy had only learned of this tradition after marrying Berto. By then it was too late: there was no way out of this insane family. She did not have the same blood in her veins. The families with *aurea sanitas* normally married into each other, to keep their bloodlines pure and avoid passing any of their extraordinary qualities on to less worthy types. But Berto had rebelled against his father and taken Daisy as his bride. Now, like everyone else, she knew the Rules by heart:

Number One: The Act of Aggression must be committed by the Aggressor himself and not by any agent or servant.

Number Two: The Act must only be committed against a man over the age of sixteen who holds a superior rank in the family to the Aggressor.

Number Three: The Act must only be committed for the purpose of advancing one's position and not out of spite, or because of insult or offense given, or to satisfy a need for revenge for an insult or injury given to a third party.

Number Four: All efforts should be made to avoid the deaths of servants while committing the Act. Good servants are hard to find.

Number Five: The Target of the Aggression can use any and all means to defend themselves, and is under an obligation to do so for the good of the family.

Number Six: Retribution against the Aggressor can only be carried out after the Act has been committed. Should the Aggressor fail in his attempt, and subsequently escape to remain at large for a full day, only the Target of the Aggression and no other person will be permitted to take Retribution.

Number Seven: No Act of Aggression or Retribution must be witnessed or reported by any member of the public. All family matters must be kept confidential.

Number Eight: Any bodies resulting from the Act must be given a proper burial in a cemetery, crypt, catacomb, or funeral pyre approved by the family.

Daisy shook her head as she and Tatiana walked away from the room where Simon was being held. The boy was a victim of the malevolent traditions in which he'd been reared. He was raised to be capable of murder.

Women could not hold positions of power in the family, but they could assist their menfolk. There were no rules to govern the killing of women—but then perhaps none were necessary. Daisy wondered if Simon's mother, Catherine, had really died of tuberculosis. If she hadn't, then one of the people who knew her real fate had written those letters to Simon. And Daisy was determined to find them.

Nate still felt a thrill of excitement whenever he made his way down to the engimal stables that lay at the back of the massive collection of structures that was Wildenstern Hall. Inside, in the low, dusty light, the place throbbed with the soft idling of engines, the exhalation of steam and shifting of restless wheels. Flash was kept at the end of the stables in one of the largest stalls. The velocycle grunted with pleasure when Nate looked over the door of the stall.

The notorious Beast of Glenmalure—named after the valley it had once haunted—was over eight feet long from nose to rump. Its tiger-like torso of metal and ceramic stretched between thigh-high wheels, its bullish head scraping mighty horns against the wooden sides of the stall. It raised its front wheel and thumped it down on the floorboards, eager to be let out. Pistons compressed and bulged outwards. Motors whirred. The creature's black and silver body parts were lined with streaks of gold and red, as well as scars that spoke of countless territorial fights and the hundreds of attempts that had been made to capture it or destroy it.

All that had ended the night Nate had hunted it down, trapped it and bent it to his will. Jumping on its back, he had managed to stay on while the creature bucked and thrashed around. Finally, he had forced it to surrender—much as a cowboy would break the spirit of a wild horse.

His cousin Gerald had since learned that, for a Wildenstern at least, feeding an engimal just a single drop of one's blood had the same effect. Gerald could have spared Nate a lot of painful bruises if he had discovered this a little earlier.

The velocycle's eyes had a subdued, but fierce, glow. Steam hissed from its nostrils.

"Time for some exercise, you great brute," Nate whispered, smiling. "Let's get you saddled up."

Minutes later, they were racing through the woods that bordered the Wildenstern estate and across the countryside beyond. The roads would have taken them to Tinahely faster, but Nate knew the inspector and his constable would need hours to reach the village in their horse-drawn brougham. There was plenty of time to wander across the mountains. Peering through the custom-made goggles strapped under his leather riding helmet, and with his riding coat whipping out behind him, he clung on as the velocycle ate up the distance.

Flash tore across a grassy meadow, its wheels leaving ragged tracks in the soft soil. It bunched its powerful body and uncoiled like a spring, leaping clear over a dry-stone wall, landing with a lightness that belied its size. Nate hung onto the horns, happy enough to give the creature its head, steering it only occasionally to keep it going in the right general direction.

Engimals. They remained an enigma. For many, they were proof of God's existence; living machines that defied man's best efforts to explain their origins. They did not mate and produced no young, so there were finite numbers of them in the world. Each one was unique; older than history, yet still very much alive and notoriously difficult to tame. Their physiology was beyond the understanding of the world's finest minds. Some of the creatures had no more wit than an insect, others demonstrated intelligence on a par with dogs, horses, or even apes. They came in a wide array of shapes, most of which seemed uncannily well suited to serving the needs of mankind. Only God could have created such creatures.

People of a more stubbornly rational persuasion—including one Charles Darwin—believed that engimals were the creations of a far superior civilization. Like fossils and ancient artifacts, they were the remnants of a long-forgotten people with extraordinary science, now lost in the mists of time.

Those who favored Divine Creation considered this idea preposterous. If this 'civilization' was so superior, where was it now? Why had no documents or other proof of this wondrous people ever been discovered? Surely, like any empire worth its salt, they would have left roads, cities and towering monuments. Even the rationalists had to admit to being puzzled by the contradictions in this theory. If someone could manufacture creatures that lived for thousands of years, why was there no other trace of their civilization to be found?

Gerald had become obsessed with the matter. He spent most of his days in his laboratory, reading and conducting experiments. Nate, blessed with a somewhat less curious mind, was happy to revel in the wonder of the engimals themselves. And Flash was one of the finest examples of its kind.

Men and women working in the fields stopped to look as the dashing young gentleman rode by on his exotic beast. Past clusters of thatched cabins he raced, along lanes lined with earthen banks topped with hedges of bramble, whitethorn, and hazel. Past the crops that the peasants would pay to his family as rent, in return for a small patch of land to grow their own. He and Flash moved as one, leaving the fields below them as they climbed into the heather- and rock-strewn hills, where only sheep and goats were farmed.

They bounded over a gate and sped towards the Wicklow Mountains.

III

NO CURE FOR CLUB FOOT

DAISY HAD CANCELED all her husband's meetings for the day. She was worried that Simon's assault had shaken Berto and she wanted him to relax for a while. It had also given her a chance to question Simon first thing, before Nate went about it like a bull in a china shop. Berto was disgusted at her attempt to spare him from his daily routine, arguing that he might be lame, but he was no poltroon. He demanded that she "get some of those dry snirps and their bothersome bloody waffle" scheduled in for the afternoon.

Taken aback by his new enthusiasm for meetings, Daisy did as she was told. But she chose carefully, and the first one of the day was with an old school friend of Berto's who wanted an investor for a railway contract. Winters checked him over discreetly before showing him into the study. Daisy excused herself so that they could get the public-school toilet humor out of their systems before getting down to business. She closed the door quietly behind her.

"Berto, old chap! Or should I say, Your Grace? What's it been? Three years? Still cutting a dash, I see!"

"Jamie! How the hell are you?"

Jamie was a tall, awkward young man with large hands which never seemed to know where to put themselves, moving from jacket pockets, to waistcoat, to hips, and on to trouser pockets before beginning their circuit again. His features were a little large for his face, made worse by his prematurely thinning red hair. His perpetually raised eyebrows always made him look eager to please, which he was. He was cheery and talkative and Berto could chat with him without feeling the need to check the shotgun was still under the desk. Even so, when Jamie walked in, Berto frowned, staring down at his friend's feet. It seemed Jamie had gone through some changes of his own.

The visitor obviously expected his old friend and host to come out from behind the desk to shake his hand; then he glanced at the wheels on either side of Berto's chair and blushed, leaning over the desk to shake instead. "Sorry, old chum. Heard about the back. Riding accident, wasn't it? Bad show."

Like so many dramatic events that went on in the Wildenstern house, Berto's injury had been explained to the public at large with a carefully orchestrated lie; in this case, a fall from a horse during a hunt.

"It's a bloody nuisance," Berto muttered, his voice tense. "Still, got the best doctors in the country looking at it . . . seeing what can be done . . . you know. You're looking well. Got that foot seen to, did you?"

Jamie blushed again and looked down, shifting his left leg, before grinning at Berto. "Bloody marvelous, isn't it? Left calf's still thinner than the right, but the foot's working a treat."

Berto was shocked to find himself jealous of his friend. Jamie had been born with a club foot. All the way through school, the other boys played sports and fought and did all the wild things that took their fancy while Jamie had limped around on a cane, his left foot turned awkwardly inwards so that he looked as if he were walking on his ankle. There was supposed to be no cure for a club foot.

Jamie obligingly lifted his foot onto the table. It was straight, although the ankle was a little knobbly. Pulling down the sock, he showed Berto the ugly scar that went up his calf and a third of the way around his ankle. "Wonders of modern medicine," he said.

"Who . . . " Berto swallowed, trying to keep himself calm. "Who did the operation?"

"Ah . . . " Jamie hesitated, licking his lips. "Thing is . . . I can't tell. Sort of a secret, don't y'know?"

"For God's sake, Jamie!" Berto shouted, but then looked at the door and lowered his voice. "It's *me*, for God's sake. Who did the operation?"

"I . . . I can't say, Berto," his friend explained, looking very uncomfortable all of a sudden. "It's one of the conditions . . . rules of the club, don't y'know."

"*Club?* What club?"

Jamie gazed back at Berto for a moment, all the schoolboy

playfulness gone from his face. He licked his lips once more and glanced at the door. For a second, Berto thought he was about to be attacked again, but instead, Jamie sat on the edge of the desk and leaned towards him, speaking in a low voice.

"Look . . . Have you heard of the Knights of Abraham?"

Berto frowned. He had heard rumors of the name in the elite gentlemen's clubs in town.

"They're . . . aren't they some kind of secret society? Like the Freemasons or something?"

At first, there was no reply. Then Jamie took Berto's pen from its holder, opened the ink pot, and, dipping the tip, wrote a name and address on the blotter on the desk.

"You're having a party next week, aren't you? Invite this man. He can explain better than I can. He can also . . . he knows better than me what to say and what not to say. Sorry; I know I'm being a complete prig, but you've no idea how picky these chaps are about privacy."

Berto thought about some of the secrets harbored within the walls of Wildenstern Hall.

"I might understand better than you think," he said, smirking. "So . . . want to talk business?"

"I suppose we must. Father will have my head if I don't come away from here with barrows of your money to spend."

"My wife will have mine if you do. Let's try and keep them both happy, shall we?"

By the time Nate reached Tinahely, his coat, boots and trousers were filthy, his goggles were dotted with dead insects and his body was tired from the drawn-out rush of adrenaline. He had taken the scenic route, but still had to wait another half-hour for the inspector to arrive.

The policeman passed no remarks about the engimal, although his constable stared in fear and awe. Engimals were rare, expensive and mysterious. Flash was all that and frightening too.

They had a further twenty minutes' ride to reach the sheltered nook in the hillside where Vicky Miller's cottage was to be found. Two more constables stood guard over the property, to keep poking noses at bay.

"I like to keep the scene clear while I'm carrying out my inquiries," Urskin explained. "Sometimes the place can tell you as much as a witness, if you know how to look. I think of it as my workshop. Don't like a herd of busybodies trampling all over it."

Nate nodded. It was the kind of thing his cousin Gerald would have said.

"The old woman died around the back," Urskin told him.

Nate got the definite impression that the policeman resented his presence, though the man would never admit it. Probably one of those who thought the lawdy-daws should keep their toffee-noses out of a working man's business. Nate had a degree of respect for this attitude in theory, but tended to ignore it in practice.

"Let's have a gander then," he prompted the inspector.

They walked around the tiny house, to where the woman had died. One of the constables walked ahead of them, and at a nod from the inspector lifted the sheet of canvas covering up the remains. Urskin had been right. You had to see the scene to appreciate how strange it was.

"Stone me," Nate said under his breath.

The remains of the old woman lay halfway between the house, with its white-washed walls and thatched roof, and the well fifteen yards away. There was no body to be seen. Instead, all that was left of Vicky Miller was a burned oval patch in the grass about two yards long with a low pile of ash along its center . . . and her lower legs. They lay there, slightly charred at the knees, but otherwise perfectly intact down to the toes.

"We're assuming that she was trying to reach the well," Urskin explained. "Although there was a jug and a bowl of water in the house . . . and a half-filled chamber pot if she was really desperate. Maybe she was in the house when it happened. Maybe not. People can do funny things in a panic."

Nate had seen some macabre things in his relatively short life, but this still turned his stomach. Suppressing the need to retch, he stepped closer.

"How did the legs survive when the rest—?" he managed to say.

"Haven't the foggiest, sir."

"And why are there no bones in the ashes?"

"Well spotted, sir." Urskin looked at him in surprise. "There should be bones. It takes a very hot fire indeed to burn bone. Hot as a furnace. Couldn't happen outside in the open with a little blaze like this. So either somebody's taken 'em . . . or the fire was not a natural one."

Nate gave him a searching look.

"And by 'not a natural one,' you mean . . . what, exactly?"

"The old spinster was well known in these parts," Urskin said, looking out over the hills. "She had a way with herbs, it's said, and some skill as a bonesetter. She kept strange hours and had stranger habits. She was more than friendly with some of the men in the area." He turned to meet Nate's gaze. "Some would have called her a witch."

Nate exhaled through his teeth.

"I was not aware that modern police work encompassed such hocus-pocus claptrap. Frankly, I'd expect more sense from officers of the law."

"Claptrap it might be, sir," said Urskin, touching his hand to his hat. "But people will gossip, and the parish priest preached more than one sermon against her. What nobody knew, however, was that she had some connection with the *noble* Wildenstern family."

If Nate detected a whiff of sarcasm in the man's tone at the word "noble," he said nothing. Following the policeman, he walked around to the front of the house and bent his head to step in through the low, open door. There were two rooms: a tiny bedroom and a kitchen. The place was small but cozy, with simple wooden furnishings and a fireplace at the end of each room, with a cast-iron kettle and a large pot (Nate resisted the urge to think of it as a cauldron) hanging from a bracket over the fire in the kitchen. There were also four bookcases, piled high with books on local history, herbs and medicine.

There was a volume on mathaumaturgy, the pseudoscience involving mathematical sequences that were thought to affect the behavior of engimals and perhaps even reality itself, if one believed that kind of thing. Nate knew quite a bit about engimal behavior, and he had never been able to understand how showing an engimal pages and pages of numbers, or flashing lights at different speeds, or tapping tones in dots and dashes like a telegraph, was supposed to have any effect whatsoever. The only effect it had on Nate was to bore him senseless.

This mathematical 'magic' was the kind of thing that excited only the most unorthodox scientists. He thought it an odd subject for an old woman to be interested in.

"We found the picture I showed you hidden at the bottom of this chest here, along with some other items that might be considered unusual for a woman of her station," the inspector continued. "And if the family connection proves to be a genuine one, it might explain how she came to be in the possession of *this*."

Reaching into the simple pine chest, he produced a small, dark wooden box with a hinged lid. It was about the size of a man's head and Nate, for one irrational second, expected it to contain just that. But when the inspector opened it Nate peered inside and saw an engimal shaped like a coiled snake. The creature was about the width of his big toe, a lustrous white in color, with hexagonal scales and lines spiraling along its three-foot length that gave it the appearance of a piece of rope. It peered up at them with sleepy silver eyes, slowly opening and closing its jaws.

"It's an engimal, sir."

"Yes, I can see that, Inspector. The ceramic skin and metal eyes are something of a giveaway. This particular type is known as a serpentine. I saw a number of these when I was in Africa. I didn't know there were any in Ireland."

"Looks in good nick too. Probably worth more than I make in a year."

"I wouldn't dare comment," Nate said. "Where do you think she got it?"

"I have no idea," the inspector replied. "But it begs the question, why was she livin' in a state of near-poverty, as it were, when she had one of these lyin' about the house?"

"Do you think she might have been killed for this? Somebody came to murder her and steal it, but couldn't find it?"

"I found it easy enough. I think there's more to this than a straightforward robbery. We didn't find a trace of anyone else. Wouldn't explain the strange nature of the fire either. Besides"—Urskin took his hat off and scratched his head, giving Nate a thoughtful glance—"she's not the first to die like this."

"She's not?"

"No indeed. And the others weren't robbed either."

"Interesting."

"Aye. What's more interesting still is that the others—at least five that we know of—all burned without a sound, in rooms in crowded tenement houses in Dublin. And they burned without setting fire to anything else in their rooms. They all died alone. And each room was locked from the inside. A couple of them were rumored to be witches too."

"You work Dublin as well? You've got a big patch to cover, haven't you?"

"I work out of Dublin Castle, sir. A couple of these women were suspected rebels. I took the liberty of requesting the case."

The worn-looking policeman was more powerful than he had let on. If he worked out of Dublin Castle, he was most likely in intelligence, tasked with hunting Fenian rebels and other threats to the government. Here was a man with hard bark and the power to use it. But why was he taking an interest in the deaths of a few old women?

The inspector stared with a disrespectful air at the youthful buck before him. There was a challenge in his eyes. It said that young gentlemen should go about their frivolous lives and leave the work of solving crime to solid, experienced men. These were matters concerning real people that could not be left in the hands of the idle rich, to be treated as passing entertainment or intellectual distractions. These eyes had seen hardship, misery and cruelty in many different forms over the years and this was a man who took his responsibilities seriously, which was more than could be said of some whippersnapper still wet behind the ears and eager for a bit of mystery. The expression in the inspector's eyes told Nate to mind his own bloody business.

Nate disregarded it completely.

"Well, Inspector," he sighed. "Until we've established just who Vicky Miller really was, her connection with the family and how her death came about, I think it would be best if you kept us informed on this one. Don't you?"

"If you insist, sir. Any help you could offer would be appreciated." Urskin dipped his head, touched his hat and almost succeeded in hiding his scowl.

"I do insist, and would be delighted to provide any help I can," Nate affirmed, glad—and not for the first time—that his was the most powerful family in Ireland. "Do you know if Mrs. Miller had any next of kin?"

"Not that we're aware, sir."

"Then if you don't mind, I'll hang onto this engimal for the moment. I have just the man to examine it. I promise you I'll return it in due course."

"Very good, sir," the inspector said, in a tone that implied quite the opposite.

There were times when Daisy would leave her husband to enjoy his rides in the country on his own. He was partial to being driven around the estate in his brougham by Hennessy, the old head groom. The two men, divided by age and class, had nevertheless become very close—far too close. Daisy had discovered the year before that they were having an affair—a crime punishable by a prison sentence in Victorian society. Berto had ended the affair, but had refused to cut all his ties with Hennessy.

And since the fateful fall that had broken Berto's back, Daisy did not have the stomach to have it out with him. She bore his disability as well as she could, despite an ever-worsening fear that they might never have children. This, and her hatred for the head groom, were the kinds of ill feelings that she considered unChristian and she tried to keep them to herself.

But her conversation with Simon that morning had left her disturbed, and Berto too seemed in a pensive mood after meeting his old school chum, Jamie. A refreshing ride in the country would do them both some good.

She and Tatiana joined the two men on their jaunt, and despite a light rain, they kept the canopy down, glad of the fresh air. The old groom avoided her gaze, keeping his attention on the horses. Daisy led the conversation, chatting about the summer ball, which was taking place the following week. It would be a huge event and both Daisy and Berto were a little nervous, unlike Tatiana, who was beside herself with excitement, her lightly freckled cheeks flushed with color.

Tatania's most prized possession perched on her shoulder, one of its feet bound to her wrist with a length of string. Siren was an engimal—a gift from Nate when he returned from Africa. The shape of a small bird, its blue and silver 'plumage' was formed of some near-weightless metal material. It had a white breast, a copper-colored beak and bright orange eyes. It could generate melodies like a music box, but had an endless variety of tunes— many of which Daisy considered highly unladylike—which it was capable of playing very loudly indeed. For the moment, Siren was projecting a repetitive drumbeat-driven tune under Tatty's blonde ringlets and into her left ear at a volume just great enough to be detected by those around her. The tinny sound was growing quite irritating, but Tatiana could not be persuaded to shut the creature up for very long.

"It's going to be such fun!" she exclaimed. "The conductor was showing me all the dances the orchestra have been practicing and we have fabulous guests coming! It's a great pity that young detective, Mr. Holmes, couldn't make it—some important case or other . . . and Sir Harry Flashman is abroad apparently— he's such a noble, heroic adventurer! They could have told us the most splendid stories. But we'll have the cricketer, A. J. Raffles, and the celebrated Doctor Jekyll . . . and lots of soldiers in the most dashing uniforms!"

"Don't be deceived by the dashing uniforms, Tatty," Berto cautioned her, lifting himself to shift his backside further into the velvet-upholstered seat. The weight of his limp legs tended to pull him forward. "Cads can wear medals too. You're a bit young yet to be dallying with men of the world."

"Berto, leave her alone," Daisy scolded him. "She's only—"

"Worldly men are the only ones who interest me," Tatty said snottily.

"Tatiana!" Daisy gasped.

The impending rebuke on suitable conversational matter for a young lady (at least, while sitting in the company of her brother) was interrupted by the rumbling grate of rolling metal feet on the surface of the road. The two horses whinnied and pulled up short, their eyes wide and ears back as they stared ahead. A low hill lined with spruce had hidden the creature and the sound of the horses' hooves had masked its approach. But now it was within a hundred yards, rounding the corner at the foot of the hill, and it was impossible to ignore.

"What the blazes is that doing out of its paddock?" Berto growled.

Trom was an engimal of notorious ferocity. The size of a locomotive and heavier still, it moved on hinged tracks that rolled around its wheels like belts, giving it superb traction. Its broad, scarred, hulking shape was gray for the most part, its extremities banded with zigzagging stripes of black and yellow. One of a breed known as bull-razers, it had a massive jaw jutting from its shoulders, capable of smashing through any building. Its dull mind made it manageable, but it was clumsy and destructive with its size and uncaring to boot. For years, the Wildensterns had used it to evict tenants who could not make the rent. It had not been out of its paddock since Berto had banned this brutal practice . . . or so he'd thought.

Standing on Trom's back, holding the beast s reins, was Berto's cousin, Oliver. A self-satisfied sneer was visible on his black-whiskered face even at this distance. Behind him, in a wagon, rode half a dozen of the family's bailiffs. Daisy glanced at Berto and then back at the oncoming enginal.

"You don't think he'd try to . . . ?" She didn't want to say it in front of Tatiana, but her sister-in-law could see it plain enough.

"I could be mistaken," Tatiana declared, the only signs of her distress showing in her pale cheeks and in the white knuckles on her hand where it gripped the side of the carriage. "But our dear cousin does seem to be approaching at an alarming pace. Is it possible he hasn't seen us?"

Siren stopped singing and huddled up against its mistress's neck.

Hennessy had pulled the brougham's horses up, but Trom was still coming. The road was barely wide enough for the monster on its own; there was no room for it to pass the carriage. High bramble hedges blocked escape on either side. Trom bore down on them, lumbering with unchecked momentum, crushing stones beneath its wide, metal, beltlike feet. The ground trembled beneath them. Oliver showed no sign of reining it in.

"Stand your ground, Hennessy," Berto said in a level voice, then to Daisy and Tatty: "The bailiffs are hired men. Oliver wouldn't make such a blatant attempt to harm me in front of them, particularly with you here. He's just throwing out his chest. Hennessy! Stand your ground, man!"

But that was easier said than done with panicking horses. They thrashed around in their harnesses, dragging the brougham in a circle, nearly twisting the wheels off their spokes and coming close to tipping the carriage over. Then as Trom rumbled closer they kicked up the dust and bolted down the road. In the careering carriage, Berto, Daisy and Tatty hung on for their lives as Hennessy fought to control the frantic animals.

IV

THE CHANGELING

CATHAL DEMPSEY WAS ENJOYING his new-found ability to breathe. It was hard to believe that only a week before he had been staring death in the face, dragging in strained, gasping breaths with the ragged remains of his lungs, coughing blood into his soiled handkerchief and feeling tight bands of pain around his ribcage with every inhalation. Now everything was different. Sucking in air through his wide-open mouth, he blew it out joyfully and shouted at the pale yellow dawn.

His mother had warned him that he was not to be seen outside for a few weeks. They were supposed to be moving to another part of Dublin where they weren't known, where people would not ask questions about Cathal's miraculous recovery.

But he was a willful boy, stubborn as a mule, and he'd had

his fill of staying inside. Nobody would be out yet—at least nobody who'd see him up here on Howth Head with his back to the quarry, taking in the view over the north side of Dublin Bay. The mail packet didn't come into Howth harbor any more, going to Kingstown instead, but the fishing boats were already heading out to sea to his left, and a paddle steamer was dragging a smudged line of smoke towards Dublin Port at the mouth of the Liffey off to Cathal's right. Out beyond the bay, Ireland's Eye was just visible as the sunlight crept across the sea.

Cathal knew he should be getting home—his ma had said they'd be in awful trouble if he was spotted—but he was just feeling so damned good. With his cropped red hair crowning what his mother called "a cheeky cherub's face with charmer's eyes," he was well known in the village for his high jinks and smart-arse ways. He never went out without his father's grubby old black velveteen coat, which was finally beginning to fit him. His pa was a second lieutenant in the Royal Navy, on a ship of the line, and was rarely home. His ma was always saying how much she missed her hard-working husband, but didn't he do them proud?

She certainly missed his belt when Cathal acted up, not that she really minded her son being a little bold—it was only to be expected, considering the way he was treated in the village. And she knew that was all down to her.

"Oi, Witch-boy!" a voice shouted from below him.

Cathal gave a start. He'd been so sure he was alone. On the path leading back into the village, he saw three boys climbing towards him. The MacGuinness brothers. Of all the people who could have seen him, why did it have to be them? The three brothers were the worst of his tormentors, both at school and in the village.

He should turn and run, but that would just make them more suspicious. There was no way he should have been able to make it up here with his lungs the way they were and they knew it. At twelve, he was younger than the three of them, but bigger than Thomas, the youngest. Cathal had been a handy enough scrapper until he got sick. Back when he was fit he could have taken Thomas in a mill, and maybe one of the others too. But not all three of them together.

"What you doing up here, Witch-boy?" Paulie, the eldest, called to him. "Should you not be at home dyin', like?"

They were glaring at him with hostile curiosity. He pretended to cough and started to walk away, mimicking the feeble movements that he'd been reduced to before his mother brought her cousin to see him. Before he was cured. But pretending to be sick meant he couldn't run.

They hurried over and surrounded him, Paulie pulling on his shoulder to turn him around.

"How'd you get up here, Witch-boy?" he demanded.

"Don't call me that," Cathal retorted, trying to force a wheeze into his voice.

"Why not? That's what y'are, aren't yeh, Witch-chit? Broomstick-boy. Yeh little feckin' changelin' yeh." Paulie looked Cathal up and down. "So, tell us: how the hell did yeh get up here then?"

Cathal coughed a bit again, but he was losing patience with

this. He thought about coming up with some fib about how he'd got here, but he was annoyed that he should have to.

"Don't call my ma a witch," he growled.

"I'll call her what I like," Paulie snorted at him. "She knows what she is and so do you. But you still haven't told us why yer not dyin', Dempsey. I think we should take yeh down to the priest, show him the color in yer cheeks. What do yeh reckon, lads?"

The lads reckoned he was right.

"Maybe he'll do an exorcism on yeh, eh?" he declared, grinning at his brothers.

Cathal's fist flashed out and he heard something snap under it as it struck Paulie's ribs. Paulie gasped in winded pain, but Cathal was already lashing out with his left foot, catching Thomas on the shin. Frank, the middle brother, got his arm around Cathal's neck from behind and started to choke him. It would have beaten Cathal two weeks ago: any pressure to his throat or chest would have been enough to make him collapse.

Thomas came at him, fists bunched, limping on his bruised shin. Cathal reached back, grabbed Frank's hair and pulled hard, bending over at the same time. Frank pitched forward over Cathal's shoulder and into Thomas's path. The two brothers tumbled together in a tangle of limbs. Cathal could have run. But he was damned if he was going to run. He had never felt so strong.

"Get up," he snarled at them. "I bloody claim yiz all. All three of yeh. Let's see if yiz have a decent set of gonads between yeh."

"He's got the bloody Devil in 'im!" Frank panted.

"I have, y'know," Cathal growled back at him. "And I'll kick seven shades of shite out o' yiz before I'm done."

The MacGuinness brothers were a tough brood, and it was unthinkable for them to lose when they were fighting together against one little gurrier. They rose to their feet, swearing and spitting at Cathal, and came at him again. He raised his fists and met them head on.

Daisy sat off to one side, staying silent as her husband dealt with the thorny issue of giving his cousin a dressing down for the run-in with Trom the previous day. The horses had galloped for nearly a mile before Hennessy had regained control over them.

The biggest obstacles to Berto's attempts to reform the family were his Uncle Gideon and his five sons, whom Berto often referred to as the Gideonettes—though not in their company.

Oliver was the second eldest of the Gideonettes—at twenty-four, he was two years older than Berto—and was a typical example of the family's burly physique, thick black hair and carefully groomed whiskers. He wore a handlebar mustache, its tips waxed into sharp points. The belligerent frown that characterized all five brothers had long ago carved a hard vertical line between his heavy eyebrows. This afternoon the line was complemented by an arrogant smirk, and Oliver was accompanied by his father.

Both wore an unseemly amount of gold jewelry, believing it would supplement their family's extraordinary health. Thick chains lay over the two men's starched shirts and heavy, jeweled rings bulged out from their thick fingers. They sat on the far side of Berto's desk, staring him down.

Daisy glanced towards Nathaniel, who was sitting in the corner behind the two men, his eyes fixed on them. He had searched them for weapons before they entered, but still would not trust them alone with his brother.

"I thought I had made it clear that Trom was no longer to be used for evictions," Berto said through his teeth. "The bailiffs know their business. I would rather it wasn't necessary at all—"

"Yes, well that's the problem, isn't it, cousin?" Oliver sniffed. "If we had it your way, no one would pay any rent whatsoever. Why, we'd be broke within a year, don't y'know. Tell me, do— how are we supposed to collect what is due to us, if the wretches can go on living in their hovels after they fail to pay?"

"Do not take me for a fool," Berto warned him. "You crushed two houses with that monster yesterday; people could have been killed. How do you expect to keep our tenants onside when we act like tyrants? You send them running into the arms of the damned Fenians! It's just the kind of thing that excites rebellion—you'll have the people thinking there's no difference between us and the British, for God's sake! Do you want those bloody rebel upstarts trying to drive *us* out of Ireland too? And as for making money out of people, cousin, I might remind you that dead men grow no grain."

"There'll be no associating with the Fenian·scum. The peasants know which side their bread is buttered," Oliver sneered. "All the more so if you give them a good spreading from time to time. Haw haw! Eh? That's what I say. I have matters well in hand. The estates are under my control and that's the way they'll stay."

"No they won't," Berto replied. "Seeing as you can't be trusted to follow my instructions—even the simpler ones like, 'Trom is not to leave its paddock'—I'm relieving you of that particular responsibility. Gerald will take over the estates, once we pry him out of his laboratory. Even with one eye glued to a bloody microscope, he'll do a better job than you. I am giving you responsibility for . . . let me see . . . ah, yes: drainage maintenance."

Oliver looked as if he'd been struck. Gideon jumped to his feet, all bristling black beard and furious red face; a fatter, older, more blustering version of his son. Daisy hated the man with a passion, not least because he represented all the worst qualities of the Wildensterns.

"How dare you insult my boy that way!" he bellowed. "It will not stand! *Drainage*? What kind of duty is that for a gentleman?"

He glanced back at Nate and, realizing he was overstepping the mark, took a step back from the desk. Oliver muttered something under his breath about letting Trom have more rein next time he came upon Berto on the road.

Berto caught the comment and raised his eyebrows.

"That. Yes, I'd almost forgotten," he said brightly. "Do you think that could be termed an Act of Aggression, under the Rules? I wonder." He reached under his desk and slapped the sawn-off shotgun down on the mahogany. "Would some retaliation be in order, d'you think? No? Sure? We can get on with it right now, if you like."

Gideon and Oliver were looking uneasily at the gun. Berto had a reputation in the family for being a soft touch, but he was still a Wildenstern—and everyone had their limits. Nate was smiling slightly, but still did not move.

"Perhaps an apology is in order," Oliver muttered weakly.

"Then I trust it will be forthcoming," Berto told him, pulling back the hammers on the weapon with his thumb. "Or something else will be."

He watched the two men fold and apologize, before gently easing the hammers back into place.

"We are forced to play such childish games, don't you think?" he said acidly.

Watching from the sidelines, Daisy was proud to see her husband giving his god-awful relatives what for, but disturbed to see how easily it came to him once his mind was set. They hated him because he had defied his father's wishes for so long, avoiding his place in the family business. Now he had all the power they so desperately craved.

Berto was changing before her eyes. Where was the carefree lover of poetry and music that she had married? It seemed to take all his optimism to keep his plans for the family on track. Was there anything of him left, now that injury, pain and responsibility had taken their toll? Daisy was determined to find out. She did not want him to succeed as Patriarch, only to lose him as her husband.

After eating some humble pie, Gideon and his son left. Berto fitted the firearm back into its clips under the desk and rolled back his chair, letting out a long sigh.

"Ye gods, this is no way to live," he breathed.

Daisy said nothing, rising and walking over to him instead, to stand behind his chair and wrap her arms around him. He squeezed her arm with one hand, but the other gripped the wheel by his hip, and she knew he was thinking how vulnerable he was, trapped in that chair.

Cathal had got a good telling off from his mother when he arrived home that morning, but it was worth it. The fight had left him feeling raw and alive and invincible. His mother had warned that there might be changes, but he'd never felt anything like this before.

Tongues would already be wagging in the village, he knew. The MacGuinness boys would have told everyone what they'd seen, although maybe not about the trouncing they'd just got from the 'witch's son.' Catherine Dempsey's lad, who'd been at death's door, coughing his lungs up with tuberculosis, had climbed up Howth Head and was standing there breathing as easy as you please.

He hadn't told his ma about meeting the MacGuinnesses. Her anger was something to behold and he had no wish to do any beholding today. It was bad enough that he'd been out at all. After the initial fireworks, she'd set Cathal to cleaning out the fire grate and sweeping and scrubbing the kitchen floor while she went back to preparing her herbal remedies. He loved the smell of the kitchen as she cooked up her 'potions,' as she sometimes called them, cackling like a witch in a pantomime. Not all of the smells were good; her cabbage tea stank to high heaven and the garlic she used could linger for days. But it smelled like nobody else's house and it always made him feel at home.

At forty-four, Catherine Dempsey was much older than the other mothers in the village with children Cathal's age. He was an only child, which was unusual too, particularly when a good stout Catholic mother could reasonably be expected to turn out eight or ten children in her lifetime. For a woman to have just one child suggested that perhaps there was *something wrong* with her.

As if Cathal's existence wasn't tough enough. So much about their lives seemed to be out of the ordinary. Sometimes he wished he was like all the other boys. Maybe they'd accept him more if his ma didn't sell herbal remedies or treat poxes and fevers, or if she didn't have 'ideas above her station,' which seemed to just mean that she wanted a better life for her family than they had now.

His chores didn't take too long and then he was bored again. He could read, but he was constantly disappointing his ma with his choice of books and she refused to buy the 'drivel' he preferred, stories of highwaymen and pirates and ghosts. Sometimes she despaired that he would turn into just another no-good gurrier, like the other lads in the area.

Their house was set apart from the main body of the village, which backed onto the grounds of Howth Castle. It nestled among some trees on a steep bit of slope with a view of the harbor. It was better than some, worse than others, but it was comfortable enough. Built of red brick, with a slate-tiled roof and sash windows, it had four main rooms: a living room; a kitchen with wood floors, patterned tiles and even a small water closet; and two bedrooms. The furniture was proper varnished stuff and they had pictures on the walls—including some real drawings and paintings and not just prints like he'd seen in other places. And they were still well off enough for him to have two pairs of shoes, which he even wore sometimes without being told to. His ma put a lot of effort into giving their home a touch of class. Even so, there were times when he found her looking around it as if it was the most depressing place in the world.

And now, of course, they were going to have to leave. Because he'd got sick. They couldn't even wait until his pa came home from the sea. Nobody was supposed to get better when they'd been as bad as he was.

"Cathal, love, don't stand in front of the windows," his ma said to him, as she weighed out portions of dried lemon balm. "You're supposed to be bedridden."

He sighed, thinking again that he should tell her about the fight. Not yet, he decided. I'll tell her later, when she's tired and can't shout as much.

"What're you brooding about?" she inquired in that I-already-know tone of voice.

"I'm bored," he said to her.

"Why don't you read?"

"I've read all the good books. Yeh won't get me the stuff I like."

She didn't reply, but he could almost hear her rolling her eyes.

"Ma!" he said abruptly, peering out of the corner of the window.

"What?"

"Father Houlihan is coming through the gate!"

She lifted her head to look through the window too. Her brow creased with concern as her eyes lit on the priest's grim visage. Mr. and Mrs. MacGuinness were with him.

"Get you to bed, and look sick," she said. "And for the love of God, put on a good show."

V

AN INQUISITIVE MIND

IT WOULD BE DIFFICULT to describe Wildenstern Hall without referring to the many ages of architecture through which it had passed, each generation leaving its distinctive mark. The manor house began life as a keep in Norman times and was then gradually broken down and repaired and extended and built upon over the centuries until its clustered buildings achieved a kind of symmetry by failing to represent any particular style or, indeed, every style.

The central tower was the latest and by far the largest addition, completed in Nathaniel's childhood, setting standards of construction that were far beyond others of its kind. At thirty stories, it was one of the tallest buildings in Europe. Its steel skeleton, anchored deep in the bedrock of the mountain on which it squatted, was the pinnacle of engineering, as were the steam turbines that drove its mechanical lifts.

With its sculptured terracotta panels, majestic arches, flying buttresses and gothic turrets, the massive building was an intimidating sight—as it was intended to be. Gargoyles perched on the ledges of this brooding structure, their gaping mouths dripping rainwater and screaming silently into the sky. When the smog enveloped Dublin, as it so often did, the Wildenstern family home rose above it as if jutting into Heaven itself.

Most of the family lived in the higher parts of the tower—the higher the rank, the higher the floor they could claim . . . and the more booby-traps they needed to set to protect themselves. But Nate's cousin, Gerald, had retreated to the vast basement in the foundations, where he had set up his rooms and laboratory, the only natural light coming from thick glass grates along one side of the ceiling. The area was filled with tables on which a plethora of experiments were taking place. Glass beakers, metal stands, thermometers, gutta-percha tubes and Bunsen burners littered the tabletops. A strange mix of smells filled the air: sulphur, ammonia, ether, blood and electricity. Among the steel stanchions that held up the rest of the house, shadows hid bizarre scientific equipment, custom-made tools and devices.

Two of the walls were lined with shelves of books, their subjects ranging from biology to mathaumaturgy—the sight of them reminded Nate that Vicky Miller had also possessed books on the mathematical 'magic.'

On some of the workbenches lay the lifeless forms of engimals, their bodies opened up and parts removed, while others waited in cages at the far end of the room. Gerald's obsession was the science that had created them, and its connection with the Wildenstern family's *aurea sanitas*—its remarkable powers of healing.

This morning, Gerald sat perched on a tall stool at a workbench under a shaft of daylight, peering into a microscope. Pale, with dark hair and two slivers of mustache, he had a pencil in one hand, poised over a notebook, and a French cigarette in the other, almost burned down to his fingers. His concentration on the slide under the microscope was absolute.

Nate waited for his attention. He needed Gerald in a good mood and his cousin did not like being interrupted. In his hands Nate held the box which contained Vicky Miller's little engimal.

As he stood there, an engimal the size of a traveling trunk scooted over to him. He recognized it as one of a breed known as self-propelling wheelbarrows. It was a rounded box-like shape, with two chunky front wheels and two smaller rear wheels that could turn through three hundred and sixty degrees, allowing the creature to maneuver in small spaces. A sandy brown in color, with stippled black markings, its flat upper body, complete with long spindly arms, formed the lid of the barrow.

It opened its lid and looked up expectantly at Nate, with small green, pleading eyes, like a dog who had brought a stick to its master to play fetch. It looked at the box and then back at him. Nate chuckled to himself. It wanted the box, but he reached over and picked up some candles from a table instead, placing them gently inside the barrow so as not to disturb Gerald. The engimal was content enough with this. It spun around and scurried away, whistling to itself, into the darkness at the far end of the room.

Gerald lifted his gaze from the brass eyepiece.

"Oh, God, don't encourage it," he moaned. "It keeps collecting odds and ends and piling them up in the corner. How long have you been standing there ogling me?"

"Long enough to need a shave. Haven't seen one of those things since Africa."

"It was found in the Sahara, actually. It was gathering rocks and forming them into piles. Made some interesting patterns, apparently, some of them stretching across acres of sand. Would love to have seen them."

"You look a bit jaded. When was the last time you were out?"

"Not sure, old chap," Gerald replied, looking regretfully at his cigarette. "What season is it?"

"You'll turn white and wrinkly. You need some sun and some air."

"I need to light up another gasper and have a few gulps of coffee. What brings you down to my little cave?"

"An altruistic concern for your wellbeing," Nate assured him.

"Ah. Need a favor, then?"

"Not exactly. I have a little mystery that I thought might pique your interest."

Gerald gave his microscope a longing gaze, but Nate knew he had been hitting one dead end after another in his experiments over these last few weeks. The two had been best friends since childhood. Apart from the very mundane fact that they enjoyed each other's company, Nate found Gerald's complete disregard for the family's fixation with money and power something of a relief. Gerald was too far down the chain to have any realistic chance of becoming Patriarch, and besides, he was much more interested in the physical qualities that made the family special, and how those qualities related to engimals. The family's wealth was merely a means to an end for him and, given a steady supply of French cigarettes, research materials and equipment—and the occasional meal—Gerald would probably have been happy spending most of the rest of his life tucked away here in his cellar.

The young scientist raised his eyebrows towards his cousin and waved to a servant to order some coffee and shortbread. As they indulged in their refreshments and Gerald lit another cigarette, Nate told him the story of the burned woman.

His cousin listened with growing fascination.

"And there were no bones?" he asked in amazement.

"None—except for the legs, which were untouched by the blaze," Nate told him. "Must have been a hellish fire. I don't know how hot it has to be—"

"In excess of seven hundred degrees centigrade," Gerald muttered, sipping his coffee. "You'd need a furnace. I can't see how her body alone could generate that kind of heat. Even putting a body on a funeral pyre isn't guaranteed to burn the whole thing. No, somebody must have stolen the bones afterwards."

"Urskin is convinced the other women they found were alone in locked rooms until they were discovered. They were in much the same state, except in a couple of cases an arm was left intact as well. The lower arm, below the elbow, in each case."

"Marvelous," Gerald breathed. "By God, I'm hooked. How do you want to proceed?"

Nate handed him the box and Gerald looked inside.

"A charming little fellow," he commented. "A serpentine, if I'm not mistaken, though its function is unclear."

"I need you to find out exactly what it is and what it can do," Nate said to him. "It seems to have been very important to this woman, and not just in monetary terms."

"I see." Gerald stared with hungry eyes at the white, snake-shaped creature, which passively returned his gaze, stretching open its jaws in a yawn.

"Don't hurt it. And definitely don't *dissect* it, Gerald."

"Very well. You can be so sentimental at times, old chum. It's not like they're people, you know."

"As if you care any more for people!" Nate continued. "To get back to the point, we need to find out who Vicky Miller was. She's not in any of the portraits in the house, but I'm sure she was a relative—she seems very familiar to me, though I can't say why. Then we need to know what caused her death. I think you should cast your keen eye over the scene and see what you can uncover."

"Jolly good. I'll take a ride over there as soon as possible."

"Thanks. There's something very queer about this whole business, but I can't give it my full attention until I've discovered who's been pulling Simon's strings and dealt with them first. Here we are trying to do away with the whole tradition of Ascension and it could be that somebody's gone and killed a Wildenstern woman without any regard to the Rules at all."

"Indeed. Some people have no sense of decorum. More coffee?"

VI

A GARRULOUS OLD HARRIDAN

CATHAL HAD PUT ON A GOOD SHOW for the priest, but neither he nor his mother thought the good father had bought it. The MacGuinnesses, for all their assertions that the Dempsey boy was up and about and looking uncommonly healthy for someone with consumption, did not dare come into the room to check for themselves. Just because he had made a remarkable recovery didn't mean the unholy little terror wasn't still contagious.

Cathal had coughed and wheezed his best for the priest, but Father Houlihan was nobody's fool. Nor was he heartless, however, and he wasn't about to go haranguing a boy who might not be long for this world on the off chance that the lad was faking it.

The priest had a grim expression on his face when he left, and it was hard to tell if it was due to the anticipation of a boy's demise or the suspicion of a witch's deal with the Devil. Cathal's mother was quiet for a long time afterwards, and he could tell she was angry with him for not telling her about the fight, but she was disappointed too and that hurt him more than any tongue-lashing.

When the Doubting Thomases had gone, Cathal stayed in bed feeling thoroughly miserable, eventually falling asleep.

He awoke the following morning to find he was still sulking. It wasn't his fault he'd been cured. And he didn't understand why it had to be a secret. If his mother's cousin could cure the dreaded disease, wasn't that a good thing? Couldn't they save thousands of lives? Couldn't she make millions of pounds from the cure?

"You're different," his mother said from the door, startling him. "You're not like other boys. You have special blood in your veins. We both have. That's how Vicky was able to cure you."

Not for the first time, Cathal wondered if his mother could read minds, or if she really was just a canny hag like she claimed. She definitely didn't look like a witch, with her round, rosy-cheeked face, button-mushroom nose, watery blue eyes and fading blonde hair. But then, he was never sure what witches were *supposed* to look like.

"Why did I get sick in the first place then?" he asked. "Why couldn't I be special enough not to catch the bloody disease?"

"Don't swear, Cathal. You know I don't like it," she chided him gently. "Vicky had to . . . to get you started. To tell your blood how to cure itself. It's not like we even know how to control this thing inside us. We grew up knowing we had it and . . . somehow that was enough, but things were different then. I couldn't raise you the same way. But if people start thinking we can do magic, they'll . . . they won't understand. People don't like folk who are different from them."

"Don't be tellin' me," Cathal snorted, pulling his knees up under the covers. "Sure, don't I get it all the time."

"That's still no excuse for getting into fights, young man."

"Tell that to the MacGuinnesses! I learned 'em though. They'll fill their britches at the thought of havin' it out with me again. You should have seen what I could do, Ma! I—"

"You *taught them*, love," his mother corrected him. "Not 'learned 'em.' And they wouldn't have been bullyragging you if you'd done as I said and stayed inside."

"But Ma—!"

"Cathal, love, this is going to make things difficult for us. You'll be a good boy and stay in from now on, won't you? Until we can move somewhere they don't know us. The neighbors gossip about us enough as it is without them thinking I've done a deal with the Devil to cure my little boy."

"Ma, I'm not little! I'm twelve!"

"You'll always be my little boy, love. Now, how about I go and get you one of those awful books you like? What'll it be? *Tom Brown's Schooldays*?"

Cathal made a face, sticking out his tongue. That was a book for 'improving' children and she knew it.

"That's all about toffs an' posh schools. I want a Dick Turpin story, or that one, *Tales of the Grotesque and Arabesque*, by that creepy fella—what's 'is name . . . Poe."

His mother made a disgusted face of her own.

"That's really not suitable, love. How about *Masterman Ready*? It's about a shipwreck on a desert island. It's very good."

"All right," Cathal muttered, sounding unsure. "As long as it's got no kissin' in it."

"I honestly can't remember, but you shouldn't knock kissing till you've tried it."

"Ma! Don't be disgustin'!" He covered his head with the blanket. "Jaysus, you'll make me sick all over again."

Nate was livid.

"But you weren't supposed to question him!"

"Why ever not?" Daisy asked.

"Because . . . Because . . . Because that's *my* job!" Nate managed at last. "Security is my responsibility."

"But we got him to talk to us!" Daisy snapped back. "Which is more than *you* could do!"

"That's beside the point!"

"No. That's the *whole* point," she said in a more measured voice. "We're trying to protect Berto—and ourselves. That *is* what we're trying to do, isn't it?"

Nate took a deep breath and nodded, but avoided her gaze. He, Daisy, Roberto, and Tatiana were sitting in a comfortable corner of Berto's study, having gathered to share their news. Nate was still put out, feeling he'd been undermined by his interfering sister-in-law.

"Honestly, Nate," Tatty scolded. "You can be ever so stubborn at times! Why shouldn't we help? We are modern women, and it's time society valued our contributions."

"Well said, Tatty." Daisy patted her hand. "We are going to

— 69 —

investigate Simon's past and discover the truth about his mother. Some of the older relatives must remember what happened to her. There should be records too."

"Aunt Elvira will remember if anyone does," Berto said, referring to Gerald's mother. "The old bird is over a hundred, but her mind's still sharp. Her tongue too—particularly when it's aimed in Gerald's direction. But she's a stickler for the Rules; if it's been covered up, she'll keep it that way."

"Well, there's the rub," Daisy replied smugly. "The Rules don't apply to women, do they?"

"True enough," Nate agreed. "I'll go with you. I want to see if she remembers Vicky Miller."

"What can *I* do?" Tatty asked, her petulant expression making it clear that she was feeling left out of the proceedings.

"You can come with me, Princess," Berto told her. "We'll see what we can dig up in the library."

"Oh, how dreadfully exciting," she said dourly. "One can only wonder how they manage to squeeze so many *thrills* into those history books. If you'll excuse me, I think I'll go and take the dogs for a walk instead."

With that, she upped and left. The others watched her go with bemused expressions.

"I swear, she's becoming more like you every day," Berto said to Nate, slapping the wheel on his chair. "She'll be running off to Africa next."

"Place has enough wild animals already." Nate smiled.

"Nathaniel—!" Daisy began, but was interrupted by a knock on the door.

Berto called Winters in. The footman announced the arrival of Mr. James Pettigrew.

"Ah, Jamie! Yes, show him up," Berto replied, his face coming suddenly alive. "If you two will excuse me . . . "

Daisy and Nate exchanged glances and rose to their feet.

"I see Jamie got his foot fixed up," Nate commented. "Nice bit of work."

"Yes, yes it is," Berto said, fiddling with his tie and straightening his cuffs, obviously keen for his brother and wife to leave. "Nothing short of a miracle. Give Aunt Elvira my love, won't you?"

"If we must," Daisy muttered in a perplexed voice. "But you will be seeing her at dinner."

They made for the door, leaving Berto to await the arrival of his friend. Nate glanced back as he walked out. Berto's features were lit up with an expression of nervous hope, his hands pushing the chair back and forth on its wheels. It pained Nate to see his brother so helpless in a house full of people willing to hurt him. They had the best science and medicine at their disposal, and still it seemed that Berto might spend the rest of his life in that chair.

And Nate would spend the rest of *his* life wishing that he'd acted sooner to stop the monsters that had crippled his brother. He closed the door on his way out.

Elvira was a garrulous, belligerent old harridan who compensated for her deafness by speaking as loudly as she could and interrupting any conversation that didn't include her. Her left arm was more developed than her right, as a result of constantly holding a listening horn to her ear. Like Roberto, she was confined to a wheelchair, but unlike him, she had lived a full and scandalous life before her body had failed her.

As the younger sister of Edgar Wildenstern, aunt to Roberto, Nathaniel and Tatiana, and the family's oldest living female, she had been generally acknowledged as the Matriarch of the family since the death of Edgar's third wife. Her seniority thus recognized, the family had then conspired to keep her from influencing any decision that might affect the future of the business, on the basis that she treated most of her relatives—regardless of their position—with complete contempt. She doted on her eldest son, Silas, but constantly derided his younger brother, Gerald, whom she neither liked nor understood.

Daisy was quite fond of her.

"I loved the dress you wore to church last Sunday, Aunt Elvira," she chirped, hoping her lie was not too obvious. "It made you look twenty years younger!"

"What?" The old woman tilted the listening horn towards her niece in order to hear.

"Your dress! At church! Made you look twenty years younger!"

"Which would, unfortunately, have reduced me only to a slightly less shriveled eighty-three!" Elvira responded in a booming voice, glowing from the flattery nonetheless. "My eighties were not a good time. I had not yet abstained from alcohol, and my bouts of sleepwalking resulted in my wandering into the servants' quarters on regular occasions."

Nate gave an involuntary shiver. The thought of being woken in the night to find an eighty-year-old Aunt Elvira standing by one's bedside, clothed in only a nightdress, was enough to give any young man nightmares. He didn't know how she had looked back then, but these days she had an eighteen-stone figure of fat and spite, topped with a shrewd and many-chinned face that had long since surrendered to gravity. Her thinning hair was hidden by a heavy wig, which she did not change often enough.

He gave a little jump when something bumped into his ankle. It was a drawbreath; an engimal not much bigger than a badger, with soft metallic fur. Mounted on a long, flexible neck was a triangular head with a wide mouth and wire whiskers. Scars marred its pelt in places. Its eyes, set into the sides of its face like a hammerhead shark, were small and sleepy and its mouth hung close to the paisley-patterned carpet, diligently sucking up all the dust and crumbs it found there. Nate knew that nothing gave this creature greater pleasure.

These were wonderfully useful creatures and the house had three of them. Elvira kept this one to herself, as much for amusement as anything else. It looked at Nate for a moment with dull curiosity, mewed softly and nudged past his feet.

Elvira's fat, wrinkled hands rearranged her weighty violet skirts where they draped over her knees, and picked up the dainty cup of tea from the little table at her side.

"I am old and I am loud, and I am sure I smell strange to your young noses! None of these things are qualities that children such as yourselves seek out in the company that you keep! I am grateful you have seen fit to call down and see me, but what do you want?"

"We're not children!" Nate retorted.

"Eh?"

"We're not *children*, Auntie!"

"I have wigs older than you, boy!" Elvira snapped back, patting her current hairpiece hard enough to drive a puff of talcum powder from it. "Don't be disrespectful to your elders and betters—you and Gerald are two of a kind: impudent in the extreme! What do you want?"

"We wanted to ask you about Simon's mother!" Daisy called into the horn. "We heard she died from tuberculosis. Is that true?"

"The simpleton's mother?" Elvira squinted at her and frowned. "Consumption? Heavens, no! She was healthy as a horse right up to the day they took her off to Richards!"

"Who's Richard?" Nate pressed her.

"Eh?"

"Who's Richard?"

"Not who—*what*! Philip Richards House! The asylum!"

Daisy sat back and shot Nate a questioning look. He shrugged.

"Why did they send her to an asylum?" she shouted into the horn. "I thought you said she was healthy!"

"In body, my dear, but not in mind," Elvira sniffed. "She was quite bats by the end. May God rest her soul."

"But how . . . in what way was she mad?" Daisy persisted.

Elvira leaned towards her, lowering the horn so that she could get quite close to the younger woman. Staring into Daisy's eyes with a chilling look, she rasped:

"Why, she was mad in the *usual* way, my dear. And you would do well not to strain your fragile little mind with such matters. You don't want to fall foul of the same malady."

With an additional raise of an eyebrow, Elvira sat back, holding Daisy's gaze for a moment longer.

"But . . . but who else would have known about this?" Daisy persisted.

"Eh?" The listening horn angled back towards her.

"Who else would have known about Simon's mother?"

"Difficult to say. The closest relatives of my generation would have been privy to the truth—though few would have discussed it. Such was the way these things were handled. And so it should be."

Nate's knee bounced up and down, his eyes roaming about the room. It felt as if something had passed between the two women, but he could not say what. He was impatient to ask his own questions.

He was ill at ease, sitting here in his aunt's boudoir. When they were children he and Roberto and their eldest brother, Marcus, would visit this room every Saturday afternoon. Tatiana had still been a baby, so she had been spared the ordeal. Elvira was deaf even then, and it was frightening to be shouted at by a massive old woman, but it was scarier still to be shouted at by her colorful macaw, which could imitate her exactly. Elvira let it fly around the room at will. It liked to perch on little boys' shoulders and pick at their ears with its powerful beak. The boys would have to make polite conversation while this parrot tormented them. If they tried to stop it, their aunt hit their shins with her walking stick. She wasn't confined to a wheelchair back then.

The room had hardly changed at all. Stuffy and dark, its windows faced north, letting in a gray light. A pianoforte with covered legs sat in one corner, the bird's empty brass cage—the size of a barrel—stood in another. The French-polished teak furnishings had not been moved in his lifetime. Bookshelves lined the walls, with any spare space taken up with family portraits. One section of wall had been left clear. Painted on it was the Wildenstern family tree going back two hundred years. Nate knew they had records going back six centuries.

The macaw was still on its perch by one of the windows. In the past, it would have savaged the little engimal that grazed on Elvira's carpet, but it didn't fly much these days. Its scarlet plumage was dull and constantly molting.

Nate looked again at Daisy, who appeared lost in thought.

"Auntie, who was Vicky Miller?" he asked.

"Who?"

He took the daguerreotype from his pocket, carefully unwrapping the muslin cloth that protected the frame. Holding it up for her to see, he asked again, "The woman with Father in this picture. Who was she? Was she a relative?"

Elvira peered short-sightedly at the silver surface of the plate. Her expression changed to one of shock. She glared at Nate, pushing the picture aside.

"That woman died a long time ago," she muttered. "And I won't have her name mentioned again in this house." Her voice lifted to its customary bellow. "These are strange questions to be asking a woman who is not long for this world! If this is some ruse to turn me against your father's memory, Nathaniel, it will not work! I know you hated him. You never understood him. But you will before the end! You and Roberto both!"

They were all silent for a minute or two.

"I am feeling weary," she sighed. Then, with a wave of her hand, "Leave me be."

And so Daisy and Nate were dismissed for a second time that day. They left Aunt Elvira's rooms with more questions than answers.

VII

A PAUPERS' ASYLUM

PHILIP RICHARDS HOUSE was a famous—some would say notorious—asylum for the mentally unwell. Its director, a Dr. Herbert Angstrom, was a leading figure in the field, trained at Bethlem Royal Hospital in London and an exponent of humane techniques such as 'moral therapy' and 'therapeutic employment.'

Philip Richards House was a paupers' asylum, but there were many within its walls who would have come from good families—committed for their own wellbeing, of course, but discreetly, so as to avoid embarrassment to their loved ones.

Angstrom still indulged in the somewhat controversial practice of allowing members of the gentry to visit and observe his patients for a nominal fee. No such charge would be leveled upon Nate and Daisy, however, as the Wildenstern family was one of the most generous contributors to the good doctor's work.

It was the day after their conversation with Aunt Elvira, and although it was Daisy who had arranged the appointment, she felt uneasy in anticipation of it. She turned her face upwards to take in the front of the building as Nate helped her from the carriage. It was a dismal brown-brick barrel with five stories above ground. Purpose-built at the beginning of the century, it was modeled on the *Narrenturm*, or fool's tower, an earlier institution in Vienna. Circular in shape, with slot-like windows, it had been constructed to house two hundred patients. It was already desperately over-crowded.

Dr. Angstrom was waiting for them by the entrance at the top of the steps. Carved into the lintel over the heavy double doors, the asylum's motto read: *To heal the body, one must first heal the mind.*

What hope was there of that, Daisy wondered, when one was trapped in a depressing little cell with no idea when one would ever be released?

The doctor was an imposing figure; tall and broad shouldered, with a sallow face pitted with acne scars and sporting a square-cut copper-colored beard and whiskers. A fine network of lines around his eyes and at the corners of his mouth marred an otherwise youthful appearance.

"Your Grace, My Lord, it is a sublime honor to welcome two of our most valued patrons to our humble establishment," he gushed, bending to kiss Daisy's knuckle and then shaking Nate's hand. "It is normally your Uncle Gideon or occasionally your Doctor Warburton, who act as ambassadors to our shores. To what do we owe this pleasure?"

His tone was warm, but slightly patronizing; something both Nate and Daisy were becoming accustomed to. They were important, even powerful, but they were still very young and this was often reflected in the way they were treated. Daisy was even more hampered by her gender. They took great pains to look at Angstrom's type of behavior and nip it firmly in the bud.

"You're very kind, Doctor," Daisy responded. "My husband, the Duke, sends his regards and his regret that he cannot make this visit himself. While Uncle Gideon delivers regular reports, the Duke is always keen to see personally how his money is being spent." She smiled, but only just. "He has sent my brother-in-law and me in his stead to ensure you and your establishment get all the funding you deserve."

Angstrom's face dropped slightly at the gently implied threat, but recovered well.

"I hope you will be suitably impressed," he said, stepping aside and gesturing towards the door.

At first glance, the interior of the asylum was less depressing than the exterior. The corridor that led straight to the center of the building and up some stairs to the attendants' area and Angstrom's office was freshly painted and well maintained. Its cold green tiles and white walls were clean, smelling faintly of bleach. The heavy locked doors leading to the corridors on either side were more suggestive of a prison than a hospital and the doctor was careful to lead them quickly past and on towards the comfort of his rooms.

A smiling orderly took Nate's top hat and coat. Daisy gave up her hat, but kept her shawl, for there was a chill in the air. One glance into Angstrom's well-appointed study told Nate that they were about to receive the blinkers treatment and he was not having it.

"We were hoping for a tour, Doctor," he said, before Angstrom could sit them down and offer them refreshments. "We're particularly interested in your female patients."

"Really? Our most fascinating cases are male. They represent the more extreme—"

"We would like to learn about the women," Nate insisted.

"Of course," Angstrom replied, without batting an eyelid. "Walk this way." He took a hefty ring of large keys from his pocket and unlocked a solid oak door at the end of the corridor. It led out into another curving corridor, which did not enjoy the same levels of maintenance as the reception areas, lit dimly by the weak yellow glow of oil lamps. Damp stained the walls and ceiling, resulting in condensation on some surfaces, small puddles on the floor and mildew under the peeling yellow paint. Apart from the accompanying smell of clammy neglect, there was the faint but unmistakable scent of old urine and vomit in the air, as well as the heavy odor of unwashed bodies.

Nate wrinkled his nose and Daisy held her handkerchief to her face. Angstrom wore a regretful expression, as if apologizing for the offense caused to their delicate sensibilities.

"We receive people within these walls who have fallen into all sorts of dire straits," he said in a low, mournful voice. "All the most unfortunate examples of humanity are represented here;

much of it unsuitable for civilized eyes and ears . . . and noses. Were there any particular conditions that interested you?"

Sounds carried to their ears along the bare, echoing corridor. All the doors were to their left as they walked counter-clockwise around the building. To their right, there was a low wall allowing them to look out on the attendants' platform. Or rather, it allowed the attendants to watch the doors of the cells on each of the floors. The cells occupied two thirds of the building. The visitors heard soft moaning, cries of anger and sorrowful wailing, sobbing and hysterical giggling. But from most of the cells there were no sounds at all. Small hatches in the doors allowed them to look in on the patients.

Both Daisy and Nate ignored the doctor's question for a minute or two, stopping to observe one patient after another. They were all women, their faces pale, with weary bags under their eyes. These desolate souls were exhausted, not from activity, but from madness or boredom or both. They were all clothed in drab, gray dresses and each room was furnished with nothing but a stool and a simple wooden bunk covered by a threadbare blanket with a bedpan tucked underneath. The eyes that stared back through the open hatch, when they responded at all, were either hostile, or hopeful, or devoid of hope.

Gone were the days when insane asylums—at least in Great Britain and Ireland—kept inmates chained or in straitjackets all day, or attempted to beat obedience into them with iron rods and sticks. It had long been accepted in civilized circles that insanity was not a kind of misbehavior that could be cured by punishment. Even so, Daisy had tears in her eyes after only a few minutes of observing these women.

Nate swallowed his distaste and turned to the doctor.

"We are looking for any women with connections to the family," he said evenly.

"The *Wildenstern* family?" Angstrom exclaimed. "Sir, this is a *paupers'* asylum. I'm sure any relative of yours who might suffer the misfortune of being afflicted with mental illness would be sent to one of the finest hospitals in Europe. We have no relatives of yours here."

"We are glad to hear it," Daisy replied, with a slight crack in her voice. "Perhaps you would allow us to view your records so that we can see for ourselves?"

She saw Angstrom's face struggling to hide the resentment that he felt. He was a powerful man in medical circles and was not accustomed to youngsters such as them making demands of him.

"If the Duke himself insists, how can I refuse?" he said with a strained smile.

"You are most kind." Daisy smiled back.

The doctor led them back along the corridor to the oak door, unlocked it and locked it carefully again once they were through. Two doors down from his study was a small clerk's office, which held all the records for the asylum in uniform wooden cabinets which held six drawers each.

"The admission files are arranged chronologically," he informed them, pointing to a set of shelves holding dozens of thick, leather-bound ledgers. "I'm afraid the patients' files are confidential, so the cabinets must remain locked, but please peruse the rest at your leisure." He turned his back on them and left the room.

Daisy cast her eyes over the ledgers with an excited sense of anticipation. Nate felt something more akin to dread.

"I was rather hoping he'd just tell us what we wanted to know," he remarked.

"Oh, Heaven forbid you should have to do any *reading*!" Daisy remarked. "It's why so many women write their most intimate thoughts down in a diary. If you want to keep a secret from most men, the best place to hide it is in a *book*."

"Funny then, that men are still running the world," he sniped back. "Oh, wait a minute . . . including the world of *education*! Some of us must read after all."

"It's the only reason you've managed to stay in charge," she sniffed. "But that will change. You mark my words; someday a woman will be Prime Minister of Britain!"

"Hah! A man will walk on the surface of the *moon* before *that* happens!"

"Now you're just being ridiculous. Let's get on, shall we? Look, this is better, Nate. This way we can investigate the admissions for ourselves, without him choosing what we see. It's a pity we can't look at the files, but . . . "

Nate glanced towards the door and then looked closely at the lock on one of the cabinets.

"I could probably pick this with my penknife," he whispered.

"Yes, but that would be committing a crime," Daisy said in the kind of tolerant voice a parent uses with an errant child. "You have more than enough property of your own to damage without resorting to somebody else's. Besides, we have lots to get through here as it is. Now are you going to help me read through these or not?"

With a labored sigh, Nate took off his suit jacket, hung it over the back of a chair and sat down at the desk.

"Where shall we start?"

"Let's begin with the year Simon's mother was committed. If Elvira says she was here, there must be some kind of record. We can go further back if we need to."

Nate glared at the lines of thick ledgers, bulging with columns and columns of names, dates and details. The thought of spending hours searching through them for some little flea-sized fact that might or might not enlighten them gave him a churning feeling in his stomach. He couldn't imagine working at it every day.

"It'd be enough to drive a man mad," he muttered.

VIII

FEARSOME AGENTS

CATHAL LAY DAYDREAMING, remembering the evening when his ma's cousin, Mrs. Miller, came calling. His ma had been in a right state, watching the consumption claim her son, and she'd sent a letter to the only person she thought could help. He was beyond the abilities of the doctor, who was not keen on visiting anyway, what with Catherine Dempsey's reputation, and her habit of taking business out of his hands.

Huddled under the bedclothes, Cathal was just wishing it would all end soon. His breathing had become loud and labored and painful. His coughing had a scraping, raw sound to it, as if it was tearing at the flesh of his windpipe. His mouth was constantly tainted with the salty iron tang of blood.

Catherine had sent a telegram to the Navy with a message for his father, but as yet there had been no reply. When he was at sea, he could be out of reach for months, even years, at a time. She sat with her son in the dim light of the oil lamp, holding his hand. Cathal never saw her show a hint of fear for her own safety, even though she must be breathing his germs into her own lungs. There was no crying now either. She was all cried out.

There was a knock on the front door, and his ma lurched from her chair, rushing to answer it. Cathal heard her crying out in relief, babbling to whoever it was about the lateness of the hour, the edge of the precipice on which he was balanced. The visitor was a woman and Cathal was surprised to hear the way they spoke to each other—yaw-yawing like toffs to the manor born. His mother's Irish accent had all but disappeared.

His ma led the other woman into the room.

"Cathal, this is my cousin, Vicky Miller. The one I was telling you about. She's going to try and help you."

The woman was older than his mother, in her sixties at least, maybe more than that. She had a proud, deeply lined face, with a long straight nose made for looking down along and a small thin mouth and eyes like a rodent's. Her thin gray hair was pulled back tightly in a bun and she wore a red shawl over a dress that had seen better days. Putting down the carpet bag she held in her hand, she sat down on the chair next to him.

"Hello, young Cathal," she said, and her voice was that of a lady, but with a harsh edge. "Let's have a look at you now."

She pulled aside the blankets and gazed into his pale face, placing the back of her hand against his brow and then lifting one of his eyelids with the ball of her thumb. She pressed her fingertips against his neck, feeling his pulse. The pressure on his throat made him break into a fit of coughing, each burst jabbing pain into his chest. He didn't get his handkerchief up in time and a light, bright-red spray fell on the white sheet.

She withdrew her hand, listening to the sound as a musician might while tuning their instrument.

"It's far along," the old woman said to her cousin. Then she tucked him in again, sat back and stared down at him. "Hear me now, young Cathal. You must forget much of what you've heard about this disease. People are largely ignorant of the working of their insides and misinterpret most of what they see from the outside. You have the benefit of a wise mother, for you could not fathom what strange ideas some have about tuberculosis. You are a boy, so you like scary stories, yes?"

Cathal nodded, although since becoming ill, he had found he had less of a stomach for stories of injury, plague and death.

"Not many years ago," Mrs. Miller began, "people believed that consumption was the work of a vampire. One person would die in a household, and not long after, other family members would become ill. They became pale and drawn and weakened and it was held that the recently deceased relative was preying on the rest of the family. When someone began coughing up blood, it was believed that they would feel the urge to replace that blood by drinking someone else's."

Cathal felt a lurch in his stomach. He certainly had no thirst to replenish his lost blood by drinking more of the same.

"Even in these modern times," she went on, "some imbeciles believe that victims are 'hag-ridden'—drained of life and transformed into a horse by some scheming witch who rides her victim to gatherings in the hills, reveling the night away with her coven, before returning at dawn. There are romantic fools who hold that artists have bouts of wild inspiration when suffering the last throes of the disease, that women become suddenly more beautiful before they die and men more creative.

"I tell you all this, Cathal, so you will understand the nonsense that is spread by ignorance." She leaned in towards him and he could smell tea on her breath. "The truth of the matter is that you have germs in your blood, and they are using your body to multiply and spread, much as humans multiply and spread across the world. That is all. There is no evil spirit in you, nothing that bears any malice towards you, simply an organism that has made a home in your body."

The old woman opened her bag and took a box from it. Lifting the lid, she reached in and pulled out the strangest engimal Cathal had ever seen. It looked like a snake—he had never come across a real snake, though he had seen them in book illustrations—but it had white ceramic skin and silvery metal eyes. Lines spiraled down its long body, making it look almost like a piece of rope, or some kind of long, flexible bolt.

The creature regarded him without expression, opening and closing its jaws. His skin crawled at the sight of it, but there was something about its gaze that was somehow . . . comforting.

Mrs. Miller pulled back the bedclothes, opened the front of Cathal's nightshirt and placed the creature on his chest. It did not weigh much, but his chest was sensitive and he felt another bout of coughing coming.

The woman started whistling. With a sense of bewilderment, he recognized the song. It was the popular ballad, "A Nation Once Again." He wouldn't have thought her the type to sing rebel songs.

The engimal uncoiled and lay flat on his chest, turning its head to one side so Cathal had the eerie sensation that it was listening to his lungs. Mrs. Miller stopped whistling. It lifted its head and a needle suddenly jabbed out of its mouth, piercing his skin. The pinprick made him jump and cry out and a cough rose in his throat . . . but then subsided, and he felt a warm numbness spreading across his chest and, for the first time since he could remember, the pain was gone.

The creature rested its head on Cathal's chest again, and to his amazement it started to sing. A soothing, low warbling emanated from its body and he felt tingling waves wash over him like warm breaths. The taste of blood disappeared from his mouth. He started crying.

"These germs in your body are just pests. They are not invincible," Mrs. Miller told him. "You have agents in your blood more fearsome than any germ. Do you believe that?"

Cathal made a non-committal grunt, barely audible over the engimal's strange singing.

"Answer me, boy! Do you believe what I'm telling you?" Her voice did not brook refusal.

"I do," he said. "Fearsome agents."

"Then say it like you mean it!"

"I've got fearsome agents in my blood!" he barked, surprised at the strength in his voice. "I'll take no nonsense from those bleedin' germs!"

"Now you're starting to sound like my kin," she said, smiling. "You'll do."

Then she pinched the back of the snake's neck and it raised itself up. The engimal's head split into three. The split extended to the base of its skull and down its back. The creature unwound like a length of rope being separated into its individual strands. Three new snakes of equal size were formed from the first. Cathal had no idea that engimals could change their shape like that.

The middle snake reared up in front of him, one eye peering from the center of its head. The other two creatures wound around his wrists, holding them gently in place. He felt a moment of terror before the middle one slid up to his face and thrust itself into his mouth. It slithered down his throat, causing him to gag uncontrollably. Cathal blacked out before the choking became too painful.

When he woke, nearly an hour later, the old woman and her bizarre pet were gone. His breathing was easier. He was still coughing, but it didn't hurt as much. There was no more blood. His mother held him and cried for a long, long time.

Thinking back on that day, Cathal reached into his shirt and felt the muscle covering his once-wasted breastbone. Whatever the thing had done to him had worked. He was stronger now than he had ever been.

Evening was falling, and with the lamp's wick turned right down and the curtains pulled over, it was safe enough to peer out of the window at the lights coming on in the village below.

His ma was late. He'd read *Masterman Ready* in no time, and despite the lack of any decent crimes, murders or battles, he'd been forced to admit it was a good ol' yarn. Ma'd had to go out to the market that afternoon and she'd promised to pick him up a couple more books, if she could find them. His ma had suggested that if he could indulge in some more contemplative stories, they might last him longer. He had assured her that he had no interest in contemplation, what with being stuck indoors with his thoughts day and night, and impressed upon her the need for a good fight scene or two to while away the time.

She should have been back by now. Cathal felt the uncomfortable hollow of loneliness starting to grow inside him. There was still no word from his father either. If Cathal could have left the house, he would have gone looking for his mother. What was taking her so long? It was really starting to get dark now. The carriage clock on the mantelpiece in the sitting room said nine o'clock. His mother was long overdue. Cathal pressed his face against the glass, willing her to appear on the path up to the house.

The day had left Nate overwhelmed with frustrated tension. After combing fruitlessly through pages and pages of entries in the ledgers of the asylum, he and Daisy had returned home to find a host of his relatives clamoring for time with Roberto—time only Nathaniel could grant, as he controlled all access to formal meetings with his brother. Every male member of the family—and a few of the females—had to be searched before being allowed near Berto and no one would permit this indignity to be carried out by a servant, so either Nate or Daisy had to do it themselves. This regime had become even more rigorous since Simple Simon's attack.

No closer to finding out what had happened to Simon's mother, Nate was seething with pent-up aggression by the time he completed his duties. He needed a good work-out. He summoned Clancy, and they made their way down to the gymnasium, where they changed into loose trousers and vests.

The gymnasium was an airy room, almost a quarter the size of a football field, with a high ceiling and small windows along the tops of the white walls that let in the fading evening light. It had a range of exercise equipment, along with racks of close-quarter weapons of every kind lining one of the walls.

The two men warmed up with some calisthenics and then walked over to the weapons wall. Nate chose a pair of tonfa, each stick of red oak about two feet long with a perpendicular handle protruding a third of the way down its length. He spun them expertly in his hands, finishing with the long sections of the sticks resting on his forearms. Moving out into the room, he stopped and waited for his opponent.

Clancy picked out a jo, a simple stick of white oak about four feet in length. He swung it around him with loose wrists, slid his hands down to one end to hold it like a sword and brought it up to guard facing his young master. They both gave a shallow bow.

The Wildensterns trained their top-ranking servants from childhood, and taught them well. Clancy had provided much of Nate's hand-to-hand instruction in his early years and still acted as a coach and sparring partner. As a result, Nate suspended the usual master—servant etiquette while they sparred. You couldn't have a decent fight with a man who was afraid of losing his job if he hit you. Nate also used these times to pick Clancy's older and more seasoned brain. He had already told his servant about Simon's mother and also about Vicky Miller.

He lunged forward, flipping the long end of his left tonfa at Clancy's right temple. The servant blocked, and almost walked into Nate's second strike—a jab with the butt of the right tonfa to the nerve cluster in the servant's shoulder. But Clancy parried that blow too, sliding the stick down and catching Nate's fingers, nearly forcing the young man to drop his weapon. They were only using light strikes, but oak still delivered a solid smack if it caught you. Nate winced and stepped back, looking for another opening.

"I'm still trying to figure out Vicky Miller's connection to the family," he said as they circled one another. "None of the old folk are talking."

"That's the family's way, sir," Clancy replied. "They are a closed-lipped crowd, and all the more so when it comes to discussing the fates of some of the female members."

"You mean the asylum?" Nate asked, striking with a right and then left jab, before spinning one stick up between Clancy's legs. The footman stepped to the side and slipped his jo straight through Nate's guard, almost catching him in the ribs. Nate sidestepped it and trapped the jo in the crook of his arm with one tonfa, swinging the other at the servant's jaw.

Clancy ducked, went for a leg sweep, and nearly succeeded in taking Nate's feet out from under him. Nate released the jo and jumped over the sweep, retreating towards the center of the room. They both hesitated, breathing deeply.

"Is there some shameful strain of insanity running through the female side of the family that I'm not aware of?" Nate pressed him. "Apart from the usual level of madness, I mean."

Clancy's rough-hewn face was as impassive as ever. It was always next to impossible to guess what he was thinking. He rubbed the point on his chest where a crossbow bolt had struck him the year before, grimacing slightly, and then raised his guard again. "A good servant is supposed to be invisible," he replied at last. "And as you're aware, sir, we see and hear a great deal that is supposed to be . . . beyond our comprehension—and most of us understand very well what would happen if we were suspected of having . . . opinions on such matters. But there are some things in this house to which even servants are not privy."

He delivered three sharp hooking blows to Nate's guard at head, knee and hip height before being forced back by a similarly swift reply, one tonfa catching him on the left elbow, causing him to lose his grip with that hand. Nate followed through, but Clancy defended well, whipping one of the tonfa out of his young master's hands.

Nate left the weapon where it had fallen. They circled again, Clancy shaking out his bruised elbow. "One such matter is the way in which women have been expelled from Wildenstern Hall," he continued. "I know only that some Wildenstern women have been driven from this house amid rumors of a cerebral disease. It must be said, however, that I myself had the pleasure of knowing three of these women during my service, and right up to the day they disappeared, I saw no notable lack of sanity in any of them. None of them have been heard of since."

"Well, if they've ever been in that asylum, there's no record of any Wildenstern women," Nate muttered. "You'll have to tell me more about them after I've finished trouncing you." Flipping the tonfa to grab its end, he took a sliding step forward, hooked the jo aside by the handle, and thrust a side kick at Clancy's midriff.

The servant took the kick with a grunt and was about to swing back with a low roundhouse of his own when a voice hailed them from across the room:

"Still fretting about our dearly departed dotards, Nate?" Oliver called, striding towards them with two of his brothers, all three dressed for training. "What does it matter what's happened to a bunch of mad old harpies? Out of sight, out of mind, that's what I say. Or should that be, *If they're out of their minds, get 'em out of sight?* Eh? Haw haw!"

His two brothers echoed his guffawing laughter. Nate and Clancy lowered their guards, resenting the interruption.

"Speaking of dotards," Oliver went on, grinning beneath his black whiskers, "how about you stop fooling around with Clancy here and take on someone your own age? The old cove looks done in."

Nate glanced at his manservant. Clancy was typically expressionless, his breathing a little fast and a light sweat shining on his face, but he was otherwise unfazed by the exercise—and by the insults. "What did you have in mind?" Nate asked, turning back to his cousin.

"A little wrestling, perhaps?" Oliver suggested. "Three falls or a submission?"

"Right you are," Nate replied, handing the tonfa to his servant.

Oliver was a couple of stone heavier than Nate and could beat anyone in the family at wrestling, but that alone was enough reason for Nate to have a go. Clancy could make sure it was all relatively clean, and in the meantime, Nate could work off some of that frustration that had been building up inside him. And if he got the chance to rip Oliver's mustache off his fat, chortling face, so much the better.

IX

SOMETHING A LITTLE MORE MARTIAL

BERTO WATCHED FROM THE WINDOW of his study as Hennessy, the head groom, went about his work. The old man was exercising one of the horses in the manicured grounds at the side of the house as the late-afternoon light settled into dusk. There was a tightness in the young Patriarch's chest as he turned his chair away from the window, a tightness he felt whenever he watched his old friend like this, or when he wondered if he would ever walk again or ride a horse again or dance again or . . .

There were so many little things he had taken for granted about being able to walk. Now, a single high step or narrow doorway could block his path. Stairs were impassable, so he could not go to any part of the house not served by the mechanical lifts without being carried by servants, a humiliating experience even when they used the sedan chair.

The secret routes through the house, the labyrinth of hidden passageways and rooms, were beyond his reach, being too narrow and involving too many steps—stairs were a curse for him to negotiate by himself. These were the ways used by the Wildensterns when they did not want even their servants to know where they were going—Berto sorely missed the freedom they offered.

Even opening and closing doors by himself was difficult—the chair got in its own way. Reaching up to shelves, or even to door handles that were set high in order to be out of reach of children, caused him no end of bother. And any soft or uneven surface outside, such as gravel, grass or cobbles—and most of the other surfaces in the gardens and the estate beyond—made the going unbearably tough. The world was not designed for someone who spent his life rolling about on wheels. As for seeing to his toilet needs and bathing . . . His hands bunched into fists and he squeezed his eyes shut, denying the tears that wanted to come.

A soft knock at the door announced Winters's entry. "Mister Gerald to see you, Your Grace."

"Thank you." Berto composed himself and nodded. "Send him in."

Gerald strolled in with his usual jaded air, cigarette in hand, a cynical smile never far from his lips.

"Berto, old bean. What's on your mind?"

"Gerald, thanks for coming," Berto replied, moving over

towards the easy chairs and gesturing for his cousin to sit down. "How are your studies progressing?"

"Still nothing that'll help you, I'm afraid, but it's only a matter of time. The healing properties of these intelligent particles are extraordinary, and if I can't crack the mystery of how they work, no one can."

"Spoken with your usual modesty," Berto said, smiling. "I'm sure you have it well in hand. On a related note, I was wondering if you'd ever heard of a fellow named Aidan O'Neill. Jamie mentioned his name to me in . . . in relation to something we were discussing. Surgery, in fact. Jamie said he was an excellent surgeon."

"O'Neill?" Gerald frowned. "No, not that I can think of. There was a famous surgeon named Aidan *Mac*Neill. A brilliant young chap over in London. But that would have been nearly twenty years ago. Pioneered a number of new techniques while he was still only in medical school. Showed extraordinary promise. Many thought he would become one of the finest physicians in the world."

"Why do you use the past tense?"

"Well, he was disgraced. Found guilty of employing grave robbers, and transported. It was a notorious case. Some say he never actually reached Australia. He had friends in high places who helped him escape, though I'm not sure I believe that part. Why do you ask?"

"Oh . . . nothing. Thought he might be worth . . . you know . . . thought I might ask for his help. Australia, you say? In a penal colony I presume?"

"Certainly. A bit harsh, in my opinion. It was in the name of research, after all."

"Hmm." Berto slapped the arm of his chair. "Enough of that, anyway. I've brought you here for another reason. Well, two actually. One is this blasted wheelchair. The summer ball is almost upon us and the whole family is going to be home. I need you to modify this thing for me—"

"Let me guess—you want to be able to dance in it. A waltz might be possible, with a few extra joints in the wheels—you'd need a short partner, of course, and one with long, strong arms. A *polka*, on the other hand, would be jolly difficult . . . "

"I was looking for something a little more . . . martial."

"Ah, yes."

"I'd have been hard put to defend myself against half the monsters in this house when I was in my prime," Berto said, with an edge of desperation in his voice. "Now I feel like a bloody fish in a barrel. Nate's doing his best, but I don't want to rely on him and Winters for everything. If things go sour and I'm caught on my own by an assailant, I want to be able to get stuck into them."

Gerald regarded his cousin with a thoughtful gaze and nodded solemnly.

"I'll see to it," he said. "Start from scratch. Do you up a proper custom job."

"Thank you," Berto sighed, looking visibly relieved. "There's one other little thing—well, not so little, to be honest. I'm putting you in charge of the estates. Oliver's tried it on one too many times, so I need you to take over his position."

Gerald stubbed out his cigarette in a crystal ashtray that stood on the mahogany side table.

"I can't, Berto. I can't spare the time," he muttered bitterly. "You simply don't appreciate what I'm on the verge of achieving here. My work is of monumental importance. It's not something that I can just dabble in whenever I get a free moment."

"Oh, come on, Ger. God, why does nobody in this family with any *decency* want any part in the business at all? Except for Daisy, of course—she has such ambitions, bless her. It's such a pity she's a woman. Look, the clerks run all the day-to-day stuff. I simply need you to oversee it."

"It's not just the time," Gerald protested. "It's the distraction of it. As it is, I don't have enough resources. I need more money, more engimals to study. It's just not right that you're putting a limit on how many I can use in my research. I—"

"I think we've spent enough on your obsessions already," Berto said sharply. "Those refrigerators you had installed didn't come cheap. God knows what they're for. Or all those electrical generators, for that matter. And the engimals you've dissected—a practice I still consider barbaric—have so far cost the family thousands. And it's not right, you know. There are no new ones being born . . . or . . . or being made, or whatever. Every time you dissect one, that's one less engimal in the world."

"Yes, but if I discover the link between the intelligent particles and the engimals, I might learn how to create new ones! Think of the possibilities! I must continue my work!"

"You know you have my support, Gerald," Berto insisted. "But it's time you took on some responsibility and put your shoulder to the wheel."

Gerald chewed his lip, gazing at his cousin with an intensity that Berto found quite unsettling. After what seemed like a very long time Gerald broke into a rueful smile.

"What did you give to Oliver, then?"

"Drainage."

"Oh, jolly good! Pity we can't make the rotter dig the ditches himself, eh? All right, then . . . I'll do it." He let out a tired breath, looking solemnly at his cousin. "So, when did you suddenly become such a tough guv'nor?"

"I don't know, but I tell you, it's an almighty strain," said the young Patriarch, looking positively miserable. "I'm afraid I'm going to end up like Father."

"No fear of that, Berto. That blackguard had a burned stone for a heart. Remember when they stabbed him in it and he didn't die?"

"Vividly," Berto said with a shudder. Edgar Wildenstern had been murdered at the dinner table, while two ancient sisters, Elizabeth and Brunhilde, held his hands, and their brother, Hugo, drove a knife into Edgar's chest. The memory brought Berto back to more pressing concerns. "Look here, you will get started on this confounded wheelchair as soon as possible, won't you?"

Nate was eating breakfast with Tatty, Berto, Daisy and Gerald when the telegram from Urskin arrived. Nate's shoulder was stiff from having been dislocated by Oliver during their wrestling bout; Nate had no doubt that the arm-lock had been applied to injure and not just hold, but he didn't care. Let his cousin get his petty blows where he could. Nate had used the fight to crack Oliver's technique and was sure that next time they sparred, he would give the miscreant a proper run for his money.

He had a gold chain wrapped around his shoulder, under his shirt, to aid the healing, confident that his *aurea sanitas* would make short work of it. Clancy—who had manipulated the dislocated joint back into place—gave his young master an appraising glance as he presented the telegram on a silver tray. The message was brief and to the point:

> LORD WILDENSTERN STOP
> ANOTHER WOMAN HAS BEEN FOUND STOP
> HOWTH VILLAGE STOP
> URSKIN STOP

Ten minutes later Nate and Gerald were riding their velocycles out along the road that led to the gates of the estate, past the cast bronze sculptures holding their gas-lamps aloft. The summer morning was still young and there was a chill in the air as it cut across their faces. The family's wealth ensured that the road between the gates of Wildenstern Hall and the outskirts of Dublin was macadamized and well maintained.

The growling mounts coasted down the gravel surface to the grand arching gates and out towards town, picking up speed on the open road. There was a private train line that led from the back of the estate to Kingstown on the coast, from where the two young men could have caught a train to Howth village. But where was the fun in that?

The countryside became more populated as the two riders hurtled towards Rathfarnham, the thatched stone or turf cabins of cotters giving way to more brick and tiled houses in areas such as Terenure and Rathmines that were being absorbed and transformed by the growth of Dublin; growth fueled by the Industrial Revolution. The roads became less consistent—from mud to gravel to cobblestones to mud again. Some parts of the city were developing faster than others.

As ever, Nate set the pace, forcing Gerald to take reckless chances in order to keep up. Gerald, who had been up most of the night working on Berto's new wheelchair, cursed his cousin's competitiveness. The mount that Gerald had chosen from the stables, Incitatus, was a lean, graceful engimal with a dark blue ceramic hide and graphite-colored legs and horns, its body spotted with leopard-like rosettes of silver.

By most standards it would have been considered a prize beast and it was one of the family's most valuable velocycles. But next to Flash it was tame, wiry and slow. Flash chewed up the miles under its wheel-like feet, snarling at carts that got in its way, panicking horses as it tore past. Young boys whooped and threw their caps in the air as they watched it roar by, girls screamed in delight or terror. Flexing its battle-scarred limbs, it threw itself into corners, accelerating out at breakneck speed, reveling in its power.

Approaching the Grand Canal, Nate spotted a group of young ladies being driven in an open-topped brougham heading towards town. He pulled back on Flash's horns and overtook the carriage with the engimal's front wheel in the air, giving the dolly-mops a dashing grin. The women gaped and blushed; their driver swore as he fought to control his horses, cursing the wealthy young buck on his ostentatious monster.

Nate dropped Flash back onto all fours and ducked his head down, pushed his toes further into the stirrups and tucked his knees in behind the beast's cowl, squinting through his goggles as they picked up speed again.

The air grew fouler; even without the smog, the exhalations of thousands of chimneys kept the streets shaded by a murky sky. The city swelled around them, with higher buildings overshadowing the streets, and the streets themselves grew busier towards the center. Horse-drawn buses mingled with coaches and carriages of every type. People picked their paths across the roadways with care. In the summer heat there was less mud, but the horse manure was still in abundance, and the stink of the River Liffey spread far beyond its banks.

Ever since the Famine in the 1840s people had been deserting the countryside for the cities, and now, as the Industrial Revolution gathered pace, Dublin was bursting at the seams. For every businessman making his fortune there were hundreds of other men working long hours in dangerous conditions in the new factories. The north of Ireland, predominantly Protestant, was getting the most benefit from the new industries, but Dublin was thriving too, many of the factories here owned by the Wildensterns and their various companies.

People came seeking work and ended up in crowded slums, where whole families were forced to live in a single room and sewage ran in the street gutters. Unscrupulous landlords charged rent for properties unfit for animals. Typhus was rife, carried by the lice in the unwashed clothes of the poor.

Nate passed a group of little gurriers playing hurling at a crossroads and was forced to duck when a ball was batted straight at his head. He shook his head in exasperation, but had to admire their spirit. It would be considered great sport to knock a swell off his mount. A stray dog scampered after them, nipping at Gerald's heels until Incitatus snarled at it, sending it cowering away.

Crossing the river over Sackville Bridge, they turned east along the quays, following the Liffey downstream. Ships lined the harbor, their forest of masts acting as perches for the seagulls and crows that wheeled overhead, combing the busy docksides for scraps of food. Stevedores yelled, sweated and swore, using pallets, cranes and windlasses to load the cargo or land it on the cobblestones of the quaysides.

On one dock stood a towering engimal, looking like a cross between a giraffe and a dinosaur, with an octopus-shaped head. This docile beast had served men on and off for centuries. Now it transferred massive loads between ship and shore with slow, ponderous ease. Its purple skin was stained dull by the pollution, blending it with the ships and buildings around despite its bizarre form.

The two riders passed all this by, but Nate could not help casting a yearning eye over the ships, envying those who sailed in them. He spent many a night wishing he could go wandering the world again.

Taking the North Strand across the Royal Canal, they rode out past Dollymount. Wherever they went, the engimals drew stares. But now the city, and its foul air, was thinning out again as they traversed the north edge of Dublin Bay. The green and purple heather of Howth Head rose above them and storm clouds glowered at them from over the hill. Howth village was around the head, on the coast, facing out east across the Irish Sea towards Wales. As they took the road that cut up behind the head and down to the village they saw the fishing boats tacking against the wind, heading back in front of the storm. The light was dropping already. The blustery breeze was picking up into something more substantial.

Both young men considered it a fitting atmosphere in which to find the body of a dead woman.

It was not hard to find the place. On the outskirts of the village, a small crowd had gathered by a copse of trees and was being kept back by a team of green-uniformed constables from the Royal Irish Constabulary. Beyond the trees was the entrance to a graveyard and the ruin of a twelfth-century abbey.

The guttural rumble of the velocycles got the attention of the crowd and they parted to let Nate and Gerald through. The cordon of policemen watched impassively as the two gentlemen dismounted, chained their beasts to a tree trunk and pulled off their leather riding helmets, goggles and mud-spattered coats.

Urskin greeted them, Nate introduced Gerald and they walked towards the crumbling stone walls of the chapel. Through the ruins, with their weed-strewn gravel floors, they found a slightly less dilapidated wooden shed behind the main buildings. This, presumably, was where the tools for tending the old graveyard were kept.

As they approached the doorway both young men gagged and recoiled from the stink of burned, smoky meat filling the dark interior. Covering their noses and mouths with handkerchiefs, they peered in with watering eyes.

"The door was barred from the inside," Urskin informed them softly. "The bolt is on the outside, but there were some sacks of grass seed leaning against the other side of the door. The only other gap is that hole in the roof the size of your fist—used to be a chimney for a stove. A man spotted smoke this morning and came to check it out. Thought it might be vagrants causing mischief. Had to force open the door. That's how he found her.

"Her name's Catherine Dempsey. The priest recognized her shoes and her satchel . . . and the ring. Pretty observant is that Father Houlihan. I find men of the cloth to be sound witnesses."

The scene was almost identical to the one in Tinahely, apart from the gardening tools and years of moldy junk stored against the walls of the shed. There was an elliptical patch of ash and burned floorboards, with nothing else around touched by the flames. At one end of the ash pile there was a pair of lower legs, burned out of existence above the knees. The feet were covered with a pair of unfashionable practical black polished shoes. But this time there was a part of an arm remaining too; the left arm, from the hand to the elbow. There was a wedding ring on the finger of the hand.

Kneeling over the woman's remains was a priest with a flushed, broken-veined face, balding head and eyes hung with premature bags. Clutching a satchel with one hand, he held a hankie up to his face with the other. Dressed in a black suit, with the traditional white dog collar, he was huddled in a dark red cardigan, shivering as if it was winter.

"Father Houlihan," Urskin said respectfully. "These were the gentlemen I was telling you about."

From the expression on the priest's face, it appeared the description had not been entirely positive.

"A terrible shock, gentlemen," Father Houlihan said, shuddering as he took the hankie down. "We've never had its like in the parish. Whatever her faults, Mrs. Dempsey did not deserve such a horrible fate."

"And what faults were those, Father?" Nate asked.

The priest looked at him evasively, biting his lip. Nate's gaze hardened. There was no doubt the priest felt compassion for the dead woman, but there was something else there too. Vindication? Satisfaction? Was there part of the man that felt this woman had it coming?

"I'll not speak ill of the dead. She was a colorful character and contributed to the . . . the wellbeing of the parish in her own way," Houlihan said. "She will be missed."

"But not by you, I'll wager," Gerald muttered quietly. Then, louder, he added: "I'd like to examine the scene if I may."

Urskin said he had already been over it carefully, but gestured to the two gentlemen to proceed at their leisure. Gerald had brought a small bag of tools and from it he took a magnifying glass, a pair of cotton gloves and some stainless-steel tongs. He had been up to see Vicky Miller's cottage, and had found few answers. The eager young scientist was hoping for more success here.

"It's very neat," Nate observed, looking at the burned area, feeling a little queasy again. "You'd think she'd have been thrashing about, spreading the flames around—even running for water, or for help. Whole place is made of wood, there's lots of smoke damage, but it should all have burned down. And why did nobody hear her screams?"

"She must have been unconscious," Gerald said thoughtfully, examining the stumps of limbs with his magnifying glass. "The position of the legs suggests she was in repose . . . I could do with more light in here. Damn these clouds."

Nate looked out of the door at the oncoming rain clouds, and then through the grime-covered window in the side of the shed. With a sharp intake of breath, he found himself staring into the face of a red-headed boy of about ten or twelve years old, dressed in an oversized velveteen coat and a floppy brown cap.

The look on the boy's face spoke volumes even before the priest exclaimed, "God have mercy! That's the woman's son!"

The face disappeared. The boy was scrambling over one of the ruined walls through the remnants of an arched window, disappearing from sight.

There was no doorway on that side of the chapel. Nate came sprinting out of the shed, leaped for the window ledge, caught hold and hauled himself over, hitting the ground hard. The lad was already through the doorway on the other side, haring through the graveyard, heading for the wall and the trees beyond. Nate took off after him.

Back inside, Urskin was shouting for two of the constables to bring the boy back. Gerald did no more than glance up before returning to his examination.

"Aren't you concerned for the boy?" Houlihan asked.

"If there's any chasing to be done, I leave it to Nathaniel," Gerald said without looking up. "He is fleeter of foot and a model of dogged pursuit. Besides, he hasn't the patience to be of any use to me here. If the boy can be caught, Nathaniel will catch him. If not, the chase will surely use up some of my cousin's over-zealous bravado. Either way, I'll be most grateful."

"I would have said that catching him would be an easy matter," Houlihan remarked, "for the boy's been housebound these last two months with consumption. It was said there wasn't much life left in him. But it seems that he's made a miraculous recovery."

"Is that so?" Gerald asked, lifting his head to regard the priest properly for the first time. "Miraculous, you say?"

"Miraculous would be the wrong word, actually," Houlihan corrected himself. "For I doubt God had anything to do with it. You see the scar on her thumb? I know the mark. And knowing the kind of woman she was, I would doubt if her son's recovery was the work of Our Lord."

"I'd be inclined to agree," Gerald mused as he examined the hand. "But for very different reasons. It's a pity; her blood will be clotted by now. Inspector, would you mind sending some more men to join the chase? It's vital we catch that boy."

"We'll catch him, sir," Urskin said, peering suspiciously over Gerald's shoulder, his eyes darting towards the open bag of instruments. "Do you mind telling me what you're looking for?"

"Whatever there is to find, Inspector," Gerald replied. "Whatever there is to find."

X

HIS MOTHER'S SHOES

CATHAL RAN WITH ALL HIS MIGHT, his legs pounding through the grass, his chest fit to burst with emotion so raw and brutal he could not put a name to it. He just wanted to run; to run away from the ruined abbey, the priest, the peelers and the two toffs who'd ridden in on their flashy engimals. And most of all he wanted to run away from that pile of ash and those two stumps of legs wearing his mother's shoes.

There were two other men, wearing long black coats and flat caps, watching from the path ahead and to the left of him. Behind them was a horse and covered cart, pulled up by the road. One fellow pointed furtively and said something to his companion. They seemed more curious than hostile, but Cathal steered away from them anyway. No point taking chances.

The blond swell dogging him was fast. Cathal could hear his footfalls through the graveyard behind him. Weaving between the gravestones, Cathal raced for the wall and bounded over it, losing his hat in the process. Crossing the path without slowing, he ducked into a copse of trees on the other side. He heard the man's riding boots hit the path seconds later but did not look back. Despite all his fancy duds, that toff could run, and Cathal knew that a fit man could outlast a youngster over a long stretch. Stamina and a longer stride would tell in the end.

But there was something in Cathal that wasn't going to stop. Strength surged through him and he felt as if he could outrun a train if he had to. He hit a path that wound up the hill and started climbing with hardly a change in pace. Still the man came after him. There were shouts from further back—green-bellies in their smart uniforms—but Cathal knew they were already too far behind to catch him . . . unless someone thought to cut him off on horseback . . . or on one of those engimals.

Rain was starting to fall now, clearing the muggy air. The toff behind him was breathing hard, but wasn't going to quit. Cathal saw a house surrounded by a high garden wall and turned towards it. Gritting his teeth, he put his head down and sprinted all out. Vaulting over it, amazed at his own agility, he cleared the six-foot wall with only one hand resting atop it, before falling over the other side. The garden below was another two or three feet lower than the ground outside. He landed easily enough in a flower bed, started forward, but then skidded to a halt and pulled up to the wall, pressing his back against it.

The rain began lashing down hard as the blond-haired man

came leaping over the wall, hands just touching the top. Cathal had an instant to admire his pursuer's grace before he landed and then the boy drove his fist with all his might into the man's groin. The toff went down like a sack of mud, letting out a gasping cry. He had Cathal's cap grasped in one hand.

Cathal seized his hat and then raced across the garden to the corner, getting a foot on one wall, launching himself across to the other and bouncing off high enough to soar over the top. In a moment he vanished into the rain, leaving the gentleman clutching his bruised goolies and hissing curses into the flower bed.

Nathaniel had gone off gallivanting after receiving some telegram or other, and Roberto only had a few meetings with clerks, which did not demand Daisy's attention, so she had been left to amuse herself. She found this a little disconcerting. When Berto had first become Patriarch, he had been hopeless at handling even the simplest business affairs and had relied heavily on her talents as a manager.

But lately he had become more confident in his position, and though she was delighted with this development, she missed being his first port of call when any problem arose. If she was honest with herself, she had preferred him when he was a bit of a noodle.

Still, it did leave her with more time on her hands, and since her visit to the asylum had turned up nothing useful she had decided to invite the Archdeacon over for a spot of archery. Tatiana had lately taken up training in some of the various martial skills that her brothers learned as a matter of course, but Daisy maintained that at least one person in this misbegotten family should remain a decent, *non-violent* Christian. She had been forced to cut someone's head off the year before—in self-defense, of course—and was still offering up prayers for the Lord's forgiveness. The nightmares she had about that time were terrible and she was determined never to corrupt her nature with violence again.

Archery, however, could be practiced for its own sake, with a view to improving one's focus, poise and mental discipline—although the strain it put on one's muscles did tend to leave one with arms like an Amazon. And Daisy had found a suitably pious teacher in the Venerable Alan Mills, Archdeacon of their Church of Ireland parish. Gentle, friendly, wise, and blessed with a prodigious memory, he was also a dead shot with a bow and arrow.

Daisy intended to improve her technique and get some questions answered into the bargain. There was a storm threatening over the coast, but it had yet to reach them, and the sky was bright overhead. Daisy, Tatty and the Archdeacon were out in the garden, using longbows to send arrows sailing towards the wooden target of painted concentric circles, some fifty yards away. It was the furthest they had ever set the targets and many of the young women's shots were falling short, but they were creeping steadily closer. Alan was still delivering one arrow after another into the central rings of the target.

A short carthorse of a man in his forties, he had receding, graying hair and premature jowls on an otherwise handsome, sallow-skinned face. An easy smile had formed crow's-feet around his eyes and he bore himself with a physical confidence often lacking in the clergy.

Daisy was trying to find a way to steer the conversation towards female relatives, but Tatiana was showing far more interest in medieval battles. Part of this gruesome interest was genuine and part of it motivated by an eagerness to make this man of God blush, which she found quite fetching.

"Is it true that an archer in the Middle Ages could kill a man at eighty yards?" she asked.

"It could be done," replied Alan, who had long grown tolerant of Tatiana's unladylike curiosity. "But it's difficult to maintain any accuracy at that range. They could have shot even further at an advancing army with a good chance of a hit. And a decent English or Welsh archer was expected to be able to shoot ten aimed shots a minute. A professional longbowman, trained from childhood, could shoot as many as twenty in a minute. Even a Henry repeating rifle would struggle to match that rate. They were a formidable force indeed."

"And is it true that the 'two fingers' gesture comes from the Battle of Agincourt?" Tatty persisted. "I heard that when the French captured any of the English bowmen, they would cut off the two shooting fingers of the man's right hand so he could never shoot again. And I heard that the archers who still had their fingers would stick them up at the French as a gesture of defiance."

"*Where* did you hear this?" Daisy asked in amazement, suppressing a smile. She could have sworn that Tatty had never even seen someone lift their two fingers.

"I would think it unlikely, Tatiana," Alan responded, looking sidelong at her as he pulled back on his bow, treating the question with a serious air. "Bowmen were commoners for the most part. They would most likely have been executed if they were captured."

"Oh. How horrid."

"Yes, indeed." Alan released his arrow, the taut silk string of the yew bow snapping forward and sending the projectile soaring in a long arc that ended in the center of the target.

Daisy watched with envy. She had only recently learned how to fire off a shot without having her wrist guard smacked by the string.

"Speaking of being horrid to commoners," she said quickly, to prevent another of Tatty's bloodthirsty questions, "I visited Philip Richards House the other day."

"Really?" He lowered his bow and looked over at her. "Not as a voyeur, I hope?"

"The family is a patron," she told him. "Roberto and I recently discovered that some of our female relatives may have been sent there."

"But that is a paupers' institution," the archdeacon said to her.

However, Daisy could see he was not that surprised. Tatiana was quiet now, listening carefully as she took her next shot.

"Even so, we think it has happened," Daisy insisted. "I'm sure you know the family is not always as . . . humane as some of us would wish it."

"Mmm," he grunted, avoiding her eyes as he pulled back on another arrow.

"We couldn't find a trace of any relatives in the records. But some of them are supposed to have died. I was wondering if you would remember any of their funerals. Or perhaps even a death certificate being filed for any of them—say, for instance, Simon's mother?"

The Archdeacon let the string of his bow go slack, the arrow nearly dropping from his fingers. He clicked his teeth together a few times.

"That is surely . . . er, surely the kind of question your family's doctor could answer," he said at last.

"Our family is very good at keeping secrets . . . particularly from its women. I'm sure the same could not be said of a devout man of the cloth such as you."

Alan turned towards her as if to retort, but thought better of it. It was clear he was mulling over what to say next. Daisy was sure that whatever it was, it weighed upon his mind.

"The Church keeps its fair share of secrets," he said softly. "But I suppose it would be best . . . it would only be . . . fair to tell you what I know of this matter. After all, your generation are responsible for the family's future." He steeled himself before continuing. "As I imagine you are already aware, some . . . influential families take a dim view of women who display low morals—particularly any kind of behavior that might bring the family into disrepute."

"Such as having an affair?" Daisy pressed him with a harsher tone than she intended. "Or falling in love with a commoner? Or . . . or having a baby out of wedlock? *Those* kinds of low morals? The kind of low morals *men* display on regular occasions?"

The Archdeacon shrugged uncomfortably. Tatiana scowled and opened her mouth to give her two-penny's worth, but Daisy made a slight gesture with her hand to silence her. It was clear there was something the man needed to say.

"It . . . it is not unusual for these women to be hidden away from society, to save face for the family. I have always suspected Philip Richards House to be just such a hiding place. If women have been 'put away' there, then they will be recorded under false names. I am not sure that, in the event of her demise, the death certificate of such a woman would bear her true name.

"You must understand," he added, taking Daisy's hand in his and squeezing it. "I have never been party to this kind of abhorrent plot."

And, standing there looking into his clear blue eyes, Daisy drew in a breath and knew that the Venerable Alan Mills was telling her a bare-faced lie. There was no way a man could have reached his position without knowing of the kinds of scandals that went on in his parish. And Daisy knew Christian churches, both Protestant and Catholic, could be extremely intolerant of fallen women.

"Do you remember what happened to Simon's mother?" she asked again. "Why was she taken away? Was she sent to the asylum? Did she die? *Is she still there?*"

He held up his hands as if they would fend off her questions, but her gaze drilled into him, her growing sense of outrage punching holes in his guilty conscience.

"Exactly what would it take for *me* to 'disappear'?" Tatiana demanded, horrified, but obviously fascinated too. "I fear there are times when my morals are not what they should be. There are times when I can be jolly rotten, you know."

"I remember when Simon's mother, Catherine Cooper, stopped coming to church—she was very pious," the Archdeacon told them. "The explanation given at the time was that she had been taken ill with consumption, but I knew it wasn't true. I would have been called. They said the disease was too infectious, but I'm certain she would have asked to see me, if only to talk through a closed door. They said she was being taken to a sanatorium—in the south of France, I think it was, where the climate was drier. But her husband and son did not go with her. Can you imagine that? Never mind her son, but her husband? And I can assure you, he loved his wife with all his heart—or at least he *did*, until he discovered she . . . " He looked uncertainly at Tatiana, as if this was an unsuitable topic for her tender ears.

A bit late for that, thought Daisy.

"Catherine had an affair?" she guessed.

Alan nodded.

"Or so the rumor mill would have it," he sighed. "I visit Philip Richards House from time to time, although it is not in my parish. I have more than a passing interest in the mental health of the poor. There are some truly miserable souls in that place. I went there about six months after Catherine had supposedly left for France. I saw a patient there by the name of Catherine Coogan. I could have sworn it was Catherine Cooper, but it was impossible to tell." He lifted his head and there were tears in his eyes. "You see, whatever state she was in when she was taken away, the wretched woman I saw in that grubby damp room in the asylum was truly a lost soul. Whatever she had experienced had driven her completely out of her mind."

Daisy and Tatiana stared at him for a long, uncomfortable moment and then Daisy took his hand in both of hers.

"I can see how much this affects you, Archdeacon," she said softly. "And though it pains me to ask, I have no choice: Alan . . . on your next visit to the asylum, you must demand that Doctor Angstrom furnish you with a list of all the women who were committed in that place against their will. I fear there is a terrible crime being perpetrated under our very noses and we must take action to stop it immediately."

"I'm sure that it's not as bad as all that," the Archdeacon said in a reassuring tone. "Doctor Angstrom is a humane man, with the best interests of society at heart."

"I have no doubt," she responded. "Though I suspect his definition of 'society' might be a little bit narrow. Not unlike his mind, I imagine."

XI

AN OUTLANDISH STORY

MRS. DEMPSEY'S HUSBAND was an officer serving on a ship of the line, on patrol somewhere in the South Atlantic, but nobody was sure where. Urskin had already sent word through the Navy to find him and inform him of his wife's death and his son's disappearance. In the meantime, the inspector had taken a decision that Nate was sure was illegal and started searching the Dempseys' house. Gerald joined in with some enthusiasm.

Nate watched but did not take part, choosing to sit at the kitchen table and rest his bruised groin as he watched his cousin going through drawers as if the rest of the Dempsey family were dead too. He looked around at the dishes on the dresser, the table with its white linen tablecloth and the counter, shelves and cast-iron stove that lined the walls. One door opened out into the short hallway, another to a small scullery with an enamel sink, a little pump and an ice cupboard, the walls hung with pots and other utensils. A third door led through into a tiny larder. Its window looked out on a well-tended vegetable and herb garden.

Nate, who had grown up in the surroundings of almost limitless wealth, wondered if this was a typical commoner's house. It was in a better state than most of their tenants' cabins on the estate. Would this house be categorized as a working-class or middle-class dwelling? In truth, he had no idea.

He kept thinking of young Cathal's face as he stared down at his mother's remains. Nate's mother, Miriam, had passed away when he was young. Weakened by the birth of her daughter, Tatiana, she had died of influenza a few months later. He and Tatty had hardly known her, and did not think of her very often. They had been raised by a distant, authoritarian father and a couple of caring nurses. But he remembered how his older brothers had continued to grieve for years. He could only imagine what Cathal was going through.

"I bloody knew it," Gerald grunted. "Did you see the scar on the dead woman's hand? It was from an operation. She must have been born with an extra thumb. Common enough type of mutation and the kind of thing that causes superstitious types—like our priest there—to mark someone as a witch. But the operation to remove it would have been expensive and must have been done when she was a child. It's the kind of little quirk that pops up in the more inbred upper classes, but they have the money to deal with it. Catherine must have come from good stock. Now, have a look at this . . . "

Nate stood up and peered over his cousin's shoulder. There was a dresser drawer full of papers and letters. One envelope bore the Wildenstern crest: a coat of arms bearing a shield on which there was an eagle holding a sword and a spear. The motto *Suffer No Weakness* was spelled out on the banner beneath it.

"Another connection to the family," Gerald observed. "We seem to keep falling over them, don't we?"

The letter was addressed to Catherine. Gerald took it from the envelope and read quickly through it. He handed it over to Nate, who was still reading.

"Bloody hell!" Nate exclaimed when he'd finished.

The letter was from Elvira, and was dated eleven years ago.

My dear Catherine,

I hope this letter finds you in good health. I regret to say that the same cannot be said of your former husband. Dear George has passed away in the most unfortunate manner, having become gruesomely impaled upon the antlers of a stag that he had shot during a hunt and mistaken for dead. The stag regained its feet as George was leaning over it to admire his accuracy, driving the aforementioned antlers into his chest.

I am sorry to say that this was not the end of the matter, as dear George was still alive and conscious as the stag attempted to free its head from his torso. A well-meaning companion fired off a shot with the intention of finishing off the stag, but the animal was thrashing most vigorously and the shot went wide, hitting poor George in the neck.

It is a testament to your late husband's strong constitution that he continued to draw breath even as this additional wound drained his life away. He could perhaps have been saved if the stag had not chosen that moment, blinded as it was by your husband's torso, to throw itself off a cliff into the river below. It is unclear if George finally died of the antler wounds, the gunshot, the fall, or drowning, but suffice it to say, he met his Maker most thoroughly.

Your son, Simon, seems to have taken his father's death reasonably well, given his limited mental capacities. The boy is in fine fettle and is showing an aptitude for drawing. You will be glad to know that he still thinks of you often.

Once more, I hope that you are faring well in your new life. Naturally, I do not expect an answer to this letter, nor do I wish for one. You will forgive me if I do not write to you again.

Yours sincerely,
Elvira Gordon

"It seems your mother knows more than she's letting on," Nate observed.

"She always does, old bean. The old battle-axe has always been the keeper of the family's secrets. She comes from a long line of Wildenstern women who know the importance of keeping their mouths shut and their eyes and ears open. Silas and I always knew where we stood—Mother's loyalty was always to her brothers first and her children second. In fact: her brothers first, Silas second and me a distant third. She still hasn't forgiven me for going to medical school."

Nate smiled. Elvira did not consider medicine a fit pursuit for a gentleman. Silas, Gerald's older brother, had taken to the family business like a fish to water, and as such had gained the delighted approval of their mother.

"I remember. She was only slightly less annoyed when you dropped out."

"Well, annoying her is what I do best."

"Charming. So, to get back to the point, Catherine is Simon's mother?" Nate frowned. "But if her husband was George Cooper, who is the boy I—?"

"She remarried," Gerald told him, holding up a marriage certificate. "Or rather, Catherine Cooper married again, but for the first time as Catherine Coogan. And she had a son by Patrick Dempsey, her new husband. Begs the questions, how, when and why did she start this new life?"

"And why did the family spread the lie about her dying of consumption?" Nate added.

"To save face, obviously," Gerald answered. "She must have got up to some mischief or other. Do you suppose George's death was an assassination?"

"I think it was," Nate said, nodding. "Oliver's first kill, if you're to believe the rumors. George was in charge of American grain imports and Oliver wanted the position. Sounds like he made a botched job of bumping off George though. God knows what he did to mangle George's corpse so badly it warranted an outlandish story like that. I wonder if Catherine even cared when she heard the news."

"Doesn't really matter any more," Gerald said, clicking his tongue as he continued to search through the papers.

Above them, they could hear Urskin and one of his constables searching the bedrooms. Gerald found a thick notebook in one of the drawers and leafed through it.

"Recipes," he muttered. "Seems Catherine was a bit of a

herbalist. The priest said she was a healer of sorts. Implied she was into pagan rituals and the like. Hmmm. Some mathaumaturgy too, by the looks of things." He snapped the book closed, looking quizzically at Nate. "Paganism and mathematical codes. Curious pursuits for a woman. So, we now know she was a Wildenstern. Supposing she was able to use her *aurea sanitas* to cure illnesses in others? It would be an extraordinary thing . . . perhaps she even discovered some way of manipulating the intelligent particles. There's nothing here about it. I'm raging that I'll never get to speak to her."

"If she did manage it, it would be enough to earn her a reputation as a witch in holier-than-thou circles," Nate mused. "Do you think all these women have been burned for being witches? That's what people used to do with them, isn't it?"

"Actually, most witches in Britain were hanged—or drowned during the 'tests,'" Gerald corrected him. "Burning was more of an Eastern European tradition. And it doesn't explain how they were burned so *thoroughly* in such small fires. No, I'm thinking this is something more . . . unconventional. Have you ever heard of spontaneous human combustion?"

"That's . . . wait a minute. That's where someone just bursts into flame for no reason?"

"There's always a reason, Nate," Gerald told him. "The trick is finding out what it is."

Feet tramped quickly down the stairs and Urskin walked into the kitchen. He was waving a small piece of card and a newspaper clipping.

"Found these in her bedside table," he said, throwing them down on the table.

The clipping was a small article about Vicky Miller's death. The card was a telegram. It read:

DEAR C STOP MAY BE ABLE TO TREAT YOUR SON STOP WILL ARRIVE TOMORROW EVENING STOP VM STOP

"So she and Vicky Miller knew each other," Nate remarked. "And the boy was definitely sick just over a week ago. His lungs are working just fine now, I can tell you. The telegram's dated three days before Miller's death, so she must have treated him just before she died."

"She cured consumption? A remarkable feat—if it's true," Urskin declared. "Seein' as no doctor can make such a claim, we can only assume she was resortin' to more . . . infernal powers. Perhaps her death—and that of her friend—was the price for such a 'miracle.' Perhaps the deal was even for their very souls."

"I wouldn't have taken you for a superstitious man, Inspector," Gerald said to him.

"I'm a God-fearin' man," Urskin replied. "As every man should be. But I believe the Devil works through *people* and 'tis against them that I have devoted my efforts."

"Quite," said Gerald. "Well, as far as Mrs. Dempsey's powers are concerned, 'infernal' might well be the right word. Because something caused that fire, and I believe that the answer to our little mystery may be coursing through the veins of young Cathal Dempsey. We have to find that boy."

XII

A FEAR OF SPONTANEOUSLY COMBUSTING

THE LITTLE ENGIMAL could walk up walls. Its agile legs ended in feet that seemed to have much the same qualities as those of a gecko lizard, allowing it to cling to smooth surfaces. It was similar in shape to a frog, but with proportionally smaller amber eyes and shorter back legs. It was roughly the size of a hatbox, a copper color, with smoky swirls of white and green traced through its ceramic skin.

"It's the mouth to which I want to draw your attention," Gerald told them. "Watch this."

Nate and Daisy were sitting on stools in Gerald's laboratory, watching as he held his little demonstration. The creature crawled sluggishly up the wall to about shoulder height and turned around to face the floor, hanging in this position with its mouth open. Gerald wet his hands under a tap at the sink beside him and then he moved and held them under the engimal's wide mouth. There was a hum, before the jaws opened a little wider. There were no teeth, yet Nate and Daisy both gave a start when the creature twitched . . . but it was merely to blow a breeze of warm air across Gerald's hands. Like most known engimals it clearly did not need to breathe. It exhaled continuously without stopping.

"You see?" he said to them. "Marvelous, isn't it?"

"It sits on its fat backside and blows hot air?" Nate asked incredulously. "So what? Half our family does the same."

Gerald held up his hands. They were dry.

"It's a superb way of drying your hands without a towel," he said.

"Or . . . you could just use a towel," Nate retorted.

"This is less likely to spread infection if one is performing an operation," Gerald told him. "And what's more, there is nothing to launder."

Daisy was gazing at the thing as if she had discovered the Holy Grail. Her fingers went up to her thick black locks.

"You could . . . " she stammered. "You could use it to dry *hair*. You must let us have it for the day of the ball, Gerald. It would save hours. My God, there are women who would sell their souls for something like this."

"No doubt," Gerald said with a dismissive gesture. "My point is this. We know that engimals carry intelligent particles in their bodies, much as we Wildensterns have them in our blood. We know that if these creatures drink even a drop of our blood, they will obey our commands because we have passed on some of our particles, and hence a means of bending them to our will. I still don't know exactly how this is possible, but it's very exciting all the same.

"Now," he continued, "engimals generate heat when they exercise, just as we do. They emit vapor, just as we do. But some of them can create heat and steam far beyond their need to regulate their temperature. This little beast can produce enough warmth to dry hands, or laundry, or . . . or hair." He nodded to Daisy as if allowing her this point. "But I've tested it and it can do much more. It can produce air hot enough to peel paint, or boil water."

Daisy and Nate regarded the creature with new eyes. It had stopped blowing as soon as Gerald had taken his hands away and now it slowly wiped its face with one paw and opened and closed its mouth a few times; the kind of gesture an old man might make while contemplating his next nap.

"How did you know it wouldn't burn the skin off your bones?" Daisy asked.

"It's house-trained," Gerald responded. "But do you see what I'm getting at?"

"Where's the heat coming from?" Nate asked.

"Exactly!" Gerald snapped, pointing at him. "It's not burning anything as fuel, as far as I can tell. Some engimals seem to feed, but most don't. Water appears to be the only thing they need for sustenance, and even that isn't true of all of them. Perhaps it's the intelligent particles themselves that create this extreme heat. And if that is true, perhaps they can create that heat within *us*."

Nate shifted uncomfortably. Daisy, who did not have Wildenstern blood, looked from one man to the other.

"You mean we could just burst into flames, like those women?" Nate's face was struggling to hide his jangling nerves. "Sounds a bit far-fetched to me."

"As far-fetched as a boy making a full recovery from a near-terminal case of tuberculosis within a week?" Gerald challenged him. "As far-fetched as seeing your six-hundred-year-old ancestors return to life?"

Daisy and Nate exchanged looks. Nobody liked mentioning the odious resurrection of the medieval Wildenstern ancestors the previous year, and the chaos that had resulted. Through some unearthly process—and a little help from Gerald—the preserved corpses of Hugo, Elizabeth, Brunhilde and Brutus Wildenstern had come back to life after being freed from the ground by a freak explosion. On regaining their strength, the ancestors (who had originally brought the family line to Ireland) had then set about trying to claim back what they saw as Hugo's rightful place at the head of the family. After some struggle, and not a few deaths, they had been defeated. Only Elizabeth was thought to have survived, her whereabouts unknown.

"I don't think these conflagrations just happened," Gerald went on. "I think these women did something to cause them. At least two of them were Wildensterns. I don't know about any of the other women yet, but I suspect they'll turn out to be related too. If we investigate every name on that list Urskin gave us, I'm sure we'll find that what they have in common is their blood.

"I have a theory that they found a way to tap into their *aurea sanitas* so that they could use it to treat others. But somehow, by releasing that power, they unleashed something they could not control and it eventually consumed them."

"And, of course, you mean to find out how they did it," Nate added.

"Of course!"

"I have always marveled at scientists' need to understand the world around them," Daisy remarked. "And their complete inability to understand the root of that need, and where it leads them. Aren't you a little worried you might spontaneously combust, as those women did?"

Gerald snorted, drawing a cigarette from the holder in his waistcoat pocket and striking a match to light it.

"Daisy, my dear, *I* am not a *woman*."

Cathal was a long way from Howth Head by the time he'd stopped running. He had stayed off the main roads, keeping to the lanes and fields until he was past Sutton. Once he had made it to the busier streets, he was able to mingle with the street urchins on the quays, feeling safe in the throng. He found shelter from the rain in a gap between stacks of cargo crates waiting to be loaded aboard a paddle steamer. He huddled up against the damp wood and cried until his throat was raw. The rain was heavier again, washing the air clean of the pungent smells of tarred wood, mildewed canvas, fish and stinking, sewage-filled river. He peered out, wondering what he was to do.

The quays made him feel more secure because he knew them. They reminded him of the times he had come here with his father. He had to get a message to Pa, wherever he was, that was clear enough. Even if he was the other side of the world some-where, Pa would know what to do. Except the peelers would be onto the Navy already, trying to get hold of him. Cathal sighed to himself. Maybe he should have stayed there and talked to them. But his parents, even though they had taught him to respect authority, had never completely trusted the green-bellies.

Something terrible had happened to his mother and he had no idea how or why, or who was responsible. Who was to say that the peelers weren't in on it? The whole village could well have turned against her. She worried about it happening sometimes, the way the priest talked about her. Maybe this was how they dealt with 'witches.'

The memory of her burned remains caused him to start sob-bing again. The noise from the docks drowned out the sound, but he stifled his tears anyway. He was alone. Until Pa found him, he was going to have to act like the man of the house.

The house. He couldn't go back there now. They'd come looking for him. But how would Pa find him then? How would he know where to look? He racked his brains. Where could he go? There was Mrs. Miller; but he didn't know where she lived. His pa had some friends, but some of them were dodgy and Cathal didn't know which ones weren't.

Ma had said there was a man in Dublin who was an old friend. What was his name? He couldn't remember. But he could recall going to the fellow's house once. Cathal had been young, so he didn't know the way, but he remembered the street because of the building stuck in the middle of the road at one end. A big church with a steeple that looked like a pepper canister. If he could find that street, he could find the house.

Not far down the quays, a giant engimal with long legs, a longer neck and a head like an octopus was lifting crates of cargo onto one of the ships. Cathal was able to watch it through a crack between two of the crates.

Over the general hullabaloo of the quays and the rattle of the rain, two voices began to carry across more clearly as they drew close to the stack of crates in which he was hiding. They spoke with thick Dublin accents and were having an argument about food. Cathal realized he had not eaten since the previous day and his ears were drawn to the conversation.

"Course there's a difference! Cottage poy is made with *beef*, shepherd's poy is made with *lamb*," a nasal, whinnying voice was saying.

"Not according to my ma," a gruffer man replied. "She made us shepherd's poy and she made it wit' deh roast beef left over from deh big house on a Sunday."

"Oi can assure yeh, Bourne, yer ma was mistaken. Shepherd's poy is made from lamb. Shepherds look after sheep, see? Hence the name of deh poy. Dey have deh raw materials to hand. Stands to reason, doesn't it?"

"Das just *stupid*, Red," Bourne protested. "A shepherd's dere to *protect* deh sheep. What kind o' job is he doin' if he's eatin' deh bleedin' tings?"

"Oh, good Jaysus, man. Yer wreckin' me head . . . Here, are yeh sure he came dis way?"

"Sure I'm sure. Don't see 'im now, dough."

It was at that moment that Cathal did the daftest thing imaginable—he stuck his head out to take a peek at these fellows who were clearly out searching for somebody. They were walking past, one tall and thin, the other shorter and stockier, both dressed in long black coats and flat caps, their shoulders hunched against the rain.

"How's it goin'?" the stocky one, Bourne, exclaimed. "Red, it's the chiselur!"

Cathal made to dart out past them, but they were quick and strong and he had nowhere to go except between the men. They pushed him back against the wet crates, each of them holding one of his wrists and gripping his collar. He kicked at them, but their longer arms kept them out of range.

"Whoa, dere, lad!" Red laughed. "Hold yer horses! We're not goin' ta hurt yeh! Calm down now."

Cathal could not break their grip and his legs were thrashing uselessly, so he went still and glared at them, ready for a chance to break free. Apart from the way they were dressed, the two men were quite different. Red had the predictable curly ginger hair, with freckles on a long, slightly flaky, pale-skinned face and stark blue eyes under almost invisible blond eyebrows. His teeth were gray and widely spaced. The flesh above the thumb of his left hand was stained with snuff. His sleeve drew back for a moment and Cathal saw that he had a tattoo on the inside of his right wrist—a pair of crossed swords with a kind of cross between them. Cathal only noticed it because of how quickly Red pulled down the sleeve to cover it up again. There was good humor in the man's expression, but some cruelty too.

Bourne's face was round, with the flushed cheeks and the

broken veins of an alcoholic. His hair was prematurely gray, hanging in a limp cowlick down his wet brow. A wobbly double chin joined a neck that was a wedge of muscle, and the strength in his stubby fingers told Cathal this man was a real hard case.

"Yer Catherine Dempsey's little fella, isn't dat right?" Red asked him.

"Blow it out yer arse!" Cathal snapped.

"Now, now. Dere's no need for dat," Bourne said in a placating tone. "Look, yer soaked to deh bone and I bet yeh could use a hot cup o' tea and some soup too. Whaddaya say? We just want to talk to yeh and there's no point doin' it out here. We're like drownded rats, the lot of us. How about we go somewhere and get some grub into us?"

Cathal's stomach growled and he shivered, the damp cold seeping through his clothes and into his flesh. He nodded, water dripping from his chin.

"Dat's the way!" Red said, loosening his grip. "A cup o' tea is yer only man. We'll get some shortbread too. Great for a chill. You like shortbread?"

Cathal nodded again. The two men held him more casually, but they did not let go.

Bourne gestured towards a tea shop further down the quays, and they started towards it. The work along the docks had eased off with the rain, so there were fewer people out as the three figures hurried along the cobbles. There was a brown mare with a black mane harnessed to a cart just beyond the lattice windows of the tea shop, the horse tied up with no driver in sight. It took him a minute, but Cathal eventually recognized the cart.

He dug his hands into his pockets. In his left was a wooden box of matches; in his right his blunt, stumpy penknife. He prized the knife blade open with the nail of his right forefinger and clicked it in place. Then he crushed the matchbox with his left hand, working the pieces around until he had the longest splinters sticking between the fingers of his tightening fist.

"Dey do a bleedin' gorgeous cream scone here, so dey do," Bourne told him with relish, pronouncing the word 'skon.'

"It's pronounced 'skown,' yeh gombeen, yeh," Red barked.

"Don't be tellin' me how to say me food!" Bourne snapped back.

When they reached the front of the tea shop the two men began to have at it regarding the proper pronunciation of the aforementioned cake. In three quick steps they had rushed Cathal past the shop and up to the back of the cart. Bourne was on his right and had a hold of his collar and Red had his left arm.

Cathal didn't wait to see what they intended to do. He started hollering at the top of his voice. Red's first instinct was to cover his mouth. As soon as his arm came up to muffle the boy's cries, Cathal jabbed the blunt knife into the man's arm as hard as he could. Red let out a yell and Cathal pulled the knife free and stuck it into the man's leg. The wounds were not deep, but they got Red's attention. Cathal's left arm was released just as Bourne got an arm around his neck. Cathal swung his left fist over his shoulder and felt a satisfying smack as Bourne got a face full of splinters. The man did not let go. Cathal stepped forward and swung his heel back into the man's kneecap, and then the thug let go. Cathal lunged forward, leaping onto the cart's tailgate, bounding across the tarpaulin that covered the flat bed and onto the horse's back. He thumped the horse's flank with his splintery fist and she reared, giving an outraged whinny, before lurching forwards and breaking into a gallop, her iron shoes kicking sparks off the cobbles.

The men shouted furiously, trying to grab the departing cart, but Cathal kept slapping the horse's flank until they had left the men behind. They came running after it as it careered down the quayside in the rain, forcing stevedores and seamen to throw themselves aside to avoid being run down. The old mare could not stay at a gallop with the cart dragging on her harness. They were bound to catch up eventually, despite slipping and tripping on the wet, uneven surface.

The cart clattered between the legs of the enormous engimal that stood on the quay. It crashed against a net full of boxes that hung from the engimal's tentacled mouth, then nearly toppled over on its side as it collided with another, bigger cart loaded with coal, sending a wave of black lumps scattering across the cobblestones. The horse staggered to a halt, heavy breaths swelling her sides. Cathal looked back and saw the two men were closing fast, their black coats billowing like bats' wings behind them.

Slipping off the horse's back onto the driver's bench, he ran up the back of the cart, caught hold of a rope that hung from the engimal's load and swung away, losing his hat in the process. He landed on top of a heap of grain sacks, dislodging an outraged seagull. Sliding down the rough fabric of the sacks, he ducked behind a row of costermongers selling their wares from carts along the street, and peeled off into a narrow alleyway. A pair of dray horses were hauling a heavily loaded cart of cotton bales away towards the city center. Keeping directly behind the driver, out of his eye line, Cathal slipped over the tailgate and under the tarpaulin on the back, disappearing from sight just as Bourne and Red came running up.

He watched through a small tear in the canvas as they swiveled one way and then the other, cursing loudly, trying to see over the heads of the stevedores and under the carts of the costermongers. As the dray horses ferried him away, Cathal wondered who these two strangers were, and why they were so desperately keen to have him to tea.

XIII

PREPARING FOR THE BALL

ROBERTO'S NEW WHEELCHAIR was finally ready after dinner on Friday evening. The Duke was intrigued to be told that it was not to be brought up to him, but that Gerald had requested his presence in one of the small training rooms on the fourth floor.

The training room was a smaller, more private version of the gymnasium, reserved for more senior family members. It was a long, high-ceilinged, oak-paneled room roughly the size of a rackets court, equipped with a rack of mock weapons such as wooden swords, padded sticks and rubber knives. A door, concealed by the paneling, led to a small armory of their more lethal versions. A row of targets for crossbow and small-caliber pistol practice were set up at one end, and some straw-stuffed fencing dummies stood off to the sides.

Winters wheeled Berto down to the room, where they found the door unlocked. Gerald was standing inside. Next to him was what appeared to be a small throne on wheels.

"It should really be painted in gold leaf and have a lot more curlicues," Gerald said, shrugging, "but that can all be added later."

Berto waved Winters away, and wheeled himself over to examine the new chair. He was not pleased. The wheels on the sides looked too small to reach comfortably, were too far forward and had no rails around their rims to allow him to push himself. They were also wide and bulky, and would catch on the sides of doors and on people's feet. They appeared to be coated in some kind of rubber, like the wheels of a penny-farthing. The rear wheels could obviously rotate to steer, but again, they stuck out too far. The back and arms and footrest appeared to be part of an ornate, purple velvet-lined chair made of French-polished wood—cannibalized from one of the house's antiques, no doubt—but the bottom was clearly a rounded metal box of some sort, hidden by a velvet skirt, and would be far too heavy to be practical. And there were no handles on the back for Winters to hold while pushing.

"I don't like it," he said.

And then Berto gave a start as the chair turned to look back at him. It moved towards him as if inviting him to sit down.

"I made it from a self-propelling wheelbarrow," Gerald told him, smiling as he drew a cigarette from his silver case. "It can move independently. Its arms are built into the arms of the chair, and I've been training it to obey commands that you tap on the three fingers on each of its hands. There hasn't been a lot of time, so you'll have to develop that yourself. Its head is between your legs—see the red netting part of the skirt?—so you'll need to keep your legs apart a bit so it can tell where it's going. It moves smoothly and gracefully and likes nothing more than to be carrying a full load—not that I'm casting any aspersions on the size of your backside, of course."

Winters helped Berto lift himself into the engimal chair, which shifted helpfully to assist them. Berto adjusted his position and found the chair very comfortable.

Gerald lit the cigarette and took a couple of puffs before continuing:

"I've had little success in teaching it to defend itself, apart from making it flee at high speed, which it does rather well. Actually, it's a rather cowardly miscreant, but that may be to your advantage. Nor have I been able to train it to attack on command. Perhaps you'll have better luck. I've included some weapons in its design, as per your original request. There are throwing knives set behind the panels of upholstery on the insides of the arms and a holster for a pistol beneath the seat on your left side. But this is my favorite bit . . . "

He got behind the chair and gently turned it to line up with one of the targets standing on wooden legs at the far end of the room. Both arms of the chair, where Roberto rested his hands, ended in a bulky carving that curved down, resembling a rolled piece of fabric. Leaning forward over the right arm, Gerald pressed the knot of wood in the center of the roll. There was a jolt, and a spinning disc shot from beneath Berto's feet, flying down the room and slicing a third of the length off one of the target's legs. The target toppled over on its side.

"Bloody hell!" Berto exclaimed.

"So what do you think?" Gerald asked.

"Brilliant!"

Berto found the creature's thin limbs tucked into a depression under the chair's arms, its hands neatly hidden within the curled carvings. Sure enough, when he touched its fingers, the chair shifted. He pressed them, seeing how the creature moved in response, jerking back and forth, spinning around in a most undignified manner and nearly hitting the wall, until he figured out how to control it. He turned towards Gerald, went too far and rotated back, went too far again and finally straightened up facing his cousin.

"Gerald, you're a bloody genius."

"I know. Thank Winters too: he helped with the upholstery and the French polishing."

"Thank you, Winters. Excellent work as always."

"Pleasure, Your Grace." The corners of the footman's mouth moved up a fraction, an expression of positively ecstatic pride.

Berto turned unsteadily to line up another target and pressed the wooden trigger. A blade shot from under his feet, took a chunk out of the sword rack and buried itself in the side wall.

"Ah," he said with a touch of embarrassment. "Perhaps a spot of practice is in order."

It was Saturday morning and long before dawn Wildenstern Hall had started buzzing with preparations for the ball that evening. It was one of the biggest events in the social calendars of the Irish upper class and Roberto had sworn to make it the best party anybody had ever attended. From the young bucks and ladies of the fast set to the grand old guard, everyone who was anyone would be there . . . or would wish they were.

Guests had been arriving all week. Their servants had been accommodated with the staff of the house, and together they were working all hours of the day and night to fulfill the visitors' needs and ready the house for the big day. The scent of freshly baked bread was already carrying up from the kitchens, the massive ovens turning out loaves in shifts that would run until the afternoon. Much of the cooking for the banquet had started and the rest would begin once breakfast was over. A few state-of-the-art gas-fired ranges had been installed in the kitchens, but there was also a need for a steady supply of coal for the older ranges. Many of the cooks still preferred them.

Before long the kitchens themselves were like ovens, with the ranges, hot-water cisterns, steam-kettles and gas hobs all adding to the stifling mix. The kitchen staff sweated and shouted, rolled up their sleeves and got stuck in. Tempers frayed, copper pots and porcelain dishes were dropped, warnings were given. The deal work surfaces were continually cleaned and scoured with sand, the steel of the knives honed with emery powder.

Elsewhere, the silver was being polished—and always, always counted to prevent theft by any light-fingered members of staff, particularly with other people's servants in the house. The breakfast dishes were washed and readied for luncheon. Linen tablecloths came down from the dining rooms, were laundered in lye, put through the mangle and hung out to dry, while fresh table-cloths were sent upstairs. Signs, painted in prominent places, aimed at improving the staff's characters, expressed such sentiments as WASTE NOT, WANT NOT, or EVERYTHING IN ITS PROPER PLACE.

Not everyone entered into the spirit of the thing—spit would occasionally be found upon a sign—but few dared risk the wrath of the butler or housekeeper. Wildenstern Hall was run like a well-oiled machine.

Daisy oversaw it all, taking time out from entertaining her guests to come down and inspect the preparations. Her reputation would stand or fall on this day. As the wife of the Duke of Wildenstern, she was not only a major figure in society, but her progressive ideas made her a model for other women her age. Her words were often quoted in gossip columns, her outfits the talk of the town. It caused her no end of irritation when she wore a new style to a ball one week, only to find everyone else wearing it the next. That said, she was looking forward to the looks her new gown would garner. Designed in Paris, its champagne-silver silk was quite different from anything else on the scene.

She could attend to all her management duties and still be ready for the ball that evening because she had a team of maids to help dress her and, with the help of Gerald's hot-breathed engimal, she knew she could wash, dry and style her hair in less than an hour.

Tatiana, on the other hand, was spending most of the day fretting over which shoes to wear with which dress that evening.

Daisy was slipping out of the drawing room, idly wondering

where her husband had got to, when she spotted him heading for the mechanical lifts in the main hallway. Winters was following protectively as Berto steered a marvelous new wheelchair across the expanse of black and white checkered tiles. They were accompanied by Berto's friend, Jamie, and another man—it looked like Dr. Herbert Angstrom. Daisy frowned, pausing to watch them as they entered one of the elevators. Berto had put Angstrom's name on the invitation list, but Daisy had assumed the doctor was just another of the family's associates—not somebody they expected to spend much time entertaining. And yet here was Berto taking the man upstairs when they had a house full of guests.

There had been times in the past when Daisy had felt compelled to spy on her husband, when she had suspected he was keeping secrets from her. And she had been right. But sneaking around after her man was not very dignified, and she did not want to be forced into doing it again.

Daisy put the matter to the back of her mind, and started up one of the wide, curving staircases for a final check on the preparations in the guests' quarters. It paid to be diligent, but it also gave her an excuse to get away from the mind-numbingly boring chit-chat one was forced to engage in with fat lords' wives, crowing society madams and doddery spinsters who constantly sought the tired ear of the Duke's wife. Sometimes, being important was a pain in the neck.

XIV

"YOU'LL SEE"

ROBERTO MANEUVERED HIMSELF over to the easy chairs, where he gestured for his guests to sit down. He had met Angstrom before. The doctor's strong face and pomaded copper-colored hair and beard were complemented by an extremely well-cut blue suit that showed off his fit frame to good effect. He sported a heavy gold signet ring on the little finger of his right hand.

Jamie sat apart from the other two, assuming a junior status in the conversation, not wishing to speak until spoken to.

Berto clapped his hands together and leaned forward, looking expectantly at the doctor.

"So," he said brightly. "This society of yours—the Knights of Abraham. Tell me all about it."

Angstrom glanced at Jamie for a moment, then laced his fingers together, crossed one leg over the other and lounged back in the armchair, regarding Berto with a critical eye. Berto saw immediately that the doctor was accustomed to commanding conversations. He was willing to let that go for the moment.

"It's a pity your father never told you about it, Your Grace," Angstrom said. "He was, at one point, a valued member."

"My father and I didn't exactly see eye to eye on many issues," Berto said, shrugging. "And we didn't talk a great deal."

Angstrom gave an understanding, if somewhat patronizing, smile. Everybody knew of Berto's hell-raising reputation before he rose to the position of Patriarch.

"Well, basically, we are a fraternity; an association of Christian gentlemen who share common philosophies, motives and goals. We cooperate with a view to improving our lives and the lives of all those in the British Empire and, ultimately, all those living under the gaze of God."

"Very admirable," Berto commented, although he suspected that some of those 'living under the gaze of God' did better out of the association than others. "I have to admit, I'm interested in what you were able to do for Jamie. It would seem that you have access to resources that even I do not."

Angstrom pulled a platinum cigar case from his pocket, flipped it open and offered it around.

"Cuban," he said. "The very best."

Jamie took a cigar; Berto did not. Angstrom snipped off the end of a cigar with a silver cutter, and struck a Vesuvian match, lighting his cigar with its spluttering flame. He handed the cutter and matches to Jamie and leaned back again, taking a long draw before exhaling the smoke in a languid manner.

"I regret to say, Your Grace, that the Knights of Abraham do not run a hospital per se; rather, we take great pains to look after our members, with a view to better serving our cause."

"I can pay any price," Berto told him sharply.

"It is not a matter of *price*, but of confidence," Angstrom replied. "Our methods are, at times, somewhat . . . unorthodox." He glanced momentarily at Jamie. "As a member, however, one can enjoy all the facilities we have to offer. In return, one is expected to exercise the proper *discretion* and to share one's resources as others share theirs. That is to say, we all help each other wherever possible, and we do so on the understanding that it is carried out *privately*. For instance, we do not involve our *women* in our affairs—talkative and frivolous creatures that they are. And we do not blow our own trumpets, so to speak. We do not announce our achievements to the world. Faith, Loyalty, Unity, Prosperity and Privacy—these are our watchwords."

"Fine," said Berto. "How do I join?"

The majestic banquet hall was situated in one of the older wings of Wildenstern Hall. Beneath its glittering chandeliers, throngs of people took their seats at the long, linen-covered tables, each place marked with a gilt-edged name card and laid with a gleaming array of silver cutlery and crystal glasses. Managed with the efficiency of a military campaign, the ball began with a lavish meal served in several courses. Servants delivered each dish swiftly and gracefully, before retreating from sight through the doors, or into the alcoves designed to conceal them along the tapestry-lined walls.

Later, stuffed with everything from turtle soup to pheasant, quails' eggs to suckling pig, dumplings to lobster, the guests started to break formation and mingle among the tables as the desserts were served. Many grabbed a plate of strawberry meringue or cheesecake along the way. A string quartet played a gentle accompaniment of the latest popular tunes.

The wine was flowing too. Gideon tried to lead some of the older men in a song at the end of his table, vigorously conducting with one hand, the other gripping a priceless bottle of 1792 Pinot Noir from *Le Clos du Bois*. The half-full bottle slipped from his hand and a nimble footman was already moving with a dustpan and brush by the time it smashed on the floor.

Berto looked out on his creation from the head of the top table and saw that it was good. This was the point in the evening he loved; when the refined Victorian manners started to go out of the window and people—many assisted by some measure of alcohol—relaxed and let their hair down, or lost the run of themselves and caused havoc. Berto didn't care which—it all contributed to the general party atmosphere.

Off to one side of the table, Tatiana was flirting with that young rake, Charlie Parnell. He was trying to terrify her with stories of the Irish rebels, while she attempted to out-shock him with the exploits of this fellow, the highwayboy she had been reading about. On the other side, Elvira was introducing Nate to a pretty blonde Prussian girl; a member of the Bismarck family if Berto's memory served him correctly. The Bismarcks also enjoyed *aurea sanitas*, and marriages between their family and the Wildensterns were quite common. When it came to arranging romances, what Elvira lacked in subtlety she made up for with sheer relentless effort.

She had ceased trying on Gerald's behalf, however, after he informed her that if she didn't, he would marry an American just to spite her.

Berto spotted Gerald's older brother, Silas, making his way down the table towards him. The reluctant Patriarch sighed; Silas ran the Company's affairs in America, and would no doubt want to talk business. He had a passion for it that Berto could not bring himself to share.

"Berto, old chap! Haven't had a proper chance to talk to you since I got back. Do you have a moment?"

"For you, Silas, always—as long as it has nothing to do with work."

Silas looked a little hurt, but quickly recovered his smile, an expression that did not suit his pale, thin face with its rigid fringe of dark hair. Almost as intelligent as his little brother, but with a good deal less imagination and character, Silas was an ideal accountant and a reliable hand on the tiller of the American business that had made the Wildensterns so rich. "Well, I *did* want to discuss this trouble that's going on across the water—the United States not being in the least bit 'United' at all, so to speak. It appears this civil war is going to go on much longer than we had hoped. And if the Union forces win, our suppliers in the South will lose their slaves—"

"Now, y'see, that sounds like business talk to me," Berto

interrupted him. "And don't expect me to feel sorry for the slave-drivers, even if it is going to cost us money. Go and chat up some girls, Silas. Let's send you back to the civil war with a new filly, what?"

"There's something else, Berto," Silas said, leaning in closer even though the noise in the room would have prevented anyone from overhearing. "I wanted to talk to you about Gideon."

"What about him?"

"He's up to something. He's been redirecting some of the ships in the fleet away from our trade routes. Ships that are supposed to be taking our goods across the Atlantic are being used for something else. He's—"

"He's in *charge* of the merchant fleet, Silas," Berto reminded his cousin, his attention drawn to Daisy, who was beckoning to him from across the room. The orchestra was tuning up in the ballroom. It was time for the dancing to begin. "It's his job to decide how best to run the damned boats and he seems to have done it well enough for years. Now go and get plastered and have a good time tonight or I'll bloody sack you, all right?"

Silas withdrew, looking a little disgruntled. Berto steered his engimal chair away from the table, with Winters gently ushering guests aside to allow the Patriarch access to the dance floor.

Nate was struggling to get away from Elvira. He was quite taken with Anika Bismarck. She was a petite, delicate beauty with cool gray eyes, straw-blonde hair and a thin-lipped but disarming smile. Her English was better than his German, so they chatted in that language, much to the annoyance of her brother, who did not share her fluency and stood glowering silently by her side.

With his smart cavalry uniform and cropped blond hair, he was every inch the *Junker*—one of the gentleman-soldier class—and bore *Schlager* dueling scars upon his face. These types of scars were worn with pride by Prussia's elite young men, and must have been hard to come by for somebody who healed as well as a Wildenstern. Nate itched to tease the man about them, but didn't want to offend the prig's sister.

"Nathaniel has become a key figure in the family since the death of his father!" Elvira was shouting up from her wheelchair into the Prussian girl's ear, selling her nephew for all she was worth. "His brother, the Duke, relies heavily upon him! I suppose you could say that Nathaniel acts as his brother's legs! And his arms! His arms too!"

Nate rolled his eyes and Anika covered up a smile with her hand. She had a very fetching way of swinging her hips gently to the music while she talked, hips swathed in a deep-blue silk, and when he heard the orchestra tuning up, Nate suggested they go through to the ballroom, confident that Elvira could not follow them onto the dance floor. Anika was eager to dance. Her brother was not.

The ballroom was even larger than the banquet hall, with a high vaulted ceiling hung with chandeliers and gas-lamps illuminating the huge room with a warm, flattering light. Arched alcoves ran down each side filled with massive bouquets of flowers and tables covered with still more food: truffles, sweetbreads, crackers, caviar, cheese, plovers' eggs and a range of other treats. Bowls of punch had tall sculptures of ice protruding from their centers. Servants wove through the crowd carrying trays of drinks, skillfully evading the drunken staggering of the guests, while still keeping the glasses within reach of their grasping hands.

The dance floor itself was a vast replica, in mosaic, of Michelangelo's work on the ceiling of the Sistine Chapel. It was only possible to see it properly from several yards above the floor. A mezzanine level had been built around the entire ballroom for that purpose. Completed during Edgar Wildenstern's reign, the entire project had cost more than all of the working-class cottages in Ireland combined. The delighted guests considered it money well spent.

To everyone's surprise, Berto and Daisy led the way onto the dance floor as the orchestra started their first number. They had had scant time to practice earlier in the day with Berto's agile new wheelchair, but to the amazement of the crowd, they began to perform an awkward, but passable, slow waltz. Dozens joined in and Nate watched with tears in his eyes as his brother danced for the first time since being crippled the year before.

Behind him Nate could hear Gideon spouting rubbish. His uncle had a habit of spewing nonsensical combinations of pompous phrases when drunk, particularly if he was talking to people he wanted to impress. Nate glanced around and saw Dr. Angstrom and the Lord Lieutenant—the Queen's representative in Ireland—listening patiently as Gideon talked balderdash.

"Of course, I believe in top-down management! You can't put an old head on young shoulders and Edgar left some pretty . . . er . . . pretty big boots to fill. Seven-league boots! We leave our footprints across this British Empire and it takes a firm hand to . . . to grip the rudder and keep this ship on the rails. There's a stampede of liberal thought tiptoeing through the governments of Europe—and Britain, God help us!—and one of those cows . . . buffalos . . . whatever . . . is . . . is holding the reins of this family!"

Nate turned away, but kept listening. Gideon was rarely discreet, but he normally kept his rants about Berto within the family circle. "We need fresh blood, fresh thinking!" he bellowed over the music, which was not that loud. "An old hand who stands for . . . for . . . er . . . for traditional values and looking to the future! If I were Chairman of the Company, I'd have a revolution—I'd see . . . I'd see to it that we go back to the way things were before that whippersnapper took charge! That's what I'd do, if . . . if it was my show. A revolution backwards! You'll see. *You'll see!*"

Nate resisted the urge to turn and look again. Gideon hadn't noticed him. 'You'll see?' Did he mean anything by that? There was no question of anyone committing an Act of Aggression at the ball, what with all the witnesses, but Nate felt suddenly uneasy. He had little time to dwell on it however, as Anika took his hand and dragged him onto the floor.

They danced for one tune, but then Berto retreated from the floor and Anika excused herself to go and powder her nose. Daisy, still eager to dance, spotted Nate standing alone and instead of waiting to be asked, took his hand and pulled him onto the floor. He grinned reluctantly, but took the lead as they whirled among the other dancers. Daisy looked beautiful, her face bright and happy, her thick dark hair pinned up and decorated with ribbons and flowers, leaving a few braids to drape over her bare shoulders. Her silver silk dress with its gold braid showed off her figure (she never wore a corset and often made scathing comments about them), the skirts flaring beneath the waist into rich frills.

Nate eventually stepped off the floor, begging to be allowed to rest and comically feigning a cramp. Daisy laughed and waved and wandered off to find a new partner. He could not identify the feeling that was flooding over him, but his back was coated in sweat. He found his hands were shaking and he was clenching his jaw shut. He was struck with a sudden restlessness, as if some animal had awoken inside him, confused by these civilized surroundings.

Anika was dancing on the floor once more, partnered by Oliver, but she looked over and caught Nate's eye. He turned away. It wasn't another dance that he needed, or more chitchat, or charming witticisms.

Gerald sidled up to him, a glass of wine in one hand and a cigarette in the other, watching the revelers with amusement and appearing to be far too sober for Nate's taste.

"You look in a bit of a funk," Gerald observed. "Music not to your taste?"

"Let's get out of here," Nate said to him.

"Out to where?"

"Anywhere," Nate snapped. "Just out of here . . . Let's go to town."

"All right then."

Some of the guests had already moved into the rooms and hallways leading off from the ballroom. Some sought drunken solitude, others a dark corner or the privacy offered by a closed door. As they walked through the house, the two young men caught glimpses of these liaisons: giggling, stolen kisses, the rustle of material under groping hands and passionate embraces. From other rooms, the smell of exotic smoke, the sight through a half-closed door of water poured over a sugar cube into green absinthe; from somewhere they detected the faint but intoxicating scent of opium fumes.

Nate and Gerald walked past it all.

"Where do you want to go?" Gerald asked.

"Monto," Nate replied.

"What do you want to do?"

"Everything."

XV

AN AREA OF ILL REPUTE

CATHAL SHIVERED. The damp cold soaking into his bones. He had walked for hours trying to find the street with the pepper canister church. Except for a small loaf of stale bread he had bought with the last penny in his pocket and an apple he had stolen from a stall, he had eaten nothing for almost two days. He was exhausted, but could not sleep. When the daylight faded and the gas-lights were being lit along the streets, he had come back to this little hideout of his, which he had discovered the previous night. It was a freshly burned-out tenement building. Parts of the walls had collapsed and most of the three floors had disintegrated, including all but the very skeletons of the staircases. Windows emptied of glass and frames gaped out on the street; anyone looking up through them could see hollow sky where there should have been walls and ceilings.

But there was a section of roof intact atop one corner over-looking the street, with some untouched floorboards beneath it—a part of the attic space that had somehow survived the fire and was protected from the worst of the wind on three sides. Climbing up into the blackened, treacherous rafters, Cathal shook ash and dust off the slightly scorched blanket he had found among the debris and curled up under the corner of roof that still offered shelter.

As the dark grip of night closed around him, he cried quietly for his dead mother. They might well have held her funeral by now; he should have been there for it. Why did his pa have to spend so much time at sea? He should have been back here looking after his son. The loneliness of Cathal's grief was almost more than he could bear. It was as if blunt claws were scraping a hollow inside him.

The sooty smell of charred wood and other scents from the recent fire assaulted his nose, but the remnants of the wooden floorboards under him were solid and dry enough and, at least up here, he would be less vulnerable to the kinds of blackguards who combed the streets looking for street urchins they could capture and put to work.

The chill breeze found every gap in the folds of the blanket, the bricks of the wall were cold where he leaned against them and drained the heat from his body. And never very far away was the fear that this building was not quite done collapsing yet. Cathal drifted off into a disturbed sleep, twitching and shifting restlessly.

He woke with a start to find his legs dangling over the edge of the floorboards into the empty space three stories deep beneath him. Scrambling back into the corner, his heart beating like a bird's wings, he pulled his knees up to his chest and dragged the blanket back over himself.

There were voices in the street below him. It was the middle of the night; a strange time to be out. Something about them sounded familiar. They were speaking softly, but the sound carried far in the clear night air.

"Yeh'll agree dat, like me, you believe in keeping deh best till last?" one voice was saying.

"Yeh know we concur on dat point, Red," the other voice replied.

"And yeh'll agree that deh fat end of the egg contains the *yolk*, which is undoubtedly deh tastiest part of said egg, it bein' the source of nutrients for the developin' chick. Dat's why dat end is fatter, to leave more room for deh yolk. Am I right?"

"I'll grant yeh dat, yes," Bourne assented.

"Well den, it follows dat yeh should always start eatin' yer boiled egg from d'udder end—the sharp end—so as to prolong the pleasure and leave more of deh yolk for deh finish."

There was a moment of silence. Then Bourne surrendered to Red's superior logic.

"When yeh put it like dat, it's hard teh argue, Red. Yer deffiney a great man for the reasonin'."

"Dat's down to me superior education, Bourne, me good man."

"Here, are yeh sure dis ting is goin' to find that little scut?"

"Diva finds *everyone* eventually. Just give 'er time. He came down dis way, dat's for sure. She'll sniff 'im out."

Cathal carefully stood up, anxious not to cause even the smallest squeak of floorboard, and peered out around the broken brick wall to look down on the street. Remembering the last time he'd stuck his head out to see these two men, he ensured that they were moving away from him before he leaned forward. He was met with a most unusual sight.

Fortunately, though the street was one of those with proper gas-lamps, the pools of light cast on the ground did not stretch up to where he was hidden, so Cathal could look down on his hunters from the security of the darkness. The two men were walking slowly down the street, following a . . . well, it was hard to say what it was.

Cathal had seen illustrations of such things in books, but had never seen one in the flesh, if 'flesh' was the right word for it. It was a drawbreath; a wheeled engimal, about the size of a springer spaniel, with a bristly pelt and a wide, triangular head mounted on a long, snake-like neck. Wire whiskers reached out from around its letterbox-shaped mouth. Its eyes were set either side of its head. He knew that engimals such as this were trained to clean the carpets in some of the grandest manor houses. What was such a valuable creature doing in the hands of these thugs?

Red held the creature on what appeared to be a leash. Its mouth was gliding along the ground, its neck moving with a lazy weaving motion that was almost hypnotic. It swayed its head from side to side as if it was searching out . . . as if it was searching for his scent. Red was holding something in his other hand, which the drawbreath sometimes turned back and studied for a few seconds before continuing.

As the men crossed the road and walked under another lamp, Cathal got a glimpse of the object. It was his hat. They were using his hat to give the drawbreath his scent.

He had never heard of engimals being used as bloodhounds, but then this last week had been one unpleasant discovery after another and this latest came as less of a shock than it might have.

"Hang on," said Red. "She's got sometin' again."

The drawbreath's head unfolded abruptly, opening out into a kind of flower-shaped funnel. There was a hissing sound, and then the head folded back up into its normal form. Cathal pulled his head back in as the men turned around.

"We've been up and down dis street twice," Bourne said impatiently.

"Could be deh little guttersnipe went back and fort' a bit."

Cathal peeked out again, gazing nervously at them as they passed the doorway leading into his building. Perhaps the stink of the ash and burned debris was hiding his scent. His ma used charcoal to soak up the bad smells her potions created in the house. Or at least, she did use it, before she died. Cathal had difficulty swallowing the lump in his throat.

"Dis is a waste of time," Bourne protested. "We should be checkin' out dat udder woman's place, out in Harold's Cross. We need to be gettin' hold of her pretty sharpish if she's to be saved."

"We'll save 'er, sure enough," Red replied. He was quiet for a while as he watched the drawbreath weave in front of him. "Dat one won't go like d'udders, Bourne. Doc says she's a cunning little wagon. She won't give up so easy. Deh Devil's fire'll be a long time waitin' for her."

"So long as we get what we want from her first," Bourne said. "She's got herself a fella wit' some money too. Did yeh see dose hedges out deh front of 'er house? Cut into all fancy animal shapes? Dat's class, dat is. Dat's what I'd like if I'd a proper house. Hedges shaped like animals. Quality, like."

"You'll 'ave fancy hedges some day," Red told him. "Just keep believin' an' it'll happen fer yeh, Bourney."

"Tanks, Red. Yer a constant source o' inspiration to me, y'know dat?"

"We look after each udder, mate. No one else will."

Their voices faded into the distance as the drawbreath led them away down the path again. Cathal sank back down the wall and huddled up, pulling his scorched blanket over him. These men knew something about how his mother had died. He should follow them and try to find out more. But his skin crawled as he thought about that engimal. There could be no doubt that if he got too close, the thing would smell him out and then they'd have him for sure.

But they knew something about his ma's death. A determined snarl twisted across Cathal's face. They knew something about his ma's death.

Monto was an area of ill repute north of the city center, a haunt for swindlers and strumpets, moneylenders and dealers in every kind of pleasure. Hidden away in its back-streets were the roughest pubs, the gambling hells and even a few opium dens. Whatever sinful desire you wished to indulge, the denizens of Monto could provide you with the means . . . for a suitable price.

It was a time of great unrest in Ireland and, as a result, there were thousands of soldiers posted in Dublin. Soldiers demanded entertainment and were willing to pay. And there were many Irish willing to take their money. Monto had become the center of this seedy business and it came alive at night—a festival of hedonism.

Nate and Gerald left the last of a long line of clubs on their trail of binge drinking in the darkness of early morning. They wandered for nearly half an hour, trying to find their velocycles, before remembering that they had taken a coach into town. This was because they had learned the year before of the dangers of riding while boozed up, and besides, Flash refused to carry Nate when its master was too buckled drunk to sit upright.

Having established that they would need to find a hansom cab to take them home, the two inebriated young men set about trying to locate one. This would have been an easier task if either of them could have managed to walk in a reasonably straight line.

"There's got to be a cab here some'ere," Nate mumbled, swiveling unsteadily to take in the dark-windowed buildings around them.

"Wizzout a doubt," Gerald agreed. "They're juss playin' hard to get."

"Nid some food to soak up dis drink . . . and the other st-stuff," Nate suggested. "Feel a bit off-kilter. Fancy a meat pie? Or some deviled ham?"

"Luvverly," Gerald said, and then turned around and vomited into the gutter.

Nate watched with mild amusement and then leaned over

and did the same. They both stood up, wiping their mouths with their handkerchiefs and feeling slightly better.

"Very dignified. Expect better behavior from such a pair o' gentlemen," a snide voice commented. "Look at yiz, spewin' yer guts up like chiselurs breakin' the pledge."

The two gentlemen looked around to find themselves facing a gang of nine teenage coves armed with wooden bats, sticks and knives. They all had their caps pulled down low over their faces and their expressions were not welcoming.

"I don't suppose you brought a pistol?" Nate muttered.

"No, didn't you?" Gerald muttered back.

"We were at a party . . . *dancing*. Dance partners tend to notice long hard shapes in your pockets."

The gang's leader, a rough-looking, red-faced scoundrel in a white shirt with rolled-up sleeves, tucked his thumbs into his braces and regarded the two vomiters with mock-disgust.

"Dat's no way to treat our streets," he scolded them. "Dis is Five Lamps turf yer throwin' up in and dere's a fine for dat."

"I see," Nate replied, feeling suddenly more sober. "And what would the fine be, exactly?"

"What's deh fine, lads? *Ezackly*, like," the leader asked, grinning.

"Send 'em home with broken bones!" the lads chanted back.

"Look here, you're coming on a bit strong, aren't you?" Gerald protested. "Couldn't we just—"

It was as far as he got. The Five Lamps boys descended on them in a rush, the leader jabbing at Nate's gut with a flick knife.

Nate's reflexes took over. Pivoting to the side, he caught the fellow's hand, bent it down and twisted his body in the opposite direction, flipping the blackguard onto his back. Nate pulled the knife from his hand and stamped on the chap's ribs, but had the knife knocked from his own fingers by a wooden stave that came down on his wrist, nearly breaking his arm. He swept the next blow aside, stepping in and slamming his elbow into the second fellow's sternum, forcing a satisfying grunt of pain out of him, before following the blow with a backfist to the man's face. A hip throw hurled the fellow into the path of a friend who was coming to his aid, swinging a butcher's knife.

Gerald pirouetted like a dancer, dodging blows and delivering swift, sure punches with stunning precision. His feet struck out, catching groins, knees and sweeping attackers from their feet.

Both Wildenstern cousins fought with a bewildering array of techniques these juvenile thugs had never seen before, striking not only with their fists, but also with the edges and heels of their hands, their fingertips, forearms, elbows, knees, shins and feet. Thinking they had come across easy prey in this pair of toffs, the Five Lamps gang were faced instead with the fighting arts of China, Japan, Okinawa and India, along with a dash of good old-fashioned pugilism. The styles of the young gentlemen were different from each other: Nate fought gracefully, but with relish; gasping and grunting, he dropped opponents with the satisfaction of a job well done. Gerald was more clinical, chillingly accurate, his movements economical, using no more energy than was necessary to dispatch his adversaries.

But what the gang members lacked in training they made up for with street-tough aggression. In a couple of minutes, the strength of their numbers was beginning to tell. And after a night of partying neither Nate nor Gerald were in a fit state for a drawn-out fight.

Nate swung a kick into the side of one lad's knee, but then took a stick to the temple from another behind him. The blow exploded across his senses and he staggered. Two more thugs piled into him, driving him into the mud of the narrow street. He thrust stiff fingers into the windpipe of one of them, driving him off, only to find the other one wrapping an arm around his neck. Nate bent three of the man's fingers back, and the chap helpfully let go before they broke.

Gerald grabbed this one by the hair and hauled him off Nate, bringing an elbow down hard on the fellow's collarbone with a loud crack. But even as Gerald freed his cousin, another two jumped him from behind. Nate obliged by picking up a fallen stave and slamming it into the kidney of one of them, causing the man to gasp before a second blow caught him in the face and shut him up most convincingly.

But they kept coming. Punches and kicks and blows with bats and sticks rained down on the two Wildensterns. Nate cried out as each nail of pain dug in more than the last, feeling the impacts against his bones, battering his torso and limbs, splitting the flesh of his head and face. Blood ran into his eyes and he tasted it in his mouth. He felt pain in too many places to block it out and eventually he collapsed into a limp heap in the gutter, bubbles gurgling through the blood in his mouth. The remaining gang members delivered a few last kicks, took the wallets from their victims' jackets and spat on the two beaten swells before walking away, supporting their limping friends, carrying those who could not walk.

Gerald was the first to come to his senses, groaning as he raised himself up, clutching ribs that were surely fractured. There was no mistaking that stabbing pain deep in his side. A grating feeling in his left forearm suggested a break there too. Finding some of the recently disgorged vomit on his sleeve, he wiped it away with disdain and crawled awkwardly towards his cousin. Nate was barely conscious, moaning pitifully.

"Well, that was refreshing," Gerald said, coughing and wincing as his ribs protested. "Much more fun than poncing around a ballroom."

Nate rolled onto his side and gagged, spitting up blood. He was in too much pain even to sit up. Despite his split lips, he seemed to still have all his teeth, and his nose was unbroken, much to his surprise. His head throbbed so much he felt sick. One eye socket was so badly bruised it had closed up, and the other was cut along his eyebrow.

Two of the fingers on his right hand were crooked and would not move properly. Dislocated. With a hiss, he gripped them tightly and pulled, screwing up his face against the discomfort until he felt their joints click back into place. Releasing them, he flexed, satisfied that they would be back in working order in a few days.

"A capital end . . . to the evening," he remarked. "By God, they . . . they trounced us good and proper. Still, we didn't do too badly, I think. There's . . . er"—he spat again—"there's a few of 'em who'll . . . who'll be feeling it tomorrow."

"Fat lot of good it'll do us," Gerald snorted, grimacing as he examined his suit. "Next time there's a party at home I suggest we just bloody stay there. At least if one of the family has a go at us, they'll have the decency not to throw us in our own *vomit* when they're done."

"Still—at least it *is* our own, eh?" Nate observed, coughing.

Gerald looked at him with an expression of weary disgust.

XVI

THE BACK-STABBING POLTROON

DAISY WAS FOOTSORE, exhausted and perilously close to being tipsy to an unladylike degree. It had been a fabulous night. She was a little concerned about Tatiana, who had disappeared off just after midnight and had not been seen since. But Daisy had faith that Tatty, for all her feckless ways, could look after herself better than many gave her credit for.

Berto led the way towards the entry hall and the elevators that would take them up to their bedrooms. He and his wife had stayed awake to the bitter end, finally surrendering after the last of the revelers had retired, collapsed, or wandered off into the maze of rooms in search of other distractions. Now Daisy was desperate to get to bed. Her shoes had been carefully chosen for the right mix of elegance and suitability for the dance floor, but she carried them in one hand as she walked alongside her husband's wheelchair. Winters walked at a discreet distance behind them, keeping a watchful eye on his master's meandering course.

"A good night, I think," Berto remarked, as he struggled to steer his chair in his befuddled state. "They'll be talking about this one for months."

Daisy smiled, sidestepping a wayward wheel before it ran over her bare toes. They were crossing the wide, checkered floor of the entry hall towards the pair of ornately decorated doors to the mechanical lifts. A sleepy and uncomfortable-looking elevator boy was waiting for them, dressed in a red jacket and cap lined with silver braid.

Sensing something was wrong, Winters stepped forward.

"What is it, lad?"

"I'm afraid the lifts is out o' order, sor," he said to the manservant, taking off his cap and keeping his eyes on the floor. "The man's been sent to look at wha's wrong with them."

"*Both* of them?" Winters asked suspiciously. He paused, and then turned to Berto. "I apologize, Your Grace. I was not informed of this. Do you wish to wait or shall we take the stairs?"

"St-stairs," Berto said groggily. "Bloody guests have broken our lifts, by the Lord Harry. We'll take the stairs. Damned if I'm goin' all the way to the . . . the top, though. Have a room prepared—as low down as bloody possible."

"Immediately, sir." Winters sent the boy off with a message for the housekeeper. She would not be happy about being raised from her bed at this hour, but then, being happy was not included in her job description. Berto and Daisy's rooms were on the twenty-ninth floor, a strenuous climb at the best of times. Doing it drunk and in a wheelchair was out of the question.

Winters was about to summon some men with a sedan chair to carry Berto, when the Patriarch called him back. He was eager to put his new engimal wheelchair to the test. Daisy and the manservant watched with some concern as Berto headed for the stairs.

"Perhaps I should get some more men, just to be safe, sir," Winters added hopefully.

"Not at all, we shall manage just fine as we are."

On either side of the hall, two wide, sweeping staircases led up to the first floor. After that, a stairwell on either side of the tower led all the way to the penultimate floor. The top floor, where Edgar Wildenstern's quarters still lay unoccupied, was only accessible by elevator and a single secured stairway.

Winters hovered protectively behind his master as the engimal began climbing. Daisy had to remind herself that although Berto was drunk, his wheelchair was not. It did little to ease her tension.

The creature extended its back legs to keep the chair as level as possible while it climbed, levering each front wheel up onto a step, following awkwardly with its rear wheels. The self-propelling wheelbarrow was unused to carrying this unwieldy weight on its back and it showed, but the engimal managed well, and once it had conquered the first few steps, it found a rhythm and soon got to grips with its task.

Daisy stayed to one side of Berto, unable to help, but

offering moral support. His face was set in concentration, as if it were only through his effort of will that the chair had made it this far.

They were nearly at the top when Gideon appeared on the landing in front of them, brandishing a crossbow. He did not waste any words on his nephew. Leveling the weapon, he aimed and fired. Daisy screamed. Blood spurted across Berto's face—but it was not his own. Winters stared down at him, a look of frozen determination on his noble face, before collapsing on top of his master's legs, the crossbow bolt protruding from the back of his skull, its point just breaking the skin of his left cheek. Gideon swore and set the crossbow nose-down on the ground, holding it with his foot as he pulled the bowstring back into place.

Berto's hand slammed the arm of his chair and a blade shot from under his feet. But the engimal wasn't leaning back far enough, and the weapon glanced off the top step, missing Gideon, who looked down at Berto in shock, and then finished reloading the bow. A second blade slashed through some banisters. Berto gritted his teeth as he struggled to control his panicking engimal.

Daisy heard steps behind her and turned in relief, thinking that help was coming. Instead, she saw Gideon's youngest son, Ainsley, charging up the stairs with a cutlass in hand.

Berto steadied the chair again, quelling its pointless attempts to turn around and run for cover, and fired another blade before Gideon could take his shot. This one was more accurate. It sliced through the side of Gideon's left shin, causing him to shriek, drop his crossbow and fall to the floor.

"Berto!" Daisy called as she unclipped her bag and reached inside.

He looked over his shoulder at Ainsley, who was only a few steps away. There was no time to turn the chair. Berto shoved Winters' dying body off his lap, pulled away the flap inside the chair's arm and grabbed a throwing knife . . . but Daisy was already raising the pistol she had taken from her bag. She fired off one shot that took Ainsley in the shoulder, causing him to drop his sword. Her second shot hit him in the side.

The gun was a double-barreled prototype Remington derringer; a tiny but effective pistol. But it was not enough to stop a strong, young Wildenstern in a killing fury. Ainsley staggered up to Daisy, knocked the gun from her hand and got his hands around her throat. Berto was about to hurl his throwing knife at the man attacking his wife, when he saw Gideon kneeling up, crossbow in hand. He changed targets, deftly whipping out his hand and sending the knife spinning towards Gideon. The older man dodged aside, but not far enough. The knife sliced his wrist, severing a tendon, and the crossbow dropped from his limp fingers.

"It'll take more than a sissy pistol to bring down a Wildenstern, you little gold-digging tramp!" Ainsley hissed into Daisy's face as he tightened his grip on her throat. "It'll take more than that!"

This was exactly why Daisy carried more than one weapon. As she struggled for breath, her hands pulled a second pistol from a pocket hidden in the folds of her skirt and pressed the muzzle against Ainsley's middle. He had a moment of shock, just an instant, in which he looked down before the gun went off. Jerking as if he had been thumped in the stomach, he stumbled backwards and toppled over the balustrade, hitting the ground below with a dull thud.

Gideon was desperately trying to lift the heavy crossbow with one hand, while keeping his balance with a torn calf muscle. A second knife spun from Berto's fingers. It struck Gideon in the chest. He collapsed again, and this time Daisy held her skirts and raced up the steps, taking them two at a time, kicking the cross-bow away from his clutching hand. The knife had not killed him, but he was having difficulty breathing.

Footmen appeared in the hall below, rushing to their aid. These were primed Wildenstern servants, wise to the family's traditions. Two were already checking Ainsley's still form, one more was examining Winters. Another had picked up Daisy's fallen pistol.

"Check that cur for other weapons, quickly!" Berto called to his wife as his whimpering wheelchair finished climbing the stairs. Then, to the men rushing towards them, he added: "The gunshots will have roused some of the guests. The noises are to be dismissed as some belated firecrackers. Remove my cousin's body, have the blood cleaned from the carpets and get my back-stabbing poltroon of an uncle here to the infirmary. He's to be guarded at all times!"

Looking down at his fallen uncle, Berto's face twisted into a mask of uncharacteristic hatred, the blood of his dead servant seeping down his neck into the collar of his shirt.

"You killed Winters, you God-awful blackguard. He was ten

times the man you'll ever be. I wash my hands of you—all of you scheming, treacherous bastards. I ask nothing more of you than to just die, you filthy piece of scum. Just die!"

Daisy listened, still waiting for her breath to return. Her heart was racing, her hands were shaking and she could not seem to breathe properly. Looking down at the pathetic bleeding, wheezing figure of Gideon Wildenstern, she raised her eyes to Roberto's face and wondered if her husband had finally lost the last remnants of his soul to these murderers.

XVII
A GENTLEMAN DOES NOT OFFER
EXPLANATIONS TO A SERVANT

CATHAL FELT THE COLD clutch his muscles in a binding grip as he followed the two men and their drawbreath. But he was still glad he had left his father's coat behind in his hideout: he hadn't wanted to get it any dirtier than it already was. So far his idea seemed to be working. By rolling in the ash of the burned building, he had camouflaged his scent, and smeared the white skin of his face and hands with the gray and black powder to help him blend into the darkness. If someone did happen to see him, he would look like a chimney-sweep's boy, fresh from the spout. He was trying not to think of the ashes as the remains of that building—and everything that had been in it. He tried not to think about his last sight of his mother.

Bourne and Red walked ahead of him through the dark streets, with Cathal keeping a corner between himself and his quarry at each turn. He was careful to keep note of where they were going; he didn't want to forget the way back to his pa's coat.

There was more going on in this part of town, even at this hour. The place had the feel of a party coming to its end. Women with heavy make-up in loud, colorful dresses stood in groups on the street; some even walked around alone, without the company of a man. Every type of fellow wandered the paths alongside the mud and cobbles; from gentlemen to navvies, groups of boisterous British soldiers to foreigners with swarthy skin and strange clothes. There were still lights on in some of the windows tucked away from the main streets, and doors were guarded by men in long coats lounging against walls.

Bourne said something to Red. The drawbreath was attracting a few looks, but Cathal supposed that engimals were not unknown in this strange part of town . . . or maybe the men themselves were known, or perhaps just their type. For even with such a valuable creature rolling along before them, they were not bothered by anyone.

The engimal pulled up in front of two young swells that looked to have had a rough night. Cathal risked creeping a bit closer, darting through the light of a gas-lamp and slipping into a shadowy doorway only a few yards behind Bourne and Red. The thing reared its snake-like neck and unfolded its head, drawing in the scent of the two gentlemen.

"Can we help you, my good men?" the thinner, dark-haired man asked.

"Sorry, dere must be some mistake, sor," Bourne replied, tipping his cap. "Our little pet here is huntin' down a young flash-tail wha' stole some money from us earlier this evenin'. I've no idea why it's shown such interest in yeh. I apologize fer way-layin' yeh, sor."

Both gentlemen appeared to have taken a beating recently. Cathal wondered if they'd been fighting each other or someone else. The engimal, unlike its master, was not apologizing. It reared again in front of the fair-haired man, bringing its head up close to his crotch, sniffing like a dog.

The man gently pushed it away, looking more amused than bothered.

"A drawbreath," he grunted, sounding a little suspicious. "A fine example of one too. How did you come to own it?"

"It's not ours, sor," Red replied. "Our employer, a kind gentleman, allows us deh use of it from time to time. Here, yer Lord Wildenstern, if I'm not mistaken, aren't yeh? Are y'all right dere, sor? Yer lookin' a bit battered, if yeh don't mind me sayin'."

The gentleman clearly did mind him saying, but let it go— and without commenting on the star-shaped wound on Bourne's face, which Cathal had noted earlier with some satisfaction. Some of the splinters from his matchbox had gone in deep. That was when he realized he knew these two men as well. The fair-haired one was the swell who had chased him away from the churchyard. The thinner one had been there too, examining the . . . the ashes left by his ma. During the chase, Lord Wildenstern must have been sweating enough to leave his scent on Cathal's hat when he grabbed it. That was why the engimal was so interested in him.

"We're fine, thank you," Wildenstern said. "We just need to find a cab. Now if you'll excuse us . . . "

"Oh, of course, of course." Red gave a little bow and backed out of the way of the two gentlemen, pulling the drawbreath after him. The creature exhaled and closed up its head with what sounded like a high-pitched sigh. Lord Wildenstern and his friend walked on, and the drawbreath watched them go with a frustrated look.

"Yeh know wha' dat was all abou'," Red growled. "Dose two were at deh church where yer one—"

"Yeah, dat's where the little beast got the scent," Bourne sniffed. "Bleedin' toffs—stickin' deir noses in where dey're not wanted. C'mon, Reddy, let's call it a night. Fancy a couple o' scoops?"

"Aye. A pint o' deh black stuff's just what yeh need after a frustratin' evenin'."

Cathal watched them walk up the path in search of a couple of pints of stout and then disappear down some steps through the low door of a dingy pub at cellar level further along the street. He sat down on the curb and thought about what he'd seen.

He was shivering with cold, and his stomach was grumbling and gurgling with hunger, scraping at his gut. From somewhere close by came the smells of bacon cooking, bread baking and with them, the warm, sweet scent of cinnamon.

Sitting there on the curb, determined not to cry, Cathal put his face in his hands and rubbed his moist eyes, smearing ash stains over his cheeks. Somebody somewhere had to know what had happened to his mother. He was too tired and too scared to follow Bourne and Red any more; he barely had the energy to make it back to his hideout.

That Wildenstern fellow and his friend—they'd seen what had happened to his ma. They seemed interested . . . and they had been with the police. Whoever Bourne and Red were working for, it wasn't the Law. Cathal had not been raised with a great love of authority, but his mother had always told him to show respect to the Church and to the Law—at least in public. She said it didn't matter what you thought of them—she avoided both where she could—but they ran things in Ireland, so it jolly well mattered what they thought of you.

Right then, thought Cathal. If I don't find this bleedin' house soon, I'll just have to throw in my lot with Wildenstern and his crowd and see what happens. Hope he's not too vexed about me punchin' him in the goolies.

Getting to his feet, Cathal started to make his way back to the hideout. He wanted to wrap himself in his father's jacket and sleep the sleep of the dead. Tomorrow, he would begin his search again.

The sun was on the rise when Daisy descended on Nate and Gerald as they staggered through the front door of Wildenstern Hall. A footman had been summoned to pay the cab driver—there was much embarrassment over their stolen wallets, but it couldn't be helped—and now the two battered revelers were eager for some sleep. They were not going to get it.

"Where the bloody hell have you been?" she demanded.

"Town," Nate replied defensively, taken aback by her unladylike language. "What's it to you?"

"*Town?* You look like you've been trying to fit spurs on a mule! And . . . and . . . Good God, what's that smell?"

"What is this, the goddamned Spanish Inquisition?" Nate protested, hoping she wouldn't notice the stains on his suit. "Save your nagging for your husband—I'm off to bed!"

"I'm fortunate to still have a husband after last night, and no thanks to you, you selfish ass!"

Nate was about to snarl a retort at her when he realized what she'd just said and how close to tears she was. His face fell.

"What do you mean?" he asked in a softer voice, a chill settling over him. "What's happened?"

And so the story of Gideon's assassination attempt was told in all its gory detail. Daisy played down her part in it, but Nate and Gerald couldn't help being impressed with her decisive action and her resourcefulness in carrying an *extra* pistol—she was definitely getting to grips with the Wildensterns' version of a family spat.

The two latecomers were permitted to bathe and change before joining Berto in his study. The mechanical lifts were working once more, their operation having been interfered with by Ainsley to force Berto onto the stairs where he would be more vulnerable.

Nate ordered some tea and toast up to his room as he got ready, the better to brace himself against Daisy's ill temper. She had well and truly mastered the ability to make him feel guilty—a skill she had no doubt honed on her husband. Even now, he could feel a vile sense of shame rising inside him.

As Clancy helped Nate dress, he was careful not to comment on the cuts, bruises and swellings on his master's body. Even so, Nate sensed the questions hanging in the air. He should have paid no attention to them; a gentleman does not offer explanations to a servant. But this was Clancy, and despite Nate's desperate attempts to express his independence, he still felt the need sometimes to seek his footman's approval, his respect.

"We were attacked by a street gang," he told his servant. "Thuggish coves, but tough. They gave us a good hiding, but we saw them off in the end."

"I have no doubt you dispatched them with gusto, sir," Clancy said, as he fitted the studs into the cuffs of Nate's white shirt and pulled the sleeves into shape. "No matter how many there were."

"There were nine of them," Nate added quickly.

"Nine, sir? A suitable match for two Wildensterns," Clancy commented. "I'm sure you could have taken more if they were to be had, sir. Like the indomitable Spartans against King Xerxes at Thermopylae, you would have given no ground."

Nate looked sidelong at his servant. There were times when he was sure Clancy was mocking him, but it was never obvious enough for Nate to pull him up on it. He winced as he lifted his chin above the stiff collar—every movement of his head made the swollen areas on his face hurt more. There was still the matter of his injuries to deal with.

"Quite so," he replied. "I'll need a couple of rings for the dislocated fingers, and some chain to wrap around my ribs when I go to bed. Have some coins ready for me for the other injuries too."

"Of course, sir." The manservant adjusted his master's tie and then helped him into his gray, pinstriped jacket.

Nate felt something catch in his throat. He coughed, but it did not help. There was a tightness in his chest and a pressure behind his eyes that had nothing to do with his injuries.

"Wait for me outside please, Clancy."

"Very good, sir."

As soon as his servant had left, Nate let the sob escape his lips, leaning forward over the chest of drawers and squeezing his eyes shut against his tears. His body shuddered with suppressed tension. He had never wanted to be his brother's keeper, but he had willingly taken on the task once it became clear how vulnerable Berto had become since he'd lost the use of his legs.

Berto firmly believed that the family could be forced to mend their ways. But he couldn't manage it on his own. Nate was not yet old enough to vote, and yet he was responsible for protecting one of the most important men in the world. And he had failed in that duty.

He had known that Gideon was up to something—Gideon was always up to something, but this time the threat had been specific. Nate should have taken action, but instead he had gone out on the town and got drunk—drunk*er*—and allowed himself to get involved in a common street brawl while his brother was being attacked.

There were so many times when Nate was tempted to just leave everything behind him and take off around the world again as he had done three years ago. But the time for that was past.

Nathaniel rubbed his eyes, straightened up and studied himself in the mirror. It was time to take care of business.

XVIII

IN THE YEAR 1833

NATE JOINED BERTO AND DAISY in the Patriarch's study. Nate apologized to his brother for his absence but Berto waved it away. Then they made their way down to the infirmary. Gideon was badly wounded, but conscious and lucid. Ainsley was in a bad way, clinging to life, the derringer's small bullets lodged deep in his torso where nothing short of major surgery could remove them. Dr. Warburton was already scrubbing up and asking time and again for Gerald, who had not yet deigned to show up. The family's doctor had been dealing with its secret casualties for decades, but he was getting old, and becoming more and more reliant on Gerald's talents as his own eyes and wits began to fail him.

The doctor's surgery was a well-appointed office adjoining the infirmary, the Wildensterns' private hospital. While the good doctor carried out his ministrations on Ainsley, Gideon was waiting in the surgery on a raised bed, with a mound of pillows propping him up. Bandages covered his chest beneath his nightshirt, and his wrist and his calf had also been treated. Nate took all of this in as he pulled a paisley-upholstered chair up beside his uncle. Both Berto and Daisy sat a little further back, leaving the nasty business of extracting information to Nate.

Gideon was about to protest that he was in no state to be in the company of a woman, but one look at Daisy's face convinced him that his pleas would fall on deaf ears.

Berto did not scare Gideon. With his blood cooled after the action, the compassionate young Patriarch was not likely to engage in any further violence against his uncle. Gideon was not so sure about Nathaniel. Nate did not sit down. Instead, he took off his jacket and gazed around the room while he removed his tie. Gideon watched uneasily. His eyes widened as he saw Nate rolling up his sleeves.

"Nathaniel, I . . . I don't know what you're thinking of doing—"

"Didn't we make it clear that no further Acts of Aggression would be tolerated in this family?" Nate asked.

"Nathaniel . . . Nate . . . I—I . . . "

"Did we not make that clear?"

"Yes . . . yes, you did. I have to explain . . . "

"Would you like a smoke?" Nate inquired, holding out a pack of Gideon's favorite Turkish cigarettes.

"What? Eh? Em . . . yes. Yes, thank you." Gideon accepted one of the gaspers and let Nate light it for him.

"Berto has no taste for bloodshed, he prefers to avoid it

whenever possible," Nate said gently as he pocketed the cigarettes. "He believes it is counterproductive. You know this.
Perhaps it makes you feel safe. I, on the other hand, am quickly
becoming convinced that violence is the only way to control
this family. And yet I failed to be at my brother's side when he
was attacked. I'm embarrassed by this failure, Gideon." Nate
leaned closer to his uncle, ignoring the pungent smoke of the
cigarette. "I'm feeling angry, frustrated. I want to compensate
for this . . . embarrassment with some violent act of my own—
something decisive, some action that will put a *permanent* end
to the current problem."

"For the love of God, Nate! I . . . I was coerced! I was *made*
to do this thing!"

Nate sat down in the chair and took Gideon's wounded hand
in his. He did not squeeze it, but Gideon was already expect-
ing him to; the pain was ready to express itself on his face. The
wound in his chest was making breathing difficult too.

"God is not here for you now, Gideon. And we're in no mood
for your lies," Nate said in a near-whisper. "There are only the
four of us in this room, Gideon. And you tried to kill my brother
and his wife this past night. Who could ever say what happened
in this room, apart from the four of us . . . sorry, the *three* of us?"

"Nate! I am not your true enemy—I was blackmailed into this
act, I swear it!"

The door burst open and Silas strode in. He looked dishev-
eled and freshly woken, his eyes bloodshot from drink and lack
of sleep.

"Roberto!" he exclaimed. "I heard about the attack! Gideon,

you bloody cur! I tried to warn you, Berto! I told you he was up to something!"

"Shut the door, sit down and clam up, Silas," Berto told him. "We're busy here."

Silas's mouth clamped shut; he was taken aback by his cousin's harsh tone. Pulling out a chair, he sat down to watch the proceedings.

"I am not your enemy," Gideon repeated. "I received a letter telling me that I had to carry out this attack or—"

The door swung open again and Oliver barged in.

"What are you doing to my father?" he demanded. "If you dare—"

"This isn't a bloody parliamentary debate!" Nate snapped. "Stand back there and keep your trap shut, or it'll be the worse for the both of you!"

Oliver started to retort, but one look at his father's face shut him up. He stood back beside Silas, seething with frustration.

"Now," Nate said mildly, still holding Gideon's injured hand. "You received a letter telling you that you had to carry out this attack or . . . what?"

"Or the writer would inform you of my . . . sideline business with the fleet."

"You seriously expect us to believe that you tried to kill Berto because a letter told you to?" Daisy scoffed. "Do you take us for idiots?"

"It worked on Simon, didn't it?" Gideon snapped back.

"Simon has the mind of a *child*, and even *he* took some convincing," she retorted.

"What was the letter-writer threatening to tell us?" Berto demanded. "What have you been up to, you old blackguard—?"

Just at that moment Tatiana hurriedly knocked and entered, followed closely by Gerald, who was sporting a tight bandage around his broken arm.

"Berto!" Tatty gasped. "Daisy! Are you all right? I heard—"

"So did everyone, it seems," Berto sighed in exasperation. "We're fine, thank you. What is this? Kingsbridge Station? Gerald, aren't you supposed to be helping with Ainsley?"

"Probably," Gerald replied, without moving from where he stood.

"Well . . . go to it, then, as soon as we're done here. Now will everyone hold their peace until we're finished, please!"

Tatiana took umbrage at this dismissal, but said no more. Gerald let her take the only remaining chair and stood by the door, picking one of his French cigarettes out of his case and lighting it, regarding his uncle with a look of mild interest.

"Carry on, Gideon," Nate pressed the wounded man. "We're all dying to hear what you've been doing—what you're so keen to hide that you'll risk your *life* to hide it."

The emphasis on the word 'life' was not lost on Gideon. He let his chin sink onto his chest and spoke without meeting Nate's eyes. Each exhalation ended with a throaty hiss.

"I've been using some of the Company's ships for . . . for other kinds of transport. For . . . well, all right—for transporting slaves. We have regular shipments supplying the southern states of America. Whoever the letter-writer is, they knew about this and swore they would tell you, Nathaniel. I have no idea who the weasel is, but they know enough to ruin me."

"Dear God," Daisy breathed.

Berto said nothing, but his hands were clenched into fists. The act of capturing and transporting people for the purposes of slavery—particularly in Africa—had been outlawed by Britain and America in 1803. When slavery itself was abolished in the British Empire in 1833, the Royal Navy had begun hunting slave ships with the zeal of the newly converted. Like so many things in the Empire, slave-trading was a hanging offense.

Gideon had already dug his hole, but it seemed as if he felt the need to make a full confession. "The passage from North Africa to America has become somewhat perilous," he continued in a low, gruff voice. "Her Majesty's Navy has been enthusiastic in its governance of the Atlantic. There have been times when a ship of ours has reached port without its cargo."

Berto closed his eyes and swore under his breath. Daisy put her hand to her mouth. Nate just scowled.

"What does that mean?" Tatty asked loudly, making them all start. "What does he mean, 'reached port without its cargo?'"

"I knew Berto would not stand for this," Gideon wheezed. "I would be exiled . . . or worse. I had no choice but to act."

"You're bloody right!" Berto shouted, striking the arm of his wheelchair with his fist. "*Slave-trading*, by God! Under my nose? I won't have it, you swine! Exiled? You're lucky I don't hand you over to the magistrate for this. Hanging's too good for you—you deserve to spend the rest of your life rotting in Kilmainham Gaol, or on some godforsaken patch of barren, sun-burned hell in Australia. You're bloody *right* you'll be exiled. You can leave this house, this country, for good. And don't go to Britain either; if I hear you've set yourself up in London or some such place, I'll have you hunted down like the dog you are! Gather up your belongings and go as far from here as your resources will take you. Never let me see or hear of you again!"

Nate kept his teeth tightly clamped together as he listened to this. Gideon deserved to hang. He deserved much worse. It was not enough that he had never harmed a slave himself; he had set up the system by which they could be harmed. He should be hanged.

But the family would not stand for Berto handing over one of their own to the Law. It was not how the Wildensterns did things. Everything would become so much more difficult to manage and Berto knew it. In order for him to reform the way the Company did business, he had to convince them all that it would not mean their own downfall. And there was much about the way the Wildensterns did business that needed changing. If Berto rushed things, he could expect to have his relatives attempt to retire him on a far more frequent basis.

"So who else would have known?" Nate growled at his uncle. "Who would know enough to be able to blackmail you?"

"We had to be able to deny everything at every stage," Gideon said miserably. "We trusted only a few ships' captains. They reported only to Ainsley in the shipping company. He reported only to me. Nobody else was supposed to know."

"But whoever it is knew about Simon's mother too," Daisy mused. "Not the kind of information a ship's captain is likely to come across."

"It seems, then, that we're no closer to finding our snake," Berto said. "And we've just lost another manager. Gerald, I want you to hand over the management of the estates to Daisy for the moment. You will take on the merchant fleet. Silas can fill you in on the basic operations."

"Oh, come on, Berto!" Gerald complained. "Have a heart! One of the Gideonettes should have it by rights—"

"But I can't trust any one of them as far as I could throw them," Berto finished for him, gesturing at Oliver, who scowled sourly. "You have to do your bit, like the rest of us. Don't test me on this, old chap. Not today. Now please, go and help the doctor with Ainsley. I'll deal with him if and when he is adequately recovered."

Gerald, seeing his beloved research drifting further and further away from him, exhaled slowly, nodded and reluctantly left the room. For a few moments, nobody else spoke.

At last, Gideon lifted his hand.

"How . . . how many servants may I take with me?" he asked timidly.

"Your man and your wife's maid," Berto barked. "I'd rather you had none at all, but I doubt either of you would survive, what with Eunice being every bit the useless parasite that you are."

Gideon went quiet again, perhaps considering for the first time what exile would really mean with only his wife for company. Theirs had been a marriage of convenience. They had hated each other from the moment they'd met.

Everyone else in the room was of the firm opinion that the couple fully deserved a long and healthy life together.

XIX

THE MORNING AFTER

WHEN INSPECTOR URSKIN CALLED on the Wildensterns on Sunday afternoon, he was taken aback by the state in which he found them.
He had heard the family threw some wild parties, but these indi-
viduals looked to have been through a war.

The Duke and his wife, just back from church, were pale and
drawn, and looked so exhausted that the weight of the world
might have been upon their shoulders. The Duke's brother,
Nathaniel, and his cousin, Gerald, looked equally drained, but
with the added misfortune of facial cuts and bruises and damaged hands that Urskin's expert eye knew could only have come
from a right good fist fight.

Even Miss Tatiana, a girl of no more than fifteen, bore the
suspicious signs of a late night and a clinging hangover.

They were all sitting in the breakfast room amidst the remains of that meal, despite the fact that it was past lunch time, and still none of them appeared to have had any sleep.

"Inspector," Nathaniel greeted him from a chair by the tall French windows that looked out on the gardens. "What can we do for you?"

"Just a courtesy call, sir . . . Your Grace," Urskin replied before bowing to Berto, hat in hand. "I wonder, could I have a quick word with you gentlemen?"

"Have it, by all means." Nate waved the policeman towards the seat opposite him. "What's on your mind?"

"It's not a very tasteful matter, sir," Urskin told him, glancing at Daisy and Tatiana. "Hardly suitable for a lady's ears."

"Our ears are not as tender as you might think, Inspector," Daisy informed him. "Do sit down. We could all do with some distraction."

The inspector took the seat offered to him, but looked decidedly uncomfortable.

"Would you like some breakfast?" Daisy asked.

"No, thank you, ma'am," Urskin responded, without adding that he had already eaten lunch. "I'm here on a matter that is not . . . not conducive to one's appetite." He directed his words towards Berto from then on, although he was obviously uncomfortable with speaking to someone of such a high rank. "I've been investigatin' the case of the . . . the burned women, Your Grace. I have since discovered two other women with . . . with reputations for paganism or arcane practices, who burned to death alone in house fires. This led me to inquire as to exactly how many women have died in similar circumstances, just in the Dublin area, over the last year."

"And how many did you come up with?" Daisy asked the worn-faced detective.

"You have to understand how commonplace this kind of death is," Urskin said first. "Oil lamps, candles, wooden structures and straw bedding, it all—"

"How many, Inspector?"

"One hundred and twelve died *alone* in fires so far this year, Your Grace. And the records are by no means complete, or indeed, accurate. Although now that insurance companies are establishing their own fire brigades, better records are being kept. Some of those fires will have been common accidents, but to me that number seems a mite suspicious."

"Indeed. But what have these deaths got to do with us?" Berto asked.

Urskin fingered his hat, turning it around in his hands, his gaze dropping to the floor for a moment. Then he lifted his eyes to look directly at the Duke.

"We have learned that at least one was not who she claimed to be. Parish records list her as Mary McDonagh, but some of her neighbors tell us that she claimed her true family name was Bismarck—a noble family from Prussia, I believe, and one that the Wildensterns have known associations with. We suspect some of the other women may have been livin' under assumed names too."

The Wildensterns were careful not to react, except for Tatty, who frowned and looked at her brothers. Many of the Bismarcks were endowed with *aurea sanitas*; another link between the Wildensterns and the burned women.

Urskin noted her expression but did not comment.

"Some of the people we spoke to believed she was a witch of sorts," he continued. "She kept strange hours, produced arcane cures for ailments and was said to be able to read the future of someone's health simply by looking them in the face. We also have it on good authority that she practiced pagan rituals and swore she would only obey ancient Celtic laws, British civilization being an offense to what she called 'nature.' This love of Irish pagan traditions over Christian ones is common among witches, so I'm given to understand."

Urskin sat up straighter, as if bracing himself for what he was going to say next.

"I believe that these women were killed tryin' to carry out some pagan ritual—perhaps even raising the Devil himself."

There was a moment of complete silence as this sank in. Then Daisy offered her opinion on the matter:

"Poppycock," she said sharply.

"I think not, ma'am. I believe that these women, in their attempts to achieve this, are going to increasin'ly extreme lengths to do so. I don't know what spell they're tryin' to cast, but they are playin' with hellfire to create it, and they are getting burned for their troubles."

"And have you any evidence for this theory, Inspector?" Berto pressed him, looking ever so slightly skeptical.

"No, sir. Not yet. But the truth will be forthcomin'. And all I can say is, may God have mercy on their souls."

☼   ☼   ☼

The news of Gideon's impending exile created another casualty. Elvira, on hearing that her only remaining brother was to be driven from the house, had a fit and fell from her wheelchair onto the floor of the drawing room. Servants rushed to help as she lay there twitching, drool running down the side of her mouth. The doctor was summoned, along with Gerald and Silas. Daisy, who had broken the news to her aunt, was overcome with guilt.

Warburton had the old woman brought to his surgery on a stretcher, where he began his ministrations. She was suffering a brainstorm, he said, brought on by the shock. There was no telling how well she would recover.

Gerald and Silas were not to be found. One of the footmen said the two brothers had gone out riding; a groom had been sent after them.

Daisy stood off to one side of the doctor, her arms folded tightly across her chest, anxiously watching the proceedings. Warburton was Elvira's cousin, and the two had been friends since childhood. He gazed down at her with concern, polishing his thick spectacles with a handkerchief. The doctor probably knew more about the casualties of the Rules of Ascension—and every other illness and injury in the family—than any person alive. When Daisy had spoken to him he had claimed to know nothing about the women sent to the asylum; but then, so did everyone.

"Is there anything I can do?" she asked the doctor.

"She may be able to hear us, even if she cannot respond,"

Warburton replied. "The sounds of her sons' voices would lift her spirits, I'm sure. And if not them, someone else close to her."

Daisy did not think she matched that description, having caused this fit in the first place. And though Gideon was Elvira's closest relative, they were a constant irritation to each other. Then Daisy had an idea. Hurrying from the surgery, she made her way to the elevators and up to Elvira's floor. There was one voice the old woman listened to every day.

The scarlet macaw was in its barrel-sized brass cage, which had been left in Elvira's bedroom. There was a cover over the cage, so the parrot was making no sound. Daisy left it covered, for she had no love for the annoying bird. Calling some of the servants, she had them carry the cage out of the door and down the corridor towards the elevators.

She was about to follow them, but stopped. Daisy had never been in Elvira's bedroom before, and curiosity made her pause and look around. The Wildenstern Matriarch was particular about her privacy and Daisy was sure that there were many secrets hidden away in this chest of drawers and wardrobes. Berto had told her there were at least two hidden doors in Elvira's rooms, and possibly a concealed trap door near the bedroom door as well, which could be sprung open by pulling on a cord hanging by the bed. The room was filled with all manner of things gathered over the ancient woman's thoroughly lived life.

The family always maintained that they were Irish first and British second, but above all, they were Wildensterns. Elvira was a royalist, however, and in regular correspondence with Queen Victoria, who was distantly related to the family and whose portrait adorned the stretch of wall between the bedroom's two windows. On the oak dresser there were many framed photographs, daguerreotypes and watercolors of Elvira with Victoria, Albert, and other members of the Royal Family, as well as more pictures of relatives such as the Bismarcks, the Rockefellers, and members of other prominent dynasties. A shotgun was mounted on the wall above the dresser, and Daisy had no doubt it was kept loaded.

There were many souvenirs from the old woman's travels: masks, spears, jewelry and pieces of sculpture. Daisy enviously perused Elvira's collection, noting all the exotic, alien places she had visited. Her gaze fell upon an oil painting with a heavy gilt frame, half hidden by the open door. Pulling back the door, she stared at the stern, middle-aged face of the woman glaring back out at her from the painting.

It took Daisy a few moments to remember where she had seen that face before. Then her jaw dropped and she read the name engraved on the plate on the bottom edge of the frame.

"You lying cow," she whispered.

In a flurry of skirts, Daisy rushed out of the room in search of her husband.

XX

BORROWING IN SECRET

IT WAS MONDAY MORNING and Daisy and Tatiana were taking a coach to Philip Richards House to examine the records again. The dark blue carriage with its gold trim and four fine black horses would have been given room on the road by almost any vehicle, but with the Wildenstern crest on the doors, it was allowed a completely clear path through every village on the way to its destination.

Daisy intended to cut just as clear a path to the truth about this asylum. After the men had all given excuses for why they couldn't spend the day looking through piles and piles of ledgers, Tatiana had jumped at the chance to join her. But there was something more pressing even than this on Tatiana's mind as they traveled down the rough mud road towards the asylum.

"So what did Gideon mean when he said that the slave ships

reached port without their cargo?" she asked her sister-in-law. "Did they hide the slaves? Is there somewhere one can conceal them and return to pick them up later? Deposit them for safe-keeping, so to speak? What did he mean?"

"What he meant, Tatty," Daisy told her in a level voice, "was that the slaves they were transporting were not aboard when the ships reached their destination. The captains of many slave ships engage in the barbaric practice of throwing their 'cargo' over-board if they are sighted by a ship of the Royal Navy, to avoid hanging for their crimes, or at the very least having their vessel confiscated and destroyed . . . " She took a breath before going on. "The prisoners are all chained together. The crew tie weights of some kind, or an anchor, to the first one and throw him over-board, pushing the rest after him. Once in the water, they are all dragged under by the weight as each one drowns in turn."

Tatty said nothing else for a moment, having turned slightly green about the gills. "Gosh," she said quietly.

"Some specialized ships can often carry hundreds of slaves across the Atlantic, chained in low, cramped spaces 'between decks' in the most atrocious conditions," Daisy continued. "Even if the ship is not threatened with discovery, only the strongest survive the voyage. Not only are the captains inhu-mane monsters, they haven't even the sense to keep their own cargoes alive and healthy in order to sell them for a better price. Cruelty is all the more despicable when it is senseless. Gideon was right to think Berto would ruin him if he found out. He was lucky to get off as lightly as he did. I would have preferred a harsher punishment."

"But we're still no closer to finding out who knew about it—who made Gideon attack Berto," Tatiana commented.

"That's not entirely true," Daisy said, shaking her head. "How many people could know about Simon's mother *and* Gideon's slave ships? I think, Tatty, that our would-be assassin has shown more of his hand than he would have liked. Perhaps he even hoped that if Gideon and Ainsley failed, they would be killed before they could talk."

Tatiana nodded solemnly, hiding her excitement beneath a veneer of ladylike reserve. Despite its seriousness, she was relishing the thrill of this mystery.

The carriage pulled up in the driveway of the asylum, but it was not Dr. Angstrom who greeted the women on this occasion. A slight man in his early forties, with a blotchy face, baggy eyes and thin features framed by lank, wheat-colored hair, was waiting at the top of the steps. He introduced himself as Aidan O'Neill, the chief attendant.

"We received your telegram earlier this morning, Your Grace, but I'm afraid the doctor is in town on business," O'Neill informed them. "He is expected to be engaged all day. If you'd like to arrange another time to—"

"No thank you, Mister O'Neill," Daisy chirped. "This morning will serve just as well. I wonder if we could have another look at your records?"

O'Neill was visibly squirming. He was obviously unhappy with someone trawling through the institution's admissions, but he wasn't sure if it was in his power to refuse a duchess, particularly one whose family helped pay his wages.

"The doctor told me you were under the impression that some of your relatives were here, ma'am, but I can assure you—"

"We will assure ourselves, thank you," Daisy told him. "If you would just show us your books, we can manage perfectly well. We don't want to be a bother."

She gave him her sweetest smile, which Tatty noted and immediately duplicated. O'Neill, faced with two very genteel but determined young ladies, surrendered and waved them inside. Taking their hats and shawls at the door, he followed them in, furiously chewing the inside of his lip as he mulled over this delicate problem.

At first he offered to find any name they were looking for, but once Daisy had made it clear that they were both keen readers and loath to disturb his work, he left them to it, retreating out of the door of the clerk's office, dragging the perplexed clerk with him. Tatty swung the door closed after them.

Daisy ran her finger over the dates on the spines of the first stack of admissions ledgers until she found the year she wanted. Pulling out the book, she laid it on the plain wooden desk and drew up a chair.

"Do you think I could visit some of the patients while we're here?" Tatty asked.

"Not this time, Tatty, dear. We have a lot to do."

Daisy was also intent on shielding the last remnants of her young friend's innocence, but to admit it to Tatiana would only have made her more curious.

"That's a pity," Tatty sighed. "I have long been concerned for the plight of fallen women."

"While many of these women may have *fallen*," Daisy

declared, "some were most certainly pushed. Now, are you going to help me or just stand there sympathizing?"

"All right then. So we're looking for Vicky Miller?"

"Yes, among others. But let's start with her."

It was Vicky's portrait that Daisy had seen in Elvira's bedroom. Vicky Miller was none other than Georgina Wildenstern, Elvira's youngest sister. Once Daisy had the name, Gerald and Silas were able to supply some more of the details. Like most children, when they were young they had secretly listened in on their parents' conversations whenever possible.

Berto's father, Edgar, had been ruthlessly ambitious. On his path to the top, Edgar had killed his brother in a duel. Georgina, more than thirty years younger than Edgar—an age gap not unknown in the Wildenstern family—was of more compassionate stock than the rest of her kin. Shocked at her brother's callousness, she began supplying money and intelligence to the peasant rebels who were proving to be such a thorn in the side of the Wildensterns. This went on for some years.

Daisy recognized the woman's motives; a powerless female in a world controlled by men, she was getting back at her brother in any way she could.

Edgar did not take such a balanced view. On discovering her treachery he saw that she was 'taken ill' and 'sent abroad for recuperation.' Daisy had come to understand just what these terms could mean for a woman in this family.

"All this death and betrayal," she sighed. "Don't you think a family would get tired of trying to murder each other after a few generations? It's all so . . . so *mindless*."

"We're sticklers for tradition," Tatty replied, shrugging. "Berto'll change things in the end."

"Unless they make an end to him first," Daisy murmured as she read down the columns. "Hah! I knew it! Here she is: Vicky Miller committed on the fourteenth of July, twenty-six years ago. Her occupation is listed as domestic servant—poor old Georgina. Diagnosed with 'hypothyroidism'—I have no idea what that is. 'Considered untreatable,' it says here. There's a little asterisk beside her name too, but I don't know what it's for—there's no footnote or anything."

There was a shelf of medical textbooks on a shelf behind her. She had to comb through the indexes of three of them before she found one that mentioned hypothyroidism. She read out loud from the book:

"*Caused by an insufficient production of thyroid hormone by the thyroid gland.* Blah, blah, blah, *lots of symptoms . . . muscle cramps, constipation,* blah, blah, blah, *hard to identify . . .* Hmm, not exactly a reason to commit someone . . . oh, wait a second. *In extreme cases, patient can exhibit inattentiveness, impaired memory and loss of brain function.* Right."

"That doesn't help us much," Tatiana commented.

"No. Let's see if Catherine Coogan—or Dempsey—or any of the other women are in here. Where's the list?" Daisy fumbled around in her bag. "Ah, here it is. Now, we have five more here. Nate and I didn't know there was a connection to the burned women last time, so we weren't looking for them."

Catherine Dempsey, Simon's mother, was easy enough to find, as they knew roughly what month she was sent away from

Wildenstern Hall. She too had been diagnosed with hypothyroidism. Daisy also noted the asterisk beside her name.

The others were harder to find. With no idea what year they might have been admitted, the two young women had to search through the ledgers one by one. Eventually, they had found all five names. Each of them had been brought in during the ten years previous; diagnosis: hypothyroidism. There was an asterisk beside each of their names too.

"Wonder what their real names were?" Tatty mused aloud.

"Who knows?" Daisy replied. "I suspect that there's another book somewhere with all the real names in it. I'm sure that must be the purpose of the asterisk—to mark out the ones whose names have been changed. But . . . I mean, look at this!" She slapped the open book. "There's nearly one every couple of pages. There must have been hundreds committed here over the years. They can't all be Wildensterns! Who are they? And, dear God, were they all just sent here as punishment, or did they really fall ill?"

"But some of them must have got out," Tatty remarked. "Vicky, Catherine and these others were all living new lives. And they all seemed to have recovered their senses enough to live normally . . . more or less, I mean. Obviously they'd become *commoners*, but . . . well, you know, otherwise . . . they seemed happy enough with their lot, didn't they?"

Daisy shook her head, not out of disagreement, but confusion. None of this was fitting together properly. There were too many pieces still missing.

"Let's not say anything about this until we get home," she

urged her sister-in-law. "Oh, and we need to take these three ledgers with us, but Mister O'Neill mustn't see us."

"You mean *steal* them? Daisy!" Tatty gasped, putting her hand to her mouth. "How could you . . . ?" She stopped and composed herself, as if spiriting away medical records was the most normal thing in the world. "And how are we going to do that? They're not exactly pocket books, you know. Where are we going to hide them?"

"The one place nobody will dare to look," Daisy told her.

She found a ball of twine in a desk drawer, but there was no way to walk in a dignified fashion with a heavy ledger or two tied beneath one's skirts.

The two young ladies did the best they could, saying goodbye to Mr. O'Neill as they took their hats and shawls and hobbled towards the exit. The steps beyond the door proved the most difficult stage of the escape, the books slapping against their thighs as they made their way down toward the waiting carriage.

"I think mine's going to drop out!" Tatty whispered, close to bursting into giggles.

"Try and hold it in! We're almost there," Daisy growled at her, pressing her own hands against her lap as if lifting her skirts, when in fact she was trying to conceal the square shape bumping against her knees.

"It's slipping! I can't hold it!"

"Yes, you can! I have two and I'm managing. Don't look back—he's watching us! Keep your head up and don't grab your skirts like that; you look like your knickers are falling down or something."

"My knickers won't make a bloody great thump when they hit the ground!"

"Tatty!"

They finally reached the steps of the carriage, where the footman helped them in with a puzzled expression. Both ladies seemed to have put on weight and were walking as if their shoes did not quite fit. The superstitious man wondered if the horrors of the asylum had somehow changed them. As he closed the door, he heard Miss Tatiana exclaiming:

"Gosh! Well, that's one for the records!"

"Yes," said the Duchess, suddenly breaking into laughter for no obvious reason. "Mister O'Neill will be . . . ha, ha . . . ! Will be most annoyed we've borrowed some of his books . . . ha, ha! Like any good librarian, he would have wanted to . . . to . . . stamp them first! Ha, ha, ha!"

Miss Tatiana squealed with mirth.

"However," the Duchess continued, "I would have had to insist that . . . that he showed me his stamp before I showed him my book!" The two young women burst into shrieks of helpless laughter.

The footman shook his head with concern and climbed onto the front. Taking up the reins, he sat down, took off the brake and urged the four horses forward.

Behind them, Aidan O'Neill watched the carriage leave, with a face that showed no trace of amusement.

XXI

"THE DEVIL'S IN THAT CHILD"

IN HINDSIGHT, CATHAL THOUGHT, he should have done it earlier. But more than anything else, he hated to sound stupid, and he was sure he would if he asked a complete stranger how to find a building that looked like a pepper canister. He could just imagine the looks he'd get. It was only when, days after his mother's death, he was suffering from sharp pangs of hunger and severe exhaustion that he finally gave in and asked a stooping, harmless-looking crone for directions.

"Deh Pepper Canister?" she replied, her toothless smile stretching her lip whisker to the corners of her jowls. "Dat's Upper Mount Street. Sure, bless us an' save us, it's only around deh corner, love. I'm goin dat way meself. Lend us a hand with dis coal and I'll walk yeh dere."

Little had Cathal realized that the church in question was a well-known landmark, famous for the distinctive shape of its steeple. Not for the first time, he cursed himself for the obstinate pride he had inherited from his mother. Despite the stale smell of whiskey wafting from her mouth, he was delighted to accompany the old dear. Hefting the sack of coal onto his shoulder, he walked alongside her as she meandered unsteadily up the street, filling his ear with stories of her gallant son, who worked in the coal yard and pinched her a free sack every week. When she wasn't talking about her son's enterprises, she nattered on about the area itself.

Upper Mount Street was a short road off Merrion Square, a wealthy district centered around a small park. Fine carriages clattered over the square's cobblestones, and police constables patrolled on every block. On the corner of the square across from Upper Mount Street was Leinster House, the Dublin residence of the Wildenstern family, and the offices of the North America Trading Company.

The woman led Cathal past this great edifice, turning right to skirt the square.

"Look at deh size o' dat house, now," she remarked. "Dat family's rich as God. And dey're spendin' a king's ransom buildin' some big museums right next door, but dey'd still take the shirt off yer back, give 'em 'alf a chance."

The Pepper Canister was situated the far end of Upper Mount Street, on a circular island right in the middle of the street. The road ran up to the little church, before splitting in two to surround it like a cobbled saucer. The two lanes united once more to cross the Grand Canal behind it. Cathal had never seen anything quite like it and it was obvious why the building had stuck in his mind.

Thanking the woman, he handed her back the sack of stolen coal and made his way down the street. Like some of Dublin's worst tenements, these were fine four-story terraced Georgian buildings with tall windows and high ceilings, but their proximity to Leinster House meant they were well kept, and occupied by some of the best families in society. There were no front gardens. Each house had black cast-iron railings outside, and a basement whose windows looked onto a recessed area set below street level. The basement, used mostly by servants or as a self-contained flat, had a separate entrance under the steps to the main door, the steps crossing the 'moat' between house and pavement like a drawbridge.

Now that he had found the street, Cathal knew where the house was. Counting the doors back from the point where the road split in two to circle the church, he found the door he was looking for. It was green with a brass knocker, and a boot scraper set into the flagstones at the top of the steps.

He stared up at the door for some time. Would the man recognize him? Would he help him? Standing there, Cathal felt increasingly nervous, wishing he knew who this man was—or even remembered his name. But his mother had trusted the fellow, and that was good enough for him. He mounted the steps and rapped the knocker on the door.

A balding manservant in a stiff suit answered, peering down with short-sighted eyes at this soot-stained ragamuffin.

"Deliveries and messages must go to the tradesman's entrance," he informed Cathal, as he went to close the door.

"The master of the house knows me," Cathal blurted out. "Tell him Catherine Dempsey's son is here. Tell him . . . tell him me ma's dead. I . . . " He felt himself starting to cry and sucked it in, annoyed with himself. "I . . . I don't have anywhere else to go."

The servant paused, examining Cathal's face, but then his gaze softened and he nodded.

"The master is not here," he said. "But I remember Mrs. Dempsey . . . and you were here once yourself, if I recall. Cathal, isn't it? I am sorry for your loss, lad. What brings you here alone like this? Where is your father?"

"He's at sea, servin' with the Navy. We . . . we couldn't get hold of 'im. An' now I'm in a bit of trouble—"

"Go to the other door," the manservant told him. "I am on my way out, but I'll have the housekeeper get you cleaned up and get some food into you—you look ready to keel over. There'll be plenty of time to tell us all about it after."

Cathal did as he was told and went back out to the gate in the fence and down the steps to the tradesman's door, where the housekeeper let him in. He refused to be put in a bath—and the look on his face convinced the housekeeper that he would not be swayed on this point—but agreed to wash his face and hands in return for a bowl of soup and some fresh bread. He had eaten only what he could steal over the last few days and thieving did not come easy to him so the food tasted like God Himself had cooked it up.

The woman told him the master would be back some time

that evening, and that Cathal could wait in the kitchen until then, but he wasn't to wander, what with the state of him and all that. She then went about her chores above stairs, leaving him to his own devices.

Roughly ten minutes passed before Cathal's impatience and curiosity got the better of him. He wanted to know who this man was and what the connection was with his mother. Out of embarrassment, he had been afraid to ask the master's name; he was also afraid that this might make the staff doubt his story, but he was sure that something, somewhere in the house would reveal the man's identity.

It was just a matter of finding it.

Creeping up the stairs to the hallway on the ground floor, Cathal crouched on the top steps, peeping up and down the length of the hall to check that the coast was clear. There was a sideboard before the door with some papers on top. A quick look through these told him nothing; they were just newspapers and circulars. There wasn't even a bill to be found.

The housekeeper could be heard singing to herself upstairs, no doubt dusting or polishing or the like. The manservant had now gone out for some messages. Walking softly to the door of the front room, Cathal reached for the handle, which was at the height of his shoulder, as was the way in these big houses. It was well-oiled and turned without a squeak. Poking his head into the living room, he saw that it was empty; a fine fireplace and comfortable furnishings, some pictures . . . nothing more.

The next door along the hall led into a study. This was a different affair altogether. The walls were lined from floor to ceiling with bookshelves holding thick volumes on a wide variety of subjects, mostly scientific in nature. There was a desk by the window, covered in papers and notes, but the writing on them was full of strange, complicated words and mathematical symbols that looked vaguely familiar to Cathal. What was it his mother had called it? Mathaumaturgy? It had something to do with talking to engimals. Ma had a book or two on it, but told him they weren't for his eyes. He'd sneaked a look at one of them, but he couldn't understand how an engimal could make sense of something that looked like complete gibberish to a human. It was like the most complicated sums he'd ever seen.

There was a stack of publications on the desk, but one well-thumbed book occupied a special place on the only space clear of notepaper. It had been laid on a black baize cloth with the reverence normally only given to the Bible. Cathal read the title:

ON

THE ORIGIN OF SPECIES
BY MEANS OF NATURAL SELECTION,
OR
THE PRESERVATION OF FAVORED RACES IN THE
STRUGGLE FOR LIFE
BY CHARLES DARWIN M.A.

He had heard of this book. His mother had mentioned *The Origin of Species* more than once. She thought highly of it, and of its author—this man, Darwin. It was causing ructions among the clergy, who were denouncing it as the worst kind of heresy. He remembered because his mother had made a gift of a copy to the local priest. Resisting the urge to pick up the book and start reading, Cathal reminded himself that he was trespassing in a gentleman's private rooms; a man he was looking to for help.

A flute sat on one side of the desk, looking out of place among all the scientific paraphernalia. Cathal frowned at it, but it held no interest for him and he ignored it.

There were more papers spread over the floor, some of them drawings of engimals, if he wasn't mistaken, including creatures that appeared to have been dissected. Some of their parts were labeled, but there were more question marks than any other symbol. One sheet caught his eye. It looked like letter-writing paper; there was a kind of coat of arms on its head, but no words, no name. The symbol took the form of a pair of intersecting swords, with a kind of cross sitting in the V made by their blades. The cross was topped with an eye.

Cathal had seen this symbol before, but he could not remember where. It was at that moment that he heard someone coming from downstairs. The sound gave him a start. It had to be the footman. He would know that Cathal had gone upstairs. With the breath catching in his throat, Cathal rushed from the room, but once out, he had nowhere to hide. The footsteps were almost at the top of the stairs. Another second or two and the man would turn and see him . . .

Panicking, he reached for the handle of the door to the front room, but it was too late.

"Well, holy God, aren't you deh quare fella! Stay still, now! Bourne! Get up here!"

That was when Cathal remembered where he'd seen the symbol before. Standing at the top of the stairs was Red, his face wrinkled in disbelief. The man didn't hesitate for long, but Cathal was already halfway into the living room. One look at the sash window told him he wouldn't get it open in time. Red was already charging after him. He lunged for the fireplace and grabbed the poker, swiveling and brandishing it at his opponent. He could feel the rush in his blood, his desperation finding that unnatural strength he had only recently discovered. They would not take him easily.

Red stopped, eyeing the iron poker. Bourne came in behind him, swore when he saw Cathal, and moved to one side of Red so that they could come at the boy from different angles.

"Put deh rod down now, lad," Red said gently. "We're not tryin' to hurt yeh. Yeh came here for help, didn't yeh? Well, we're the ones who'll help yeh if yeh'll let us. Isn't dat right, Bourney?"

"Dat's deh God's honest truth," Bourne said, nodding.

"How come you're here?" Cathal growled. "What's this place to you?"

"Dis is our boss's place," Red told him. "He's a gentleman, a pillar o' society, and you were right to seek out his help. We work for him . . . but we are all three of us in God's service. We know wha' happened to your ma, son. 'Twas our master helped set her up in her new life. We may be dee *only* ones who know deh truth abou' deh fire. It was down to the Devil's work, lad, and yeh need to be educated in his ways. Yeh want to know deh truth, don't yeh?"

"Not from you," Cathal snarled, jabbing at them with the

poker. Part of him did desperately want to know what they knew, but his instinct for survival told him these men were not to be trusted. Whatever he could find out here, the cost was too high.

"You're bein' silly, lad," Red cautioned him. "Put deh poker down, eh? Yeh've nowhere to go."

"I can go *through you*," Cathal retorted.

The two men were embarrassed at being faced down by a boy, but they had both seen the savagery with which he could fight and were determined to acquire as few bruises as possible while capturing him. They edged closer, hands raised. Cathal went very still, waiting.

Bourne moved first, leaping forward, trying to grab the poker. He was fast for such a stocky man, but Cathal saw the attack coming, pulled the iron rod away and swung it back into the man's wrist. Bourne roared with pain, and even as Red darted in, Cathal acted on reflex, bounding back against the fireplace and *leaping over Bourne's head*. Red froze for a moment, stunned, but lashed out with his fist as Cathal landed. Cathal ducked the blow and whipped the poker back, catching Red across the shin. Red yelped and sprawled forward, rolling and curling up to clutch his leg.

Cathal didn't waste a moment. He could not hold out against a pair of professional heavies for long. Bourne was already coming at him again. Cathal gave off a bellowing cry that surprised him as much as the two men. A feeling of surging, boiling energy rushed through him. Sprinting towards the window, he jumped onto the sofa, launched himself off the back of it, bunched up and crashed through the top pane of glass, hurtling out over the empty space beyond. It was a ten-foot drop to the ground in front of the basement windows, but his momentum carried him across the gap and his toes reached the ledge on the other side as his hands caught hold of the railings. He flung himself over the spikes on top in one lithe movement and hit the ground running.

By the time Bourne and Red had rushed out of the front door, Cathal was away off down the street. They hadn't a hope of catching him. They both looked in amazement at the broken window and the yawning gap in front of it. No normal young boy could have made such a jump.

"Deh Devil's in that child," Bourne muttered.

"Den it's our job to save him," Red said grimly.

XXII

INAPPROPRIATE ACTIVITIES

TATIANA'S KEEN INTEREST in the family's mode of self-defense training had some unanticipated consequences. Her female instructor had been sent home the week before with a broken ankle, one maid who had volunteered to act as a sparring partner was now in bed with a cracked rib and another had, only the day before, been sent home after suffering a dislocated elbow.

It seemed that Tatty's enthusiasm sometimes got the better of her.

Inappropriate though it might be for a man and woman to spar together, Nate had offered to train with her until her instructor recovered. And so Tatiana had donned a pair of trousers and a shirt and led him to the quiet hidden room in the east wing of the house where she took her instruction. It was a decision he was to regret. Tatty was more than able to maintain incessant conversation while learning the art of unarmed combat.

Her chatter was made all the more galling because she claimed she couldn't do anything without listening to her music at the same time. Siren, the bird-shaped engimal that was her constant companion, flew around them, surrounding them with a noise that Nate had come to think of as that made by innocent instruments in bondage to the rhythms of some African witch doctor.

"What's going to happen to Simple Simon?" she inquired as Nate demonstrated a hip throw on her, gently lowering her onto the sprung floor. "You're not going to exile him too, are you? He's such a sweetheart really; I can't believe he meant any harm."

"We're going to send him to one of the island estates for an extended holiday," her brother reassured her. "Achill, perhaps. He's not a bad sort; he's just been misled. I think he needs some time to come to his senses, but he'll be all right. Some fresh sea air will do him good."

"I think you're right." She nodded sagely as she stood up again. "What about all these Good Samaritan thingies we're doing? Have you made all the changes you wanted? Are we saving the poor yet or not?"

Part of Nate's job was finding the problem areas; the parts of the business where his cousins and other relatives were defying Roberto's wishes and engaging in cruel or unjust business practices. He was the 'fixer,' and trying to enforce reforms that endangered profits and still keep the family onside was no easy task. At the same time, he had to stop the Fenians from causing trouble for the family's interests in Ireland—for many of the rebels, there was little difference between the Wildensterns and the British—and he also had to deal with the interference that the civil war was causing in the not-so-United States. Gideon's slave operations were a typical example of errant family behavior.

"It's not as simple as all that," he replied, helping Tatty to her feet. "Your turn—remember, keep your head up and don't spread your feet too wide, that's it." He checked her stance before continuing. "The family's business is like a huge ship—it turns slowly. Berto's forcing everybody to bring in a lot of reforms, and some of them don't like it one bit."

"Oh!" She went to tuck her arm around him and lift him off his feet, but her hip slid off his thigh. "Bother!"

"You didn't pull me off balance," he told her. "Here, I'll show you again."

"I'm not as strong as you!" she protested.

"It's not about strength. Watch what I do."

He held her right sleeve with his left hand and the collar of her shirt with his right. Tugging her towards him to break her balance, he stepped around to her left and brought his right hand up behind her back. Pulling her into the space he'd made, he stuck his hip under hers as she tipped forward. Nate then straightened his legs and lifted her off the ground. He let go of her, balancing her on his hip and flexing his knees to show how well she balanced there, indicating the next part of the move. She giggled and then he flicked his hips, flipping her onto her back, controlling her fall as he did so.

"You see? No strength. It's all in your positioning: how you place your feet, how you move, and how you make your opponent move. Get those steps right, then you can learn to do it in one quick spin." He helped her onto her feet. "And don't forget to break your fall by slapping the ground. Your opponent won't always be so considerate. Now, try again."

Tatty's hunger for gossip was able to operate independently of her body. As she faced her brother again, she continued her questioning.

"Daisy says the family's rotten to the bone and she'd like to see half of them put out to pasture—"

"You're mixing metaphors," he managed to say before he was lifted off his feet and slammed down on the floor.

"Don't interrupt, it's rude," Tatty chided him. "She says there's not a decent Christian among them. Do you think she's right?"

Nate winced. His sister had no control, and being thrown by someone smaller was often more painful than the same technique performed by a larger opponent. The victim flipped around faster.

He got up and gestured for his sister to have another go.

"I don't know, but I'm sure *she* thinks she's right."

"She usually is, Nathaniel. And you could certainly take a leaf out of her book when it comes to worship. We hardly ever see you in church. Anyone would think you didn't enjoy it."

"Hmph!"

As he hit the floor once more, Nate restrained himself from pointing out that half the reason that Tatty attended church was to see what everyone else was wearing that week and to trade the latest gossip afterwards. And her taste in music was hardly what one would call pious, as Siren continued to demonstrate.

He jumped to his feet again. His shirt was torn under the arm and three of the buttons on the front had been ripped off.

"That was better. You're getting the hang of it now," he said with a smile. "Do it a few more times and then I'll show you a finishing strike from that position."

"Couldn't I just stamp on your head?" she asked innocently.

"Eh . . . yes. Yes, that'd do it, all right. But, em . . . why don't we give you some options, eh?"

They performed the move five more times and then Nate showed her an arm-lock to hold the opponent in place while she delivered a combination of strikes.

"It's very complicated," she declared. "I'd much rather just kick you in the face or stand on your throat or something."

"Hell's teeth, you're a bit bloodthirsty, aren't you? I'm rather hoping you never have to get into a scrap at all, never mind having to use hip throws and kicks to the head."

"Yes, but if I do, you'll want me to *win*, won't you?"

"I don't know. Frankly I'm starting to worry about the other bloke . . . or girl . . . or whoever."

But there was no arguing with her logic. They went on to leg sweeps, and Tatty quickly learned how to draw her opponent onto one leg before scything it out from under them with a deft sweep of her calf or thigh. As she practiced these throws on her brother, her thoughts returned to their earlier discussion.

"So do you think Daisy's right, that our family's not very Christian?"

"You're the one who wants to stand on someone's throat, my dear."

"Be serious. Most of us go to church. Goodness, I mean, we even built our own church to go to. Everyone I know prays to God. My governess makes me read from the Bible every day . . . "

"God, yes. I remember when Mr. Trent tried to get Gerald to learn passages from the Bible; Ger told him he would do nothing of the sort. Said it was dead knowledge and not worth committing to memory. He preferred to reserve his mental faculties for more fruitful pursuits. Started quoting Newton's three laws of motion instead."

"Really? What happened?"

"Trent commended him on his grasp of physics and then caned him to within an inch of his life. He couldn't sit down for three days."

Tatiana burst out laughing, missing the sweep so that Nate was able to reverse it and drop her to the floor. The soft impact just made her laugh harder.

"I think . . . ha ha ha ha . . . ! I remember that. Didn't he . . . ha ha ha . . . ! Didn't he bring an extra cushion to the dinner table for a few days? God, he even walked funny!" Her laughter subsided and she wiped away a tear. "What . . . what did he mean by 'dead knowledge'?"

"It's something he still goes on about," Nate said as he helped her up and demonstrated an arm-lock, followed by an elbow to the chest and a foot sweep. "He doesn't believe anybody should take any knowledge as . . . well, as gospel." Nate grunted as he hit the floor, but was on his feet a second later. "He says society won't advance as long as it obeys dogma, and advancing is everything in Gerald's eyes. Progress is his religion." Tatty locked up his arm, slammed her elbow into his chest and floored him again; he was a bit slower getting up this time. "Knowledge isn't something that's set for ever in print. It changes and grows. He has no tolerance for any religion, including Christianity. He says they haven't done any fresh thinking in two thousand years."

"Yes, well, he's not the most . . . tolerant type, is he?" Tatty grunted as she dropped her brother one last time. "But what do *you* think?"

Nate stayed sitting on the floor, catching his breath. He didn't reply immediately. He stared down at his feet. Siren, sensitive to the change of mood in the room, let its music settle into a calmer tempo. It fluttered down, settling in its favorite position on Tatty's shoulder.

"I try not to think too much," Nate sighed. "Ger's got a point, you know. But how can so many people be so wrong? Life would be so much easier if someone did have all the answers, but I haven't met anybody who does. You let this get into your head and it just goes around and around in there. I have enough on my plate without all that balderdash. I'm hard put every day, trying to keep my brother alive and change this family's ways—pound to a penny they're defying us in a thousand different ways in all those little details we can't check on all the time."

Tatiana sat down beside him, taking his hand in hers.

"Your heart's not in it," she said tenderly.

It wasn't a question.

"I'm trying my best, Tatty," he whispered. "I really am."

"Everyone knows it, Nate," she assured him. "Even Daisy— though she might not show it. She's always saying that Berto would be lost without you. Don't let on I told you this, but she said once that between the two of you, you make the perfect man."

"She did?"

"Yes, although she tends to think of you as the brutish, caveman half."

"I see."

"So . . . enough about you. How do you think I'm doing in my training?"

"Splendidly," he said, giving her a warm smile. "You're coming along very well."

"Oh, good! Because it's my intention to ride into the mountains, seek out the highwayboy and capture him single-handed."

"Oh, excellent."

XXII!

THE KNIGHTS OF ABRAHAM

BERTO TOOK HENNESSY with him when he went to meet Jamie Pettigrew and Herbert Angstrom at the plush lounge of the Members Club in the Royal Dublin Society. The head groom had barely enough training to pass as a footman, but with the loss of Winters, Berto wanted someone with him whom he could trust. Clancy would have been the obvious choice—his martial skills would certainly have offered more reassurance—but he knew that the servant's first loyalty was to Nathaniel, and Berto did not want his brother to know about this outing just yet.

Evening was falling. After half an hour of brandy, cigars and hobnobbing, Angstrom led them outside to a carriage with curtained windows that waited in the gathering dusk. There was an awkward moment as the matter of what to do with Berto's wheelchair was resolved, by Hennessy lifting Berto into the carriage and the wheelchair being stowed on the luggage rack at the back. Hennessy himself was to ride up front with the driver, but he was blindfolded, the brim of his bowler hat pulled down to hide the blindfold in its shadow.

Berto was permitted to ride without his eyes covered, but the curtains on the windows remained closed for the duration of the drive. This jaunt lasted nearly an hour; though Berto was certain that they turned back on themselves many times, ensuring that he could not try and guess their destination. The three gentlemen made only occasional conversation, the tension in the carriage's luxurious interior adding uncomfortable weight to every word.

Darkness had settled over the city when they finally pulled into a small courtyard. The men had to wait until Berto's wheelchair was unloaded and brought inside. Hennessy was led in and allowed to remove his blindfold. Then the carriage was drawn right up to the door so that Berto could not see the courtyard as his man helped him out.

They entered a shadowy but comfortable antechamber, with only a few framed maps of Ireland and Britain on the walls. The door leading further into the building bore a crest painted in red and gold on white showing two intersecting swords with a Coptic cross—a cross topped by a circle—between the blades. The circle held an image of an eye rather than the traditional second cross.

"Your man will wait here," Angstrom said to Berto. "Only brothers and initiates may proceed past this point."

Hennessy's fingers brushed across Berto's hand before he stepped aside. Angstrom knocked slowly three times on the door with a miniature wooden mallet and waited. A small hatch at face height opened and a voice said:

"Who are ye, who wish to enter this place?"

"Three men of decent intent," Angstrom chanted back. "Two brothers and one initiate, who is faithful, loyal and humble before God."

"Have you protected your approach against cowans and eavesdroppers, that the way may remain safe?"

"We have."

"Enter then, brothers, and may God be with you."

The door opened. The space beyond was pitch black and Berto could not see who had let them in. Jamie lit a single candle, casting enough light for Berto to tell that they were in a long passage with stone walls. They followed it down, with Angstrom leading the way to another door that also bore the society's crest.

Once more Angstrom knocked, was challenged, and answered with the passwords. The door opened into a much bigger room, lit only by Jamie's candle. Its walls were hung with tall red curtains stretching from floor to ceiling. Berto's wheelchair barely fitted in the doorway, the engimal grunting as it squeezed through. The floor was paved with marble flagstones, a large mosaic of the crest dominating its center. The candle was placed on the floor over the crest's eye. It was only when Berto was inside that he saw there were figures in dark red robes blending into the curtains on either side, pointed hoods hiding their faces.

Angstrom had vanished in the darkness. The door closed behind them and Jamie's tiny candle sputtered in the draught made by its movement.

"Who proposes this initiate for entry into the Knights of Abraham?" a voice asked from the darkness.

"I do," Jamie said in a toneless reply.

"What are you?"

"A Knight of the First Degree. Faithful, loyal and humble before God."

"And as for you, Initiate, what came you here to do?"

"To learn to subdue my passions and improve myself in brotherhood," Berto answered as he'd been instructed.

This was the easy bit. The next part would prove far more testing. There were several more ritual questions that demanded ritual answers.

"Do you come of your own free will?"

"I do."

"Do you believe in God the Almighty, and in his son Jesus Christ?"

"I do."

And then the one he had been dreading:

"Are you of sound mind and body?"

Berto hesitated. Jamie prodded him in the back. The Duke of Leinster was a great name to have among the ranks of the Knights. He had been assured that they would not reject him because of his useless legs, but here, now, surrounded by these hooded figures, he doubted everything he had been told. There was an air of menace about this place.

"I am," he said at last.

The figures seemed to take this without a murmur, and the questions continued until it seemed to Berto as if hours had passed.

"Prepare yourself for the passing through."

Berto started to undress. Handing his jacket, waistcoat, shirt, vest and tie to Jamie, he hesitated again. The clothes were handed to a red-robed figure that retreated back into the shadows. He was supposed to pass through the next doorway naked, but given his condition, it had been agreed that he could leave his trousers on. Even so, he felt terribly vulnerable with these masked strangers all around him; Berto struggled to keep his hands from shaking, his teeth from chattering. The embarrassment of his thin, wasted legs almost made him cry.

Jamie picked him up and carried him to the next door, one covered with red baize. It opened silently and they moved through into an even larger room with a high, vaulted ceiling decorated with carvings of scenes of Heaven and Hell.

This time there were golden candlesticks on a pedestal in each corner, seven candles in each. Jamie and Berto had to pass through a circle of the robed figures, each of whom held a sword with a gold hilt vertically in front of them.

In the center of the circle, Berto was lowered into a chair before a low carved stone table that resembled an altar. On it lay a cross, a sword, a length of rope, a gold coin, and a wax seal bearing the crest.

"These are our symbols: Faith, Loyalty, Unity, Prosperity, and Privacy. These are our watchwords."

It was Angstrom who spoke, but Berto could not see his face for he had donned a purple robe, its pointed hood cloaking his features in shadow. Berto was terrified. It was unthinkable for a Wildenstern to allow himself to be caught in such a situation:

semi-naked and unarmed, surrounded by men with swords—he was utterly defenseless. If this was a plot by some of his relatives to murder him then he was finished.

But that was how these Knights of Abraham wanted him to feel. That was the point. He had to surrender to them, as each man here had done before, and in that way, give them power over him. This was what kept the brotherhood strong—the individual's surrender to a greater calling.

Angstrom drew a dagger from inside his robe and walked around to Berto's right side. He placed a small piece of parchment, a silver egg cup and a quill on the altar in front of the initiate.

"Do you submit fully to these proceedings?" he asked.

Berto heard the voice as if from a great distance. There was a ringing in his ears. Fat lot of good it would do if I said no, he thought.

"Yes," he croaked.

Angstrom took Berto's right arm and made a slit with the blade across the back of it, just deep enough to draw blood. Berto drew in a steady breath and held his arm over the egg cup so that the blood could dribble down into it. Again, this went against every fiber of his being. Wildensterns guarded the secret of their blood, their *aurea sanitas*, jealously.

It also went against the grain to spill one's own blood, rather than someone else's.

More questions followed. He answered them automatically. Then, taking the quill, he dipped it in his blood and signed his name on the piece of parchment. Angstrom picked up the paper and struck a match. He dropped the burning parchment into the egg cup, where it disintegrated into ash and dissolved into clumps in the blood. Suppressing an urge to gag, Berto picked up the little cup and knocked back the contents as if it were a glass of whiskey. Swilling spit in his mouth to try and shift the mixture of metallic-tasting blood and dry, bitter ash, he managed not to throw up.

"So you relinquish your old life and are reborn," Angstrom declared. "Brother Roberto, welcome to our temple. Welcome to the Knights of Abraham!"

When he looked up, the swords had disappeared. The figures around him applauded. Jamie draped a red robe over his shoulders and slapped him on the back. A handkerchief was given to him to press against his wound and a glass of wine was put in his hand, which he gulped down gratefully, washing the vile taste from his throat, neglecting to savor the wine's excellent vintage. His clothes and wheelchair were brought in.

He was taken out of the chamber into a well-appointed, ordinary-looking corridor where servants were waiting to lead him to a spacious bathroom; here he was helped to bathe and dress. He joined the other Knights in the temple's lounge and was offered a glass of brandy and a Cuban cigar.

Angstrom was waiting for him with a warm smile on his face. "An uncomfortable experience, I know, Your Grace. But I hope you will, in time, see its necessity."

There was another man standing silently behind the doctor; a thin man in his forties, with heavy bags under his eyes, a flushed complexion and wheat-colored hair. Angstrom did not introduce him.

Berto took a sip of his drink and gazed around the room at the different groups of men talking in an animated fashion. Some were obviously waiting to speak to him. From where he was sitting, Berto could see two British generals, the Lord Mayor of Dublin, several distinguished police officers, the Archbishop of Armagh, and a dozen of the most powerful and influential industrialists in this part of the country.

He felt a jolt as he found himself looking into the eyes of his cousin, Oliver. Gideon's son was staring at him from across the room. Oliver looked away when he realized Berto had seen him and Berto shifted uncomfortably in his chair. What other members of the family were Knights of Abraham? If Oliver was here, then it was possible his brothers were members too—and most likely Gideon as well. Berto did not like the idea of his relatives having allegiances to anyone but the Wildensterns. He noted that Oliver did not come over to congratulate him.

"It's good to be here," he said quietly.

"It's good to have you here, sir," Angstrom replied. "And it pains me to bring this up so soon after your initiation, but it seems we have an urgent matter to discuss. Your Grace, I regret to say that your good lady wife has been interfering in some delicate matters—matters that concern us all. I urge you to curtail her activities . . . And I must impress upon you, sir, the very existence of this brotherhood may hinge upon your actions."

XXIV

RICH MEN'S SKELETONS

BERTO SAT BROODING in his coach on the way home. He was giving Jamie a lift back to his house, which was on the way. Jamie sat opposite, gazing out of the window at the darkness. The interior of the coach was lit by an oil lamp, the flame of its wick flickering with the movement of the vehicle over the bumpy road.

"Why didn't I meet any of the surgeons?" Berto asked.

"I don't know, old chap. I mean, Angstrom does some of the work, but there are others too . . . "

"So he doesn't do the operations on his own, does he? Which bloody genius fixed your leg? That's what I want to know. Are they holding off because of what Daisy's been up to?"

"I don't know," Jamie repeated.

"They bloody are, I can tell," Berto growled. "The nerve of

'em. What's all that about anyway? What are they up to that they're so defensive about?"

"I don't know, Berto. I'm only a First Degree Knight like you. There's a lot the Third Degrees don't tell the rest of us."

Berto grunted and stared out of the other window, facing away from his friend. Then he turned back again.

"You say that Angstrom is the Grand Master? Over all those other men?"

"That's right."

"How can that be? He ranks over the generals? The Mayor? Over the Archbishop, for goodness' sake? He's a *doctor*! He runs an asylum—"

"Among other things," Jamie pointed out. "He has at least one orphanage too, and a number of businesses. I'd say he's got a lot more than that if you looked hard. But it's the asylum that is the focus of his interests."

"Then how has he gained so much power?"

"Berto," Jamie sighed, "I think the question you need to be asking is: 'Over *whom* does he *have* power?'"

"What do you mean?"

"Haven't you heard any of the rumors about what goes on in that asylum?" Jamie locked eyes with his friend. "It's a dumping ground for every family mistake, every embarrassment . . . any . . . any poor wretch who threatens a noble family's reputation.

"The Knights of Abraham are made up of the great and the good of society, Berto, and Angstrom has all their skeletons hidden in his closet."

✿   ✿   ✿

The turf cottage where the witch lived was situated in a clearing within a copse of woods not far from the village of Blessington. A single track, just wide enough to walk down on foot, led down to the cabin; a stream bordered the clearing on the other side. It was a quiet, attractive spot, whose inhabitant lived alone, minding her own business.

It was early, not long after dawn on a Tuesday morning, and the birds were celebrating the sunrise with a cacophony of varied tunes. Nate could have named most of the birds, though his interest in wildlife had waned since he'd resigned himself to a life of protecting his brother. It was another regret that he forced himself to suppress as he followed Inspector Urskin and two constables down the narrow path leading into the clearing.

Nate had been invited along because this was Wildenstern land. The woman they were here to talk to was a leaseholder. They were miles from the nearest town, and some said this was rebel country. The constables kept looking around nervously. Nate was more at ease; he had done deals with the Fenians to keep the peace on the Wildenstern estates. If his family knew, there would have been uproar. It was the official position that Irish nobility did not negotiate with violent peasant rabble.

Urskin talked as they walked, showing no sign of anxiety.

"Frankly, some of these rebels need killin', if you ask me. They can be a bloodthirsty lot. But I find it's always better to take a man and break him than to turn him into a martyr. We Irish love our martyrs. The roughest thug can become the prettiest-spoken statesman simply by dyin'. You can be more noble, more heroic, dead than you can ever be alive, 'cos only your virtues'll last in people's memories once those who really knew you are gone. And there's no debatin' with the wisdom of dead men. They don't have to stand by their words."

The men reached the door of the cabin. With two small windows in its turf wall on the front, and a thatched roof that needed tending, it was much like thousands of other cabins in the country. Urskin rapped on the door. A moment later it was opened by a wizened, middle-aged woman holding a kettle. "Good morning, ma'am." The inspector greeted her with a friendly smile. "Inspector Urskin of the Royal Irish Constabulary. We've had some reports of—"

The smile was smacked from his face when the woman swung the kettle at his head. He managed to deflect the main force of the blow with his arm, saving his skull from a good cracking. But the enraged biddy swung at him again, shrieking like a banshee, and he stumbled backwards. At her third swing Urskin caught the kettle and pushed the woman to the ground. The pair of grinning constables took her by the arms, enduring her spitting and curses until she turned her fury back on their boss.

"Come back here! Come an' face me like a *man*, yeh green-bellied heretic . . . yeh guttersnipe shite-stirrin' West-Brit hoor!" she screamed. "Yer mother's a Liverpool strumpet an' yer father's a *goat*, yeh fat crawling Prod shillin'-taker!"

The breathless stream of abuse brought sheepish smiles to all who heard it, even the inspector as he stepped back, rubbing his sore head and flexing his arm.

"Ah, the Irish mother," he exclaimed to Nathaniel as the

constables bound her hands. "By God, if we could make an army of them, we could conquer the world! We've yet to see if her practices are as poisonous as her tongue, but she seems like a good candidate."

"A capital operation, Inspector," Nate declared wryly. "What will become of her now?"

"Ach, we'll search the house and grounds and find out what there is to see. Her son is a known troublemaker so we'll see how far the apple has fallen from the tree."

"Very wise," Nate said. "Thank you for allowing me to observe, Inspector."

"Just doin' my job, sir." The inspector touched the rim of his bowler hat. "Distasteful and all, that it is."

Nate put on his hat, nodded his head in return and set out for the trees again, turning his back on the drama. The scene had left him disturbed. Whoever the woman was, she was no witch. Nor did she have the *aurea sanitas* that might cause her to be accused of it. The knuckles of her hands were swollen with what appeared to be rheumatoid arthritis—she could barely hold onto that kettle, despite being hardly older than forty-five. Nobody with the health of a Wildenstern would have suffered from such a condition at her age.

Spinning on his heel, Nate strode back up the path. One of the constables had stayed with the prisoner; the other had joined Urskin to search the inside of the house. Nate ducked his head to step in through the door. The place was a hovel, with an earth floor, bare walls, and only a couple of rough stools and a table for furniture. Some aged pots hung on the wall over the fireplace. He quietly asked the constable to step outside. The man glanced once at his superior and then left without a word. Urskin was busy rooting through a wooden box.

"Stop this," Nate said.

"Sir?" Urskin replied, looking up.

"We're not going to find any answers here," Nate declared firmly. "Look around you, Inspector. This is no witch's den. Let's leave this woman be. If she is guilty of anything, it is a mere hatred of the police, and who can blame her when you—when *we* treat her like this. Let's not waste any more of our time here, Inspector."

Urskin was about to retort, but seemed to pull himself together. His head dropped for a moment, and then he sighed and stood up straight. He stuck his hands in his coat pockets and chewed the inside of his cheek, sizing Nate up with careful eyes.

"You don't give much credence to the paranormal, do you, sir?"

"I've seen things you wouldn't believe, Inspector. But none of them would lead me to believe this poor woman is a witch. And I don't think the ignorant superstition of commoners is a sound basis for police work."

"'The ignorant superstition of commoners'?" Urskin chuckled to himself. He shook his head and gazed at the floor for a few seconds before lifting his head again. "Tell me, sir. Have you ever heard of the Knights of Abraham?"

"I have heard the name mentioned," Nate replied, struggling to remember where. "Are they a secret society of some kind? Some branch of the Freemasons, perhaps?"

"They are a semi-religious organization with tentacles

reachin' into every area of power," Urskin said. "I am sure you come across their members in your everyday dealings without ever realizin' it. And though I can't prove it, I know that some of my own men serve this 'brotherhood.' I am sure that the Knights influence law enforcement to their own ends. Huh! As if the rich were not above the Law already. It's ironic, but the more important you become, the more you need the services of ordinary folk. There are rumors that the Knights of Abraham have unholy rituals, ones that include blood sacrifice. These are the kind of men who seek influence at any cost, sir. And I have heard from reliable sources, sir, that some of these men are thankful to the Devil himself for their privileged lives. Perhaps you should consider that before you scoff at ignorant superstition."

"Really? And where might I find some of these Knights?"

"Look close to home, sir. Find the ones with the tightest grip on power, those who will hold onto it no matter how many bodies they leave in their wake."

"We're not all bloodthirsty tyrants, Urskin," Nate sighed.

"No, sir. But lookin' from down here, where the 'commoners' are, it can be hard to tell the difference."

XXV
AN UNCOMMONLY BRIGHT
EXAMPLE OF HER GENDER

BERTO WAS THROWN through the window, thirty stories above the ground. His scream followed him out through the spray of broken glass and wood. The pistol fell from his hand and he flailed for a grip, anything to stop him from falling. Falling . . . falling . . . Nothing but empty space below him. His scream was cut short by an impact that sent a shock through his body. Something snapped in his spine. Berto knew what it was. He had been here before. With one hand, he managed to grip onto the stone gargoyle that had broken his fall—and his back. Far below him, hidden in the darkness, the ground waited for him to finish his drop. Berto denied it the pleasure.

He caught a glimpse of the woman through the broken window, saw her tall bearing, pale skin and her long black hair. She took only a moment to admire her work, glancing out through the window before turning away. The white shapes, the infernal creatures that had hurled him through the glass, wafted gently around her. Then Berto started to slip off the gargoyle's back . . .

Berto awoke with a shout, trying to sit up and failing. It happened the same way every time. He would wake from the nightmare always forgetting that he was crippled; try to sit up and flop back, moaning with exhaustion and despair. The dreams were always at their worst when he was enduring great stress—particularly the kind that came from facing down his family.

The room was dark, dimly lit by the moonlight seeping through the gaps in the curtains. Rolling onto his side, he worked himself up into a sitting position, piled some pillows behind him and sighed. Like all civilized upper-class married couples, Berto and his wife slept in separate rooms. It was a pity; he could have done with a bit of a chat. It would take him some time to get back to sleep.

"It's all right," he called to the manservant who tapped lightly on the door. "Just the usual bloody nonsense."

For the thousandth time, he cursed Elizabeth and her cur of a brother, Hugo. They had unmanned him. An explosion had freed their mummified bodies from the ground and they had gradually come back to life. They brought with them their ancient appetites for bloodshed and power. After killing Edgar, they had set about getting rid of his sons. Berto had been first in line. They had almost succeeded, though the fall that should have killed him left him with a broken spine.

His mind went back to a story Angstrom had told him as they sat sipping brandy in the deep armchairs of the temple's lounge.

"I have never trusted women," the doctor said after a long drag on his cigar. "It is a conviction I have held since childhood. Tell me, have you ever heard of the succubus?"

Berto blew out a smoke ring and frowned.

"Some kind of she-demon, wasn't she?"

"There are those who say she took the form of a beautiful woman who bewitched men and stole their seed," Angstrom said. "But there are other versions of the legend. And you are wrong to use the past tense, for I believe they are still among us. I myself was tortured for years by one."

He gazed at Berto, his eyes challenging the younger man to question or ridicule the suggestion. Berto didn't take the bait.

"I suffered from night terrors," the doctor went on. "I believe they were a manifestation of the Devil's attempts to control my very soul. Almost every night, from the age of thirteen onwards, I would wake to find a wretched old crone sitting on my chest. I would lie there paralyzed, my body frozen in place, her weight bending my ribs, crushing my chest. She would lean over me, her hateful, wizened face hovering above mine as she sucked the breath from my lungs. Imagine the effect this had on a young boy; night after night of torment. I lived each day in horror of the night ahead."

"I can only imagine," Berto sympathized. "How did you overcome these terrors in the end?"

"Prayer," Angstrom told him. "Prayer and an iron-clad faith in the Almighty."

As Berto lay in bed, his heart slowing down to a normal rhythm after his own recurring nightmare, he gazed up at the ceiling, its rococo plasterwork just visible in the gloom.

Closing his eyes, he began to pray.

Daisy read the Archdeacan's letter one more time, trying to contain her disgust. She had thought Alan Mills a decent soul; not only a genuine man of God, but a gentleman to the core. After the conversation they'd had during their archery practice with Tatty, she had hoped that Mills would provide her with some much-needed answers. It seemed that, like so many men before him, he was to disappoint her.

The letter was full of platitudes, but it contained a passage that rendered all the others meaningless:

> *I regret to inform you that, after some discussion with the Archbishop, I have been persuaded of the inappropriate nature of your request that I make inquiries into the patients at Philip Richards House. It is considered that the accusations you have made against Dr. Herbert Angstrom can have no foundation. Such unfounded allegations could needlessly sully the reputation of a gentleman who has performed many a great service for society and ultimately cause you a great deal of embarrassment as the source.*

There was much diplomatic padding either side of the passage, but the implication was clear. Alan Mills had been stepped upon. His letter went on to express his hope that they would continue to be firm friends, despite this 'difficulty.' Daisy had grave doubts on the matter.

She was standing in the conservatory gazing out at the gardens through the speckled lens of the rain-spattered glass. The room could comfortably seat fifty people, and the white painted iron latticework framing the glass was decorated with molded ivy leaves and curlicues. A summer shower fell lazily from the sky, the raindrops descending without any apparent haste as if confident that they would dampen everything with sheer weight of numbers.

The letter was crumpled in her fist, her nails piercing into its surface. Unfolding it, she flattened the paper out with her hands, before changing her mind and tearing it to pieces, tossing the shreds onto the mosaic-topped table that stood to one side.

Her fury was nurtured by the certainty that if she was a man, her suspicions would not have been met with such a casual dismissal. Not for the first time, she felt a fervent hatred of all men . . . and wished she were one.

She was under no illusions that if she had not held the lofty position of Duchess of Leinster and wife of the Wildenstern Patriarch there would have been repercussions for her intrusion into Dr. Angstrom's affairs. If the Archbishop himself had taken an interest, she was dealing with the highest spheres of influence. The implications of that set her nerves on edge. Was the Church involved somehow? Or was this something the Archbishop had a personal interest in keeping under wraps? Were there other powerful men involved in this conspiracy? If so, how long would Daisy's position protect her?

That was how Berto found her, her lips pressed tightly together, her hands clenched into fists as she glared out through the windows, lost in her thoughts. He knew his wife well; he saw the warning signs and wondered if perhaps this was not the time for the conversation he intended to have with her. But in truth, there was no good time to make his attempt and this way she would be more angry than hurt, which always made him feel a little better when he had to deliver bad news. He could never bear to hurt her, and though her tempers could be fearsome, they never lasted very long. He cleared his throat.

"Darling, I wonder if I might have a word?"

Daisy did not answer him at first; giving no indication that she had heard him except for a quiet indrawn breath. It was enough to convince Berto that this was a very bad time indeed. But it was best to plow ahead with matters such as these, once one had made the decision to do so.

"It's about these inquiries into Philip Richards House—you know, Doctor Angstrom's place? I . . . I . . . wanted to, eh . . . to ask you to . . . to exercise more, em . . . eh . . . discretion . . . " He winced at his lack of nerve. He was the master of his house, after all. Bracing himself, he continued in his sternest voice: "Now look here, Daisy, it's got to stop. You're causing me no end of embarrassment in certain circles and from what Doctor Angstrom tells me, you have even descended as low as . . . as *theft*! He claims that you stole some record books from the asylum. It's simply not on. You must return them forthwith. We can't go around just helping ourselves to whatever we please . . . we have lawyers for that kind of thing."

He hoped that his little jest at the end there would inject some levity into the situation, but feared it would not be enough. The expression on his wife's face had not changed one whit while he said his piece—never a good sign. Berto was prepared for a range of reactions: anything from a hurt, betrayed silence to an angry tirade, laced with disgust. He was not prepared for what he got.

Daisy turned to him, her eyes as cold as glacial water for one moment before she gave him a sweet smile and said:

"Of course, dear. I'm dreadfully sorry for causing you any embarrassment. You know I would never intentionally do anything to undermine you. I hope I have not cost you the good opinion of anyone important. If I have, I give you my most sincere apologies."

And without waiting for a response, she left.

Berto sat staring out at the rain for a minute, digesting this. Then he swallowed the lump in his throat and turned his wheelchair around to make his way back to his study.

"Oh, bugger," he sighed quietly.

Gerald stood behind his desk in the laboratory, a French cigarette burning in one hand, the other clasping his chin as he gazed down at his notes and the other articles that were laid out carefully on the desktop. He had spent the day before learning the ins and outs of the Wildensterns' shipping business and had confirmed that it would bore him senseless if he was forced to devote his attentions to it. The idea of having to deal with problems caused by a long chain of imbeciles was also too much for him to bear.

For instance, the number of ships lost at sea merely because they were overloaded was absurd. On reading the figures, he decided that the captains and managers were not to be trusted, and ordered the hull of every ship in the merchant fleet to be marked with a load line. This would show how low in the water the boat could sit and still sail safely.

After hearing the managers' protests, Gerald made it clear to them that bigger loads—and the associated profits—were of no advantage to the Company if they ended up at the bottom of the ocean. Anyone who disagreed was welcome to seek employment elsewhere. Shaking his head at their failure to apply some basic reasoning, he then strode out of the shipping office on the quays of the Liffey and rode his velocycle at high speed back to Wildenstern Hall, where he had taken refuge in his research.

Now, after a long morning of reading up on pagan rituals and their possible connections to mathaumaturgy, he was once more pondering the fate of the women who had died in the mysterious fires. He was wondering if they had somehow, through some unintentional act during one of their rituals, provoked the intelligent particles into igniting. But he felt he was no closer to the truth than when he had started.

Daisy found him there when she came to inquire on his progress. He seemed glad of the question, as if it diverted him from obsessing over a problem he could not solve.

"I have examined the scenes of the last two deaths," he told her. "The rooms where the others died were already let to new tenants. Their habitation would have destroyed any meaningful evidence. What I've gathered from the scenes of the deaths of Vicky Miller and Catherine Dempsey has yet to produce a clear picture of their fates."

"So what have you got?" Daisy asked. "Perhaps I could help?"

Despite his firm belief that women were best left out of any business requiring a cool intellect, Gerald knew Daisy to be an uncommonly bright example of her gender, so he did not immediately dismiss the possibility of her offering any assistance. Regarding her for a moment, he shrugged and began to lay out what he had thus far discovered.

"For a start," he said, "there are the ashes of the corpses themselves. They contained fragments of bone, which suggests that the bones did indeed burn in the fires, rather than being removed afterwards. That puts the temperature of the fire well above anything that could be achieved by normal ignition.

"Then there are the remains of the limbs: normally, when someone dies, the blood in their body, no longer propelled through the vessels by the heart, settles into the lower regions. This often causes an effect not unlike bruising where the blood has pooled. If you're lying on your back when you die, you see discoloration on the back, the backs of the legs, the heels, et cetera. There was none of that here. So I opened up the remains and examined them. They were almost entirely free of blood."

"What does that mean?" Daisy prompted him. "Where did the blood go?"

"If the victim was extremely cold, or if she had suffered a major wound, the body's defenses might have caused much of the blood to be drawn from the limbs to gather around her vital organs before she died," Gerald explained. "But it's impossible to be sure with so little of the cadaver left to examine. Certainly there was no sign of great pools of blood at the scenes, around the bodies, nor was it excessively cold on the evenings of their deaths—even given a woman's tendency to feel a chill on the balmiest of days. I am inclined to think that neither explanation is the answer.

"The natures of the fires themselves provide some clues. The fact that the shed where Catherine Dempsey was found did not burn down suggests that, while the fire must have been extremely hot, the flames were not high enough to burn the ceiling. It is an odd thing. Perhaps the fire did not burn fiercely, but over an extended period—for as many as eight or ten hours. I am becoming increasingly convinced that it is the work of intelligent particles, though I cannot ascertain how or why. It is a most perplexing problem.

"I'm sure that Catherine Dempsey's son could provide many of the answers—his lightning recovery from consumption is proof enough that he carries the particles in his blood—but we don't know where to even start looking for him."

Gerald gazed down at a candle sitting in a candlestick on one corner of the desk. In a room illuminated by gas-light, this extra flame seemed unnecessary, but Daisy suspected that he had been staring at the light as if it would offer answers to the questions posed by somewhat greater fires. Childhood habit caused her to reach out and pass her index finger through the flame, testing how slowly she could do it before the heat burned her. After a few passes there was a dark smudge of soot on her fingertip.

Gerald watched her, appearing distracted, as if struck by some extraordinary thought. He blinked and shook his head slightly, gathering his thoughts once more. There was a cage on the shelf above his desk and he took it down and opened it. Inside was the snake-like engimal—the 'serpentine,' as Nate had called it—that had been found in Vicky Miller's house.

"This serpentine is proving to be another conundrum. All engimals have a function, a means of being useful to mankind; I am certain of this. It is their purpose in life to serve our needs. The function of most engimals can be deduced by their shape, their behavior, et cetera. But the purpose of *this* creature eludes me. I'm sure Berto's mother had one years ago, but the family got rid of it when she died. I'm beginning to understand why. It doesn't seem to want to do *anything*."

"Perhaps it only serves its mistress," Daisy suggested.

"I fed it a drop of my blood in some water—that's normally enough for an engimal to bond with someone. But it just sits there, looking at me."

"It does look sweet, though," Daisy said, smiling at the small creature.

"*Looking sweet* is not a purpose in itself—even flowers have a practical purpose. This thing must do *something*; I'm just damned if I know what it is."

"I'm sure you'll find out sooner or later."

"Better sooner than later, given that there may be more women meddling in affairs they cannot understand," he grunted. "Actually, there was one more thing. I suspect there was a man in Vicky Miller's cottage not long before she died."

"What makes you say that?"

"I found this underneath the dresser in the kitchen," he said, holding up a cufflink. "The floor of that house was spotless; she must have swept it every day. So this had been dropped recently. It tells us something of the man too . . . "

"He uses cufflinks rather than buttons on his shirt cuffs, so he's not a working-class man—or at least he doesn't dress like one," Daisy observed, studying this new clue. "But the metal is cheap, the quality poor, which suggests someone who dresses above his station."

"Exactly," Gerald said approvingly. "Perhaps he was a client of hers, or a lover? Perhaps a man of God, come to teach her the error of her ways?"

Daisy targeted him with a harsh glare.

"You say that as if you suspect the Church of foul play, and yet there's no reason to believe it! Religion is responsible for so many great things, Gerald. Why do you hate it so?"

"Why do you love it?" he retorted. "It has done little for women these last few centuries. You can worship, but you can't be a priest or minister. You are belittled, patronized, kept from power and even, in the case of the so-called 'witches,' perse-cuted. You are blamed for mankind's first and greatest sin, and everything that came of it. Now, you are expected to do nothing more than keep the home and turn out babies.

"In those pagan times the Church so often condemns, nature was worshipped in the form of the Earth Goddess. Women were thought to be at one with nature because their cycles were in tune with the moon and the tides. They prac-ticed religion as priestesses, helped develop metallurgy and chemistry, and even fought in battle alongside their men. They could try a man out for a year of marriage then dismiss him if they weren't happy with him. Compared to all of this, what does Christianity do for you?"

"It gives us something greater than ourselves to believe in," Daisy replied evenly. "Because I don't believe that mankind has all the answers to life. Reason cannot explain why a certain piece of music can fill me with emotion. Science does not preach love or kindness or tolerance or generosity."

"Perhaps, but in a more rational world there would be less need of them."

"Yes, and we know how *rational* that world is today, don't we? Besides, since when did you become such a supporter of women's rights? You've always prided yourself on being the most awful bigot."

"I'm no great fan of your cause, but that's not because I want to keep you subdued," he admitted with a languid shrug. "It's simply a matter of evolution. You are the weaker sex; you are dominated by your emotions. That is why the world is ruled by *men*. If our two sexes were gathered into separate groups, divided by an ocean of water, it would be the men who would set about building ships to cross that divide. You can be sure the women would just dress up, make themselves pretty and wait for the menfolk to arrive."

"Perhaps you're right," Daisy sniffed. "But if the women *were* to just wait, sitting around amusing themselves, safe in the knowledge that the men would make every effort to reach them . . . who would you really think was ruling the world?"

And with that, allowing herself just the hint of a smile, she spun around and glided out of the laboratory.

XXVI

A MATTER OF BREEDING

THE PROBLEM OF IDENTIFYING who was plotting against Roberto was uppermost in Nate's mind when he went to visit Aunt Elvira as she nestled on the sofa in her living room, recovering from her collapse. He had first made sure that Gideon and his wife were busy packing for their one-way trip to as-far-away-as-possible. They were under orders to go without any fuss, and they didn't put up much argument. The couple wanted to leave with as little shame and as much dignity as they could muster—the fewer people who saw them off the better.

Ainsley, too, would be exiled, though he would be allowed to recover before leaving. Elvira was still visibly upset at the loss of her brother and was not in a mood to cooperate with Nathaniel. Besides, what her generation got up to was no business of Nate's generation, and he could go and rot if he thought otherwise.

But he did think otherwise.

When Nate walked in with a ledger tucked under his arm, Silas was sitting in a chair by his mother's side. A silver teapot and some scones sat on the coffee table before them. Elvira glowered at Nate, tilting her listening horn towards him, but then turning to address her son instead:

"Inform Nathaniel I do not wish to speak with him."

"Mother, there's no need to be unpleasant," Silas chided her.

"Eh?"

"I said there's no need to be unpleasant! Nate is only abiding by the Rules. Gideon could have been put to death for what he did—"

"Do not think to lecture your mother on the Rules of Ascension, nor any other matter of etiquette," she snapped back, gesturing dismissively at him. "While I know it is every generation's fate to be swept aside by their offspring, I did not expect—"

"My patience has worn thin, Elvira!" Nate barked at her, cutting off another self-righteous tirade. "There were few enough who knew the shenanigans surrounding the women in the top ranks of this family and half of those are now dead. We have a conspirator in our midst, and the list of suspects is growing steadily shorter!"

"Ask your cousin," Elvira croaked to Silas, "if he is suggesting that I am somehow involved in the attempts on Roberto's life."

Silas looked at her and then at Nate, holding up his hands in a helpless fashion.

"You heard me," Nate said forcefully, ignoring his cousin and keeping his gaze fixed on his aunt's face.

"Silas please convey to Nathaniel my heartfelt disappointment at his suspicions," Elvira said, staring at the nails of her free hand, "and my hope that he may quickly clear his senses of the cloud that so obviously obscures them."

"What would my father have done? I wonder," Nate asked, almost as if speaking to himself. "Faced with a bloody-minded woman whose silence threatened the life of his brother? Do you think he would have been as understanding as I have been?"

"Mind how you go now, Nathaniel," Silas uttered in a low voice. "There's no call for threats, is there?"

Elvira did not respond this time, but her listening trumpet was still held to her ear and the belligerent expression had melted from her face.

"After all," Nate continued, "we don't do away with our women, do we? No, we just *put* them away. In places like Philip Richards House." He slammed the ledger down on the coffee table, making the other two jump. "Did you ever think about what happened to those women, Auntie? We know that you wrote to at least one of them after she escaped. How *did* she escape? I wonder. Were you involved? Did you ever worry that you might be the next guest in the asylum? You know what Father was like—catch him in a bad mood and anything you said could have set him off.

"You must have lain awake some nights fretting that you had crossed him one too many times. I always knew how loyal you were to him, I just never understood why."

"Do not say a word against your father!" Elvira bellowed. "He was ten times the man you or Roberto will ever be! He was our shining light, our protector, our shepherd in the family's worst times. We would have been lost without him. Edgar did not have to negotiate for my loyalty; I loved him with all my heart!"

"And just in case you didn't, there was always the threat of being thrown into a living Hell to help keep you in line," Nate snorted. "He had a strange way of showing his love in return, don't you think? But still, we mustn't speak ill of the *dead*, must we? Even if I do wish the old bastard was here to explain how he could send healthy women to a pit of an asylum simply because they defied his wishes. But he's not here, is he? He doesn't have to explain anything. No, there's only you left now.

"Tell me who else knew about the women, Auntie."

They glared at each other, the air freezing between them, as Silas sat and awaited an outcome, playing with the watch chain that dangled from his waistcoat pocket. Ruthlessly efficient in business, he was always at a loss when it came to disputes within the family.

"Apart from Gideon, I do not know," Elvira eventually declared, appearing almost relieved at the surrender. "He orchestrated all of the 'committals.' That was one of his duties. I imagine his wife knew, and possibly some of his sons. Warburton as well, I'm sure. As my generation has dwindled, so too has the number of people trusted with the family's darkest secrets."

"Then perhaps it's time you started spilling them, Auntie," Nate suggested, "or let them die with you. Berto and I are intent on getting our house in order, and to do that, we need to know what rugs have had things swept under them, and what dark corners need light shone into them. It seems our traitor is managing to keep a step ahead of us the whole way."

"There's another possibility you haven't considered," Silas added. "Have you thought that it might be someone outside of the family who is engineering all of this? Though we take great pains to ensure that our family's enemies do not slip spies into the fold, it's always a risk. The East India Company has tried to infiltrate this house on more than one occasion, as have the British government and the nationalist rebels.

"Our personal servants share some of our closest secrets. Some of them know far more about our private matters than many of the family members, and our clerks and secretaries could give away much about our business. The Devil's in the detail, Nate, and we have so many details to manage, we have to rely on a great many hands and eyes whose loyalty is based on nothing more than a regular wage.

"If somebody was truly determined to discover our guiltiest secrets, their best chance would be to mingle with those who help us dress, change our bed sheets, serve our food and balance our accounts. Look to the staff, Nathaniel. And ask yourself how many of them you would trust to watch over you while you slept. I'd wager that they would be small in number."

Nate found himself thinking of Clancy, and how much he relied on his manservant. He literally trusted the man with his life. And Nate was so used to his presence that he forgot sometimes that Clancy was not a member of the family, that the servant's upbringing in a working-class home in Limerick had been utterly different to his. And yet Nate would, at times, speak his most private thoughts out loud while Clancy was within earshot. A good servant was there when you needed them and invisible when you didn't. But, of course, invisible did not mean deaf.

Nate sighed and flopped down in an armchair.

"By the Lord, sometimes I wonder if it would be better to be poor."

"And be ruled by the likes of us?" Silas chuckled, brushing his floppy dark fringe out of his eyes as he got up to take his leave. "I hardly think so. Better to be the rider than the horse, old bean. Listen, I leave for New York at the weekend. Will you try and get Berto to sign those contracts I gave him before I go? I can't get him to focus on anything at the moment and he's more likely to listen to you. Has his mind set on this operation, no doubt?"

"*Operation?*" Nate frowned. "What operation? I thought Gerald had done all he could do for the moment."

"This is something else, I think," Silas replied. He kept his voice low so that Elvira couldn't hear, though she seemed too lost in her own thoughts to pay any attention. "Another doctor's going to have a go, apparently. Some fellow named O'Neill. I don't think I'm supposed to know; Berto just let it slip yesterday while I was pestering him. I assumed you were in on it. Keep mum, won't you? I'd hate him to think I was being indiscreet. Gerald probably wouldn't take it very well either."

"Of course." But Nate was taken aback that his brother had sought out another doctor without telling him. How was he supposed to protect his brother if he was planning *surgery* without even mentioning it to him? And where had this Dr. O'Neill come from, all of a sudden?

His thoughts were interrupted by Clancy, who appeared in front of him out of nowhere.

"Begging your pardon, sir. But there's a young lad downstairs who is demanding to see you."

"Oh, for God's sake, what now? Who is he?"

"He says his name is Cathal Dempsey, sir," the manservant replied, his eyes fixed on the wall behind Nate. "He said he 'wished to apologize for any injury he might have caused to you and your privates on your last meeting, and hoped that there was no permanent damage done' . . . sir."

"Good Heavens, Nathaniel! Where on earth did you meet this boy, and under what circumstances?" Elvira exclaimed, her listening horn directed at Clancy's words. "In my day, young men could liaise without any risk to their private parts whatsoever. That they can no longer do so is a poor reflection on modern society!"

But Nate was already out of the door and running towards the mechanical lift.

"It all comes down to a matter of breeding," Angstrom declared.

The declaration was made in the smoking room of the Temple of the Knights of Abraham, where Roberto was taking brandy with the good doctor. They were surrounded by shelves lined with books of science, a discipline which apparently was merely a means of understanding the works of God and thereby mapping a path to His Glory. To illustrate this, Angstrom was using the example of Darwin's *The Origin of Species* and how it related to perfecting the human race.

"You will have noticed how men seek out an attractive partner with whom to produce offspring, whereas women are drawn to men of quality, status and intelligence. This is how it should be. Should a couple prove to be a successful combination of these qualities, the offspring that results will have an advantage over his peers."

"Naturally," Berto agreed, wondering where this was leading.

He found Angstrom to be an interesting and stimulating companion, if a trifle chilly. The man had some novel ideas and expressed them well. But Berto had joined the Knights for one reason and one reason only and he was keen to learn whether this discussion would offer any further news on his impending operation.

"Women are searching for a man whose qualities compensate for what they themselves lack. Men are seeking a healthy womb and a nurturing home for their progeny. This process has been going on for centuries, the process by which God has been perfecting mankind. And the peak of this evolution is to be found here in Britain—in the English gentleman . . . and the English lady with which he can breed."

Angstrom, needless to say, was English. Berto, being Irish first, British second, and not very English at all, wondered if Angstrom included him in this evolutionary elite. He could only assume so, having been taken into the man's confidence in this fashion. And though this appealed to the vanity in his nature, Berto thought the theory painted a damned unfair picture for those unlucky enough to be born more geographically challenged than himself and the doctor.

If it was true, it seemed that God, like Berto's own father, had favorites among His children. It also suggested that, like Edgar

Wildenstern, God had a poor opinion of women in general and foreign women in particular—a position with which Berto could not entirely agree, having met some formidable women in his time, both foreign and otherwise. He had even gone so far as to marry one of them. The fact that his father had disapproved of the marriage had been a nice little bonus.

And if it was the case that God was dissatisfied with any of the results of His own Creation, then Berto could not help feeling it was churlish of Him not to take responsibility for His mistakes. Either He was all-powerful or He wasn't; He couldn't have it both ways. To create someone as a barbarian and then dislike them *because* they were a barbarian seemed at the very least unfair, if not downright petty. One shouldn't go about painting a picture and then blame the *picture* for being rubbish.

And like God, Edgar Wildenstern had to take some of the responsibility for what Berto was.

For Berto had his own reasons for considering the Creator's tastes a trifle unfair. His thoughts went to Hennessy, who was waiting downstairs for him. The British—the *Christian*—world could never tolerate their love for each other. If Daisy had chosen to expose their affair, it would have taken all of Berto's power and influence to keep himself and his lover out of prison. No one in Christian society would be preaching forgiveness then . . . at least not in public.

And there was another aspect of this 'evolution' that disturbed him. Angstrom's idea was not a new one. The Wildensterns had been breeding their way to the top for centuries. That breeding had created the implacable tyrant that was Edgar Wildenstern.

"Our society, our empire, is proof of its evolutionary superiority," Angstrom continued. "God helps those who help themselves. His rewards to us for our faith, strength and valor are the power we have gained, our level of civilization, and our assurance of future greatness. And it is largely due to the actions of a few dedicated men, Roberto. Men like you and I."

Berto did not point out that he had been born into his position, and had spent most of his life trying to avoid it.

Angstrom stopped to take a few puffs on his cigar. The fire in the hearth was settling into embers among the gray ash. Berto noticed that the doctor did not summon someone to stoke it. He studied Berto for a moment before speaking again.

"I think I am right, sir, in deducing that, like me, you prefer the company of men. Tell me I'm mistaken!"

"No, for the most part, you are right," Berto admitted. "Though I count a number of women among my closest friends."

"A social necessity," Angstrom sniffed, waving this aside as something unfortunate but forgivable. "Childbirth and domestic issues aside, women are largely extraneous. Plato believed that the love between men was the purest kind; wise, rational and measured. It was he who laid the foundations for modern civilization and I read his words whenever I seek inspiration."

The doctor stubbed his cigar out on the ashtray by his chair and uncrossed his legs, before crossing them the other way. O'Neill, Angstrom's deputy at the asylum, appeared at the door, his hands behind his back. He waited politely to be invited before joining them. Angstrom nodded, but said nothing. He swirled the brandy around the inside of his glass with a gentle motion of his hand, breathing in the vapor before sipping it delicately. Then he gazed at Berto again.

"I think we are on the verge of a new era, Roberto. We are poised to take an evolutionary leap and that leap is being made here, within these walls. For the first time, it is within our power not simply to heal injuries, but to *improve* a man, mentally and physically and spiritually. It is my contention that, God willing, we can create a breed of man superior in every way to the average human. A man who will finally meet God's exacting requirements in every respect. I believe it *can* be done, not in a thousand years, as Charles Darwin would claim, but in two or three generations."

Putting down his glass, he stood up and stepped in front of Berto.

"It is nothing short of a revolution, Your Grace. Can we count on your support? Are you with us?"

Berto glanced up at O'Neill and then back at Angstrom. Something told him there was only one right answer to this question, but he had no doubt that there was a price to be paid. And he suspected that—as had been the case for most of his life—someone else would be doing the paying.

His hands clenched his lifeless legs, squeezing limp muscles that were atrophied from lack of use, completely lacking sensation despite the fact that his nails were digging into his skin through the material of his trousers. They were nothing more than weights hanging from his crippled torso. He could not bear to live like this any longer. He could not.

"Yes," he said.

XXVII

"WHATEVER THEY WISH TO DO"

IF CATHAL HAD BEEN AWESTRUCK by Leinster House, he was absolutely dumbfounded on his arrival at Wildenstern Hall. After escaping Bourne and Red for the second time, he had wandered at a loss for a long while, before finally resolving to go to Lord Wildenstern, determined to find out what the young gentleman knew about his mother's death. He had nowhere else to turn.

On presenting himself at the door of Leinster House on Monday afternoon, it took him some time to convince the butler that he was neither a street urchin, a thief, nor a chimney-sweep's boy, that he was honorable in his intentions and that Lord Wildenstern was indeed looking for him. This difficulty was compounded by the fact that Lord Wildenstern spent most of his time in Wildenstern Hall, only using the Dublin residence for parties with his town set.

It was decided that Cathal could travel up to Wildenstern Hall with the messenger the following day. He was given a filling meal of stew, a bed for the night in the servants' quarters of the manor house and a long thorough bath, administered by a tough old maid who knew even more bad language then he did. Cathal eventually capitulated on the basis that he would not hit a woman—and she had made it clear she would continue to box him around the ears until he got into that tub.

A proper outfit had been found for him; it was not a good fit and the collar was stiff and uncomfortable but his old clothes were thrown out before he could protest. The old maid told him that even if they were deloused, no amount of lye could get the stink out of them. After he had extracted a promise from her that his father's coat would be spared and stored safely, Cathal had gone to bed with a full stomach and skin so clean it was almost raw.

The messenger drove his cart out of the gates early the following morning, and set off for the Dublin Mountains. He was a garrulous man of about forty, eager to compare and contrast Cathal with each of his eight children, but harmless enough for all that. As soon as Cathal discovered that the man was not looking for a discussion, but merely a set of ears to listen to him go on, it was a simple matter to drop in the occasional "Yeah," "No," or "Is that right?" at the correct moment, and otherwise be left alone to his own thoughts.

On reaching Wildenstern Hall, those thoughts could best be described as:

"Holy Jaysus!"

"Aye!" the driver acknowledged with a faint smile.

The enormous house towered into the sky and even from a distance it was clear that there could be no other building like it in Ireland. Up close it was even more impressive, with countless windows, and its walls layered with sculpted terracotta panels. Gargoyles looked out from the eaves high above them and Cathal was left with an impression of the kind of castle he had only read of in books, where princesses were kept locked in high towers and evil sorcerers practiced their craft. The sudden appearance of a dragon would not have seemed out of place.

He was taken in through the servants' entrance around the side, and a footman took charge of him. Cathal gaped at the size of the downstairs section of this house, where an army of servants worked to provide for the family's needs. He wondered what these toffs did all day that required so much help.

On asking the footman, he received the blunt answer:

"Whatever they *wish* to do, whenever they wish to do it."

But though the building was impressive, Cathal had been brought up to put little stock in the trappings of luxury. His parents had drilled into him the awareness that neither wealth nor fine duds nor a fancy house made a gentleman. The rich could be every bit as sinful as the poor, they said. He had often wondered where his parents had come upon their familiarity with the gentry, but he'd be keeping his eye on these lawdy-daws all the same, in case they had a mind to treat him with anything less than respect.

Left to wait in a hallway with the footman while Lord Wildenstern was informed of his arrival, he stood observing his surroundings with as much of a contemptuous air as he could muster. He was eventually brought to a mechanical lift, a modern wonder that comprised a small room that carried them down three stories to a long corridor in the basement, which in turn led to a kind of laboratory.

The footman preceded him through the door.

"Master Cathal Dempsey, sir."

"Thank you, Mahon. That will be all. Hello, Cathal. I suspect you'll remember me, yes?"

And so Cathal found himself facing the man who had given chase to him on the day his mother died. But he had barely time to recognize the man, or to register the other three people in the room—two young women and the man who had accompanied the young lord in Howth—before Cathal noticed the laboratory itself.

He had never seen so many engimals in one place, though many of these appeared to be dead and in a state of dissection. On the walls around him were drawings of the insides of these mysterious creatures, much as there had been in the house near the Pepper Canister church—the house that belonged to the man who employed Bourne and Red. There were other similarities too. He spied sheets of paper with those mathaumaturgical symbols on them, and on the desk next to him he saw a copy of that book, *The Origin of Species*.

Cathal began to fear that he had just made a terrible mistake.

"Do you think he has a tongue in his head, or is he a mute?" the youngest woman asked.

"Tatiana, don't be rude, dear," the older woman scolded her.

Cathal looked at the younger one; she was an attractive girl with blonde hair and rosy cheeks, a little older than him, and she regarded him with the kind of expression one might reserve for a mad dog.

"I can talk just fine . . . miss," he replied, trying to ignore the lead weight in the pit of his stomach.

"We never doubted it for a moment," Lord Wildenstern assured him, clapping his hands. "Why don't we get you something to eat? A sandwich, perhaps? And some soup? I think we might well have a lot to talk about."

And as the gentleman spoke, Cathal was dearly hoping that he had found himself among friends this time—for there were no windows in this room fit to jump out of . . .

Berto's recovery from his operation was extremely rapid, as he would have expected. Despite his paralysis, his body had retained its hereditary healing abilities. As he drifted back from the ether-induced unconsciousness, he became increasingly aware of a stabbing pain in his back.

He had been here before. Gerald had attempted to restore the connections in the damaged nerves in his spine, to no avail. Berto had consulted with the best surgeons in the world and they had assured him that spinal injuries such as his were beyond anyone's skill to repair.

The bedroom was dark, the afternoon light blocked out by heavy velvet drapes. Dr. Angstrom and Dr. O'Neill were sitting in easy chairs by his bedside, observing him as if he was a bit of fascinating theater.

"Welcome back, Your Grace," O'Neill whispered, his mottled face glowing in the low light of a nearby lamp. "The operation went well. We have done all we can. It is in God's hands now."

Berto was lying on his front in the bed, his head turned to one side. Reaching behind him, he felt up under his nightshirt for the stitches binding the swollen, puckered lips of a wound that traced a line from his buttocks to a point below his shoulder blades. The pain of moving made him grunt, but it was satisfying too. He sought out any sign of sensation below the base of his spine; there was nothing. He had been here before.

His body was exhausted and he blacked out, unconsciousness easing into a healing sleep. A few hours later, he awoke again. The doctors were gone, but there was an attendant standing by the door. This time Berto was able to roll onto his side and sit up by himself, waving the attendant away while he assessed his own strength. His hips and legs were still unresponsive, but they felt different now. Instead of lifeless lumps attached to the base of his spine, he was more aware of them somehow. As if, instead of being paralyzed, they were simply numbed.

After another hour he managed to move the big toe of his right foot.

Two more hours later and he was dressed and back in his wheelchair, sitting in the temple's lounge. He was not wearing shoes, preferring instead to watch his stockinged feet as he painstakingly willed his toes to flex, which they did with twitches from time to time.

"Your recovery is remarkable," Angstrom told him, sipping on a fine whiskey. "This was the most challenging operation we have ever performed. I have to say, my own humble skills aside, credit must be given to O'Neill's blood."

"What has his blood got to do with anything?" Berto inquired.

"It's not actually *his* blood. It is donated and used as part of our treatment. O'Neill has a process he performs on the blood that we use for transfusions during the operation. You lose so much of your own, it is necessary to replace it. Apart from my techniques, it is the chief element in aiding recovery."

Berto wondered what O'Neill could be doing to blood that would match the healing properties of *aurea sanitas*, but he didn't say anything. Angstrom was as good as his word. He had proven himself where other men had failed. And to think that most of the world's finest surgeons had not even been willing to try. Berto continued to watch his toes twitch, tears welling in his eyes.

"Your Grace," Angstrom continued. "I know that you will be tired, but if you could indulge me for a moment, there is someone I would like you to meet."

"Of course," Berto replied.

Angstrom made a gesture with his right hand and a footman came forward, leading a young boy by the hand. The lad could not have been more than six years old.

"This is William," Angstrom said. "Say hello to His Grace, William."

The boy stepped forward and bowed.

"Hello, Your Grace. It is an honor to meet you, sir."

"And it is a pleasure to meet you, William," Berto said in reply.

With another tiny gesture, Angstrom had the footman take the boy by the hand again and lead him away.

"A very well-mannered boy," Berto observed.

"I'm glad you think so, sir," Angstrom said. "He is also a vital part of our research."

"Really? How so?"

"He is one of twins, Your Grace. William and his brother are orphans—recently given into the care of an orphanage of which I am the main patron. William has been well raised as far as it goes, but from this point on, he is to be part of something much greater than himself. And I hope that you will agree to play a part. I wonder, Your Grace, if I could ask you to foster the boy."

Berto frowned, looking to Angstrom as if this might be some kind of a joke. Clearly it wasn't. He paused for a moment, digesting the bizarre request. He was taken aback; he had known there would be a debt to repay to the Knights, but this was the last thing he had expected. Even as he considered it, he thought of Daisy. She dearly wanted children. They had talked around the subject many times, without ever facing it head-on. With Berto in the state that he was, adoption looked to be the only choice open to them. He shook his head in indignation.

"Bloody hell, Angstrom!" he protested. "I'm just over an operation, and you ask me this? Couldn't it wait?"

"I'm afraid time is a vital factor, sir," Angstrom told him, as he sat down in the armchair next to Berto. "William no longer has any family and it is important that this be rectified in order for me to start studying the contrast."

"What contrast?"

"The contrast between *his* existence and his brother's. You see," Angstrom explained, "identical twins provide the best resource for my research. By having them develop differently, I can study them both and see how their childhoods influence their development. William will grow up in a good family; he will receive the best of everything: education, opportunities, connections, et cetera. His brother, on the other hand, will be kept in the orphanage, where his existence will be in stark contrast: brutal discipline, deprivation, neglect and a future with no prospects. By studying them both, we will learn more about what makes a fine example of a man, and what makes a vagabond."

Berto listened, but he could not believe what he was hearing.

"Everyone knows that you have been phasing out the use of child workers in your factories," Angstrom went on. "You have been praised for the humane way in which you treat your tenants and for the way you do business. You are considered a gentleman in every respect and we believe you would make an excellent father. Provided you follow the plan I have laid out for William's development, you could produce a model son."

"And in the meantime, you condemn another boy to a life of misery?" Berto growled.

"It is a necessary condition of the experiment." Angstrom shrugged. "At least one boy will do well out of it. Sacrifices must be made to achieve greatness, and I am working for the good of mankind. Christ has promised us he will come again, Your Grace. The world did not treat the last Messiah very well. When he descends to Earth again, I want the human race to be worthy of Him. Tell me this is not a noble goal."

"*Noble?*" Berto had to restrain himself from shouting. "What part of tormenting children do you consider noble? Do the rest of the Knights know about this? I cannot believe that they would all stand for it. It makes me wonder, sir, what other *experiments* you are carrying out. I find myself in something of a quandary, for it seems I am in debt to you, Doctor Angstrom, but I *will not* take part in your monstrous explorations! Indeed, I will do everything in my power to ensure that they are stopped!"

"You would do well to remember that debt, Your Grace," Angstrom said with exaggerated care. "You are one of us now. All those who truly matter in our society are privy to the plan. Even the Wildenstern Patriach, the Chairman of the North American Trading Company, must walk with care among the Knights of Abraham. It would not do to set yourself against us."

"And you should mind your tone, sir," Berto responded, his fingers resting lightly on the arms of his enginal chair, in case he should need to engage its weapons. "Do not make the mistake of thinking that my injury has deprived me of a backbone. It's a foolish man indeed who chooses to cross the Wildensterns. We are not to be trifled with. I shall take my leave of you now and I do not expect to return. Goodbye, sir."

And with that, keeping a watchful eye out for anyone who might stop him, Berto made his way from the room. It was only when he reached the courtyard, where Hennessy was waiting in the gatehouse with some of the other servants, that Berto realized he had left without his shoes. After he was installed within the safe confines of his coach, he stared at his toes all the way back to Wildenstern Hall.

XXVIII

AN UNPLEASANT REUNION

AS THE CARRIAGE CARRIED Nathaniel, Daisy, and Tatiana towards Dublin, Nate sat reflecting on their conversation with Cathal Dempsey. The boy had eaten his lunch with a prodigious appetite, speaking between mouthfuls as they attempted to divert his attention away from the food long enough to get some answers to their barrage of questions. During the consumption of a hot beef sandwich, a bowl of soup, a piece of steak and kidney pie, two scones and a bunch of grapes—his eyes had nearly popped out of his head at the sight of the exotic fruit—he had divulged some invaluable pieces of information.

The full identities of Bourne and Red would not take long to discover, particularly since they were employed by one of the Wildenstern's neighbors off Merrion Square. The fact that Nate and Gerald had actually met the two men after their ill-fated street fight was a bit galling, but would at least help in recognizing the hoodlums when the time came. The tattoo on Red's wrist, the same symbol Cathal had seen in the house on Upper Mount Street, was that of the Knights of Abraham. It could apparently be worn as a secret mark of honor by a few of their most trusted servants. Gerald had found a reference to it in one of the books in the family's library.

Gerald had shown the boy the serpentine, but the lad had denied any knowledge of it. It was easy to see that he was lying, though they had not pressed the matter—there would be time enough for that when they got to know him better. The boy certainly seemed to have *aurea sanitas*. They could see it in his complexion, in his eyes and in the way he moved. Gerald would test his blood to be sure.

Possibly the most useful piece of information he had imparted was the whereabouts of the next woman being sought by Bourne and Red—the one they spoke of *saving* at a 'place out in Harold's Cross, where the bushes were cut into all sorts of shapes.' Men had been sent out to search the area and by late afternoon Nate had received a telegram announcing that three houses matching that description had been found. Discreet inquiries had established that only one was inhabited by a woman—the wife of a company clerk.

A clerk of the North America Trading Company, as it turned out.

It had been decided to leave Inspector Urskin out of the matter until it had been investigated further. Any possible connection with the family had to be established and dealt with first;

things were getting complicated enough as it was without the law taking an interest in Wildenstern affairs.

Men were sent in advance to watch the woman's house, with particular instructions to keep an eye out for anyone matching Bourne and Red's descriptions.

Gerald had opted to stay in the laboratory with Cathal and see what else the boy knew. The young scientist had also muttered something about having to find a pig, but Nate knew him well enough not to inquire as to the need for said pig; no doubt it would all become clear in time.

Nate, Daisy and Tatiana were now riding in a carriage to Harold's Cross to speak to the woman who, it appeared, had caught the attention of the Knights of Abraham.

Tatiana was using the time to discuss the mysterious boy and declare—at length—her lack of interest in him.

"I mean, I know his mother was a Wildenstern, so strictly speaking he is family, but he seems a bit *rough* to me. And his manners leave a lot to be desired. I suppose his style of dress can be excused due to his circumstances, but he could surely have made more of an effort before turning up on our doorstep! Sometimes I think boys have no conception of what to wear without a woman to guide them. If he is to stay in the house I would have to insist that he be introduced to a good tailor at the earliest opportunity. I could assist him in choosing some fabrics . . . if it was absolutely necessary . . . and Nate could tell him where to get some decent shoes . . . "

The house was a nondescript brown-brick, two-story affair

with slate tiles and small windows. Flower boxes adorned the sills, but it was the topiary in the spacious front garden that grabbed the eye. Examples of shrubs and hedges, from box to bay, laurel to privet, were all shaped with meticulous care to create a wide range of animals.

"It's not as nice as ours," Tatiana observed critically. "They don't have an elephant or a giant butterfly or anything. But it's really quite pretty for a commoner's garden."

"This is a work of passion for someone," Daisy commented. "I've always thought it a pity that topiaries went out of fashion. Look at the care they've taken! I think it's lovely."

"If you like that sort of thing," Nate sniffed. "If you ask me, it looks like a children's garden."

"Well then, you should feel right at home, shouldn't you?"

Clancy, who was riding with the driver, opened the door for them and Nate stepped out first to help the two ladies down. They walked up the path and Nate rapped on the door. It opened a second later—obviously their arrival had been noticed. A maid stared out at them like a rabbit caught in the gaze of a speeding velocycle.

"Good day," Nate greeted her, handing her his card. "I am Lord Nathaniel Wildenstern; this is the Duchess Melancholy Wildenstern, and our sister, Miss Tatiana Wildenstern. Please inform your master that we have urgent news that we must share with him immediately."

"Yes, m'lord!" the maid yelped in a high-pitched voice. She closed the door, then opened it quickly again. "Eh . . . will you come in, m'lord? M'ladies?"

"Thank you," Daisy said to her.

"Mr. Nevin is not home yet. I'll inform Mrs. Nevin of your . . . your imminent . . . eh . . . your illustrious . . . eh . . . I'll tell 'er you're 'ere!'"

"Marvelous!" Tatiana said in a voice that mimicked the maid's excitement.

The maid shot off down the hall and through the door to the drawing room with a speed that almost shook the mobcap from her head. They heard her shrill tones, and then those of another woman, one who spoke calmly and with stern authority.

The maid was back a few moments later, looking chastened and positively deflated.

"Mrs. Nevin will see you now, m'lord."

Nate and Daisy exchanged glances. It seemed that the maid had been too excited on her mistress's behalf. Mrs. Nevin was not the type to be overawed by those of a higher station. They followed the maid into the drawing room, where she announced them to the lady of the house.

Mrs. Nevin was standing in the middle of the small room, waiting for them with a serene expression marred only by her cold smile. She was a tall lady with clear, pale skin and hair like black satin. Her three guests stopped in their tracks, their tongues frozen in their mouths by the sight of the woman in front of them.

It was Elizabeth, sister of Hugo Wildenstern, the medieval founder of the dynasty and the murderer of Edgar Wildenstern. Her six hundred years did not show; she looked no older than mid-thirties, and handsome with it. It was Elizabeth who had thrown Berto from an upper window of Wildenstern Hall onto the stone figure of a gargoyle—the fall that had broken his back.

"My family have come to visit at last!" she exclaimed. "Can I offer anyone tea? A glass of sherry, maybe? Or perhaps, from the looks on your faces, you could use something stronger?"

XXIX

A NEW KIND OF RELATIVE

NATE'S FIRST INSTINCT was to grab the woman and drag her—by her bloody hair if necessary—out to the carriage and back to Wildenstern Hall. Daisy's hand touched his arm as if anticipating this hasty reaction and counseling against it. Tatiana looked fit to explode.

The ancient woman carried herself with a majestic air that did not quite fit her middle-class surroundings. Her dress was fashionable enough—cotton with a woven flower design, spreading below the waist over oval hoops—but unremarkable in its cut. Her hair was worn in a long braid that was, no doubt, the best style her maid could conjure. It was clear from Elizabeth's expression that the sheer mundane nature of it all was difficult for her to bear. But they were on her territory, such as it was, and that was to be respected.

"Why, Elizabeth!" Daisy exclaimed. "How lovely to see you! We did wonder what had become of you."

"I have no doubt," Elizabeth responded with equal warmth. "I believe you had men combing every inch of the Pale and beyond for me. It gladdens my heart that you were so concerned for my welfare."

"We were so dreadfully worried," said Daisy. "Heaven forbid we should allow any *harm* to come to our kin in such turbulent times."

"I'll give her bloody *harm* . . . " Nate growled.

Caught between the two women, he was as yet unaware that there was a very different kind of confrontation taking place.

"Remember your manners, Nathaniel," Daisy cautioned. "There's no need for hostility. Is there any need for hostility, Elizabeth?"

"None whatsoever. Please do sit down. Won't you have something to drink?"

"Probably bloody poisoned," Nate muttered.

"Nathaniel." Daisy hushed him. "Tea all around, I think, Elizabeth. That would be lovely."

"Splendid. Mary, some tea, please. And see if we have any of that delicious shortbread Mr. Nevin's mother so kindly made for us."

"Probably stones in it," Nate muttered again.

The maid curtsied and swept out of the room on a wave of relief. Tatiana and Daisy made themselves comfortable on the sofa, while Nate took the free armchair. Elizabeth settled back into her seat, arranging her skirts over her knees, handling the fabric as if it was the finest silk, instead of cotton.

"So, you must tell us how you've been," Daisy urged their hostess.

Elizabeth eyed them for a number of slow breaths before smiling again.

"I almost died that day, at the train wreck," she said in a low, chilling voice. "You broke my neck, Nathaniel, you do know that, don't you? A normal woman would have perished. But we Wildensterns are quite another breed, aren't we? I managed to crawl away through nettles and brambles, hiding in the long grass beneath a hedge until the mayhem had subsided.

"I watched them take my sister's body away. I did not see what became of my brother, though I heard his cries. I lay there all night. By morning there were fewer people around the site of the crash; just a couple of men examining the wreckage. I waited, trying to hold my neck in place as it healed. It still aches now when I am cold. When the way was clear, I crept down the railway track to Kingstown. There was a shop there that dealt in rare objects and antiquities. I sold one of my leaf-lights there, for enough money to pay my way for a few days."

Nate twitched at the mention of the leaf-lights. Looking around he saw what appeared to be sheets of paper laid out on the windowsill. Their stillness did not fool him. He bore tiny scars on his arms and neck from their last encounter.

"They are never far from me," Elizabeth told him, noticing his glance. "After all, one never knows where peril lies, does one?"

He glared back at her, uneasy about having the engimals at his back.

Elizabeth continued her story:

'My neck was steady enough for me to hold it upright, but I had to buy a scarf to bind it. I was alone in a world I scarcely knew or understood. I needed an ally. So I sought out James Nevin. I had made his acquaintance while in Wildenstern Hall— he worked in the conveyance office there—and I don't think it too conceited of me to say that I had made an impression. I have always found that it pays to make friends with useful men. I knew the rough whereabouts of his house, and he had told me about his rather bizarre hobby—you will have noticed the appalling garden.

"I told him that my brother had outraged the Patriarch and had disappeared. I had fled in shame. I had nowhere else to go . . . I was desperate . . . only he could help me . . . you know, all that nonsense that men want to hear. The scandal of giving an unmarried woman lodgings in his house could have ruined his reputation, but he risked it just to have me close. I posed as his wife until we were able to make it a reality.

"And now here I am, Lady of the Manor . . . so to speak."

"I see," Daisy said in a thoughtful voice.

For a few moments, no words were uttered.

"I like your dress," Tatiana commented to break the silence. "Did you make it yourself? It has a rather *home-made* quality. I think it's admirable that a lady should put her needlework skills to good use when she finds herself in reduced circumstances."

Nate suppressed a smile. But they were here on serious business, and since Daisy clearly did not think it appropriate to drag this harpy back to face justice in Wildenstern Hall they would have to proceed in a more roundabout way.

"Elizabeth, we believe you might be in danger," he said to her.

"Goodness gracious—is that right?" she responded, with mock-fright. "You mean from someone other than you? Who might they be, and why would you feel the need to warn me?"

"You may well be putting yourself in danger," he replied frostily. "Have you . . . have you been experimenting with mathaumaturgy at all? Dabbling in any practices of a . . . a pagan nature? Rituals and so forth?"

"Mathaumaturgy?" She looked puzzled.

"It is a new science . . . or so some claim," Daisy explained. "A means of communicating with the elements using mathematical language. I . . . believe one can use flashing lights, or . . . or a telegraph machine. Apparently some engimals even react to pages of mathematical symbols . . . "

She hesitated, feeling somewhat embarrassed and at a loss to explain something she did not believe in herself.

"I have not heard of it," Elizabeth replied. "And I have never indulged in unchristian practices of any kind. Why do you ask?"

"Because there are a couple of very unsavory characters who believe that you have, and they are intent on saving your soul," Nate told her. "A number of other women have died recently because of these *practices*. We don't know what the men's involvement in this is, but we're sure they are up to no good."

"Well then, you must afford me all the protection I need." Elizabeth smiled. "I am no damsel in distress, but I am somewhat vulnerable here, in my *reduced circumstances*. I must return to my rightful home . . . in Wildenstern Hall."

"To the dungeons, perhaps," Nate snapped, "but it will be a cold day in Hell before you take dinner at our table again."

"But, Nathaniel, you of all people should be determined to welcome me back . . . " She laughed, before favoring him with a sly smile. "Now that we share such a special bond."

With that, her eyes turned towards a large writing desk in the corner of the room. But it was not the desk she was looking at. Tucked beside it was a small baby carriage. Daisy drew in a sudden breath. How had they not noticed it before? Almost as if on cue a cry rose from the pram and Elizabeth glided over to pick up the child that lay within. It was a beautiful baby—with white-blond hair and blue eyes. It looked around at them with sleepy curiosity. Tatiana let out a gasp of delight.

"I . . . I . . . Congratulations," Daisy stammered.

"Thank you, my dear," Elizabeth replied. "This is my angel, Leopold. Leopold, may I introduce your Aunt Melancholy . . . sorry, I mean, 'Daisy,' and your Aunt Tatiana. And this, Leopold"—she gestured gracefully towards Nate—"this is Nathaniel Wildenstern . . . your father."

Nate felt as if he was suddenly detached from the ground, as if overwhelmed by a floating numbness. The only thing his eyes could focus on was the infant in Elizabeth's arms.

"Wh-what did you say?" he whispered.

"That is an outrageous claim!" Daisy cried. "How could even you stoop so low as to try and—"

"But it's quite true, my dear." Elizabeth interrupted her. "Poor Mr. Nevin thinks it's his, but he's mistaken. I was pregnant when I sought him out. It was another reason to marry quickly."

"Nate!" Daisy protested. "Have you nothing to say about this? How can you let her make such a claim? As if you could ever sink to such depths as . . . " She turned towards him. "Nate? Have you lost your tongue? You mustn't stand for this! You mustn't . . . Nate?" Daisy stared at him, taken aback by his expression. "Nate—you didn't . . . ? Did you?"

Her eyes stretched open as far as her lids would allow and her jaw dropped in a most unladylike fashion. "*You did!* You did! Oh, my God! Dear God in Heaven! You mean this *is* your child?"

"I don't know," he rasped. "I suppose, eh . . . I suppose it could be."

"You *suppose*! You . . . He supposes!" Daisy shrieked at Tatiana, who was still reeling from the surprise and unprepared for her sister-in-law's hysteria. "He *supposes* it's his child! Truly, you are a Wildenstern, sir, when you cannot recognize your own son without a nanny to point him out to you. How could you have let this happen?"

"What are you shouting about?" he barked at her. "It was before Father's death. I didn't know what she was at the time, what she was about to do. How could I? It was nothing—a momentary fling."

"I'm flattered," Elizabeth remarked with raised eyebrows. "As I remember, you seemed eager for the attentions of an older woman."

"I'll say she's older!" Daisy exclaimed, turning on him again. "Try *six hundred years* older! You grew up surrounded by conspiracies, Nathaniel. Could you . . . could you not have refrained from tipping such . . . such . . . such old velvet for just one moment to take time to consider that perhaps, just perhaps, you were being played for a fool?"

Daisy gazed at him, terrible dismay written across her face.

"I . . . didn't think," Nate said, trembling.

Daisy covered her face with her hands. Tatiana continued to observe the proceedings with uncharacteristic silence.

"Do not be too hard on him, my dears," Elizabeth said soothingly. "Such is men's weakness; and I have seduced far greater men than he. Nathaniel will have plenty of time to think on it now—the rest of his life, to be exact. In the meantime, there is my reintroduction to consider, so that you can all share in the delight of watching our son grow. I am tired of this mediocrity to which I have been condemned. It is time Leopold met his relations."

"But what kind of relation is he?" Tatiana wondered aloud. "A nephew? A cousin? My brother has had a baby with a centuries-old ancestor. I fear we shall have to invent a new word for it."

"Indeed!" Elizabeth laughed as the maid shuffled in with a tray. "Ah, and here's the tea, at last. Who's for shortbread?"

Cathal followed the two servants who were carrying the dead pig on a stretcher along the corridor. Gerald walked ahead of them, holding a camera, with another footman behind him bearing the tripod and a leather case of scientific instruments. This strange procession made its way down through the house and out to the gardens. Once outside, Gerald took them to the shelter of a little-used bandstand, where he directed the footman to lay down the pig.

Cathal had been having a strange afternoon. Gerald had used a needle to take some of his blood, which he had examined under a microscope, and had seemingly been very pleased with the results. He had let Cathal look through into the instrument's eyepiece; Cathal had not known what to make of the little blobs he saw, which Gerald told him were blood cells or the mist that flowed around them—the intelligent particles of which Gerald thought so highly. The scientist had then put him through some tests to assess his health—exercises, reflexes, breathing and so forth—until Cathal had thought it quite enough and declared it in no uncertain terms.

Gerald had agreed to postpone any further testing until another day.

That was when the footmen arrived and informed them that the pig was ready.

Now Cathal and Gerald, with three of the servants watching from a discreet distance, prepared the pig for Gerald's experiment.

"Why have they gone and put a dress on it?" Cathal asked.

"To present us with circumstances as close to reality as social convention will allow," Gerald replied. Looking at Cathal's frown of incomprehension, he added, "Dead *human* bodies are not so easily obtained. A pig's physiology is sufficiently close to a human's to simulate the effects I am looking for. The victims of the fires were all wearing clothes of some kind when they died."

Cathal had suspected that this was connected with the fires they had all been talking about. There was a churning in the pit of his stomach. He wanted to find out what had happened to his mother, but this was making him very uncomfortable.

"It's a very grand dress, isn't it? Looks expensive," he observed, looking at the swathes of peach-colored silk, trying to take his mind off what they were about to do.

"It cost a small fortune, I believe," Gerald responded. "It is my mother's favorite outfit."

"And you're *burning* it? Will she not be awful angry?"

"She'll be absolutely livid. I only wish she could be here to see it. I would have preferred it if the pig could have worn the gown for a few days beforehand, but it would have required taking the dress in by a considerable amount. Still, one must be thankful for small blessings. I shall make sure she sees the photographs."

Cathal wondered how anybody could be so mean to their mother.

"Are you going to eat the pig afterwards?" he asked.

"No, this is for the purposes of investigation only."

"Seems a waste."

"Scientific endeavor is never a waste, my boy," Gerald said sternly.

He opened a small bottle of paraffin and splashed it all over the pig's evening gown.

"I have been looking for answers to this mystery along complex and convoluted lines, when I should have started simple. Simplicity is the essence of experimentation. How can a body burn hot enough to cremate bone? I ask. And so, I must theorize and then experiment to test those theories."

Cathal looked around at the wooden floor, posts and roof of the bandstand.

"Will this not catch fire?"

"If my theory is correct, I think not. It remains to be seen."

Once the paraffin had been sprinkled evenly across the material, Gerald took out some matches, struck one on a post of the bandstand and paused solemnly to savor the moment, watching the flame creep away from the tip of the match. Then he dropped the match onto the oil-soaked dress.

As the flames rose up and crept across the material, Cathal felt a constriction in his chest. It was suddenly difficult to breathe, and he became frightened, thinking his consumption was returning. But it was not illness that was causing this, and he knew it. His mother might well have burned like this. Bile rose in his throat.

"What . . . what do we do now?" he asked.

Gerald checked the time on his pocket watch and began setting up his camera. "We wait," he replied.

"I need to go for a walk," Cathal told him, feeling as if his recent meal was attempting to climb back out of his mouth. "Can I walk around the gardens?"

"By all means," Gerald murmured, his attention focused on the burning pig. "I have read the future in your blood, young Cathal. Believe me when I say that our home is your home."

XXX

THE BABY IS SAVED

NATE, DAISY, AND TATIANA each sat stewing in their own thoughts as the carriage drove away from Harold's Cross. Daisy had not said a word since leaving Elizabeth's house. There had been no question of taking Elizabeth with them there and then, but there seemed no option but to allow her to come back to Wildenstern Hall at some point. She seemed very ready to desert her husband if they did not wish to include him; to be quite frank, she had told them, now that she was being welcomed back into the bosom of her true family, Mr. Nevin was surplus to her requirements.

None of them liked the idea of living with that dangerous, conniving woman under the same roof. Nate, in particular, sat with his fists clenched, his jaw muscles flexing as he stared out of the window.

It was too much of a coincidence. Whoever was conspiring against Berto had access to information shared with very few members of the family and perhaps—*perhaps*—their closest servants. They knew the ways of the Wildensterns: the personalities, the Rules of Ascension, the family's obsession with keeping their secrets from the outside world.

In the short time she had spent in Wildenstern Hall, Elizabeth had shown a rare ability to wheedle information out of everyone she met. She had her brother's cunning and ambition, but had been considered less of a threat because she was a woman. That had been a mistake. She had befriended the women around her. Daisy had been fascinated by her past, Gideon's wife had been eager to impress her, Tatiana had told her stories of how Edgar had risen to power. Had Elizabeth listened to any gossip from the other women? Had she been taken into Elvira's confidence?

Because if she had, and could now combine it with her husband's knowledge of the business . . .

Nate did not share Gerald's low opinion of women. He knew exactly how much of a threat they could be. And Elizabeth had more than enough reason to want revenge.

He did not want to think about the child. He would not let himself. He did not dare. There was no shortage of gentlemen who spawned bastard children and then covered it up; paying off their mistresses, sending them away or even threatening them with ruin. But Nate was not afraid of scandal or the Church. Public opinion held no sway over him. There was more than enough room and enough servants to accommodate one more child in Wildenstern Hall.

But why did it have to happen with her? Why *her*? He cursed his own stupidity. Still, he thought, at least she has gone and married someone else. She needn't entertain any ideas of trying that with him. Whatever plan she had concocted, he would not allow her to carry it through.

"Confounded woman!" he muttered to himself.

Daisy turned to look at him and her eyes were rimmed with red; she had been crying. The sight enraged him further. What did she have to cry about? This was his problem . . . and he would deal with it his way. He thumped the wall.

"Clancy! Stop here! I'm getting out."

"What are you doing?" Tatty asked as he opened the door and stepped down.

"I don't know," he said honestly. "But I'm not letting that woman back into our home until I know what she's up to. Go on without me. I'll take a cab back."

His manservant made to go with him, but Nate waved him back.

"No thank you, Clancy. Stay with the ladies. I'll handle this alone."

Nate watched the coach drive away and then walked back towards Elizabeth's house. Dusk was settling over the day, shadows overwhelmed by the gloom.

It took him less than fifteen minutes, but he knew something had changed here since he'd left. He had sent three men ahead to guard the place; two of them should have still been positioned out on the street. Walking around to the alley behind the house, he saw that the third sentry was missing too. They were reliable men; they would not all have left their posts at the same time like this.

Instincts fine-tuned from years of life in Wildenstern Hall told him foul play could be the only explanation. He patted the reinforced hip pocket of his jacket, feeling the reassuring bulk of the six-shot Navy Colt concealed there. If there was to be trouble, then let it come.

Rather than approach the front door, he made his way down the alley, careful to avoid being seen from the back garden. The garden was more conservative than that at the front of the house, but well-tended and surrounded by a five-foot-high brick wall. Keeping his head low, Nate opened the gate in the wall a few inches and peered inside. There was no one to be seen. As he crept up the path, he saw a pair of feet sticking out from behind the garden shed. A quick inspection revealed the dead body of the man who should have been on guard in the alley. Bruises on his throat told Nate that he had been strangled by a head-lock from behind.

He had been an able man; it would have taken more than one assailant to overcome him so easily. Nate drew his pistol and continued making his way up to the house, keeping under the foliage of the crab-apple trees that lined the side of the garden.

The scullery door at the back of the house was open. Just as he reached it, even as he went to peek into a utilitarian room with glazed brick walls, a tough-looking ginger-haired man stepped out. Nate reacted instantly, jabbing his stiffened fingers into the man's throat to silence his cry of alarm and then striking him across the temple with the butt of his gun. The man slumped to the ground, out cold. He was carrying a sack. There was something moving in it.

Nate was about to look inside, when he heard a voice speaking in an urgent whisper:

"Where's Red? Tell 'im to fetch deh ting. We've got deh witch. She was a righ' wagon and no doubt. God knows wha' deh babby'll grow up like. Where's Red? Tell 'im we're waitin' on 'im!"

"He's gone outside. I'll get 'im," another voice answered. "Mind dat mad cow. Remember wha' dat Miller hag did to Gentleman George!"

Red's slumped figure was lying in the doorway in full view. There was no time to hide him. Nate took a deep breath, raised his gun and jumped in through the doorway. The door to the kitchen was open and he had his weapon trained on it when a club came down on his forearm with a force that nearly broke it. He cried out as the pistol clattered to the floor. His reflexes saved him as the club swung at him again, aimed at his head. The attacker had been in the pantry, hidden behind the open rear door. Stepping to the side, Nate arched his back, leaning under the club and then regaining his balance as he kicked out hard, his heel catching the attacker across the kneecap.

The man yelled in pain, falling backwards onto the flagstoned floor. Nate went to finish him off, but a third cove was already charging through the kitchen door. Nate had barely a second to glance around for his missing gun before the thug was upon him, fists swinging.

Nate blocked the man's blows, ducking past and getting an

elbow into the thug's ribs before shoving him into a set of heavily laden shelves that collapsed onto him. Nate was far enough into the small room to see through to the kitchen beyond. Elizabeth lay unconscious on the tiles. Under other circumstances, Nate might have congratulated the three men. A fourth appeared through the door to the hallway and let out a curse, drawing a knife, holding it blade-down before approaching with more care than his fellows.

He fitted the description Cathal had given of the man named Bourne: broken-veined cheeks, graying hair and a stocky build. With his broken nose and his big hands with their scarred knuckles, he had the look of a bare-knuckle fighter about him, and Nate knew he would not be an easy opponent.

Bourne stopped in the middle of the scullery floor. Looking over Nate's shoulder, he called to the men behind.

"You two! Get off yer arses—we've work to be doin'!" Then to Nate he added, "Come on den, boy. Oi 'aven't got all day."

Nate realized he had allowed himself to be cornered. The two coves behind him got to their feet with murder in their eyes, blocking his escape. He looked around quickly for his pistol, but it was gone, under one of the dressers, perhaps, or lying out in the garden. Grabbing a cast-iron frying pan from its hook on the scullery wall, he stepped into the kitchen.

Staying side on to the door, Nate kept close enough to it that the men in the scullery would have to come at him one at a time. The smell of paraffin hit his nostrils. They meant to burn the place.

"My good fellows," he said. "I *would* urge you to reconsider this course of action . . . but quite frankly, with the way things have been going lately, I could do with giving someone a good thrashing and you three will do quite nicely." He raised his guard. "Let's get on with it."

The first attack came from the taller of the two in the scullery, the gaunt-faced man who had been thrown into the shelves. There was a knife in his hand and he slashed at Nate's arm, getting close enough to cut the sleeve and draw a line of blood. But Nate jumped back; he smacked the knife aside with the frying pan, brought the edge of it up to connect sharply with the man's elbow, jolting the arm straight, then over and down on his wrist, knocking the knife away. The thug screamed as his wrist shattered, but was cut off when the pan hit him squarely in the face and sent him flying back into the arms of his friend, who was coming through the scullery door after him.

Nate dropped into a crouch in time to avoid the attack from behind. Bourne's knife arm swung over his head, but changed direction instantly, stabbing downwards. Nate rolled away, slamming the edge of the pan into Bourne's ankle, then jumping up and deflecting a third strike of the knife. Bourne swore, flexing his injured leg, but kept coming.

The third cove, a swarthy Mediterranean type who had cast his fallen comrade aside without so much as a glance at his smashed-in face, hurled himself at Nate. But his damaged kneecap was slowing him down: he swung a punch, only to have it strike the frying pan with a loud clang. He yelped, shook out his damaged knuckles, but kept coming.

Stepping back over Elizabeth's body, Nate found himself

retreating against the solid oak barrier of the kitchen table. He rolled backwards over it, his feet flipping away just as Bourne and the Mediterranean trampled over Elizabeth and crashed into the edge of the table. Nate landed upright on the other side, heaving the table over into them as they tried to follow.

The Mediterranean was back on his feet first, roaring as he came after Nate again. Nate reached up to the row of presses by his head and snapped one of the doors open in the man's face, before jabbing the hard edge of the frying pan into his groin and then delivering a kick to his sternum with such force that the thug was thrown from his feet, falling against the iron stove and cracking his head on its open door.

"Yeh can handle yerself, lad, I'll give yeh dat," Bourne observed, not sparing a moment to check on his fallen comrade as he picked up a poker used for stoking the fire in the stove. "But it's time we finished dis."

With the poker in his left hand and the knife in his right, he closed on Nate. Instead of meeting him, Nate backed through the door into the hallway. Elizabeth's maid lay unconscious near the foot of the stairs. The door to the living room was closed and he could hear a fluttering sound from within.

"Don't . . . " Bourne said, pulling up short.

Nate opened the door. A whirlwind of white shapes swept out and past him. He covered his face with his arms, gritting his teeth and waiting for their razor-sharp edges, but his guess had proved to be right. Somehow, they had read his intentions. They weren't interested in him.

Bourne was enveloped in what looked like a storm of paper

sheets. These wafer-thin engimals fed on daylight, lying around and soaking up the sun's radiation. Individually they were just flimsy creatures, but together they formed a bewildering flock of swift, sharp edges. Bourne cried out, flailing at them with his arms. His knife cut some of them; his poker knocked others to the floor. But the cuts on his hands and face spread as if his flesh was trying to burst from its skin; tears appeared in his clothes, blood soaked into his shirt and trousers.

Rushing into the living room, Nate looked into the pram. The child was gone. He staggered back, completely at a loss. In all the commotion, he had simply assumed the baby was where he had last seen it. His son. They had taken his son. His mind went back to the bag Red had been carrying. There had been movement in it.

He turned, about to leave, when he saw an engimal squatting under the pram. It was a drawbreath, the same one he had seen on a leash when he had first met Bourne and Red. It gazed up at him, looking somewhat forlorn. Its bristly back was marked with dozens of shallow cuts.

"They used *you*," Nate said almost to himself. "They used you to distract the leaf-lights so that they could take Elizabeth . . . and the child."

He went to grab it, but it tried to squirm past him. Catching hold of its body, Nate picked it off the floor. The drawbreath's snake-like neck suddenly broke off its body, and he nearly dropped it in surprise. The head folded back along its neck and the creature wriggled away with startling speed. Nate went after it, but it slithered over to the fireplace and into the fire burning in the hearth. Seemingly insensitive to the heat, it disappeared up the chimney.

As he was distracted, the other half of the creature scuttled out of the living room, heading for the back door.

"Well, I'll be damned," he breathed.

He had heard of engimals that could change their shape, but had never seen one before. That snake-like section of the drawbreath could account for the women found in rooms locked from the inside. If the creature could be trained to turn a key—which some engimals could—and it could get in and out through chimneys . . . Nate emerged from the room to find Bourne crying now, calling out for someone to help him. The leaf-lights kept whirling around him, slitting his skin wherever it was exposed.

And then they stopped, rising calmly to hover near the ceiling.

Bourne was on his knees, sobbing. Elizabeth glided up silently behind him, grabbed his hair and pulled his head back. She pressed the blade of a bread knife against his throat and hissed into his ear in a voice as cold as an arctic wind:

"Where. Is. My. Son?"

"Wait," Nate exclaimed, barging past them and making for the back door. "The child's outside. And we know where this cur's master lives. You don't have to—"

"You're too late," Bourne gasped through bleeding lips. "Deh babby's saved, but you won't be. An' may . . . may God have mercy on your twisted souls."

Nate had his back turned to them, but out of the corner of his eye, he saw the spray of blood that came from Bourne's opened throat. It painted a spattered line across the wall. The man's corpse sprawled onto the floor, twitching, blood pooling beneath it. Nate ran through the kitchen and the scullery to the back door. He felt his heart give an almighty thud.

Red was gone—and so was the baby.

XXXI

THE DRAGON'S TEETH

DAISY AND TATIANA HAD ANOTHER ERRAND to run before they returned to Wildenstern Hall. Tatiana was as curious as she was upset by the discovery of Nathaniel's illegitimate son, but Daisy was badly shaken. They were almost at their destination by the time she had regained her composure and she kept her face turned towards the window, leaving the curtain almost completely closed. Tatiana chatted to her as if nothing was wrong, but was careful not to say anything that required Daisy to answer. This was not a difficult task for her.

The address they were looking for was a small terraced house in Kimmage. They were calling on another woman, one whose background was as different from Elizabeth's as it was possible to be.

Mary Behan was in her seventies, still hale and hearty, despite failing eyesight, a bad hip and arthritic ankles. She greeted the two ladies politely, but with barely disguised suspicion. A gaggle of children aged from three years to eight were wandering around the house and she shooed them upstairs.

"Me grandchildren, Your Grace," she explained. "I mind 'em while their mothers are out workin'."

Her living room was the type that was rarely used, set aside for formal visits. The family life of the small house centered around the kitchen, warmed by the stove and filled with the smells of stew and baking bread.

Daisy and Tatiana were ushered into the living room. It was a modest affair, with threadbare furniture and cheap prints of Pope Pius IX, Wolfe Tone and Daniel O'Connell on the walls. On the mantelpiece was a brass plaque carrying the old Irish proverb, *Níl aon tinteán mar do thinteán féin*—"There's no fireplace like your own fireplace." It was the kind of ordinary sentiment that Daisy missed in the grandness of Wildenstern Hall.

The house was well-kept, despite its simple décor, and Mrs. Behan made no attempts to apologize for it. Her tone, though civil, was brusque. An air of hostility glowed about her. After some tea had been served and the necessary pleasantries had passed between them, Mrs. Behan waited expectantly for them to get down to brass tacks. Even though it was her house, she was not in a position to ask the purpose of their visit, but the question was written in every line of her face.

"You will no doubt be wondering what brings us here, Mrs. Behan," Daisy said eventually. "We both know that this is not an entirely social visit. Let us put formality aside for a moment and speak as one woman to another."

Mrs. Behan resisted the urge to snort in derision. It was all very well for a duchess to speak of 'putting formality aside.' Daisy's airs and graces would be enough to keep old Behan in her place, but the old biddy had learned some shrewdness in her time, and she saw that there was an opportunity here. The Wildenstern women were up to something—as usual—and she might well profit from it.

"I am overwhelmed, Your Grace, with this honor of having you in my humble house. I cannot imagine what good fortune brings you to my door," she declared, squinting short-sightedly at the pair in front of her. "Though my service to the Wildenstern family ended some years ago, I am delighted indeed that you have seen fit to remember me."

"We are here regarding your long years of service with Lady Elvira Gordon," Daisy said tentatively. "Her wits have been failing her of late, and we believe that you might be of some assistance to us in tidying up some of her affairs. In her twilight years, she has become very morose, haunted by what she sees as her failure in matters concerning her sister and other women in the family."

"Oh, aye?" Mrs. Behan raised a wire-brush eyebrow, her polite tone dissolving into Dublin scorn. "Well, formalities aside, Your Grace, I never saw dat woman morose in all deh fifteen years I served her. Broody, yes. Offended, often. An' obstreperous for most of deh time she was awake . . . but never *morose*. An' I somehow doubt dat her wits are sufferin' failure of any meanin'ful sort. Deh Devil hisself will 'ave his hands full defendin' his ears from her tongue. But if it's secrets yer lookin' fer . . . well, some I know and some I don't. Elvira Gordon was not a kind mistress, but I know which side me bread is buttered. If I cross her, me life won't be worth livin'."

She leaned closer and Daisy resisted the urge to flinch away from the scent of rotting teeth.

"I've seen tings dat would shake your delicate sensibilities," Behan snorted. "I was wit' her when she had to be dragged drunk from servants' rooms in deh middle o' deh night. I was dere when she almost died from opium poisonin', an' I was dere on deh day she realized she'd grown too fat to reach around and wipe her own arse an' I knew I'd be doin' it for her from dat day on. Dat ol' wagon has deh waist of an elephant an' deh memory of one too. She has deh Devil in her an' I'll not be crossin' her in a hurry. I give you me Bible-word on dat."

"Do not think you can shock my 'delicate sensibilities' with the ugliness of life, Mrs. Behan," Daisy told her with an edge in her voice. "Before I knew this great wealth, I helped raise my siblings in hard times; while still a child, I tended to a sister dying of influenza because my mother was too sick to help; I dealt with the victims of horrific accidents in my father's factories; I have a husband who is paralyzed, and I do not have to describe to you the unique perils of being married to the Wildenstern Patriarch. I have seen things that would challenge even your stout stomach."

Daisy did not mention that she was also responsible for the grisly death of a woman the previous year. Some things were best left unsaid.

"Daisy killed a woman too, last year, you know," Tatty piped up helpfully. "While defending herself, of course. Chopped off her head with a sword. That was pretty shocking!"

Mrs. Behan raised her eyebrows. She had heard that particular rumor but had not believed it. Daisy sighed quietly and gave her sister-in-law a hard stare before continuing.

"You need not worry about Elvira," she said to Mrs. Behan. "I can assure you, that dragon's teeth have been well and truly pulled. Wildenstern Hall has a new mistress . . . and she understands the importance of loyalty."

She made a show of listening to the children playing upstairs.

"How many grandchildren do you have?" she asked.

"Fourteen," Behan responded. "Two more died last year, one in the cotton mill, another from consumption."

"I am very sorry for your loss," Daisy said. "Let us ensure that they are the last to pass away at such an unfair age. What if I were to promise you that all of your grandchildren will be provided for most generously? They will not have to take time out of their education to work; each will go to a good school and, if they so wish, will learn a profession. We will assure their futures."

Mrs. Behan's chin trembled as she turned her head away, her eyes flicking back to Daisy as if she was trying to judge the truth of Daisy's words by catching the lady off guard. But the old woman's indecision did not last long. She gazed at Daisy with tears welling in her eyes.

"I-If you can protect me from her, Your Grace," she uttered through a throat constricted with emotion, her professional manners reasserting themselves, "I'll tell you all I can. What do you want to know?"

"We want to know about the women who were sent away," Daisy replied. "We want to know everything."

Cathal watched the engimals sweeping across the grass. There were three of them, lawn-cutters, gardeners steering them by their tails as they ate their away across the spacious lawns, trimming the grass to perfect uniformity. He admired the way their trails left alternating stripes of darker and lighter shades of green and wondered at the cost of having three such creatures simply for cutting the grass.

He had been avoiding the burning pig as best he could, but morbid fascination drew him back from time to time to check on the fire's progress. He headed back towards the bandstand once more. More than four hours had passed, and most of the pig's carcass, complete with peach-colored evening gown, was still intact.

It was getting dark now; the air was filled with the stench of slow-burning fat. Footmen set up lanterns around the bandstand. Cathal found Gerald checking the temperature of the smoldering flesh with a meat thermometer.

The young scientist made a note of the temperature and took the lens cap off the camera to expose the slide. Once the photograph was taken, he carefully stowed the delicate collodion negative away in his case before setting up a shot from another angle.

A man wearing a top hat and long coat appeared, striding across the lawn towards them. He bore a close resemblance to Gerald, though he was a few years older and slightly more conventional in manner. Cathal had seen him briefly before; it was Gerald's brother, Silas.

"Where is everybody?" he asked as he reached the bandstand. "I have to leave for New York within the hour and have not said goodbye to anyone. Where are they all?"

"Running errands," Gerald replied brusquely, annoyed at being distracted from his work. "I'm sure they did not mean to be absent for your departure. Perhaps you should just wait for them. You run the Company's business in America; I hardly think the ship will leave without you."

All three of them stood around the burning corpse as if it was some bizarre campfire. Silas glanced at Cathal. They had not been introduced and, given the boy's age, they did not expect to be unless it was absolutely necessary.

"I despise poor punctuality," Silas responded at last, slipping on a pair of gray silk gloves. "The ship has a schedule to keep and I will not waylay it. But I am not pleased; I am not pleased at all. Sometimes I think this family spends their entire time indulging their whims while I endeavor to keep them rich . . . and with dashed little appreciation."

"So you are always saying," Gerald murmured, engrossed in framing his photograph.

"Yes, well it's not good enough. It's not right that some of us do all the work while the rest sit around sponging off the family coffers and getting fat as butter. And don't think you're excluded from that category, Gerald. You can't waste your whole life on these . . . these pointless inquiries. Hang on . . . Is that Mother's dress? She'll have a conniption when she hears about this! What is all this *about*, anyway? It's creating the most God-awful stink."

Gerald withdrew his gaze from the viewfinder, but did not look up at his brother.

"You've never understood my work, Silas, and I suspect you never will. You lack curiosity. Like so many in the world, you haven't the imagination to see the bigger picture. Why don't you hasten to your ship, lest it fail to keep to its schedule? I will pass on your best wishes to the others and urge them to show you more appreciation in future."

Silas stared at his younger brother for a moment. Something unspoken passed between them as if in final realization that something they had lost years ago would never be found.

Silas clicked his teeth together and nodded. If nothing else, brothers always understood each other's temperaments.

"Goodbye then, Gerald."

"Goodbye, Silas."

Cathal watched the older brother walk away. He was just deciding that Gerald would probably want to be alone when the gentleman started speaking to him.

"The high water content of flesh makes ignition difficult," he said in a dry tone as if reading from a textbook. "Under normal circumstances, a body that is set on fire will not continue to burn until it is consumed. That would ordinarily require a fire of much greater intensity, such as a furnace.

"But just as a candle can be kept alight, so too can a body. Instead of having a wick running through its core, a human body can be kept alight by being wrapped in an *external* wick . . .

— 313 —

clothing. Spray the clothing with paraffin and set fire to it, and the flesh slowly ignites. The body's fat does not burn immediately, melting instead into the clothing before catching fire itself. As the flames consuming the flesh start to die, the burning fat in the material reignites them. This happens over a long period, smoldering slowly, extending the fire's life. The heat within the body builds to an intensity I would not have thought possible. The fire reaches a temperature at which it can burn bone. Seven hundred degrees centigrade."

Gerald gazed into the low flames eating through the dead pig as if in a trance, no longer heeding the smoke wafting into his eyes or the terrible pungent, oily smell.

"The fat is the key. That is why parts of the limbs were left. There is little fat around the elbows or knees; they are composed mainly of bone, ligament, sinew and skin. If the limbs were not lying against the body, there was not enough fuel to carry the flames down to the lower arms or legs.

"The peculiar combination of circumstances, along with the fact that all three women were endowed with *aurea sanitas*, leads me to believe that these could not have been accidents. These women were murdered, and each killing was carried out in such a way that their deaths would provoke superstitious rumor. They were murdered by someone who hoped to gain from the deaths themselves, but who also had a greater agenda. Exactly what that was, we have yet to discover."

Gerald blinked as if regaining his senses, and turned to find Cathal huddled in a ball, his back against one of the struts of the bandstand. The boy's shoulders were shaking; quiet sobs emitted from deep inside him, his face was pressed between his knees. Gerald nodded in sympathy but did not move from where he stood, switching his attention back to his experiment and the answers it was beginning to provide.

That was how Daisy and Tatiana found them. Daisy's first reaction was to crouch down beside Cathal and put her arms around him.

"You poor boy," she whispered. "What have you been going through?" She looked up at Gerald. "What in Heaven's name have you done to him? He's terribly upset."

"I explained to him how his mother died," Gerald replied. "His reaction is perfectly natural. But better he hears the truth straight out than beating around the bush. He'll make a full recovery, given time."

"Spoken like a true cad," Tatty told him. "Sometimes I think you have no heart at all, Gerald."

"I can assure you, I have. And I have the pulse to prove it. Oh, speaking of bulging blood vessels, Silas left for New York a little earlier. He said to say he felt mightily unappreciated and told me to wish you all goodbye. Now tell me how your investigations have been progressing."

While Tatiana filled Gerald in on everything that had happened, Daisy took Cathal away and directed the servants to find him a good room and put him to bed. He was to have whatever he asked for. She came back to find Gerald wearing a bemused expression as he lit a cigarette off the flames issuing from the pig's torso.

"Gerald, that's disgusting!" Tatty exclaimed. "You did that on purpose!"

"It was the most convenient flame," he retorted. "So tell me again about Mrs. Behan's claim, I want to—"

He was interrupted by the sight of Nate and Elizabeth striding towards them, flanking Berto in his wheelchair. All three had looks of urgent determination about them.

"The child . . . my son . . . The . . . the child has been stolen," Nate spluttered, struggling to find the words. He turned to Gerald. "I have a son."

"So I've heard, old bean. You *have* been busy."

"What do you mean, he's been stolen?" Daisy asked. "You just let someone waltz in and kidnap him?"

"Nobody waltzed in anywhere," he snapped back. "There was a great deal of violence involved. But that is beside the point. They have him and we have to get him back. And we think we know where he is."

As he said this, he glanced down at Berto, who glowered back at them with an aggression that hid his shame.

"Our people have informed us that the house Cathal escaped from is owned by Aidan O'Neill," he told them, "Herbert Angstrom's assistant at the asylum. Those hoodlums work for him. You've been making inquiries into the Knights of Abraham—well . . . he's a member. And Angstrom is the Grand Master."

"Really?" Gerald looked surprised. "How do you know?"

"Because I joined them not long ago," Berto said through tense jaws, speaking quickly as if he needed to release some great pressure. "It is a decision I sorely regret. Angstrom has been carrying out operations . . . He's been achieving some incredible things, but . . . but he's got some hare-brained scheme to breed the perfect human being. I think he means to *create* a Messiah, by providing a vessel for God. He made this whole 'improved human' thing sound plausible at first, but the more I listened . . . His early advances were built upon the development of a special kind of blood . . . "

"It's *aurea sanitas*," Nate said. "He's creating stockpiles of our blood and using it for transfusions. Elizabeth told me her husband is a member of the Knights of Abraham too. She says he's prone to boasting about how he married into the Wildensterns. The men who came for Elizabeth—they had hypodermic needles, rubber hoses and jars. They meant to subdue her with chloroform and . . . and . . . "

"And bleed her dry," Daisy finished for him, her voice shaking with emotion. "And now they have your baby. What do you propose to do about it?"

"I mean to find him," Nate replied in an emotionless voice. "And kill anyone who thinks to hurt him."

"And hardly a moment too late," Daisy said under her breath.

XXXII

AN ASSAULT ON THE ASYLUM

IT WAS A RARE SIGHT INDEED: a group of six engimals tearing down an Irish road, the beams of their bright eyes stabbing into the darkness. This was the largest group of velocycles in Europe; the Wildenstern's stables could be bettered only by a few of the richest families in the United States or a couple of the dynasties in Asia.

Nathaniel led the way, resisting the urge to let Flash stretch out and unleash the full extent of its power along the road so that the others could keep up.

Behind him rode Gerald on Incitatus. The smaller engimal occasionally nipped at Flash's heels as they raced along, but was careful not to try the lead engimal's patience. Flash did not tolerate rivals to its position as pack leader. Velocycles tended to be

aggressive creatures and were not always happy to run in packs—
they were fiercely independent and territorial in the wild. And
though the remaining four beasts—ridden by Clancy and three
other well-armed footmen—were accustomed to working as a
disciplined group, there was always the possibility that Flash's
overbearing nature could spark a fight for dominance. The
resulting high-speed running battle between these six ferocious
engimals could leave their human masters as sprawled debris
along the roadway.

Nate had already sent a telegram to Urskin, telling the inspector about the men they had left behind in Elizabeth's house. He
had told Berto and Daisy to send another to the inspector about
Angstrom's connection—but not until Nate had time to reach the
asylum first.

Daisy had informed them of her conversation with Mrs.
Behan. Elvira's ex-servant had been most helpful. One of the
pieces of information she had supplied was that Angstrom kept
a book of admissions with the real names of all the women he
had incarcerated. Mrs. Behan had seen this book herself once,
when Elvira had gone on a rare visit to the asylum. Between the
Wildensterns and other wealthy families in Ireland and Britain,
there were dozens of noble women imprisoned in the asylum at
any one time. Angstrom was paid a healthy sum for 'accommo-
dating' each, and for keeping quiet.

He provided a similar accommodation service for illegitimate
children, hiding them away in an orphanage that he ran not far
from the asylum. Angstrom was a useful man to have around if
you had embarrassing relatives to conceal.

Mrs. Behan believed the doctor even operated on the brains of some of his patients, to ensure their submission. Gerald had been reading some of the doctor's published papers and thought that Angstrom might know enough about the workings of the thyroid gland to induce hypothyroidism—possibly through some surgical procedure. If so, he could effectively induce insanity with the cut of a scalpel, giving a family the perfect excuse to institutionalize the woman.

According to Behan, Angstrom would know who else in the Wildenstern family was privy to the fates of these women. He could provide the missing link in the search for the traitor.

And now this man had Nathaniel's son.

Nate still did not know how to feel about the knowledge that he had a son. Despite the fact that his head was boiling with thoughts, he was sure he felt no emotional bond with the child; he had never so much as held him. But Nate had always planned to have children. It was what a man was supposed to do, after all. And he had strong feelings about a father's duties to his child. First among them was to keep it safe—no matter what.

He was afraid that the family might use this new vulnerability against him. A son would make an ideal hostage. But he did not countenance such concerns for long. Nate did not know what kind of father he would be—particularly with Elizabeth as a mother—but he would not be like his own father. He would not be like that.

The depressing brown-brick vat of a building hove into view. This five-story fool's tower appeared as a fortress now, its circular walls suggesting the tower of a Norman castle, an impression heightened by its slot-like windows. The pack of velocycles roared along the driveway, through grounds tended during the day by some of the less-troublesome patients. The six creatures swept up to the steps of the entrance in a spray of gravel, steam rising from their nostrils, their mechanical muscles quivering with energy.

The asylum's motto, written in stone above the heavy double-doors, seemed now to be laced with irony.

"*To heal the body, one must first heal the mind*," Gerald read aloud as he swung from his mount and took off his leather helmet and goggles. "A noble sentiment indeed. One wonders what state those women's minds were in as their bodies burned. No doubt Doctor Angstrom will be able to offer an informed opinion. Nate, old chap, how do you wish to proceed?"

"I favor the direct approach," Nate replied.

"But, of course. Why change the habit of a lifetime, eh?"

The four footmen dismounted, removing their goggles and gloves, but holding back as Nathaniel strode up to the foot of the steps. Flash rolled alongside him. Nate took a small blue blanket from his pocket and held it to the velocycle's nostrils.

"Breathe it in, Flash," he said softly. "Get the scent."

The engimal inhaled and gave a low growl of affirmation. It raised itself up slightly, looking intently at the asylum door.

"That's it," Nate said, patting its flank. "That's it. Go on now! Find the baby."

The engimal's back wheel spun, gouging into the gravel and launching the creature up the steps. The stout wooden doors gave way like cardboard under the force of the beast's charge. Flash disappeared inside and Nate hurried up the steps after it.

"Come on!" he called, drawing his pistol. "I want to see the looks on their damned faces when it lands on them!"

The engimal had already bludgeoned its way through three more doors; the sound of splintering wood, its growling engine and various screams announced Flash's passage through the building. Nate followed the trail of wreckage, dazed orderlies and skid marks along corridors and up and down steps, deep into the *Narrenturm*.

Tough-looking orderlies ran from all parts of the hospital to investigate the commotion, but Clancy and his men kept them at bay with pistols and shotguns. Ahead of them, Flash was growling softly. The engimal had come to a halt.

Gerald followed at Nate's heels as they made their way cautiously along the corridor towards Flash, weapons at the ready, until they came to a low oak door bound with iron bands that appeared to lead down to a cellar. Flash squatted before it, engine idling. Even it could not ram through this one. From the other side of the door, they could hear raised voices. Whoever it was, they had not heard the invasion upstairs.

Nate examined the lock. It was sturdy but simple. Taking some tools from his pocket, he inserted a hook pick and felt around until he had pushed up the pins in the lock. Then he slid in a tension wrench, twisting it to hold the pins in place, freeing the hook pick. Feeling around with this, Nate pressed it in further, and twisted. The lock opened with a click.

"Clancy?" Nate said softly, as if his manservant could not be anywhere else but behind him.

"Yes, sir?"

"Don't let anyone else down here."

"As you wish, sir."

There were steps beyond the doorway, and they descended further down than one would have expected for a normal cellar. This room was deep underground. Gas-lamps lit the way. Leaving Flash and Clancy behind them, Nate and Gerald crept down the stairs, pistols raised. They could hear two voices, both raised in anger, and with them, the sound of a baby crying.

"But where the hell did it come from?" one was demanding. Nate recognized Angstrom's commanding tones.

"What does it matter?" the second replied, shouting to be heard over the baby's cries. "I've provided you with the blood time and time again, but the supply is limited. And I'm telling you, this child could be the answer to your prayers. We've hit a dead end in our research. This infant represents the way forward!"

At the mention of the child Nate's hand tightened on his gun. That was all he needed to hear. He continued down the steps into the room below.

"What has the child got to do with the blood?" Angstrom asked. "You said that was produced using a chemical process, a formula. *Why have you brought a baby to my laboratory?*"

"You never complained about the other subjects!" The second man retorted plaintively. It was Aidan O'Neill, Angstrom's deputy. "You were happy to bring all those old beggars down here and cut open *their* heads!"

"A different kettle of fish altogether! They were miscreants, the dregs of humanity." Angstrom waved his hand in a dismissive fashion. "Sacrificed for the greater good. Who would—?"

He broke off as he realized they were not alone.

Nate and Gerald leveled their pistols at the two men.

"You were saying?" Nate prompted them. "No, no, don't stop there. We're fascinated. And while you talk, you can hand over that baby, you goddamned toerags."

The baby lay wrapped in a rough blanket bawling its eyes out on the hardwood table between the two men. The rest of the room resembled a doctor's surgery, with trays of steel and copper instruments, anatomical drawings on the walls and shelves containing rows of jars, full of what looked like pickled body parts.

The space was enormous, with doors leading off on every side, suggesting a larger complex. It must easily have stretched to the limits of the building above it and perhaps even further. There was room for fifty men to work in comfort. The room was musty with the scent of old blood, preservatives and other chemicals. On counters around the sides glass beakers, test tubes and other scientific paraphernalia sat neatly arranged. Despite a few cobwebs in the corners of the ceiling, the place was remarkably clean. Whatever Angstrom was up to here, it had little to do with his duties as Director of Philip Richards House.

"How the bloody hell did you get in here?" Angstrom barked, disregarding Nate's rank.

"The baby," Nate said calmly, ignoring the question and motioning with his gun. "Step away from him. And then kindly explain what the Devil you're playing at in your little dungeon."

"I don't know what you're doing here," Angstrom said, gathering himself together and speaking in a quieter, more confident tone, "but you need not concern yourself, sir. Indeed, it would be best for all concerned if you just returned from whence you came. Do not make the mistake of thinking I am a mere doctor in an asylum, sir. My influence reaches much further than you would believe."

"As the Grand Master of the Knights of Abraham—I know," Nate replied. "Stand away from the child and start talking. Right now your influence doesn't extend past the barrel of this gun, and I'm inclined to make things a damn sight hotter for you if I don't get some answers, sharpish."

Both men took a step back from the table, glaring at the Wildensterns with hate in their eyes, but said nothing. Nate moved forward and scooped up the baby, holding the delicate bundle in the crook of his left arm while he kept his gun trained with his right. The degree of noise the little mite was capable of producing was astounding. And the sound was immensely irritating.

"Let's start you off, then," he went on. "You have some hare-brained scheme to build the perfect human and you have been using the expertise of O'Neill, here, a brilliant, but disgraced surgeon. A man convicted of employing grave robbers. You've used what you've learned to cure some of your most important members of disfigurement or injury or the like. But even with O'Neill's expertise, you couldn't have succeeded without transfusions of a type of blood that has the most wondrous qualities, blood that your thugs drained from the bodies of helpless women. A process that was fatal to the donors. And you burned their bodies to hide the evidence and perhaps even provoke some superstition into the bargain."

"What kind of preposterous accusations are these?" Angstrom bellowed, holding himself up straighter, his copper-colored whiskers seeming to bristle with indignation. "We are not in the business of *stealing* blood! We are not *vampires*, sir! O'Neill here produces the improved blood through . . . through . . . through a chemical process . . . he . . . "

The doctor's tirade faltered as he looked across at his colleague. O'Neill had turned quite pale beneath the blotches of pink on each cheek. Angstrom stared at him in what appeared to be genuine shock.

"What's come over you, man?" the doctor rasped. "You don't mean to say there's truth to their insane claims? Speak up, damn you!"

"You never understood," O'Neill muttered, his head hanging low, his baggy eyes angled up at his employer, dark with contempt. "You have fanciful notions of the level of your intelligence, *Doctor* Angstrom, but we both know you are no real man of science. You do not have the capacity to enact the plans that you hatch. I have been carrying you for years. Perhaps, now that we are exposed, you will be forced to admit it."

"You mind your tone, O'Neill," Angstrom snarled at him. "Do you forget who I am?"

"How could I forget, when I helped make you what you are?" O'Neill responded. "I have helped you gain wealth and power and influence through the cursed souls in this building. You are a master blackmailer, sir, a manipulator—but no scientist. Your vain, fantasist scheme to engineer a Messiah was doomed to failure from the start. God does not *favor* you. There is no Divine Power directing your actions. Your theories are poppycock, balderdash. Your finest moment was when you recognized my brilliance and saved me from being transported to Australia. You made use of me, and I returned the favor, for it served my purpose to mix with the rich and powerful."

"But the miracles we performed!" Angstrom protested, his face going a deep red, his cheeks shaking with rage. "We cured the incurable!"

"It was the *blood*," O'Neill explained, enunciating the words slowly as if to a child. "That was what *I* was studying. We were able to perform the surgeries because, with that blood in their veins, the patient could recover from almost any wound. And that blood came from women who died from the lack of it."

He turned to face Nate and Gerald.

"Women abandoned in this hellhole by families such as theirs," he said, waving at them with scorn. "There is something in their blood that is nothing short of supernatural. Some kind of . . . of benevolent parasite. I helped these women escape, and in return they let me take samples of their blood to study from time to time. At first it was enough. But then the demands of the Knights of Abraham grew too great and, one by one, the women had to be bled to death to meet the needs of you and your chums."

"But before that, the women learned from you too," Gerald said, his voice distant, as if his mind was somewhere else. "They discovered how to use their own blood to cure illness and injury."

"Some of them," O'Neill admitted. "They should have been more careful. People did not understand the nature of this wonder. Word got out about their abilities. That was why they became known as witches."

"Parasites . . . witches . . . the blood of the insane," Angstrom wheezed, leaning against the edge of the table. "What have you involved me in? This is what we used to cure some of the greatest men in this land? All my work, my research . . . based on the blood of *witches*? We infused the great and the good with the blood of Devil-worshippers?" He staggered around the table, his hands curled into talons. "What in God's name have you done to me? I am ruined. *I am damned!*"

"Hold on there!" Nate shouted, but to no avail. Angstrom was beyond reasoning.

The doctor's hands closed around O'Neill's neck, seeking to choke the life out of him. O'Neill punched and clawed at the bigger man, but Angstrom felt nothing, such was his fury. He paid no heed to the guns pointed at him, even when Nate fired off a shot. The baby started screaming louder. Nate went to grab the enraged doctor and then, fearing for the baby he cradled in his arm, held back. But Gerald was already moving. He aimed his pistol and fired a shot into the back of Angstrom's calf.

The doctor screamed and fell back, his head cracking against the edge of the table. He was unconscious before he slammed into the flagstoned floor.

"Bugger," Gerald grunted. "I didn't mean for him to hit his head. We might need it."

"Good riddance to him," O'Neill gasped. "I hope he never wakes up."

The baby was still shrieking at the top of his voice and they all winced at the sound.

"How do we get him to stop?" Nate called out over the noise, still keeping his gun on O'Neill.

"I don't know . . . feed it?" Gerald suggested.

Nate regarded the screaming bundle for a moment.

"With what?" he asked.

"It needs its mother," Clancy called from the top of the stairs. "Shall I take it from you, sir?"

"God, yes," Nate replied, heading for the stairs. "Send a telegram to Daisy; tell her to come quickly and to bring Elizabeth." He looked back. "Gerald? Make sure that blackguard stays put for the moment. I need to sort all this out. This could turn into a God-awful mess if the Knights of Abraham get involved. Berto's going to have half the country banging on his door."

Then he was gone, with Clancy and the baby, and silence settled over the underground laboratory. Gerald pulled up a chair and gestured to O'Neill to sit down in it, which the older man did, rubbing his bruised throat and coughing. Leaning against the table next to him, O'Neill looked up at Gerald with an expression of defeat in his tired eyes.

"So," said Gerald, "you studied our blood."

"I did. And if you really are Gerald Gordon, then you will know what I found. I have read your articles on immunity in *The Lancet*. They were quite brilliant. I noticed how careful you were not to mention your family's special qualities, however, even though you must have explored them yourself.

"Angstrom never understood. He experimented on beggars down here in his 'laboratory'; trying to understand how their brains worked; fumbling around inside their skulls. He never comprehended the importance of the blood that kept his sub-jects alive.

"I realized it, of course. After Vicky Miller went under his knife—had her thyroid gland worked on—and then made a complete recovery only a few weeks later. I never told him, but I helped her escape, and many more like her. In return for my help in starting new lives—and keeping their secrets—they each gave me some of their blood on a regular basis. Their healing powers were extraordinary. But in the end they couldn't give me enough to serve the needs of the Knights. I had to start having them drained completely."

"The burnings hid the evidence—the importance of their blood," Gerald added.

"Yes." O'Neill nodded. "The whole 'witches' story was a useful distraction, though I suppose there was some truth in it. Vicky, in particular, was a formidable woman—no shrinking violet, that one. And startlingly intelligent. I loved her, you know. My men took plenty of others before I could bear to send them for her, but in the end I needed what she had. The most potent blood flowed in her veins."

He put his head back, his eyes closed, as if fondly recalling a childhood memory.

"You know she killed one of the men who took her blood? She was barely conscious, her dress already smoldering, and she crushed his throat with a blow. The other men fled, but she burned anyway, it seems. My chaps tidied things up later, but we've been more careful ever since."

Gerald was studying the diagrams on the wall, hoping to learn more about O'Neill's research, but there was nothing there that offered anything new.

The other man watched him, a smile playing on the corners of his mouth.

"I do most of my own work at home," O'Neill told him. "I would very much like to pay a visit to your residence at some point. Your laboratory must be a fascinating place. Are the rumors true? That in families such as yours, you prey on each other? That your powers are such that you brought some of your ancestors back from the dead? The woman—Elizabeth—she was one of them, wasn't she? I would have loved to study her child."

"Yes, I am deeply moved by your heartfelt sorrow over the deaths of the women," Gerald snorted. "I'm sure you would have treated the infant with suitable tenderness."

"I would not have hurt him—he is a marvel, something to be treasured."

"We guard our pedigree jealously," Gerald replied. "There are few outside the family who are party to our secrets. Your research cannot be allowed to continue."

"Naturally . . . your benevolent parasites give you a superb advantage. It would be foolish to give it up."

"'Benevolent parasites'? Is that what you call them? An interesting name, but short-sighted, I think. And I do not think they are alive, in the normal sense of the word. I prefer to call them *intelligent particles*."

"A suitable term, though I prefer my own. Where do they come from, do you think?"

"I don't know. Nor can I understand why a civilization that

could create these wonders did not leave buildings or roads or the like, as other ancient civilizations have. It is the most sublime mystery. But certainly, I think the engimals are key to understanding the particles."

"I agree absolutely; they are the stepping stones. Tell me, have you had any success in replicating these particles, or perhaps *communicating* with them?" O'Neill asked.

"Communication? You mean with mathaumaturgy? If I had, why would I tell you?"

"Because like me, you relish the thrill of scientific discovery. We could work together, pool resources and share ideas. Numbers are definitely the key, the alphabet, if you like. But the mathematics are so incredibly complicated and unwieldy, aren't they? And how do we make these clunky numbers into reality, eh? You have to wonder if there might not be a more . . . *instinctive* way of transmitting your intentions. I don't think you have managed to crack these tiny enigmas; I must admit, nor have I. Perhaps, together, we might."

"Perhaps I am happy to work alone," Gerald responded. "And I don't care one whit for your methods."

O'Neill nodded slowly.

They fell silent. There was so much that each man wanted to talk about with the other; neither had ever had such a kindred spirit and both regretted the circumstances under which they now met. A minute passed as they regarded one another, and then O'Neill started to whistle.

It immediately made Gerald uncomfortable.

"Stop that," he said.

But O'Neill persisted in his whistling. Gerald recognized the tune; it was "La Campanella" by Liszt . . . or was it Paganini? He couldn't remember. "Stop it," he said again.

It was a catchy little number. Gerald found it very hard to keep his concentration on anything but the whistled notes. They sent his mind whirling into flights of imagination; raindrops and birds, feet dancing in puddles . . .

He came to his senses to discover that he had laid the pistol down on the table, within reach of O'Neill's hand. For an instant he was so stunned he did not move. O'Neill lunged for the gun. Gerald's foot kicked out across O'Neill's forearm, breaking it against the edge of the table. The older man cried out as the bones gave with a dull cracking sound, but he had reached far enough forward to snatch the gun with his other hand.

Gerald brought the edge of his own hand around hard onto the side of O'Neill's neck, stunning him. Taking O'Neill's head in the crook of his arm, much as Nate had cradled the baby, he hesitated.

O'Neill pursed his lips to whistle again and, with an abrupt twist, Gerald broke the man's neck. He let the limp corpse slump to the floor. Straightening his rumpled collar, Gerald took his cigarette case and a box of matches from the pocket of his coat. He waited for his breathing to settle and then he struck a match, lighting one of the gaspers. As he smoked, his eyes fell on the pistol where it still lay on the table.

"So . . . an instinctive way of transmitting your intentions," he said to himself. "Yes. That was *very* interesting."

XXXIII

A BIZARRE APOLOGY

DAISY MADE HER WAY SLOWLY along the corridor towards the conservatory. She was in no hurry to keep this appointment. Ainsley had asked to see her. What with him helping Gideon in the assassination attempt on Berto and all that, she had little interest in talking to him. Once she had assured herself that the derringer bullets she had shot into his body had been removed and he was likely to live, she had not set eyes on him again. It would not be long before he was well enough to travel; then his exile would begin. And not a moment too soon, as far as she was concerned.

She gazed absent-mindedly at the paintings on the walls as she walked. The artwork in most of the corridors of Wildenstern Hall had a theme. This corridor was lined with Orthodox Christian icons from Russia, painted with egg tempera onto wooden panels, embellished with gold or silver leaf. They were flat images, stylized and serious, giving the hallway a somber feel. She had always liked them before, but now she was not so sure.

Her thoughts turned to Angstrom—a so-called man of God. He was being tended to by Dr. Warburton in the family's infirmary, but he still had not regained consciousness, a full day after the raid on the asylum. Warburton was beginning to suspect he never would.

Inspector Urskin, suspicious of the family's motives, had demanded that Angstrom be moved to a more neutral location. Petitions to reinforce these demands had been sent to Berto by two distinguished police officers, a British general, the Lord Mayor of Dublin and even the Archbishop of Armagh.

So far, Berto had ignored them all. But it was a political nightmare and it was not going to go away. Berto, Nate, Gerald and Daisy were all determined to hold onto Angstrom until he woke up and could be persuaded to tell them all he knew about the Wildenstern women. They feared that if he were allowed to leave he would disappear before he could stand trial for his crimes, aided by his powerful friends.

And so the Wildensterns were wielding some power of their own.

Nate had found Angstrom's admissions book. Daisy had still to study it properly, but there were hundreds of women's names there; nearly thirty years worth of miserable incarceration. Not just Wildensterns, but many others from prominent families too, including dynasties like the Bismarcks and Medicis, who hailed from outside Ireland.

Elizabeth and her husband had been brought into the house,

much to everyone's discomfort. Nathaniel still did not seem to know what to do about the fact that he had a son.

Daisy wanted to get this conversation with Ainsley over and done with. For Mrs. Behan had supplied another useful titbit of information: Edgar Wildenstern had kept a journal. And though Elvira had never known where it was hidden, she had clues to its whereabouts. If they could find Edgar's diaries, they might not need Angstrom after all. Nobody else had been told yet. Nate and Berto were on their way upstairs to Edgar's study now, and Daisy wanted to join them as soon as she could.

Ainsley was sitting in a wheelchair—Roberto's old one—bathing in the golden afternoon light that flooded into the conservatory. His brother, Oliver, was there too. Daisy took a long breath and glided in.

"Ah, Daisy!" Ainsley exclaimed. "Thank you for agreeing to meet me. Oliver, would you give us a moment?"

Oliver glowered at his younger brother; but then, he glowered at everybody and it had ceased to have any effect. He stood, brushing some imaginary lint from his suit jacket. As he passed Daisy, his hand went up to the waxed tip of his handlebar mustache for a moment, and he paused beside her.

"Do you think you can exile everyone who crosses you, hmm?" he muttered. "A family will not go against its nature, that's what I say. Driving Ainsley away will not achieve a thing. Be sure of that. We will not let you bring down the empire that Uncle Edgar and my father spent their lives building. Their legacy will stand long after Roberto has gone the way of the dodo."

She gave him her best chilly smile.

"Shouldn't you be supervising some ditch-digging some-where, Oliver? We would not want our land to be swamped by your slurry."

He scowled at her again, then turned on his heel and left.

Ainsley watched him go and sighed with a rueful smile.

"Pay him no mind," he said, breathing with difficulty. "He has not taken the departure of our father well. Not that they got on at all, but he feels there's a principle to be observed. He's been throwing abuse around left, right and center, but it's all wind and water. Thank you for coming to see me."

"How are you feeling?" Daisy inquired, forcing herself to be polite. "I'm sorry I haven't been to see you before this."

Ainsley gave a grunt that could have been a laugh.

"Can't really blame you, can I? That's why I asked for you. I wanted to apologize."

"*Really?*" Daisy's tone was skeptical.

"No, it's the truth. Attacking you was a most un-gentlemanly act. You were not supposed to be there and I would have pre-ferred to wait until Berto was alone, but my father is an impulsive fool. No lady should be witness to such violence, and should cer-tainly never be the victim of it. I am dreadfully sorry."

"So . . . you are apologizing for attacking me, but not for attempting to murder my husband," Daisy replied. "I have to say, it is quite the most bizarre apology I have ever received."

"It is the best I can offer," Ainsley said, shrugging. "I acted according to my family's values—it is . . . it is how I was brought up. And now I face exile . . . and I deserve my fate. But I won-dered . . . I thought perhaps . . . "

His voice drifted off. Daisy lifted her eyebrows, but said nothing.

"I was wondering if I could write to you . . . and . . . and you to me?" he asked gently. "My parents are already in exile and my brothers . . . well, they are not exactly the writing type. I would very much like to keep in touch with the family in some way."

There was sincerity in his eyes and in his voice, and Daisy was touched by it. Perhaps Berto was right. It was possible for this family to change.

"All right, then," she agreed. "Then I shall write to you on occasion. And in return, perhaps you could tell me who drove your father to this senseless assault."

"I wish I knew," Ainsley replied. "For I would very much like to catch the blackguard myself. I'll tell you this, though: Edgar Wildenstern may have kept this family together when he was Patriarch, but he got to where he was by playing his relatives against each other. And then he took the spoils. Whoever this blighter is, he's an apt student of Edgar's, and he's working the game in the same way—pitting us against each other, but staying out of it himself. I'll warrant that he won't be content with removing Berto. What, and just move up a rank or two? No. This one wants rid of us all."

Nate stood beside Berto's wheelchair in the middle of their dead father's study. This place brought back unpleasant memories for both of them—most of which had to do with meetings with their father.

Apart from a light dusting from time to time, the room had

not been changed since Edgar's death. The place was huge, with a vaulted ceiling braced by carved oak beams. The walls were lined with bookshelves, paintings and hunting trophies, and above the fireplace, a display of edged weapons from all over the world.

Both Nate and Berto looked to the corners of the room, where two elegant black men would always have stood. Edgar's personal servants, they had been taken as young children from a Maasai tribe in Kenya. There had always been two of the four waiting in those corners—each nearly seven feet tall and dressed in immaculate black uniforms. Trained from childhood to serve and protect their master, they would wait silent and unnoticed until he beckoned them. After helping to avenge Edgar's death, the Maasai servants had returned to their homeland.

Apart from the footmen, the space had been shared with three bull mastiffs, hulking dogs with square heads that treated the place as if they owned it. They were gone now too, but Nate was sure he could still smell them.

Edgar Wildenstern's desk was nearly ten feet wide and made of solid teak. The tall teak and leather chair still stood behind it, and it was easy for them to imagine their father sitting there once more, a cigar clamped between his teeth, his white-whisker-lined face like that of a wild boar glaring back at them. The crab-like engimal claw that had replaced his right hand would click when he was irritated. His bass voice was not often raised, but when it was, they would have sworn the ceiling shook with it.

"Do you remember we used to hear screams from the attic?" Berto said quietly. "I thought—I hoped—it was just the wind because we were so high up here, but I think now they were screams. I still shiver to think of it."

Nate nodded. His brother had never moved into this study—it made him uncomfortable, and Nate could not blame him. Ever since the deaths of Edgar and their eldest brother, Marcus, this room had taken on a haunted quality. It had been left here like this until they could decide what to do with it.

"We should take this place apart and do something useful with it," he said at last. "It's a beautiful room and its windows have the best views in the country. It's a crime to waste it like this."

"Yes. And it might seem to some that we've created a shrine to the old monster," Berto said, "and we can't have that. But let's find these diaries first. I thought we'd combed his lair for anything useful: it's a wonder we didn't come across them. What was it Mrs. Behan said again?"

"She said Elvira always referred to Father 'hiding his secrets beneath the roses.' Thought she was being terribly clever, apparently."

They looked at each other for a moment.

"Well, I think we can assume that she wasn't talking about actual *flowers*," Berto declared. "It being Father and all that."

"Obviously."

They both lifted their eyes to the ornately shaped plasterwork of the ceiling. There were four small chandeliers, each hanging from the center of a ceiling rose, a circular plaster decoration of leaves and flowers. The plasterwork was a good twenty feet up.

"Too high to be convenient," Berto said.

"Not these ones," Nate replied, walking over to the nearest wall.

Most well-appointed rooms in this era had dado rails running at about waist height along the walls. This room was no exception. But the architects had gone one better, decorating the plaster above the wooden rail with intricate carvings that included tiny little plaster roses. They went all the way around the room. Nate ran his fingers over one. "Any of these could operate a latch of some kind."

Both young men were well-accustomed to using secret doors.

"There's got to be a few hundred of the wretched things," Berto retorted. "Where do we start?"

"Where would you put a hidden door, if you were Father?"

"Given the number of people who wanted him dead, I'd have it as close to hand as possible."

Nate went around to the wall behind the desk. Running his fingers over the little circular features, he found one that was slightly grubbier than the others—from being pressed many times over the years, no doubt. He pushed on it gently and felt it give. There was a click and he expected a door to open in front of him, but nothing happened.

Then, to his surprise, the entire room started to move upwards.

The section of floorboards he was standing on sank quickly into the floor, gliding down quietly on greased rails. Somewhere, a counter-weight mechanism was operating. A spring-loaded trap door went to close over the opening above him, but he reached up and caught it, pushing it back into place so Berto could see down into the little room that he had found.

There was a low door off to one side which, Nate was certain, offered a quick escape route down through the building, but the rest of the wall space was taken up with shelves and shelves of leather-bound notebooks.

"Oh, well done, old chap!" Berto called down.

Nate took one out at random and opened it, recognizing his father's handwriting.

The peasant unrest grows as the water mold known as 'potato blight' spreads, rotting the vegetables in the ground. Hardly a crop seems untouched. The lowest of humanity have been hit hardest; soon there will be no food for the winter. They know they will starve, and they aim their anger at the landed gentry. Harsh measures will have to be taken to maintain order. This is not the first time in our history that the rabble's food has become infected, and it won't be the last. It will change nothing in the long run.

Nate looked at the date. November 1845; the year the Great Famine began.

"There's a lot of them, isn't there?" Berto muttered. "I suppose the old bugger did live for more than a hundred years—do you think it's all in there? Looks like someone's going to have to do a lot of reading."

"We can't allow anyone else to see these," Nate called up to his brother. "At least, not yet. God knows what's in here. We have to get them out of the house and put them somewhere only we know about."

"Agreed."

Nate replaced the notebook where he had found it and located the lever that would send the mechanical section of floor back up to the study. He was about to pull it, when he noticed something. There was a thin film of dust on everything down here. Obviously the cleaning staff did not know about this room, and even though it had not been used for some time, he doubted if his father would have allowed it to be cleaned much when he was alive.

Where his fingers had brushed across the spines of the notebooks to take the one out, Nate had left three barely perceptible streaks in the dust. Only a foot away from them, he saw a similar mark. Looking around him, he found others. There was a small oil lamp sitting on the floor in one corner. He stooped down and picked it up. Opening it, he sniffed at the wick.

"Berto? Someone's been down here recently."

"Well, that won't do. Right, come on up out of there and let's get these bloody things moved."

Nate was rising back through the floor when Daisy entered with Tatty on her heels.

"In any other house, that would be unusual," Tatty commented.

"We've found the journals," Berto announced.

"We've found something else," Daisy replied, holding up Angstrom's admissions book. "Nate, Berto . . . your mother's name is in here. She was held for over a year in the asylum before being taken out again . . . by your father."

Nate and Berto were dumbstruck. They leaned over the desk as Daisy laid the ledger on the surface, opening it to the page she had marked.

"You see? Miriam Wildenstern, it says it right here: *Committed by her husband, Edgar Wildenstern, on 14 June 1846*, a few months after Tatiana's birth, and then further on, just over a year later: *Released into the care of Edgar Wildenstern, 10 October 1847.*"

"But . . . but she was dead by October 1847, wasn't she?" Tatty asked her brothers. "She died of influenza after I was born. I mean, there was a funeral and everything, wasn't there? You were at it, you said. She died after I was born, didn't she?"

"That's what we were told," Berto murmured.

Nate didn't say a word. He flopped back into his father's chair and stared up at the ceiling. "This can't be right," he rasped. "Father loved her. We all know that. He hardly felt a thing for anybody except Marcus, but he loved Mother. Everyone said it about him. He was devastated when she died. Marcus used to say that a part of Father went with her when she left."

"Perhaps," Berto said in a thoughtful tone, "she didn't go so very far at all. Do you remember, Nate? The screams from the attic. Perhaps our dearly departed mother was closer to us than any of us realized."

XXXIV

A SAD MELODY

ROBERTO SAT NERVOUSLY in his wheelchair, drumming his fingers on its arm. He had asked his manservant to leave him alone for a few minutes. Sitting in his dressing room facing a full-length mirror, he gazed at the picture it presented. He was the Wildenstern Patriarch, dressed in the finest tailored suit money could buy, his blond hair coiffed, his face freshly shaven, his useless feet resting in shoes that cost more than some peasants would pay for a house. Roberto Wildenstern was a physically broken man, a cripple.

Or so everyone thought.

He had taken to pinching the flesh of his thighs when no one was watching. It had been so long since he had any feeling below his waist. But that sensation was coming back.

The irony did not escape him. Angstrom and O'Neill had built their research on *aurea sanitas*, though it seemed that Angstrom had not known it. Berto's own healing powers had failed to restore function to his spinal cord. And, despite their understanding of *aurea sanitas*, neither Warburton nor Gerald was skilled enough to surgically repair the damage. Other, more accomplished surgeons—unaware that they would be aided by the Wildenstern's special qualities—would not even attempt the operation. Instead, the Knights of Abraham had unknowingly transfused Berto with his own family's blood and the skills of Angstrom and O'Neill had achieved the rest.

He felt the shame over the women's deaths lying on his skin like chilly, greasy slime, and dismay that this shame could not blot out the elation of his ongoing recovery.

Roberto allowed himself a little smile. He could flex his toes now; feel the footboard of the wheelchair beneath his soles. His legs were suffused with a heavy numbness that was gradually fading. The flesh he pinched between finger and thumb felt the beginnings of pain.

He would announce it at dinner. But there was something he had to do first. Gripping the arms of the wheelchair, he edged his hips forward, then, lifting his legs at the knees, he slipped one foot off the footrest and then the other. The engimal anticipated his intention and its arms extended, gripping Berto's waist as he pushed himself up. It caught him by surprise for a moment, but he gratefully let the creature support him. Grunting with the effort, he shifted his weight onto his feet.

The atrophied muscles in his legs only just managed to hold

them rigid. His knees were weak and he had to place one hand on the wall and tip himself forward until he could lock his knees and hold himself upright. His hands were braced against the wall, but he was doing it. He was standing. He was standing!

Berto panted, catching his breath, a near-hysterical laugh expelling from his mouth. He was standing! Tears formed in his eyes. Staring at himself in the mirror, his first thought was of Hennessy. He couldn't wait to show his old friend. But Daisy should know first. And Nate. He would show them all at dinner.

It was at that moment he thought he heard violin music. Yes, he was sure of it. It sounded like Chopin's Nocturne in C-sharp minor. It was a piece he loved, though it always made him think of his mother, who used to hum it when she was doing her embroidery. Its sad melody sent a shiver down his spine. With a start, he realized that if he was caught standing up, it would spoil the surprise at dinner. He hurriedly lowered himself into the chair and lifted his legs onto the footboard.

The music was not coming from the hallway, he realized. Or his bedroom. Instead, it seemed to be coming from the wall. There was a secret passage on the other side of that wall. Only he and Nathaniel and a couple of trusted servants knew of its existence. Berto turned his wheelchair to face the section of walnut paneling that disguised the entrance to the passageway. He curled his fingers around the arm of the chair, caressing the trigger of the hidden blade-thrower. The engimal tensed beneath him.

The music stopped, and there was a click on the other side of the panel. The violin started playing again as the panel swung open.

"What the Devil are *you* up to?" Berto exclaimed, thumping

the arm of the chair. "You nearly gave me a heart attack, you blockhead, bursting in like that! What are you doing here? How did you know about that passage . . . ? And since when did you go in for the violin?"

As with so many events in a manor house, the servants found out first. Berto's man made the discovery and told Clancy. Clancy hurried to Nathaniel's side, leaning in to whisper in his master's ear as Nate sat waiting for his brother to appear at the dinner table. Berto was often late. It had not occurred to him to be concerned. With a hoarse cry, he jumped to his feet, his chair falling over and skidding backwards. He turned and raced out of the room and along the hallway to the mechanical lifts.

Nate waited for the elevator to carry him up the twenty-six floors to Berto's rooms. His fists were clenched so tightly that his nails pierced the skin of his palms, drawing blood. The boy working the lift turned away, cowering from the expression on the master's face. His terror escalated when the master began making a growling sound from behind his bared teeth. Nathaniel's body trembled as he stared intently at the polished brass doors of the lift.

The bell chimed, and Nate forced his way through the doors before they were fully open, sprinting down the hallway to the entrance to Berto's dressing room. Berto's new manservant was standing outside, struggling to maintain his composure against the consternation he was feeling. He flinched as Nate strode past him and pushed the door open.

Roberto sat in his wheelchair, his body in calm repose. His head had been cut completely from his neck and sat in his lap, his face frozen in an expression of mild surprise. The single bullet hole in his forehead explained the remarkable lack of blood. His heart had stopped before he'd been decapitated. The assassin had simply wanted to be sure he could not recover from the bullet wound. He was a Wildenstern, after all.

Even so, the collar of his shirt, his shoulders, back and chest were soaked with blood and his head had bled out onto his thighs. Nate staggered forward, falling to his knees in front of his brother. For seconds, no scream would issue from his lips . . . and then it scraped up his throat and grated from his mouth like a petrified breath bursting from its bonds. He tried to inhale, but couldn't, choking on his shock, his shoulders twitching as his lungs fought for air.

At last, it all came out in a wail of pain and sobs that shook his body. For a while Nate could manage no words. And then they emerged. At first they were unintelligible. Then the servants were able to make out what he was saying: "I'm sorry! Oh, God . . . God . . . my poor brother, I am so sorry! I am so sorry! Look what they've done to you, my brother. I am so, so sorry! *Look what they've done!*"

There was a scream from behind him. The servants had been so focused on Nate that they had not noticed Daisy approaching. She stood in the doorway, and let out a shriek. Her legs gave way beneath her and Clancy was there, supporting her and calling for some of the maids.

"*Noooo!*" she screamed. "Oh, my love! My Berto! No, dear God, no!" Her cries broke down into hysterical sobs. She uttered a few more gasping words: "What have you monsters done to him? Oh, my love, oh . . . *Dear God, no!* What have you monsters done?"

Her shrieks carried on down the hallway as the maids tried to drag their mistress away from the horrific scene. Daisy fought them, clawed at them, tearing at their hair, trying to get back to her dead husband. But she grew weak, lifting her head as she was carried away, wailing at the ceiling like a banshee.

"Clancy!" Nate coughed.

"Here, sir."

"Tatty mustn't see. She must not see him like this. Make sure of it."

"Of course, sir."

Instructions were issued. The door was shut. Only Clancy remained in the room with Nate and his dead brother. Nate hugged Berto's calves, laying his head against the corpse's knees, weeping uncontrollably.

He did not know how long he knelt there, but when he raised his eyes, he found himself staring into the face of his brother's decapitated head.

"I will find them, Berto," he said through his teeth, spit flying from his mouth. "I swear on my life, I won't rest until I've found the bastards who did this to you. And when I do, they'll *pray for death* before I'm finished with them. They will breathe blood and beg for death. *They will beg for Hell itself.*"

Nate got to his feet, staring with a dull expression at his brother. He felt empty, exhausted and without hope. Clancy was still standing by the door and Nate, not knowing what else to do, went over to him and said in a voice like a child's:

"My big brother's dead."

Clancy pulled him close and held him tight. Nate wrapped

his arms around his manservant and clung there as if his grief might wash him away.

"I'm sorry, lad," the older man said to him. "I'm so sorry."

Nathaniel and Daisy walked in the garden, both dressed in black, heedless of the rain that fell around them. A day had passed since Roberto's murder. Tatiana had taken to her bed. She was inconsolable, crying constantly, rejecting any offers of comfort or support.

The wind had a chill quality that bit through Daisy's damp dress and shawl, but she ignored it.

"I am sick to my stomach of this family," she was saying, her throat raw from sobbing. "Tatiana and I are going to leave after the funeral. We will stay with my family in Ballsbridge until we decide what to do with ourselves."

"Don't take Tatty away from me," Nate said hoarsely. "She's the only thing that can keep me human."

Daisy did not reply immediately. There was an ever-present pressure behind her eyes and nose, a stricture in her throat that threatened to cause her to burst into tears at any moment. Speaking was still a struggle.

"I would think that sparing Tatty's character from any more horror is more important," she said at last. "You should not take this on yourself, Nathaniel. Let the Law handle the Wildenstern crimes. It's about time. If you look for revenge, then someone else will seek it against you. Let the Law into the house and have the courts deal with it."

"The courts would not be capable of it. Have you any idea how complicated these knots of conspiracy are? The family would just unite against any outsiders. Nothing would be accomplished."

"I still say revenge is not the answer. It is not what Berto would have wanted. We should serve these animals up to the Law and pray for Berto's soul."

"*Berto's* soul?" Nate exclaimed, coming to an abrupt halt and turning to face her. "Berto was the best of us. He was kinder, gentler and more forgiving than any of us. He still had faith that this family could change long after you and I gave up. He *tried* to be a good Christian, even when Christians would happily have thrown him in prison. If God is not welcoming his soul with open arms, then what hope is there for any of us?"

He started walking again, faster this time, his long strides forcing Daisy to lag behind at the more dignified pace demanded by her dress and shoes.

"If there is a God," he went on, "He cares nothing for what is good or right. Either we are pawns in some great entertainment, or Gerald is right, and none of it means anything at all. The Bible and its like are the contradictory ramblings of some long-dead preachers who are saved from having to argue their case. Whichever it may be, I will pay no more heed to the wisdom of dead men, no matter how holy they might be."

"As if you ever did!" Daisy called after him. "At least Berto *tried*!"

"Yes, and look where it got him!" Nate retorted, spinning around to glare at her. "Take Tatty away then, if you must. I will stay here and clean up the mess. But then I'll be leaving too. And I'll be going a damn sight further than Ballsbridge!"

They stood there in the rain, some ten yards apart, gazing at each other. Then they each chose a different path back to the house.

Daisy's course took her close to the stables. Beyond the low building, she saw a figure standing with a horse near the gate to the main paddock. She recognized the slightly stooped form of Hennessy. Despite her dislike for the man, she thought she should go over and say a few words to him. She could never forgive him for being the reason for her husband's unfaithfulness, but he too had lost someone dear to him. They had that in common at least.

The middle-aged man was standing with his brow pressed against the horse's neck. The horse did not move, paying no heed to the rain pelting down on its back, perhaps content to have this contact with the kind man who never failed to tend to its needs. Daisy stopped a few yards from the pair and cleared her throat.

Hennessy pulled away with a start.

"Beggin' Yer Paardon, Yer Grace," he said in his broad Donegal accent, wiping what might be tears or rainwater from his face. "Ah didnae hear yeh comin' up on mae. Ah haven't had the opportunitae to offer mae condolences, ma'am. Ah'm sorry for yer loss."

"Thank you, Hennessy. And it is I who should apologize for sneaking up on you so," Daisy replied. She hesitated, unsure of how to continue. The groom would not be comfortable relating to her in anything other than their normal mistress—servant manner, but he was entitled to better than that.

"Hennessy, I know you are familiar by now with the etiquette of our funerals. It would not normally be appropriate for staff to come inside the church or to attend the graveside."

"Of course, ma'am," he said, nodding. "We all know our places dinestairs. Ah've seen more deaths in this family then most. But this wan must surely be the worst of all of 'em. Et's . . . et's desperate saad."

Like any good servant, he avoided her gaze without looking so far away as to seem disrespectful. The horse nuzzled his neck and he gently pushed it back.

"We will naturally need pallbearers to carry the coffin," Daisy told him, taking her turn to look away awkwardly, clasping her fingers tightly together. "The Duke's brother has insisted on being one himself. I would very much like you to be another. I know the Duke had a . . . a fondness for you. It would require you to be close at hand, both at the church and by the graveside."

"Et would be an honor, Yer Grace," he uttered through a constricted throat, his face quivering. "Thank you, ma'am."

"Thank you, Hennessy," she replied, before turning and walking away through the rain.

Nate crouched beside Leopold, watching the child play with the wooden blocks. Leopold was strong, healthy and extremely perceptive for his age, as all Wildensterns were expected to be. He handed a block to Nate, who took it and passed it around behind his back and out the other side, as he done seven times before in the last few minutes.

Leopold laughed as if he had never seen the trick before. This was his favorite new game. Nate gave him back the block. Leopold put it behind his back and then took it out the same side. Looking at his other, empty hand, he seemed disappointed with the result. He picked up another block and handed it to Nate.

"Again!" he demanded excitedly.

"Nathaniel, to what do I owe the pleasure?" a voice asked from the doorway.

Nate stood up, straightening his jacket. Elizabeth stood there, looking resplendent in a long red silk gown embroidered with roses.

"Is that how you dress when you're grieving?" Nate asked sourly. "Your Patriarch is dead."

"I'm not grieving, I'm celebrating," she replied with a smile. "I'm back with my family. But I am sorry for *your* loss, of course. My condolences and all that."

"Yes, Your Grace; my wife and I offer our most sincere condolences." The nondescript man in a black suit and tie spoke from over Elizabeth's shoulder. "It is a most terrible loss."

James Nevin had completely failed to make any kind of impression since coming to live in Wildenstern Hall. As a clerk, he was lower in rank than anyone in the house other than the staff. And he had the extra curse of being married to the most hated woman in the family. On top of all this, the fact that he had no discernible personality conspired to make him almost invisible.

Nate ignored him.

"I am here on an important matter," he said to Elizabeth. "We have still not discovered who killed Roberto, and since I am now Patriarch—"

"Yes, isn't that fortunate for you!" Elizabeth exclaimed.

"Since I am now Patriarch, I am likely to be the assassin's next target. As Leopold is my son—or so you claim"—he looked to Nevin to contradict him, but nothing was forthcoming—"then he is now the Heir, which makes him a target too."

"And what do you mean to do about it?" Elizabeth asked.

"You need to hide somewhere until the funeral is over and I have time to deal with you properly. That's no easy task; it needs to be somewhere neither my family nor the Knights of Abraham can find you. Thankfully, I have just the place in mind."

"Really? I trust this refuge offers a level of comfort appropriate to someone in my position?"

"No," said Nate. "It doesn't."

XXXV

PLANNING FOR THE FUTURE

ORGANIZING A WILDENSTERN FUNERAL was no simple matter, and the funeral of a Patriarch posed the greatest problems of all. Berto had been unpopular among the old guard in his family, but he had been well thought of by many more. Hundreds, perhaps thousands were expected to attend. Unlike the funeral processions of his forebears, the family had not insisted that all their employees and tenants line the route. But still, the sides of the road between the gates of the house and the family's chapel, a mile down the hill, were thronging with people by mid-morning.

Members of the family had come from all corners of the country; a few had even made it over from mainland Britain in time. Of the immediate family, only Silas was not present. Being out in the middle of the Atlantic, he could not be contacted.

All these extra relatives had to be accommodated, along with the dozens of other guests and hundreds of friends, colleagues and business associates. Some of most important figures in the land would be attending and had to be made comfortable before the service. The Lord Lieutenant of Ireland, two archbishops—one of whom would handle the service personally—industrialists, generals from the Army, admirals from the Navy, mayors and members of parliament. On top of all the grand funeral arrangements, food had to be laid on, the house had to be cleaned from top to bottom—even more than usual—and every piece of brass, silver and gold polished until it gleamed. The staff were pushed to their limits.

And Daisy oversaw all of it.

In the meantime, Nate was responsible for security. With thousands of people in and around the estate, protecting the great and the good of Irish society was paramount. The Fenian rebels were still active throughout the country, harrying the British and anyone who dealt with them. He had a meeting with some of the Fenian leaders to ensure that no foul play would be committed, but he took precautions anyway. Armed guards, some in uniform, but many in plain clothes, supplemented the huge police presence.

The year before, a massive explosion had caused carnage during Marcus's funeral. That had been an accident, but it had highlighted the risk a well-placed bomb could pose. Clancy had led a team of men in a search for any trace of explosives in or around the church and graveyard.

It was his own family that Nate most feared, however, and he only allowed those he trusted most to deal with the important elements of the funeral. It was late morning before everything was ready and the family was preparing to leave the house and make its way to the chapel. They were all gathering in the hall-way, awaiting Daisy, Tatiana and Nathaniel.

The two young women were adding the finishing touches to their appearance. They had been so busy with everyone else's needs, they themselves were running behind. Nate had gone looking for Cathal, who had disappeared. He found the boy in Gerald's laboratory, sitting on a stool holding Vicky Miller's ser-pentine in his hands, and stroking it tenderly. The snake-like engimal had coiled its white three-foot length around the boy's arm and shoulder, and looked completely at ease. It lifted its head and regarded Nate with its silvery eyes.

"I knew it," Nate said when he found the lad. "You've seen this thing before. Why didn't you tell us?"

"Ma said it was secret," Cathal replied. "No one was to know. Don't suppose it matters now. She's not yours, anyhow. Her name's Apple. Mrs. Miller would have wanted me ma to have her; Ma was the only one close to her. And Ma would have left it to me. You can't just go takin' things that aren't yours, y'know."

Nate took Cathal's arm and helped him down off the stool. Examining the lad's new suit, he nodded in approval and took the serpentine from him.

"You're right, of course. But we needed to know what this creature did, and for that, Gerald had to examine it. Not that he's had any luck. But *you* know, don't you? Why won't you tell us, Cathal? We're on your side. You're family, whether you were brought up to think it or not."

"I've seen what happens in your family," Cathal retorted. "I'll not be havin' any of it. I'll take me snake back now, if you please. You've no right to take it—and I don't trust that Gerald fella with it. I've seen what he does to engimals. He'll cut it open, give 'im half a chance."

"I haven't time to be arguing with you," Nate snapped at him, taking the serpentine from the boy and putting it back in its box. "Come on. I've a brother to bury today."

He was just closing the lid of the box, when the snake started singing. Nate stopped, staring down at the engimal. It fixed its eyes on him, swaying its head from side to side. Nate felt a warmth wash over him, touching him to the core. Tears welled in his eyes. With an abrupt movement, he closed the box.

"If you're sick, Apple makes you well," Cathal said. "It sings you better. It's like it talks to these things inside of you. The singin' is a way of tellin' them what to do. Your fearsome agents, an' all that. Can even stick new ones into you if you need 'em."

Pushing the boy ahead of him, Nate strode out of the laboratory.

"Come along now, I've more than enough 'fearsome agents' to contend with, without that thing singing up more. And I can assure you, I'm not the one who will need healing."

Nate and Cathal came out of the mechanical lift and were about to emerge from the corridor into the main hallway, when Nate stopped, grabbing the boy's shoulder and pulling him into an alcove next to a medieval suit of armor. There were over fifty Wildensterns in the hallway, and Nate could hear snippets of their conversations from where he stood.

"It's well and truly blown things wide open, don't y'know," Oliver was saying. "Things are going to change around here now. Perhaps we can start undoing all the damage that Berto's done to the business, that's what I say."

"Eh?" Elvira shouted.

"I don't think he's done so badly," Ainsley argued. "Our profits have hardly dropped at all, and there's been no trouble from the Fenians in the last year. But you're right, it's a new dawn. I don't know if Nate has what it takes to run the Company."

"That's what we said about Berto, and look what happened!" Elvira bellowed. "Nate will snatch the reins just to spite the rest of us. He won't take this well at all. But it is apparently Daisy's intention to leave after the funeral. Nate will struggle to manage without her! The fellow is not a reader; he has no aptitude for business. You mark my words, he won't be able to keep up with things and there will be much room for maneuvering."

"Nothing can change until Silas comes back, anyway," Oliver said. "He controls the whole American side of the business, after all. It's damned inconvenient of him to be abroad at such a juncture."

"Yes, somebody timed that well," Ainsley observed. "Everything is put on hold and we all stand around wondering who did it and whether there's more to come. Everyone gets to have a good stew. I don't suppose anyone's going to own up to the dastardly deed?"

The room suddenly went much quieter. Berto had been intent on putting an end to the Rules of Ascension, and everyone was sure that Nate would follow suit, so confessing to the Patriarch's murder would not be a wise move. The silence only lasted a few seconds.

"The peasants will already be idolizing him, of course," Ainsley said. "He put so much effort into being nice to them, and now he's dead. There'll be trouble over that. You know how they love their martyrs."

"Martyrs!" Elvira barked. "They'll be the death of us! Still, it can't be helped."

"It was an admirable piece of work, whoever did it," Oliver commented. "In and out without being seen or heard, a clean kill—Warburton says they left Berto's head on his lap. A great sense of staging. Someone with a sense of style."

There was general agreement that it had indeed been an exemplary assassination.

Nate listened with his eyes closed, hating each and every one of them for what they were.

Cathal looked up at him, and then peeked around the corner at the crowd.

"That's a fine family you've got there, sir," he whispered. "Tell me, how old do I have to be before I need to start fearing for me life?"

Nate opened his eyes and straightened himself up.

"To be frank, Cathal, it would be best if you started immediately. Let us join our beloved relatives."

There was a noticeable lull in the chatter as Nathaniel came through the double doors. Everyone turned to look at him with varying expressions of sympathy, grief, gloating and calculation.

"Are Daisy and Tatiana here yet?" he asked by way of greeting.

"They're on their way," Elvira informed him. "It is the widow's prerogative to be late if she wishes."

"You'd know more about that than I would, Auntie, having been in the position three times in relatively quick succession. Becoming a widow has long been a family tradition. Berto had hoped to discard that particular practice, but it seems it is not to be the case. Let us hope I find the culprit while there are still some male members left in the family."

"Indeed!" Elvira declared. "To lose one brother, Nathaniel, may be regarded as a misfortune. To lose both looks like carelessness. Perhaps you will take your responsibilities more seriously from here on in."

"I can assure you I will be quite *ruthless* in the execution of my duties, Auntie, both in the family and in the business. Have no doubt about it."

The happy banter was interrupted by the arrival of Daisy and Tatiana, both dressed in black crepe dresses and wearing jet jewelry. They also wore veils on their black bonnets, ready to be hung down over their faces when they went outside. Both young women were pictures of dignified grief, make-up concealing eyes rimmed red by crying, cheeks pale from the chill of loss.

Siren was sitting on Tatty's shoulder. Elvira objected most strongly:

"Surely you are not considering taking that *thing* to the church, dear?" she said. "The choir will be made up of the most angelic voices and that creature would destroy their harmony. It's like the Devil himself playing on a telegraph machine. I dare say Hell's torments could not ask for better accompaniment. I insist you leave it in the house!"

"She can take it where she likes," Nate told the old woman. "And you will no longer have any say in how this family is run. You've given up that right. Let us make our way to the carriages. The day is getting on."

Gerald was standing outside, away from the family, smoking a cigarette. Nate nodded to his cousin on the way out and he joined him, Tatty and Daisy as they climbed into the carriage that immediately followed the hearse. It was being pulled by four velocycles, their engines running on silent, their eyes dimmed.

It was raining heavily and Elvira grumbled loudly about the unsuitable weather.

Gerald was the last one into the lead coach; he threw the cigarette away and stopped as he was mounting the steps into the carriage. He put his hand to his throat and coughed, then gagged and coughed again.

"You all right?" Nate asked.

"Yes, yes, just dandy," Gerald replied, waving the question away. "It's nothing. I think . . . think it's just something stuck in my throat. I'm fine."

The funeral procession moved slowly forward as each section of the family boarded their respective carriage. All the other vehicles were pulled by black thoroughbred horses, the brass of their tackle shining, the leather highly polished, black ostrich feathers on their heads. The plumage had also been used to decorate the hearse, which was surrounded by flowers to such an extent that they almost hid the coffin, despite the glass walls of the carriage.

Attendants dressed in long black tail-coats, black gloves and tall-crowned hats walked solemnly alongside the coaches. Mutes wearing gowns and carrying wands led the funeral procession in a model of Victorian tragedy.

Nate sat staring out of the window at the estate as they passed slowly through it. The lampposts along the way were hung with wreaths. People lined the road on either side, their hats in their hands. It was all so like his mother's funeral, his brother's funeral, his father's funeral, but this time there were thousands more who had come to pay their respects. In his short time as Patriarch, Berto had worked to improve the lot of the ordinary people working on the Wildenstern estates, and they had come now to acknowledge everything he had done. Perhaps they even realized that he had died for it.

Nate turned his mind to the murder and what he had discovered so far. Berto had been killed by someone he knew; that much was certain. He had been taken by surprise in his own dressing room, by someone who knew about the secret door into that room. The door had been booby-trapped, but traps could be evaded. He had not fired a single shot from his wheelchair, or tried to use any of his other weapons, when he would only have needed a second to react. So, he had hesitated in defending himself and he had not felt threatened enough to shout for help.

He had been killed by one shot to the head, with what appeared to be a pistol. The shot had to have been silenced; the Wildensterns were pioneers in the use of silencers for firearms and it would not have been difficult to get hold of one. Then an edged weapon with a long blade, probably a short sword, had been used to remove the head to ensure Berto would not recover. It had been done with one clean stroke—again, a degree of skill that spoke of years of training.

The assassin had placed the head on the victim's lap and then escaped the same way he or she had arrived. It had been a perfectly executed murder.

Nate struggled to keep his head clear of emotion, to look on the facts with a clinical logic. There were some strange factors in all of this. Berto's manservant had left him alone for less than ten minutes, but he swore he had heard violin music from the dressing room. Chopin's Nocturne in C-sharp minor, he'd claimed. "A suitably somber piece, sir, if you don't mind me saying," he'd said. Berto could play the violin, though he didn't do it very often. But his instruments were not kept in the dressing room and none was found there after the murder.

If the murderer played the violin, that narrowed down the suspects: not many in the family studied it to any serious level. Nate's nerves felt as if they themselves were being played like a violin—harsh, jangling strokes that juddered his bones.

There were also three faint bruises on Berto's right arm, and similar marks on the right side of his face. They suggested finger marks, as if someone had come from behind him and held down his arm—presumably to stop him engaging the chair's weapon—and covered his mouth. But he had been shot at from the front—the ugly exit wound was testament to that. Had there been two assailants? It might account for the fact that he had not put up a fight.

Berto had long been secretive about his affair with Hennessy. Could he have had another lover no one knew about? Someone with more sinister motives? Nate quickly dismissed the idea. His brother had been a true romantic—breaking his wife's heart had been almost more than he could take.

The funeral procession was approaching the church. Nate found his train of thought profoundly depressing. He had no wish to be Patriarch, and if Tatiana and Daisy left him to face his relatives alone life would become unbearable. With only Gerald to keep him company, he would quickly lose the run of himself.

Gerald's coughing was getting worse, his face red, either with embarrassment or the effort of breathing, Nate could not tell. The carriage came to a stop outside the gate of the church and Nate got down to help carry the coffin inside. Four footmen pulled it from the hearse. He took the front right corner, and noticed Hennessy was diagonally opposite him at the back corner. Nate gave him an almost imperceptible nod as they took their positions.

Once the coffin had been laid at the head of the church and everyone had taken their positions, the Archbishop began to speak. Nate was not paying attention, seated in the front pew beside Daisy, Tatiana and Gerald, his mind focused on the murder again, and the threat the entire family faced by being in one place like this. Everyone was here except for Gideon and Eunice, now in exile, as well as Silas and a few other relatives who were too far away to make it. This church was a tempting target indeed.

The afternoon light had a murky brown quality to it, even as it passed through the stained-glass windows. Nate had to stand and speak to the congregation soon. He tried to listen to the arch-bishop, waiting for his cue. Instead, he found himself going back over the details of the assassination again and again, and the murder attempts before that. He was missing something important, he was sure of it.

The choir started to sing, a beautiful, floating song . . . Schubert's "Ellens Dritter Gesang"; Berto's favorite piece of music. Hearing it caused Nate's breath to catch in his throat. Beside him, Daisy started to cry silently. Tears streamed down Tatiana's cheeks. She put her face in her hands, and as she did Siren reacted to the music, sensing the mood. It joined the choir in their song, taking their deep notes deeper, their high notes higher, its voice seeming to use the stone, the statues, the multi-colored windows of the church to make its sound. Tatiana's sobs broke the flow of the music, causing waves in its surface.

The hair on the back of Nate's neck rose. What was it Cathal had said? "It sings you better. It's like it talks to these things inside of you. The singin' is a way of tellin' them what to do. Your fearsome agents, an' all that. Can even stick new ones into you if you need 'em."

Nate's thoughts were racing. He knew it was possible to make an engimal obedient by feeding it a drop of one's blood. The intelligent particles had something to do with how the engimal's body and mind worked. So, by introducing a person's own particles into its system, that person could claim a creature's loyalty. If the serpentine could cure a patient's ills using song to communicate to the particles in their body, could music somehow be used to *control* these microscopic enigmas? Could engimals be controlled with *music*? Music *was* a kind of mathematical code, wasn't it? Was it possible to transmit thoughts or commands with a tune? It was certainly the most direct way of affecting human emotions.

Suddenly he knew what had caused the marks on Berto's arm and face. It wasn't a second attacker, or at least not a human one. It was his wheelchair. The engimal had held him down while his assassin stood in front of him and shot him dead. And somehow, the violin music had commanded the wheelchair to do it.

Gerald's coughing cut into the music now, getting progressively worse. Nate looked over at him. Gerald winced an apology and stood up, hurrying along the side of the church, his handkerchief pressed against his mouth to muffle the noise.

Nate's eyes followed his cousin towards the door. He leaned over to Daisy and spoke into her ear.

"Get everyone out of the church—now."

"What?"

"Someone's about to be killed. It could be us. Get everyone out of the church. Do as I tell you. Do it now." He didn't waste any more words. Leaping to his feet, he sprinted out of the church after Gerald.

Daisy turned to Tatiana, who was staring after her brother with a mystified expression.

"Tatty," Daisy asked in a breathless voice, looking at Siren. "How loud can that thing scream?"

Nate was ready for anything as he came running out through the doors of the church. But his cousin was not waiting to attack him. At first, there was no sign of Gerald. Nate ran out far enough to see around the corner of the building. Gerald was a hundred yards away, out of sight of the entrance to the church, walking quickly through the graveyard towards his velocycle, which waited in the shadow of a tree.

The crowds gathered outside the church grounds were watching curiously. It was a bit early for mourners to be emerging from the service.

From inside the church, there came a deafening, high-pitched scream. The singing stopped.

Nate advanced on Gerald who, now standing on the other side of Incitatus, was busy securing saddlebags on the engimal's back. The rain was easing off, but the skies overhead were promising more to come.

"It was you, wasn't it?" Nate snarled at him, his voice shaking, tears welling in his eyes. "It was you all along. You treacherous bastard! You killed Berto! You . . . you cut off his bloody . . . his . . . his bloody head! What . . . who the bloody hell *are* you, Gerald?"

Gerald raised his head to face him, regarding him with an expression that could almost have been sympathy. There came the sounds of panic from inside the church. He frowned, took out his pocket watch and glanced at it.

Nate stood waiting for a reply. He had sworn an oath to his brother, but he wanted answers before he carried it out.

"I'm someone who serves a greater cause, Nate," Gerald said, holding up his hands and shrugging. "That's all. It was nothing personal. I had hoped you'd understand that, but obviously you can't. Something had to be done about this family and neither you nor Berto had the stomach for it. Actually, truth be told, Berto's stomach came in very useful in the end. That and the rest of his ample corpse, I should say."

Nate gaped at him in confusion, then his face fell and he looked back at the church.

"What the . . . what the hell have you done?"

"It's more what I'm *about* to do, old chum," Gerald told him, looking at his watch again. "Right about . . . now."

He ducked down behind the velocycle. Then a massive explosion burst through the end wall of the church, blowing out every window in the building and ripping off half the roof. Nate was lifted from his feet like a rag doll and thrown against the tree next to the engimal. Shattered tiles, shards of stained glass, fragments of wood and stone and torn body parts came raining down. The crowd of bystanders let out a chorus of shrieks and fled, trampling over each other in their panic. A cloud of dust and smoke rose from the center of the explosion, mushrooming and settling over the area carrying hats, veils, gloves and shreds of clothing that floated down at a slower pace.

Even as Nate regained his senses, Gerald was climbing onto his velocycle and kicking his heels into its sides. He raced away through the rain of debris.

Less than half the church was still standing. Rafters, broken beams and stone blocks continued to collapse into it. Bodies littered the space around it and screams pierced the air. The horses and engimals had bolted, dragging their drivers and carriages with them.

Nate clawed his way to his feet using the trunk of the tree, a roaring sound in his ears. He had been here before. He knew this feeling: reeling senses, deafened, dizzy, his throat full and his brain trying to burst out of his skull. He had to ignore the pain in his battered body, the blood flowing into his left eye from a wound in his scalp. He started to walk, but had to fall back against the tree until he got his balance again. Think. *"Think!"* he said to himself over and over again. Help the ones inside.

Clancy and his men had searched every inch of that church. There was no way a bomb could have been planted there. But they had not searched the *coffin*. Warburton and Gerald had prepared the body, and Warburton delegated just about everything to Gerald nowadays. How difficult would it have been for him to pack the body with explosives? Not hard at all, it seemed. Nate, Hennessy and the other pallbearers had carried the bomb right up to the front of the church where all the most important members of the family would be seated.

Standing there gazing at the carnage, Nate was overwhelmed. Tatty. Daisy. Clancy. Cathal. They were all in there. They were probably dead . . . dead because he had been too stupid, too slow.

No, he thought. There's nothing you can do about that now. If they're alive, there will be help for them. If not, it's too late for me to do anything anyway. Gerald is going after Elizabeth and Leopold. That's why he didn't stay to take me on in a straight fight. He's already done for most of the rest of the family. Now he means to kill Leopold.

The only people Nate had told about Elizabeth's refuge were Daisy, Tatty . . . and Gerald.

Nate's instincts told him to go and get Flash, to give chase and ride Gerald down before he could reach Elizabeth's hiding place. He shook his head. No, he thought. He knows I'll come after him to stop him. He'll be ready for me. He's smarter than me—he's probably even planned for it. He always plans ten steps ahead.

Nate started running up the hill through the graveyard, taking the most direct route to the house. He would hunt Gerald down all right, but if he recklessly threw himself into a duel with his cousin, he would pay with his life.

Running past the stables, he headed for the rear entrance to the house instead. He needed to be prepared. Nate was not afraid of fighting Gerald. He was terrified that he would die before he even got close.

XXXVI

DEATH RIDES AT HIS HEELS

IT WAS ONLY WHEN NATHANIEL finally charged out of the stables on
Flash's back, setting off for the hills, that the full immensity of
Gerald's betrayal started to eat into him, burning every nerve in
his body. Nate's brother had been murdered by his best friend.
He shouted and roared into the wind, sounding like a madman as
he raced along roads, past cabins and pubs and farmyards.

The sound of the explosion had carried for miles, bringing
people out of their houses to stare at the column of smoke rising
into the sky. Not long after these events, a new term would enter
the English language: 'Like a Wildenstern funeral,' a phrase that
would mean the worst kind of disaster. Now, however, the vision
of this deranged man riding the Beast of Glenmalure caused a
flurry of rumors to spread outwards like shock waves from the

explosion. They knew Nathaniel Wildenstern and his mount by sight and they had all heard the bloodthirsty myths about the Wildenstern family. There were some who claimed they had the second sight, who swore that when they spotted him that day, they saw Death himself riding at the young Duke's heels.

Nate urged his mount ever faster, the wind pressing his goggles against his face, whipping at his riding coat and whistling around his leather helmet. Flash could sense its master's mood and hurtled along the road at a terrific pace, taking corners at breakneck speed and sending sprays of mud, dust and stones flying from under its wheels. It bellowed in time with its rider.

Nate knew the hills better than Gerald. He cut across country, leaping hedges and dry-stone walls, smashing through thickets, through bramble and heather, following animal trails and cart tracks. Flash's wheels ate up the miles.

Soon they were making their way along the edge of a cliff covered in grass and ragged bushes that looked down into a picturesque valley, which ended ahead of him with a towering waterfall nearly four hundred feet high. This was part of the Powerscourt Estate, where Elizabeth and Leopold were hiding in a little-used hunting cabin not far from the top of the falls.

The hills on either side of the valley continued to rise beyond the waterfall. High up to the left was the hulking shape of Djouce Mountain. Nate could see the roof of the cabin just over the crest of the slope . . . and there on the hillside above it was Gerald, standing out against the sky playing a violin.

Nate slowed, waiting to see what would happen next. As Flash's engine grew quiet, Nate could hear the music—a lively reel. He glanced over his shoulder in time to see Elizabeth's leaf-lights coming at him from behind, fast and silent like a flock of flying blades. Spinning Flash around, he reached into the saddle-bag with his left hand and pulled out a large bottle. He hurled it up into the path of the engimals. They swerved in different directions to avoid it. Nate whipped a sawn-off shotgun from the holster behind him with his right hand, raised it and fired. The bottle exploded, spraying acid in every direction. He shielded his face as droplets fell towards him. The delicate leaf-lights were devastated by the corrosive liquid, many falling in pieces or swirling away injured and disoriented.

Nate quickly swiveled to aim the shotgun at Gerald. His cousin was still playing, the instrument tucked under his chin, the bow sweeping in graceful strokes back and forth over the strings. The notes of the dance tune carried an ominous warning through the clear mountain air. He was too far away for Nate's short-range weapon to have much effect, but he might just . . .

Gerald raised the tempo. Flash suddenly bucked, pivoted and bucked again, throwing Nate off its back. He landed hard on his shoulder, but rolled on instinct, his reflex saving him as the horse-sized velocycle barreled past him. Flash did a skidding turn and came at him again. Nate dived to one side, but Flash was fast, fast enough to hit Nate's foot as he leaped aside. Nate felt something snap and he cried out, dropping the scattergun. The engimal was already turning again. Struggling to his feet, stinging as much from Flash's betrayal as he was from his injury, Nate picked up the gun and limped along the path. He was making for a steep section of bank where he might climb out of Flash's reach. He heard the engine roar, and the beast charged after him again.

"You can't help yourself, my friend," he said under his breath. "But I don't have time to care."

He spun around and fired the shotgun into Flash's face. The creature screamed, its momentum carrying it forward. Nate stepped to the side and Flash hurtled out over the edge of the cliff. With a wail, it crashed and tumbled down through the heather, bushes and scree to the valley floor.

Nate heaved in a few breaths, pulling off his helmet and goggles. He threw off his coat, forgetting about the thing he had concealed in the hip pocket. He reloaded both barrels of the shotgun and swapped it to his left hand, pulling a revolver from a shoulder holster with his right. Then he started to limp up the hill towards Gerald. From the feel of it he had broken one of the bones in his foot. It was already healing, but not fast enough to be ready for this fight.

Gerald stopped playing and lowered the violin, carefully placing it in the case at his feet.

"You did better than I expected," he said, straightening up and flexing his fingers. "But then, you were always smarter than the family gave you credit for. I used to think you appreciated how important my work was, you know. The way the engimals fascinated you, I thought you felt the same way I did. I really hoped you'd take over if I got Marcus out of the way for you. But you still wouldn't grasp the nettle, would you?"

"You killed Marcus too? I thought that was Father—or his

men defending him, at least," Nate said as he drew closer, puzzled that Gerald had not drawn a weapon.

"No, no; that was me." Gerald gave a rueful shrug as if owning up to some foolish prank. "Marcus was extremely gifted, but short-sighted. Your father was already letting him make most of the business decisions. And Marcus would have just stood in my way, as Berto has done, or worse, he would have kept my discoveries secret and used them to help the family gain even more power. He would never have grasped the enormity of what my work could achieve, so he had to go—omelettes and eggs and all that. I needed much more of the family's resources to take my research further, and he wouldn't have given it to me. It was so frustrating—I couldn't make him understand.

"I thought with him gone, you'd take what should have been yours," Gerald said in a weary voice. "But you had to go and let Berto run things. And who'd have thought he'd turn out to have such backbone? I thought *you'd* be the power behind the throne, but instead, you became Berto and Daisy's lapdog. I was so sure you'd support my work in a way that none of them ever would.

"But you all forced my hand, Nate. I never wanted to be Patriarch. I don't crave the power. I just needed . . . I just needed the family's money to complete my work. And then I met O'Neill and . . . and saw what he could do—I was terrified to see how far he had progressed. And I knew there might be others around the world working on this too. None of you understand! There may be no limit to what we can achieve if we can learn to control these intelligent particles. And if this power falls into the wrong hands, Nate . . . I mean, my God, there may be no limit to the horrors some villain could visit on mankind!"

Gerald's face was bright red, spit flying from his mouth as he punctuated his sentences by thumping the palm of his hand. "Imagine if the likes of Angstrom and O'Neill had got there first—or someone even worse! Think what they might do! Everything must take second place to this—everything! If people have to die, well . . . well, so be it!

"I'm trying to change the world, Nate, and I had hoped you'd want to change it with me, once I'd cleared the way for you. You were never supposed to know, of course. All these terrible things I've had to do for a cause that is bigger than all of us. You were never supposed to know.

"But now you see what I've done. And I know you haven't the vision to look past these few petty deaths and see what really matters. I've changed my mind about you."

"The feeling's mutual," Nate said, as he came level with Gerald and raised both his guns. "It's over, Gerald."

"Of course it isn't," his cousin replied, gesturing down the slope behind him.

Nate moved closer and looked down. From here he had a better view of the cabin. Out on the stretch of grass in front of it squatted Incitatus, its engine running on silent. Bundled up in a blanket and lying just in front of the velocycle's front wheel was Nate's son. Leopold was gazing up in wonder at the engimal looming over him, gurgling to himself. Nate stared down at the scene and his heart sank.

"What have you done with Elizabeth and her husband?" he asked, unable to think of anything else to say.

"Still alive, but tied up inside," Gerald told him. "They might yet be useful."

He walked down towards the velocycle, heedless of the weapons pointed at him.

"Why don't you put those down, Nate? You've lost. You know you have."

"No," said Nate. "You'll kill the child anyway. He's an obstacle—that's all that matters to you. As long as he's alive, you can't be Patriarch."

"Don't be foolish; I never *wanted* to be Patriarch. I just want to get my way. I'm happy for somebody else to run the wretched Company, as long as it's funding my experiments."

He was standing beside the engimal now, his hand on one of its horns. Nate hesitated for just a second, and then fired his pistol. The shot should have hit Gerald squarely in the chest. Instead, a blur of movement blocked its path, the bullet smacked against something hard. Incitatus was rearing, changing, unfolding at a speed that defied belief. In moments, it had wrapped itself around Gerald in a new shape. Its arms and legs molded themselves to Gerald's limbs, its hide opening, unwrapping and closing protectively around him, shielding him with its own skin. In a matter of seconds, the velocycle had become a bizarre suit of armor. Gerald stood nearly nine feet tall, encased almost entirely in engimal hide, even around his joints, neck and head. His hands were metal claws. His feet were the size of anvils.

Nate fired the remaining five shots with his pistol, and then emptied the shotgun at this monstrosity. The shots tore its hide, but did not penetrate it. The damage healed quickly into scars.

Leopold still lay defenseless at Gerald's feet. Nate only belatedly realized that any one of his shots could have deflected towards his child. Gerald flexed arms that looked strong enough to lift a horse.

"Oh, bugger," Nate breathed.

"You'd think that it would be awkward to move in, but it's not," Gerald commented. "It's actually amazingly responsive. Almost like a second skin."

He leaped forward, crossing the distance between himself and Nate in an instant, his armored hand striking Nate in the chest. The impact was like being hit by a sledgehammer. It broke two of his ribs and knocked him back several yards, sending him sprawling to the ground. Clutching his chest, Nate got to his feet and started to stumble away. He did not know where he was going, but he knew this fight was lost. He had to escape and . . . and . . . he didn't know what he was going to do. Nate had no idea how to fight this thing.

"The music was the key," Gerald went on, calmly watching Nate stagger down the hill. "The engimals are capable of so much more than we know; we simply have to learn how to communicate with them. I'd been working with mathaumaturgy for so long, but the mathematics were just too complex. The numbers needed to form the simplest command were too complicated to be worthwhile, too time-consuming."

With a single bound, he jumped right over Nate and landed ahead of him, crunching down on the rocks by the edge of the narrow river. Nate felt the impact in the ground through the soles of his feet.

"But music, now that is mathematics at its most graceful, its most instinctive." The armored hand came down on Nate's left shoulder, smashing his collarbone. Nate fell, one sharp fragment of the bone jutting through his skin.

Gerald kept talking while his cousin screamed.

"Somehow, by playing music, we can transmit our intentions to the engimals. Simply by thinking about it as we play, we can send messages in the music. They understand and obey us. It's quite remarkable. I'd love to take the credit for the discovery, but actually it was O'Neill who tipped me off. He almost managed to do the same to the intelligent particles in *my body*. Isn't that something? I still haven't figured out how he did that."

Gerald gazed down at his cousin, who lay on the ground writhing in agony. They were now standing near the top of Powerscourt Waterfall.

Pain coursed through Nate's body; he could feel the fragments of bone grate against one another in his shattered shoulder. His ribs felt like shards of broken glass. Every movement was fiery agony, but the pain made it impossible to keep still.

Gerald looked out over the lush, picturesque valley.

"This would be a good death, Nathaniel," he said sadly, reluctant to deliver the final blow to his best friend. "I'd rather you came with me. I'm going to build a new future and I need someone to appreciate it with me. But you'd only try and stop me, wouldn't you?"

Dropping onto one knee, he took hold of Nate's head in one

massive claw. Nate felt the strength of it start to crush his skull. He let out a pathetic whimper; he couldn't help himself.

Gerald pushed back the visor covering his face and looked into Nate's eyes, speaking over the noise of the rushing water.

"I'm truly sorry, Nate."

"You bloody should be!"

Nate moved fast—almost fast enough. His wrist flicked back. The long dagger concealed in a spring-loaded scabbard in his right sleeve shot forward into his hand and he stabbed upwards. Gerald flinched back, his other hand coming up to shield it. The tip of the blade cut through his cheek, slicing the skin from the corner of his mouth up towards his eye. He shrieked and stood up, clumsily trying to stem the spurts of blood with his huge engimal hands. But the wound was not fatal.

Nate made a futile attempt to crawl away. Gerald kicked him over onto his back, grabbed the dagger and drove it hard into his cousin's chest. The blade pierced Nate's heart, and a scream froze in his paralyzed lungs. The world started to go dark.

Gerald was shedding his armor, trying to free his hands. Incitatus unfolded itself again, disentangling itself from his body so that only his legs were covered. Gerald pulled off his jacket and tore a sleeve from his shirt, folding it into a pad to hold against his face. He was crying, howling with pain.

Even with a knife blade through it, Nate's Wildenstern heart kept beating. He thought he could hear another cry, besides Gerald's screaming. Was this what people meant about the banshee's wail? Was there really a faerie woman whose mournful cry heralded your death?

This was no banshee. Something was moving beside him. He turned his head to the side, his short breaths coming in wheezing, gurgling red bubbles. There was Apple, Cathal's serpentine, sliding through the grass towards him. Nate had taken her with him to the church, tucked into his jacket pocket. He hadn't known what he intended to do with her, but he was sure she was important somehow, and right now he didn't want Gerald to have her if . . . if he failed. And now she was wailing at him like a siren.

The white snake-like engimal slipped over the gravel with slow easy grace, climbing up over Nate's chest. As she reached the handle of the knife protruding from between his ribs, Apple's head split in three, and her body unwound, separating like three strands of a rope. Each of the three mouths started to sing in a sweet, warbling voice. A flush of warmth flooded through Nate's body. One of the strands crept up towards his face, and he gasped as it raised its head over him. Then it curled over and darted into his mouth.

Already struggling for breath, Nate gagged as the full length of the creature slid down his throat. He tried to grab at it, but he was too weak. Sobbing around it, he choked, spasming uncontrollably. The other two strands of the creature wound around the three inches of blade still visible above his chest, braced themselves against the hilt of the knife and started to drag the dagger out of his body.

The blockage in his throat cleared and Nate was able to breathe fitfully again. He could feel the thing inside him, doing things to his body. It was fixing him. Images flickered across his vision. He saw things that had nothing to do with this place and time. Somehow, the part of Apple coiled inside him was leaking memories. Nate saw its past. At that moment, he couldn't care less.

Give me my heart back, he begged silently. I can still beat this cur; just give me back my heart.

The two pieces of the serpentine dropped the dagger then one pushed its way into the wound. He felt his flesh knitting back together. It withdrew its head and sutured the lips of the wound and the flow of blood reduced to a trickle.

It was still singing, and Gerald finally heard the song. He looked back at Nate and gave a frustrated snarl. His legs were still encased by the engimal, the rest of the creature suspended above his waist behind him. He strode forward and snatched the two serpentine strands from Nate's chest with one hand, the other still holding the improvised dressing to his torn face. Looking at the closed wound and then back at the two pieces of the engimal, Gerald quickly interpreted what he was seeing . . . and the implications.

"This is it," he rasped. "This is the missing link I've been look-ing for!" He glared down at his cousin. "And you *knew*! How could *you* see it when I couldn't?" Pausing for a moment, he added: "It was the bloody boy, wasn't it? He told you. Still, it doesn't matter now."

Nate was up on his knees, crawling towards the river. Gerald bundled up the squirming engimal segments and shoved them into a storage compartment in his velocycle's side. Then he went after Nathaniel. He lifted his foot high over Nate's back, ready to bring it down, crushing his cousin. Nate looked up and a sound burst from his mouth, two sharp tones that froze Gerald in his tracks and bent his leg violently upwards against the knee. Ger-ald's leg snapped and he fell backwards with a scream.

Incitatus seemed to be completely paralyzed. Gerald

struggled free of the engimal and crawled after Nate, dragging his limp, broken leg. He had to let go of his dressing and blood poured from his wounded face. He caught up by the side of the river and tackled Nate from behind. But Nate was ready. His left arm was almost useless, his broken ribs and collarbone made any movement torture, but he blocked Gerald's punch with his right, grabbing his cousin with his left hand and hanging on as tightly as he could. Two jabs to Gerald's bloody mouth caused his cousin to clench his eyes shut and it was enough for Nate to get his arm around Gerald's neck and heave him into the river.

The water was cold, knocking the wind from their lungs. Nate got his head above the surface and caught a breath, but Gerald swallowed water. Their momentum was strengthened by the swift current. They rolled over and over in the shallow water, thudding against rocks, grinding over gravel, water foaming red around them as they fought like blood-crazed animals. The river carried them ever closer to the edge of the falls.

Nate saw the danger and grabbed a rock. But it left him open. Gerald had one hand on Nate's throat and now he pounded the other into his cousin's injured shoulder. Nate lost his grip and the water took them again. Gerald pushed away, kicking with his good leg, trying to shove Nate over the edge. The water was weakening them both now, stiffening their muscles, chilling their blood, draining their energy. Nate fought back, trying to breathe against the onslaught of the water, sliding towards the precipice. Gerald caught hold of another boulder and clung on, kicking out hard against his cousin.

Nate managed to get his head above the water. He sucked in air and seized Gerald's foot, gripping it under his arm.

"I know where they came from!" he shouted. "I can tell you what they are!"

Gerald stopped for just a second, an expression of doubt on his face. It was all Nate needed. He grabbed his cousin by the testicles and wrenched him free of the rock. Seizing Gerald's neck with his other hand, he summoned up a burst of inhuman strength and hurled his best friend over the edge of the falls. Gerald's screams were cut short as he bounced against the rocks on the way down.

Nate nearly surrendered to the force of the water, he was so exhausted. But he hauled himself, inch by inch, up the bank and onto the grass. Semi-conscious, he lay there shivering, his body racked with pain. The snake was still inside him, doing things to him. Its memories were still seeping into his consciousness, causing him to hallucinate. He rolled over onto his back, staring at the sky. But what he saw was altogether different.

Visions of an alien world flashed before his eyes, a world that had once existed on this earth. The engimals were just the last remnants of it; they gave hardly a hint of what had come before. Nate blinked, wishing the visions away. The engimals had been mere tools, perhaps even just playthings, created by children. The true wonder of this civilization had been the intelligent particles. And they had also been the seeds of its extinction.

It was then that Nate understood: the serpentine had its own reasons for saving him.

EPILOGUE

THE ORIGIN OF SPECIES

DAISY AND TATIANA STOOD GAZING at the ruins of the church in the fading evening light, taking in the full scale of the destruction. Fragments of the multicolored stained glass still hung from the remains of the window frames, with strips of lead protruding like insects' legs. Half the roof had been blown off and most of the rest had collapsed afterwards. Wooden beams lay at strange angles against the stone rubble, or jutted from the tops of the walls as if awaiting the return of the roof. Fire had eaten much of what was left, consuming all but a few of the oak pews. Flames still licked half-heartedly at the last of the charred wood, embers glowed in the ashes. Melted pools of gold from the religious artifacts had mingled with the ash and debris on the mosaic floor.

Even now, hours after the fire had died down, the floor was warm beneath their feet.

"Do you think Gerald was making some kind of statement by destroying a church?" Daisy wondered aloud. "Or was it just a happy coincidence for him that the whole family were gathered together in this one place?"

"Pardon?" Tatty asked, with one hand to her ear.

She was still partially deaf from the explosion. They were both filthy, bedraggled, covered in soot and stained with smoke. They had barely escaped with their lives. Daisy had reacted quickly to Nate's warning and, using Tatiana's songbird to shriek at the top of its voice, had brought the proceedings to an abrupt halt. As soon as silence had been achieved, she had ordered an immediate evacuation and, leading Tatty by the hand, quickly demonstrated the most direct route to the door.

The Wildensterns, aware of common family practice, did not question the announcement. They left their seats in hasty fashion and rushed out of the church. The Archbishop, along with some other important personages, had stood there questioning the propriety of abandoning a funeral in such a manner. Their hesitation was just long enough for them to be caught and killed in the blast.

Thirty-two had died in the explosion, and many more were injured. The casualties were being seen to up in Wildenstern Hall. Daisy had come back down here to get away from the family's bickering. They were already arguing over how this had changed the structure of power, and it sickened her. She was desperate to get away from them, from all of this.

Tatty had come along to keep her company. She could not hear the bickering very well anyway, and she found she could not sit still, what with all the muddled thoughts and emotions in her head. She was quite beside herself and the walk would do her good.

"We can't stay here, Tatty," Daisy said, raising her voice. "The monsters in this family have committed so many atrocities; it won't be long before we lose all sense of what is normal and decent. Even now, I'm finding it hard to appreciate how truly horrific this is."

"It's pretty awful, that's easy enough to see," Tatty replied loudly, reminding Daisy of Elvira's booming voice. "What's more, I'd have to say that Gerald has well and truly blown the Rules of Ascension out of the water. I haven't seen quite so much devastation since . . . well, since *Marcus's* funeral. Or perhaps the train wreck that Elizabeth and her lot caused . . . "

Her voice drifted off as they spotted Elizabeth and her husband riding in a brougham towards them through the evening mist. The horses whinnied, snorting at the smell of the burned church. Elizabeth appeared almost distressed. Nevin reined in the animals and helped Elizabeth down. She was cradling Leopold in her arms.

"Then it's true," she said, and it was unclear whether she was speaking in shock, awe or admiration. "Gerald blew up the entire building. One has to appreciate the strength of his will. He was a man with a purpose."

"'Was'?" Daisy repeated. "You mean he's dead?"

"It would seem so," Elizabeth replied. "We did not stop to study the body, but Nathaniel threw him off a four-hundred-foot-high waterfall. The broken thing we saw at the bottom was in no state to dance a jig, that's for certain. Nathaniel came back to where we were imprisoned, untied us and put the baby in my arms."

As she said this, she gazed down fondly at her son.

"Father came to rescue you, didn't he, my sweet? Father loves you so much!"

Nevin was still standing a few yards back. He looked awkwardly at his feet.

"Nathaniel gave me a message to pass on to whomever was left in the family," Elizabeth continued. "His exact words were: 'I have something to do, and may be gone for some time.' He said no more, but he seemed to me to be in something of a confused state. Perhaps he will come back and elaborate when he regains his senses."

Daisy and Tatiana exchanged looks. After everything that had happened, it was a bizarre way to behave. They were not sure they believed Elizabeth either. The woman was a ruthless, conniving harpy, after all. And she held the Wildenstern Heir in her arms. This was a dangerous situation indeed, what with the Patriarch missing without explanation. Elizabeth was now in a uniquely powerful position, and she was the sort who would take full advantage of it.

"Then we will wait for him to come back," Daisy declared at last. "No matter how long it takes."

"That's right," Tatiana agreed. "Nathaniel is the Patriarch, and it is up to us to keep things in order until he comes back. It is what my brother would want."

"And I shall, of course, look forward to listening to your counsel," Elizabeth said generously.

"We would not *presume* to lay much responsibility on your shoulders," Daisy retorted. "You will have your hands full raising your beautiful son. It will be our solemn duty to see that you are never bothered with all the tiresome matters of business."

"And it will be *my* duty to see that the family's business receives all the attention I can give it," Elizabeth responded with a calculating smile.

The three women regarded each other for nearly a minute.

"Well, that's that settled," Tatty said at last. "Let's get away from this place—it's in a terrible state and my dress is quite ruined. I'm sure my hair will smell of smoke for days to come."

"Yes, we will have to rebuild the church as soon as possible," Daisy said as they walked away from the bombsite. Glancing at Elizabeth, she added: "I have a feeling we're going to be needing it."

Nate stumbled along the road in the darkness, his vision awash with strange images. The agony was gone, even though he could still feel his injuries. Somehow, he was being spared the pain. He felt as if he was in that muddled state between sleep and wakefulness, where nothing is clear. His feet were leading him towards Dublin, towards the docks.

Nate saw what had once been. He understood now why the engimals were the only trace left behind by the civilization that had made them. Only the things made of certain materials had survived: metal, ceramic and other inorganic substances. But most of what these people made was *grown*; whole buildings formed in harmony with the environment, roads of condensed earth that followed the shape of the landscape; architecture, infrastructure that changed itself to suit the needs of its occupants.

On the road ahead of him, a fox scampered out, looking around for prey, or some garbage to root through. It gave a long, shrill bark and then, noticing this lone, limping man on the road, disappeared into the hedge with hardly a rustle.

Nate could not believe some of the things he saw: clothes that changed shape and color, vehicles that seemed to form out of the elements themselves, people with untold agility, able to run across water, others who could *even fly*. And it was all made possible by the intelligent particles. He felt the serpentine move restlessly in his intestine. These people had been capable of magic.

He wandered through more heavily inhabited areas now, past houses, shops and pubs. Along another stretch of fields he saw some men digging drainage channels with spades and mattocks, and he realized it must be morning. Sure enough, there was the sun lifting over the eastern horizon. He hadn't even noticed.

Before long he was walking through town, his movements more comfortable now, his injuries already difficult to detect as Apple, the serpentine, did its—her work. The city was waking up around him. Carriages and horse-drawn buses passed him by. Dogs barked and circled him to investigate this strange figure. People looked at him with interest, this young gentleman out walking first thing in the morning without hat or coat.

He reached the docks, still plagued by these strange

visions. The ships' masts towered above him. The stevedores were already busy loading up, the sailors on deck carrying out cleaning and repairs to their vessels. The engimal crane that reminded him so much of a giraffe or a dinosaur strode over-head, lifting and placing its feet carefully either side of him as it carried a net of crates down the quay to a waiting ship.

Even as he observed this, Nate watched the hallucinations that laid themselves over these more mundane sights. The intel-ligent particles, the same elements that gave his family their extraordinary power, had enabled their creators to perform mira-cles. But they had been a curse as well as a blessing. Nate walked down the quays, looking for a ship of the Wildenstern fleet—one which would suit his purposes.

It was becoming increasingly difficult for him to think clearly, so confusing were the images, the emotions he felt, the memories inflicted upon him by the serpentine. There was nothing left for him now. Gerald had betrayed him. Berto had been beheaded. Daisy and Tatiana had died in the explosion . . . hadn't they? Yes, he thought, I would have seen them come out. I'm sure of it. They're dead. There's nothing here for me now. It's better if I go.

This ship. This was the one. He gazed up at it. It was the *Banshee*, a square-rigged clipper with three masts. It was nearly two hundred and fifty feet long, with three decks. When he had returned home from Africa, this was the ship that had carried him. How fitting that it would now take him back. That was where he had to go—back to Africa, where the roots of that ancient civilization lay.

One of the officers recognized him and waved. He waved

back. He was the Patriarch; he could do what he wanted with this vessel. They would take him back to Africa. The visions swirled before his eyes, obscuring his view of the ship. The serpentine wanted to show him how it could all be made real again. But he had to be careful.

Those ancient people had lost control of the intelligent particles and their mistake had destroyed them.

As Nate walked up the ship's gangplank, the serpentine squirmed in his gut and conjured up more images of the people who had created her. And, as Nate began his new life, Apple showed him how theirs had come to an end.

ACKNOWLEDGMENTS

You write a book alone, you publish it with a team, and you sell it with a community. I'd like to thank my family first, as always. They are the root of everything that is good in my books. From the stories we enjoyed when my brothers, sisters, and I were children, to the conversations and lively arguments we have today, I am reminded constantly that I was blessed with a fantastic childhood that fueled my imagination. It was the kind of childhood my wife and I hope to be able to provide for Danu, our brand new baby daughter.

Thanks to my wife, Maedhbh, for understanding why I have to keep weird hours, and my stepson, Oscar, for being such a big help with his little sister when I'm away, or even when I'm just upstairs at my drawing desk or hammering at the keyboard. My brother, Marek, continues his dedicated management of my website (www.oisinmcgann.com) despite increasingly eccentric demands and constant nit-picking.

I'm indebted to my agent, Sophie Hicks, along with Edina Imrik and everyone at Ed Victor Ltd, for keeping a sharp eye on the small print and making sure I never lose sight of the bigger picture. It's a real pleasure to work in this industry, and Sophie and her team help to ensure it stays that way. Thanks also to all

ACKNOWLEDGMENTS

the people I meet at events and visits, whose passion, commitment, and positivity make this such a fun job.

And finally, a special thanks to Emma Pulitzer and Tim Travaglini at Open Road Media, for their work on the US edition of this book, and for their diligence in making sure I was involved in, and kept informed of, every stage of the process.

Oisín McGann

ABOUT THE AUTHOR

Oisín McGann was born and raised in Dublin and Drogheda, County Louth, in Ireland. He studied art at Senior College Ballyfermot and Dún Laoghaire School of Art, Design & Technology. Before becoming an author, he worked as a freelance illustrator, serving time along the way as a pizza chef, security guard, background artist for an animation company, and art director and copywriter in an advertising agency.

In 2003 McGann published his first two books in the Mad Grandad series for young readers, followed by his first young adult novel, *The Gods and Their Machines*. Since then, he has written several more novels for young adults, including the Wildenstern Saga, a steampunk series set in nineteenth-century Ireland, and the thrillers *Strangled Silence* and *Rat Runners*.

A full-time writer and illustrator, McGann is married, has three children, and lives somewhere in the Irish countryside.

THE WILDENSTERN SAGA

FROM OPEN ROAD MEDIA

Available wherever ebooks are sold

OPEN ROAD
INTEGRATED MEDIA

Open Road Integrated Media is a digital publisher and multimedia content company. Open Road creates connections between authors and their audiences by marketing its ebooks through a new proprietary online platform, which uses premium video content and social media.

Videos, Archival Documents, and New Releases

Sign up for the Open Road Media newsletter and get news delivered straight to your inbox.

Sign up now at
www.openroadmedia.com/newsletters

FIND OUT MORE AT
WWW.OPENROADMEDIA.COM

FOLLOW US:
@openroadmedia and
Facebook.com/OpenRoadMedia

CPSIA information can be obtained at www.ICGtesting.com
Printed in the USA
BVOW02s1104091115

426152BV00002BA/2/P